"There is nothing acceptable about our being here, my lord, is there?" Meg Smiles asked. To be less than honest would rob her of any joy she might hope to take away from the night.

"Not unless we convince each other there is. If we forget who we are, how we are different—even how we are the same—and grant ourselves permission to accept whatever we have to offer and take, then I believe our actions are not only acceptable, but necessary." He tilted his face to the ceiling and expanded his lungs. "I am a man who is torn between two countries, and between what is expected of him and what he craves for himself. The responsibilities I am ordered to assume weigh heavily. I would like to please those who expect these things of me. But my heart is elsewhere, and I do not know what to do."

"My lord," Miss Smiles said softly, "I feel for you in your struggle."

Yes, Jean-Marc believed she did. "These matters are most private. I have not shared even a hint of my true feelings with anyone else."

"Why do you share them with me?" Only a gullible person would refrain from asking, Meg thought. "A stranger?"

"Are you a stranger?" He smiled to himself. "I suppose that is so in hours and minutes, but in here—" he struck his chest "—it is as if I have been coming toward you for a long time. Oh, I didn't know it, but I do now. You are familiar to me. Familiar yet mysterious, and I want to know you.... Meg, I should like to know you very well."

"Full of mystery, betrayal and complications, Cameron's tale comes complete with an eccentric cast of characters, including a meddlesome, match-making ghost and enough villains to keep readers thoroughly entertained."

—*Publishers Weekly* on *More and More*

STELLA CAMERON

ALL SMILES

MIRA

ISBN 1-55166-615-4

ALL SMILES

Copyright © 2000 by Stella Cameron.

Visit us at www.mirabooks.com

nted In U.S.A.

For the folks at www.stellacameron.com
who wanted to return to Mayfair Square.
And for all the Rebels—you know who you are!

_____ Prologue _____

7 Mayfair Square, London, 1821

Sir Septimus Spivey here:

It's not easy being a ghost.

One must put up with being overlooked, ignored, forgotten, or worse yet, spoken of with heartless disrespect as if one weren't there.

Well, yes, of course I'm not there anyway, but in light of who I am—was—surely my name should evoke nothing short of reverence.

I have suffered too much, for too long, and this must stop.

I should have listened to my father. He warned me that my generous spirit would bring nothing but disappointment.

Hmm. Of course, my father never reached, or even approached, the level of my own successes in life. Nevertheless, he was right in this instance. I built a beautiful house for my family—and only for my family. The fact that circumstances have forced me to take up residence elsewhere—in a manner of speaking—is no excuse for the way in which my granddaughter and her nephew now abuse the jewel in my professional crown.

I was knighted for my accomplishments as an architect. Number Seven Mayfair Square is the best of my extraordinary designs. Hester and her nephew, young Hunter Lloyd, are despoiling their inheritance. They have jeopardized their own reputations, their

*own standing in society, and thus tainted the very air that touches
the face of my precious creation. More importantly, they have
sullied a peerless man's memory—mine.*

*In Mayfair Square, address of addresses, golden carrot before
the noses of the most ambitious of well-bred noses, the stuff of
dreams for those who look longingly but know they are unfit—in
this square, at the triumph that is Number Seven—there are lodgers!*

Hester and Hunter are letting rooms.

*I am as angry as I can be and I refuse to tolerate this state of
affairs any longer.*

*This is insupportable, you know. I have reached a stage at
which I should need to do nothing but occupy my favorite vantage
point in the fabulously carved staircase I myself sketched for the
craftsmen. The faces of members of my family are depicted there
in great detail, and so is mine. That is where I retire to rest, and
where I should be left in peace to admire what I have accomplished. But, no, no, thanks to my ungrateful relations it's not yet
to be. No matter, I shall prevail.*

And I have a plan.

*Meg and Sibyl Smiles live at Seven B. They are sisters, orphans
of some country clergyman. I cannot even remember the name of
the village. Somewhere forgettable in the Cotswolds, I believe.
Oh, the shame of it all. They try to disguise the truth that Number
Seven is being used like a lowly rooming house by speaking of
Lady Hester's "resident protegées," if you can imagine such foolishness. Since when have protegées paid their champions? And
who, may I ask, champions seamstresses and pianoforte teachers—or shopkeepers—or failed painters? Oh, we have them all
at Number Seven Mayfair Square, my friends.*

*Meg Smiles has certain troubles, I understand. For these I am
profoundly sorry. I wish life were treating her better. Regardless,
I intend to assist in her removal from my house for other parts.
Sibyl will accompany her. Toward that end, this is what I intend:*

There's a new fellow at Number Seventeen, name of Count Etranger—Jean-Marc. Fancies himself more English than...than whatever they call people from Mont Nuages. Country about the size of Hyde Park on the border between France and Italy. Anyway, Etranger wants a home away from home, I should think, so he's brought his sister to London for the Season. Intends to marry her off to the wealthiest, most elevated contender and use the resulting connections to weasel his way into the best places, don't you know. Good luck to him, that's what I say.

The sister is Princess Désirée. She understands fiddle-all of the ins and outs of going about in Town, and Etranger knows this is so. He needs absolutely trustworthy assistance with the girl's preparation. Someone, or more than one, who can guide the young lady in basic areas without having any pretensions of their own. Who better to fill the post—posts—than the sisters Smiles?

They will do well enough as companions expert in questions of style (although they have none), elocution, voice training and mastery of the pianoforte. After all, how much experience could be necessary to fill such posts?

Of course, companions are also for the purpose of keeping their charges company. To this end they must move to Number Seventeen. My task will be to ensure Meg and Sibyl do not return to Number Seven.

Trust me. They won't.

1

"**S**ingle ladies should not discuss eligible gentlemen so...*intimately*," Sibyl Smiles told her sister, Meg.

Seated on the very shabby rose-colored chaise in the parlor at 7B Mayfair Square, Meg rearranged the black lace mantilla with which she'd draped her head and face and said, "Who should discuss them intimately, then? *Married* ladies?"

"Oh, fiddlesticks," Sibyl said. "I think you want to shock me and it's really too bad of you."

"I want to say whatever I'm thinking—when I'm thinking about it. That is whenever I'm forced to abandon my meditation for matters of the mundane world. And it isn't as if I were discussing an actual man, for goodness sake. Simply men in general and why one might or might not find one man in particular more attractive than another man in particular. These are things I must be clear about, and very soon."

"*Why?*" Blond and ethereal, lovely Sibyl fluttered over Meg.

This was where caution became imperative. "Don't worry so, Sibyl. There is no absolutely clear direction for all this. I'm gathering information, simply gathering to broaden my understanding." Slight understatements, or even fabrications could occasionally be justified. "I should think a man's hands would be most important, shouldn't you?"

"Yes."

"But why do you think so, Sibyl?"

"I... Well, if you must know, I do not at all care for men with *soft* hands. There, now you know. They are not manly to me.

And I do not like *small* hands. That is more difficult to explain except to say that I should prefer a man's hands—if I were interested in him at all—that is, if I noticed him at all—I should prefer a man's hands to be larger than mine. Much larger. There is something inside me that insists this is important, yet I don't know why. Yes, large, strong, well-shaped, long-fingered—perhaps blunt at the nail—yes, yes, that is what I prefer.''

Meg watched her sister's deep concentration and smiled. "Hmm. I agree." And all this from dear Sibyl, who didn't think they should as much as have an opinion on a gentleman's person.

"I also dislike those small, neat feet some gentlemen seem to take pride in. But again, the reason is beyond my reach. It's just that I know it could be important.''

"Hmm. Yes."

"Height is not of such great importance. But a good carriage is essential, and fine, strong-looking shoulders—legs that look well without padding, particularly when the gentleman is on horseback and the muscle is flexed. Yes, very pleasant. One doesn't, of course, tend to see a gentleman's chest other than when he adjusts his waistcoat, but there are those moments. A solid-looking chest. Firm, with good muscles again. Oh, yes, that is quite the thing. And I do warm to a charming smile. I shouldn't care for a man who smiled all the time since I prefer a serious side in all acquaintances, but a charming smile so becomes a handsome gentleman's face, don't you think? And dimples here?'' She touched her own face just below each cheekbone.

Meg scarcely dared move one of her own muscles, or take the smallest breath for fear of diverting Sibyl from this absolutely wonderful revelation. Sibyl was human. Sibyl had *longings*. Sibyl was no different from Meg in reacting to certain qualities in the male.

"Meg?" Sibyl said. "Do you agree?"

"Oh, I do, I most definitely do. Oh, very much so, I assure you. But do go on.''

"Go on? What do you mean?"

Fiddle dee dee, the spell was broken. "Nothing. I didn't want to interrupt if you had more to say. I thought you might have an opinion on, um, well, a gentleman's...*derriere?*"

Aghast came close to describing Sibyl's expression.

"No," Meg said rapidly, "I see you don't. But I do. Muscle is important there, too—only to ensure the fit of the trouser, of course. But, moving on to another subject, I'm going to make certain our affairs turn out well. It's just that I have things to learn, and quickly. Because I do have a plan."

Sibyl's blue eyes sharpened with worry. "Oh, no, no, Meggie. I don't know what you intend, but already you frighten me. This is all part of this, this—" she waved a hand at Meg "—this new preoccupation with strange, foreign notions. Oh, do take that thing off your head, Meggie. I can't think what's come over you of late. You are quite changed."

"A grateful parishioner brought the mantilla back for Papa," she said, still hoping to deflect any alarm. "From a long sea journey. It never had any purpose before. But it does now. It calms my inner self and helps me achieve a serene state. Familiar objects can do that, Sibyl. And if I am changed it's because the world has changed me—for the better, I prefer to think. I am a woman of spirit, a woman with a backbone. I am a woman who will not sit with her hands crossed, waiting for disaster—waiting to become destitute. I *am.*" She closed her eyes and took a deep breath.

"You are what?" Sibyl whispered.

Meg breathed in again, long and deep through her nose, and repeated, "I *am,* that's all. One day, when you are ready and no longer frightened of anything you don't understand, one day I shall begin your instruction in abstraction."

"I cannot bear it," Sibyl said, pacing the drab floral carpet. "If Papa were alive he would put a stop to it. This is what comes of women attending lectures by foreigners. They get foreign ideas. I'm not at all certain all this *abstracted* thinking, and muttering of *mantram,* or whatever you call these meaningless words you chant, isn't, well… I'm just not sure, that's all. I thought you only chanted when you assumed you were alone, but now you are perfectly content to worry me with your muttering and humming, and with assuming such completely unladylike poses at any moment at all. They just—''

"Are," Meg finished for her sister.

"There, you see?" Sibyl planted her feet and pointed at Meg. "You do it all the time. Dear, dear. I'm just not sure what to do about you. We won't discuss the subject further at this time."

"Good for you," Meg said. "Now do sit, Sibyl. I have something wonderful to tell you. I was going to wait, but perhaps it will cheer you, and since I am expecting a message on the subject, we might as well get the explanation out of the way."

Sibyl shook her head. Her serviceable gray morning gown became her, but then, anything became Sibyl. "You are afraid," she said. "No, don't interrupt me, please. You were experimenting with this strangeness before, but now—since the…you know what—you've only become so, so *obvious* since that."

Since she had been pushed into the path of a coach near the Burlington Arcade. "I will not lie to you," she said. "There are moments when I want to make my mind so busy there is no room in there for being frightened."

"If we only think good thoughts," Sibyl said, "then we cannot possibly be frightened."

With a great deal of effort, Meg held back a retort that would upset dear, good, Sibyl.

"There, you see now?" Sibyl sounded triumphant. "You can't argue with the truth. Papa—God rest his soul—would be so pleased and proud of you that you are willing to examine your motives in this."

"I wish Papa were here now," Meg said.

"Oh, so do I."

"If he were," Meg continued, "I should give him a piece of my mind and he would not be at all pleased with that."

"Meggie, you are disrespectful."

"I am practical. If Papa had been sensible enough to find a way around leaving our home to a wretched male relation, we should not be in our current dilemma. *My* current dilemma. We should be safe in dear little Puckly Hinton, not in rented rooms in London, trying to support ourselves while someone tries to...*kill* me." The time had passed for mincing words.

Sibyl halted her agitated pacing. Sun through the window shimmered on her hair. Her soft mouth trembled. "You cannot be certain someone pushed you. It's perfectly possible that in such a crush, you tripped, or imagined you were pushed. After all, you do have an active mind, Meggie."

"We won't pursue the subject further at this time," Meg said. "My plan is the result of a letter I received from Finch in Scotland."

"You heard from Finch?" Sibyl was instantly distracted. She plopped down beside Meg on the chaise. "You didn't say she'd written. How is she, and His Lordship? How is Hayden faring—and dear little Oswin?"

Finch had been Finch More when they'd all met. Her brother, Latimer More, still lived in the rooms beneath Meg and Sibyl's. Latimer was at 7A Mayfair Square whereas the Smiles lived at 7B. Above them were Lady Hester Bingham, owner of the house, and her nephew Hunter Lloyd, Barrister at Law. Adam Chillworth, artist and Meg's friend, lived in the attic. That was 7C. Lady Hester might be on the third floor but her address was 7, since it was her house. Finch had married Ross, Viscount Kilrood, who owned Number 8, and they were currently at their Scottish estates.

"Meggie? Do tell."

"Sorry. I've rather a lot on my mind. They are all well. Finch mentions Hayden often and is glad His Lordship took him in." Hayden had come to Viscount Kilrood as a street urchin paid to carry a message. And he'd stayed, together with his dog, Oswin. "I miss them all. But I've no doubt they'll be back in London sometime during the Season." The Season, which was all but upon them, and which Meg intended to exploit in order to provide the Smiles sisters with the opportunity they urgently needed.

"It will be lovely to see them," Sibyl said. "Meggie, forgive me if I am sometimes sharp. You know, the mantilla becomes you. Your eyes sparkle most mysteriously through the lace."

Meg said, "Thank you," and reached to embrace her sister.

"Your hair!" Sibyl's mouth opened and remained so.

This had been inevitable. "Let me tell you what is about to happen," Meg said.

"What have you done to your hair?" Sibyl was not to be diverted. She peered through the mantilla. "Why didn't I notice it before? Meggie, it's turned red."

"Don't be silly, it's brown." Meg swallowed. "Finch's letter arrived yesterday. She knows of the people who have moved into Number Seventeen—across the square. They are from a small country on the border between, er, France and Italy, I think. Mont Nuages."

"Your hair is *red*," Sibyl announced. "The sun is shining on it and it *glows* red."

"The man's name is Count Etranger and he has brought his young sister to make a London Season. Anyway, he is not well equipped to guide her in preparing for the whirl to come and is in need of assistance. A companion for the girl, someone who can instruct her in matters of fashion and deportment. She is also—although I cannot imagine why—but she is not accomplished at the pianoforte, nor does she sing appealingly although she has a pleasant enough voice."

"You sew brilliantly," Sibyl said, distracted. "And no one has better sense of style or is more informed of current fashions." Meg's girlhood skills as a seamstress had provided them with some meager wages since they came to Town. However, she was not well known—did not wish to be—and the ladies she sewed for took advantage by paying her very paltry compensation for excellent work.

"And you play brilliantly," she told Sibyl, "and sing brilliantly. What could be more perfect?"

"Please tell me what has happened to your hair."

"Ooh, you are not to be silenced on the matter, are you?" Meg said. "Very well. I shall tell you and then I wish to hear not another word on the subject. There is a certain small shop behind a milliner's establishment on Bond Street. It is known to young ladies—and certain others—as a discreet place from which to obtain advice on matters of personal delicacy. At Mme. Suzanne's one need never fear saying, or asking anything. So, when I went to seek that lady's assistance she was most helpful. As you have said, my hair is brown, the dull brown of a dull brown mouse. Not good enough. I need excitement, Sibyl. I need that mystery you mentioned. Red hair is mysterious."

Sibyl fell back on a cushion. "But—but ladies do not do whatever you have done to achieve such a thing. And why do you need it, Meggie, why?"

"I have told you what I've done to my hair. Now I must move on to more important things. Before someone comes with a message."

"Before *who* comes with a message?" Sibyl moaned. "What are you talking about? What is wrong with you? What is to become of us?"

She would remain calm, Meg told herself. "Early this morning I had a letter delivered to Count Etranger at Number Seventeen Mayfair Square. I informed him that I had heard through a mutual friend, Viscountess Kilrood, that he was in need of a companion for his sister. I offered my services in that capacity and assured him that with my help he need have no further concern about the Princess's wardrobe, deportment, or her understanding of the social intricacies she will meet while she is in London."

"You didn't." Sibyl's voice was faint.

"Buck up, Sibyl. I most certainly did. We are all but penniless and I will not remain in this house for one moment longer than we can afford to pay rent."

"Lady Hester would never make us leave."

"No, she would not. And I know it pleases her to insist to her friends that all of her lodgers are her protégées, but it isn't true. She must need the money, and we understand such situations, don't we? Of course we do. So, I have decided to find employment."

"You will also teach... Princess? Did you mention a princess?"

Meg composed herself and sat absolutely still. "Princess Désirée of Mont Nuages. The Crown Prince's daughter."

"And *you* have put yourself forward to be her companion?"

"They will find none better."

Sibyl covered her face. "You applied for work. Oh, what have we come to? What will become of us? Perhaps we should go to Cousin William and ask for—"

"We will ask William Godly-Smythe for nothing. We are going to become advisers to Count Etranger, for which he will compensate us out of gratitude."

"We?" Sibyl squeaked.

"Well, you are the pianoforte and voice teacher, not I. So the Count will be doubly fortunate. Between the two of us, we will turn his drab, graceless, bad-tempered sister into a charming creature."

Sibyl stared, but then she smiled, smiled more widely, chuckled, laughed more loudly than Meg ever recalled her laughing before. When Sibyl was at last in control of herself again, she dabbed at her eyes with a lace handkerchief and said, "You are incorrigible. You frighten me with your wild words. Undoubtedly your abstracted thinking is responsible. It causes you to imagine your dreamings to be true. How foolish of me to believe you even for a moment."

"Believe me."

"Yes, yes, of course. You wrote to someone you do not know, a count from Mont Nuages, and offered to become his sister's companion—his sister, the princess, that is—her ultimate adviser in making a successful Season. Certainly, you did. And I suppose your decision to do whatever you did to make your hair red has something to do with this plan.''

"It does now."

"I see." Sibyl giggled afresh.

"No, you don't." Meg had not meant to sound so cross. "I intend to use this wonderful opportunity to our own ends. In order to do that, I must make the best of my less plain attributes. I have been told I have good skin—so I shall take special care of it. And, so I understand, I have fine eyes. I am deciding how to use them well. I'm pleased to hear my mantilla may be useful on occasion. My hair is thick and shiny, but it is brown. As I have already told you, I've done something about that. And then—" she looked at the floor and felt her face grow hot "—then I have, well, I might as well get it said. After all, we're both women, and sisters. We should be able to say anything to each other. I have a passable figure. Rather a lot of bosom, I always thought, but, since I'm told many gentlemen are extremely attracted to such things, well then, I intend to flatter that aspect of my person."

"Meggie."

"Oh, don't swoon, dear. Not now, when there is so much to consider."

"You are not yourself. You can't be. So much worry has turned your mind. Where shall I go for help?"

"Help will be here at any moment," Meg said, matter of fact. "I expect a prompt response to my letter. After all, I wrote to the Count that I am a friend of Finch, who is the wife of his long acquaintance, Viscount Kilrood. It was the Viscount who helped the Count's father locate a suitable establishment from which to launch his sister, you know."

"You mean Finch suggested you approach the Count?"

"Well, no, not exactly."

"So you fabricated in your letter? You implied that had been the case?"

Sibyl was too intelligent to be deceived by any effort of Meg's to cover the truth. "I did. Just a little. But only out of desperation."

"Nothing will come of it." There was more hope than certainty in Sibyl's voice. She got up and took a poker to the small fire that burned in the grate. March, always an uncertain month, was proving pretty but cold. "I am hopeful of finding new students, soon. Lady Chattam is so pleased with her Teddy's progress. She has said she will recommend me to others of her friends who are having difficulty with their children's music lessons."

Poor Sibyl. So talented, yet reduced to spending tiresome hours with the untalented and spoiled offspring of the wealthy.

"It will not be necessary for you to take on more nasty Teddy Chattams. I will make sure of that."

Sibyl dropped the poker. It clanged on the green stone hearth. "Meg." She spun about. "Oh, no, you cannot possibly be planning such a thing. Say it isn't true."

Meg frowned at her sister through the mantilla. "What isn't true?"

"You haven't spun some fantasy in which you will..." She tottered back to sit by Meg. "You haven't—aren't—*won't* pursue any notion of getting this Count to...to *marry* you?"

Now it was Meg who laughed loud and long. When she could speak again, she said, "You silly goose. We both know a man like that would never consider marrying the daughter of an English country clergyman. No, nothing of the kind."

Sibyl let out a breath. "That's good then. But...Meg, you wouldn't. You couldn't. Could you?"

"Speak plain, Sibyl. I am tired by my abstractions, and more tired by the matters of this world that interfere with my inner improvement. Do not speak in riddles."

"Very well." When pushed, Sibyl could become quite the rigid little tyrant. She sat straight and drew her lips in tight and pale. "Do you seek to become Count Etranger's ladybird?"

There had been few occasions when Sibyl had shocked Meg, but this was one of them. She pulled up her slippered feet and crossed her legs beneath the loose, scarlet robe she had sewn to wear during abstraction sessions. "Mystery," she said, "that is the answer." And she rested her upturned hands on her knees, in the manner illustrated in the book she had secretly obtained and which she kept hidden.

"So, you do not deny it?"

A rap on the door preceded the slow entry of Old Coot, Lady Hester's aged butler. He fixed his bulbous eyes on Meg and shook his head. "Unsuitable behavior," he said, as certain as always of his place in the world and his right to say whatever came to mind. "Can't imagine what things are coming to. A person to see you, Miss Meg. Are you receivin'?"

"Of course," Meg said promptly.

"Then I'll send M. Verbeux up."

Old Coot withdrew to be quickly replaced by a slender, dark-haired man with a black mustache that curved downward at either side of his mouth. He wore spectacles with small, round frames that barely revealed all of his brooding dark eyes. M. Verbeux was...compelling.

"Oh, Meggie," Sibyl muttered.

M. Verbeux did not as much as glance at Sibyl. "Miss Meg Smiles," the man said to Meg, with only the faintest trace of a French accent.

Meg managed to stop herself from shooting her feet back to the floor. "I am Miss Meg Smiles, if that is who you seek."

M. Verbeux studied a thick piece of paper in his hand and grunted. "He'll see you. Now. Accompany me, please."

"The Count?" Meg said, scarcely able to breathe at all.

"Answers only. No questions. He tolerates nothing more." M. Verbeux turned his handsome back and retreated.

"Help me change," Meg said the instant the door closed again. She worked to unhook the satin frogs on her robe. "I must be quick."

"Quick to run to a rude man, *with* a rude man who does not know you but who orders you about as if you were a servant?"

"I am prepared to be a servant," Meg said, tossing aside the robe as she entered the bedroom she and Sibyl shared. "I am prepared to become the Count's most pleasing servant, for which I shall be well compensated."

2

Number 17 was not at all like Number 7. In fact, whereas Number 7 was a single terraced house, albeit shabby but of grand proportions, Number 17 consisted of two houses made into one. There was no longer a Number 16 Mayfair Square.

"Grand" hardly did justice to Number 17.

Meg sat where M. Verbeux had indicated she should. The dimensions of the brown, brass-studded leather chair she used were enormous. If she were a considerably taller person, tall enough for her head to reach the chair's wings, she doubted she could see to either side. As it was she perched, stiff-backed, at the very edge of the seat, surrounded by the lustrous dark paneling of a galleried library and study. Four narrow windows, curtained with fringed green velvet, soared at the opposite side of the room from where Meg waited. Indeed, the windows were so far away as to cast slim oblongs of sunlight that didn't reach her toes.

Her toes barely made contact with the green and gold Aubusson carpet.

Perhaps she had been hasty in approaching the Count.

Footsteps rang from the stone-tiled foyer outside the room, from behind Meg. Measured footsteps. A man's measured footsteps—no doubt made by his boots. They paused somewhere out there. She could not risk peering around the side of the chair in search of a person.

The footsteps continued, drew closer, changed in tenor as heel left stone and descended on wood, then thudded on carpet.

Meg sat as straight and tall as she could.

Perhaps she should stand. Yes, that's what she should do.

With as much grace as possible, she slid even farther forward and, using a slight but embarrassing jump, made audibly solid contact with the floor. She prepared to curtsey.

"Sit, if you please," a man's voice ordered. A deep voice with the faintest of French accents.

Intriguing.

Terrifying.

Meg worked her way back onto the seat of the chair in time to look up at a person who would undoubtedly fit Sibyl's list of desirable male attributes—only this man wasn't smiling, so Meg couldn't say whether or not his smile might be charming, or produce fascinating dimples somewhere.

He clasped his hands behind his back. "Miss Smiles, I presume?"

This was no time or place for the fainthearted. "I am Meg Smiles."

"But of course you are." He bowed very slightly and reached for her hand. When she thought to raise it, he took her fingers in his and passed his mouth within a breath's distance of her skin. "Charmed," he said.

His hands must be the actual hands Sibyl had described. Meg raised her eyes to his and felt hot and cold at the exact same time. His eyes were as dark as his hair—which was very dark. He had an exceedingly handsome face, in a commanding way.

"Count Etranger," he said, and released her hand.

Meg didn't recall her hand being kissed—in a manner of speaking—by a count before. Meg didn't recall her hand being kissed by anyone before.

She remembered to return both hands to her lap and tried not to stare at this tall, imposing, somberly dressed man who would render Sibyl into an ecstacy. He had absolutely no effect on Meg. Well, almost no effect.

He put some small distance between them. But his regard didn't waver.

Miss Meg Smiles conducted herself well, Jean-Marc decided, but the effort cost her considerably. Given her unorthodox and impertinent approach, he had expected someone different, someone more…bold. In fact, despite her mention of his old friend, Kilrood, he would have ignored her letter had she not offered exactly the type of services he urgently needed, including some he hadn't even identified before she mentioned them.

He propped an elbow on the opposite forearm and tapped his chin. The question was, could she really accomplish what her proposal had promised? And would she command the respect she must command in order to relieve him of the onerous duty of spending too much time on Désirée's debut? Naturally, he would assume the essential responsibilities, but what did he know of bringing out a seventeen-year-old girl?

Miss Smiles was not remarkable, other than for what he could see of her thick, red hair beneath the brim of a fashionable bonnet the color of lemons. Now that was startling, in fact—the contrasts. She achieved a sort of brilliance with her choice of bright colors against that very fascinating hair. He strolled to view her from the opposite side. Only once had she looked at him direct. Memorable eyes of a light brown, perhaps the brown of good cognac. Nice mouth. Full, but not too full. And she had good skin, pale but with color high on the cheek, and a bloom of health. That was appealing—important. It was important that she be healthy. Her yellow pelisse had a stand-up collar faced with satin. Jean-Marc rarely took overmuch notice of such things, but the impression she would give was of the utmost importance.

Her clothes seemed to him to be highly fashionable, if devoid of excessive ornament, and of fine quality. For the first time since his arrival in London he felt a lightening of the heart.

Only with extreme difficulty did Meg sit still and endure the Count's examination, his rather rude examination in her estimation. He strolled to look at her from first one, then another direction. Meg felt when his regard was on her face, and when it progressed to other parts of her person. She had only recently finished the outfit she wore. The pattern she had made herself, using French fashion plates as her guide. The ensemble might be a trifle girlish, and somewhat too noticeable, but it was in the latest style and the Count might want to feel confident that she could manage the acquisition of a most up-to-date wardrobe for his sister. The Princess could, in fact, already have most items she would need, but there must always be additional purchases at such a time.

Count Etranger assumed yet another angle on her person. Meg reached into her beaded reticule for a handkerchief and touched it to her nose. Sitting just so while he observed her with such... His regard was rude.

Her half boots had caught his attention. Meg blushed. They were not new, a fact that the small, yellow satin roses she'd sewn at the ankles would not hide from a sharp eye. And he couldn't fail to note that even though she pointed her toes, she could scarcely reach the floor. Hardly a dignified situation.

Miss Smiles was short.

In other circumstances that would be of no importance. As it was, it could present a problem. She would have to have presence. "Kindly stand, Miss Smiles. If you don't mind."

The manner in which she moved her nether regions to the edge of the chair before launching into a jump that landed her on the carpet was unfortunate. Particularly unfortunate since the combination of that jump, and the concentration that knitted her brow, might cause a less composed man to laugh.

She did look at him direct then, and said, "The chair is sized for a much larger person, Your Lordship. I fear it makes a spectacle of me," and she smiled just a little—and he liked her smile. With the explanation, and that smile, she regained her dignity, a feat he admired. Evidently there was some shortage of blunt, though. Something would have to be done about the worn boots— if he decided she was worth a trial.

"I should like you to walk, Miss Smiles. Perhaps toward the

desk, then around the desk to the windows. You might move a curtain to look down upon the street."

Meg wasn't certain she could move her legs at all. The reason for all this observation, which required that she endure his scrutiny, eluded her. Never had she suffered such acute awkwardness, such stinging of the skin all over her person, such heat in her face, such lack of feeling in her hands and feet.

However, she had a plan, and that plan could very well benefit from practice such as this. She must become accustomed not only to enduring the attention of gentlemen, but to seeking it out. The thought brought a painful glow to her already overwarm face.

Collecting herself, she inclined her head at the Count, stiffened her spine yct again and progressed, eyes high, toward the desk. And promptly tripped.

In one stride the Count was at her side, catching her about the waist as she would have fallen. "You might want to have the bottoms of your boots inspected," he said. "Possibly a seam has become unstitched." He released her at once.

He *had* noticed they were old. "Thank you," she said, breathless. And he had held her about the waist. "I shall take your advice." Lifting each foot in a manner that felt ridiculous, she continued her progress toward the desk, and around the desk to the windows, where she pulled a heavy, looped drapery aside and looked down upon the shiny, black metal railings fronting the flagway. A gate in the railings led to steps descending to the basement and the servants' domain.

Meg waited to be told to return. The Count made no such request. Rather he came to stand some feet distant, his arms crossed, his dark, arched brows pulled down in a frown. She inclined her head as if to look toward the gardens in the middle of the square. "A lovely time of year," she remarked while the pulse in her throat felt painful. "Crocus and primrose, and so much budding. Spring can be so delightful."

"You speak well," he said.

"So do you." The instant the words left her lips she looked at him, aghast.

He actually smiled, and he did have a dimple beneath each cheekbone.

"I apologize," she said. Oh, would she never learn to curb her careless retorts?

"You are perhaps overly outspoken, but I accept your apology."

Such generosity of spirit, Meg thought. Would she actually manage to navigate her way through this difficult interview, obtain the position and turn it into the result she and Sibyl needed if they were to survive with any degree of dignity?

"I am half English," the Count said, surprising Meg. "Which may account for my command of the language. I was educated in England, and I have property here—on the Thames at Windsor. It has always been my delight to spend as much time as possible there."

She nodded with genuine interest and smiled. "My travels have only been within this country, and those over short distances, but my love for England is a deep thing that brightens my heart."

The Count took a long time to respond, and while he was silent he concentrated on Meg in a most disconcerting manner. "I think you may do quite well as my sister's companion," he said at last. "At least from the manner in which you present yourself. Tell me about your accomplishments."

These had been glossed over in her letter, Meg thought. How insignificant they were bound to seem when explored. "I, er, have a flair for design. Of ladies' clothing. I am self-taught—to pretend otherwise would be foolish. But I am always informed of the latest fashions and I am adept at making patterns from fashion plates and producing wardrobes that bring great pleasure to my small number of clients."

"But you are not well known?"

She looked away. "No. My father is dead, but he was a minister and did not approve of drawing attention to oneself. He would have been embarrassed that Sibyl—my sister—and I are forced to work.'' She regarded him. ''We are forced to work, Count Etranger. And we work hard. We were brought up as ladies, but that is not enough to guarantee that one may placidly expect to be taken care of. We are understated women, but accomplished in our own small way.''

His expression didn't change from one of mild interest.

He was not touched by her description of herself. Tension mounted for Meg. She needed this position—needed this position as a stepping stone to something more, or she and Sibyl would surely descend into poverty.

''I will do my utmost for the Princess,'' she said, hearing how hurried she sounded, and how eager—too eager. ''I believe I will be able to win her confidence and help her enter what must be a disconcertingly demanding time in her life, with a sense of assurance.''

''A commendable speech,'' he said, but he was frowning again.

''After our father died, Sibyl and I decided to come to London. This sounds somewhat silly, but we no longer had a home and we came to seek our fortune. We intended to make the best of the talents we have. Sibyl is a most accomplished musician, an excellent teacher of the pianoforte and also a voice teacher. I'm sure your sister needs little help in these areas, but my sister is available and she works well with young people.''

''Yellow becomes you, Miss Smiles.''

Meg forgot whatever else she had intended to say. She glanced down at her pelisse and said, when she could gather her wits, ''Thank you.''

This was a pretty muddle, Jean-Marc thought. The girl was a minister's daughter, probably from some insignificant place where society consisted of the odd musicale in less than elegant surroundings. Yet she had courage and style and she might just do.

It wasn't as if he'd had any luck finding someone more qualified who was at all interested in the post.

"You also walk exceedingly well. Do you feel qualified to…to ensure that the Princess's deportment is without flaw?"

"I do indeed," Meg said. She would approach Lady Hester Bingham for any extra advice she needed. "Oh, absolutely." She wondered how often she would see Count Etranger—if he retained her. Often, she hoped—although she shouldn't hope for any such thing.

"In matters concerning toilette. Coiffeur and so on. What of those?"

"I'm sure—"

"Kindly remove your bonnet."

Meg swallowed, but she slowly untied the ribbons beneath her chin and slid off the bonnet. Sibyl had been right when she'd said Meg's experiments with Mme. Suzanne's product had produced a startling result. What if the Count found the color garish?

Count Etranger came toward her and bowed his head to regard her at a singularly discomforting proximity. "Yes, indeed, your own hair is most fetching. Do you dress it yourself?"

"I do," Meg said. Did he think she'd be looking for employment as a companion if she could afford her own maid?

Etranger made one of his slow progressions around her, studying her hair from all sides. "I don't think I've ever seen hair of a brighter red hue. Extraordinary."

Artificial. "Thank you."

"How well it sets off your white skin."

Yet again her white skin felt scorched. "Thank you."

"Think nothing of it." He stood inches from her right shoulder and she would have to be blind not to note that his attention rested where she'd made the rash decision to follow the fashion plate to its most extreme feature by including a keyhole cutout that revealed her décolletage. After all, she had decided not to disguise the full bosom with which she had been endowed.

Jean-Marc realized he had contemplated Miss Smiles's interesting—or rather, her somewhat arousing display of bosom for too long. It wasn't as if it was obviously presented. Oh, no, the girl had merely created a wicked little peephole beneath the collar of her pelisse, a peephole just large enough to give a glimpse of the way her plump breasts pressed together above the neck of her gown.

"Very white," he murmured. "And you have a few freckles." He shifted his gaze to her nose. "Yes, I do think you may be what I need—for my sister."

If Miss Smiles noted his correction, there was no change in her expression. She appeared vaguely bemused.

"Very well, my dear," he said, deliberately hearty. "We shall discuss what I require of you, shall we?"

Meg said, "Yes," and enjoyed his hand beneath her elbow, and the manner in which he guided her to a chair facing the huge expanse of an ebony desk, the legs of which ended in gold claws. The Count settled himself on the opposite side of the desk and pulled clean paper before him. The silver lid of his crystal inkstandish clicked open beneath his fingers and he dipped his pen.

"Sibyl—my sister—is very musically gifted and—"

"So you have said. I will consider giving her a trial. But first we must be clear on what I expect you to accomplish and plan how you will set about following my instructions."

He absolutely had to agree to take Sibyl, too. Not only did Meg need her sister's support, but she had vowed to remove her from the odious business of teaching badly behaved children.

Jean-Marc reached into a drawer in the desk and produced Meg Smiles's letter—her well-composed letter written in a strong, beautifully formed hand and with evident understanding of such matters as appropriate forms of address and so on. "Now," he said, tossing the two sheets of good quality paper on his blotter, "let us dispose of the details. Princess Désirée is barely seventeen and brilliant. Her knowledge of world affairs is probably more developed than that of many men, even men of her class and position."

Meg murmured appreciatively. But surely Finch's letter had hinted that the Princess's disposition was other than pleasing?

"Princess Désirée is very quiet by nature," Jean-Marc said, deliberately nonchalant. "But she is charming nevertheless, and ready to learn those graces she will need. Not, of course, that she lacks grace, but she has had little need to use it in social situations. Mont Nuages—our home—is a small country. Our intimate circle is also small."

Miss Smiles murmured again.

"Princess Désirée is witty. In fact, when she is in one of her ebullient moods, it may be necessary for you to subdue her tendency to become overexcited and to laugh too often and too loudly."

Miss Smiles said, "I see."

"Of course we must understand her enthusiasm at the prospect of making her debut. And she loves clothes. She has so many. However nothing will suit her but that she acquire a completely new wardrobe. You are confident you can supervise such an extensive undertaking?"

"Yes, yes. It will be my pleasure."

"Good." Very good, Jean-Marc thought. The idea of having to take part in any of this foolishness had all but undone him. "Spare no expense. Princess Désirée learns quickly, so, if you should see some area of her development that appears to need considerable attention, do not panic—she will understand your concerns and set about fulfilling your instructions at once."

"I am not given to panic," Miss Smiles said.

"Good. Princess Désirée is malleable. She wants to please. She will want to please you. But you are to do whatever you think necessary to make her the success of the Season."

Meg smiled. "I will," she said. Evidently she had misunderstood Finch. She began to look forward to the prospect of working with a high-spirited person. "And, if I may say so, your admiration for your sister is a heartwarming thing to see."

He raised his eyes from the notes he was making. "I'm glad." One moment he smiled and looked approachable, the next he became forbiddingly cool. "Family loyalty is expected, isn't it?"

He was putting her in her place. "My father taught us that love of family should be second only to love of God."

Apparently Count Etranger found her comment noteworthy. He wrote for quite some time. Meg liked the sharp bones in his face, and the manner in which his eyebrows flared upward at the ends. His white neck cloth was simply tied and stark against an unrelieved black coat and waistcoat.

She must not be caught watching him. "How fortunate that you found such a lovely house to rent," she said, admiring the shimmer on dark wood, the acres of leather-bound books, the elegant furnishings, most of them French and old.

"I understand it was not so lovely when it had no furniture. But you are right, it is quite fine now."

"It... Yes, indeed." So, what she saw belonged to him. Though she shouldn't be surprised that he would choose to go to such lengths for a stay of a few months.

"I take it you understand who we are?" he said, still writing. He allowed a few seconds to pass before continuing, "Our father, Prince Georges, rules Mont Nuages. Do you know where that is?"

"Yes," Meg said.

"Good. Princess Désirée and I are his only children. It is at my father's request that I am here to attend to bringing my sister out."

The manner in which he informed her of these facts did not invite a response.

"Very well." He pushed back his chair and rose. "I shall send Princess Désirée to you so the two of you may become acquainted."

Meg became anxious all over again. "You will be with her, Your Lordship? To make sure she is comfortable with me?" There had been entirely too many strangers for one day.

"No. You must exert authority, you understand? Not without respect for my sister's status, but authority indeed. I shall hope for a suitable degree of friendship between you, but, as with any undertaking where one must follow the instruction of another without question—absolutely without question—rank must be established.''

Meg wasn't at all certain how she felt about that. "Surely—"

He wagged a finger to silence her. "Think of battle, dear girl. How would it be if a soldier were to challenge his commanding officer at the height of battle? Tell me that, hmm?"

"Battle—"

"It would be disastrous." Without so much as glancing in her direction again, the Count went toward the foyer. "Deferentially in command, that will be the nature of your position with Désirée. Oh, do you speak French?"

Praying he wouldn't change his mind, Meg said, "As well as a person taught by her English father can. A person who has never spoken French with a French person. Schoolroom French, I suppose I should say."

"Ah." He turned back. "Then I should remind you that the purpose of your position here is not to improve your command of French. Under no circumstances will you speak French in this house. Is that understood?"

What a vexing man. A contrary man. A confusing man. "I hadn't thought—"

"Well, think of it now, Miss Smiles, and all will be well. Désirée's English is perfect. Almost perfect. If she becomes uncertain about something, she may stumble a little. But she will be anxious to practice, and she must. She must practice a great deal. So—" he inclined his head and smiled "—not a word of French. We are agreed?"

"Agreed," Meg said, hoping he wouldn't hear her relief.

The Count's purposeful footsteps departed across the stone floor in the foyer and Meg heard a door open, not too distant a door, and the sound of muffled conversation.

A longcase clock ticked loudly. Meg remained facing the door, a pleasant smile in place. A princess was bound to be sure of herself, but still it was always nice to be welcoming.

The ticking seemed to grow even louder. Meg could barely hear the voices now.

More minutes passed, and more. She took a few steps while humming notes from a waltz Sibyl had played. It might be a good idea to improve her dancing skills, Meg thought, just in case. Of course, the waltz was very new and daring and she doubted she would ever have an opportunity to enjoy it herself.

She held her arms as if she were dancing with a gentleman and whirled around, and whirled around again. Really, she might become skilled at this. "Thank you," she said to her imaginary partner, and laughed. "You are too kind. Why, yes, it is warm. You think so, too?" Meg laughed again. "Of course, you are right."

Her next twirl took her past the oversize leather chair, then around it. She had always loved music.

Count Etranger stood near the door, at the edge of the carpet.

Puffing a little, Meg stood still. There was nothing she could do about either her blushes or the erratic beating of her heart. *Oh, fiddle, fiddle, fiddle, the mortification of it.* "Practicing," she said in a silly little voice that shamed her.

"So I see," the Count said, and there was no doubt that the corners of his mouth twitched. "Very industrious of you. I thought better of what I said and decided to bring Princess Désirée to you myself, as you suggested. Come along, Désirée."

He leaned outside the library wall, then left the room entirely, to reappear holding a girl by the wrist. "Désirée, this is Miss Smiles. Miss Smiles, Her Royal Highness, Princess Désirée of Mont Nuages. Please remember everything I've told you, particularly the part about rank, and battle."

This time he closed the door behind him when he left, closed Meg and his sister inside the room together.

Meg dropped into a deep curtsey and wondered how one gave orders from such a position. When the princess failed to make any comment at all, Meg straightened and reapplied her smile. "I am honored to meet you, Princess Désirée. Your brother has told me so much about you. He has said you are very excited by all you are to experience here in London. We shall work only as hard as we must to make you ready for all the wonderful parties and balls, and so on. The Count said you are to have an entire new wardrobe, and I shall be thrilled to help you with your selections.''

Princess Désirée watched Meg, appeared to listen, but showed no sign of the exhilaration her brother had insisted she felt.

An unpleasant premonition assailed Meg. She might fail here. If she did, and that failure was noted too soon, she would have no time to take even a small advantage of her hard-won opportunity.

''Deportment will be simple, of course. And most of the so-called required graces. You must already know a great deal about those.''

Not a word.

Before Meg stood a thin girl, a thin girl who must be at least six inches taller than her new ranking officer. Princess Désirée's hair was not exactly brown, but neither was it blond. Light brown, perhaps, and straight. Probably straight. Parted at one side and pulled flat over her ears, it was plaited. Two long plaits fell forward over the girl's narrow shoulders. Not a hint of color brightened her features. Sallow might be the description employed by someone less charitable than Meg.

''Do you enjoy music?'' she asked.

The princess looked at her feet.

Meg cast about for some means to ease the girl's obvious shyness. How could such a plain, gangly duck be turned into a swan—in so short a time? That was such an unpleasant description. But the princess was gangly, pallid, rather plain, dressed completely in gray—apart from a white chemisette—and resembled a schoolgirl recently soaked in a storm and dried out with her clothes on. And she drooped. Everything about her drooped. No spark showed in her. If she had any figure at all, the walking dress—which was indeed much too large—did a fine job of disguising the fact.

Even if she hadn't been pleased by Meg's plan, poor dear Sibyl's only hope was for this seemingly impossible venture to be a success. Persistence would be the key.

"Come here, please," Meg said, summoning a little of the authority she'd been told she must employ. Rather than wait for her wish to be obeyed—and it showed no sign of any such thing—she went to the princess and looked up into her face. "What beautiful eyes you have. Gray. A fine color. We must experiment with your hair. It's time for it to be put up. Some favor a great many curls. I do not care for that myself, and I think we will see how we do with a smooth coiffeur for you. Your hair is fine, but—" and limp "—but there is plenty of it. We shall see. Perhaps we might begin getting to know each other? I should like to spend our first hours together in conversation. If you would prefer a smaller, more intimate room, I'm sure the Count would be more than agreeable. I want you to talk to me about your expectations. About your hopes. The things you like about London so far, or don't like about London. Most of all, we must deal with those things you do not understand. Once those are cleared away, the rest will be simple." Meg widened her smile, although the princess wasn't actually looking at her. "Shall we summon your brother?"

Princess Désirée lowered her eyelids.

"Come, come, now," Meg said. Her stomach felt so unpleasant. "I will make the decision for both of us. A more intimate room. I'll ring for someone."

"Qu'est-ce que vous pouvez bien faire ici? Qu'est-ce que vous voulez?"

With one hand on the satin bellpull, Meg froze. She worked her way slowly through what she'd just heard. What on earth was she doing there, and what did—she—want? Not a word of French, the Count had instructed her. He had also assured her that the princess's English was excellent. "We must speak English," Meg said. "Your brother insisted."

The thin face rose, and Meg was given the questionable honor of a flat stare from her so-called charge's light eyes. *"Je n'y comprends absolument rien."*

Nothing? Surely that was wrong. Princess Désirée could not mean she didn't understand any English at all.

The door opened again and the Count strode in. His smile was brilliant but did not allay Meg's horror at the certain failure that confronted her.

"You are getting along," he said. "Good, good. I have always found that I can trust my instincts in such things. Are you available to start at once, Miss Smiles? This afternoon?"

Meg looked at the Princess, then at the Count. "If you think that's a good idea."

"Of course it is." He bent to bestow a kiss on his sister's cheek. "Remember what I have told you, Miss Smiles. My sister can be very quiet, but she will soon come to trust you—as I already do. The sooner she will chatter away, the better. I am most concerned that her English be as perfect as I know it can be. And I should like to see a pretty new coiffeur when I return home this evening. You shall show it off at dinner, Désirée. Miss Smiles is to retain a modiste for you—an army of modistes. She is extremely knowledgeable in these matters and will supervise all decisions. Yes, I shall look forward to dinner. You shall join us—"

"Jean-Marc, je suis—"

"English," the Count thundered at his sister. "I thought we both understood that was to be your language until I say otherwise.

"I must go to Windsor," he said to Meg. "But only for the briefest of visits. The ride both ways will be hard in such a short time, but I'll expect to see you at dinner. We did not discuss all our arrangements. Remuneration. You will leave that matter to me. I assure you it will be adequate. And your sister will receive the same sum.''

"Thank you, Your Lordship.'' Meg hovered between ecstacy and doom. He would employ them both, and pay them both. They would manage again—as long as she didn't weaken.

"The other Miss Smiles may remain where she is, at Number Seven, is it?''

Meg nodded.

"Just so. And you will decide appropriate times for Désirée's musical instruction. You, of course, as Désirée's companion, her right hand, my right hand, her teacher, her confidante, her mother while she is without her own, you will share her suite and be with her at all times. *All times.* You will live with us.''

3

"Old Coot told me Barstow's in a flap," Hunter Lloyd said when Sibyl answered his knock on her door. "I realize Meg can't possibly have been lured away by a suspicious, quite possibly dangerous foreigner, but I assume something unusual has happened."

Privacy was impossible at Number 7. Mrs. Barstow, Lady Hester Bingham's housekeeper and personal maid of many years—a cost-reducing measure everyone knew Lady Hester preferred—managed to be aware of almost every move the lodgers made. "Come in," Sibyl said. "I hope Barstow hasn't upset your aunt."

"Aunt thrives on being upset," Hunter said, advancing only feet inside the door. "She waits for whatever gossip others provide. But we do enjoy her, don't we? Some people live their own lives. Some are threatened by reality. My aunt is of the latter persuasion."

Sibyl liked Hunter a good deal. Already a distinguished barrister, he affected no airs. The reason for his continued presence at Number 7 was a puzzle. Although he hadn't been heard to complain, Lady Hester was a trial to her nephew. He must certainly be well fixed, and he was undeniably handsome. Meg and Sibyl had long expected to learn he planned to marry and set himself up elsewhere.

He inclined his head and said, "What was Barstow chattering about?"

"Nothing, I should think," Sibyl said. "At least…well, nothing." She was so frightened for Meg that she longed for wise advice and support, but Meg would be horrified if she discovered Sibyl had discussed their problems.

"Sibyl," Hunter said, his green eyes serious, "Barstow informed Coot that you've been standing in the window for some time. And she said Meg left in a great hurry, and—according to Barstow—dressed as if for an, um, assignation. Barstow's words, not mine, of course."

Sibyl felt a cold shiver. "Meg looked lovely. She always looks lovely. How could Barstow make such a suggestion? Just because she wore her new yellow and her hair is—" Sibyl slapped a hand over her mouth.

"Her hair is?"

"Nothing," Sibyl said, blowing out through pursed lips and avoiding Hunter's regard. "Oh, bother. I shall have to explain. I know I need not ask you to keep what I tell you a confidence. Meg is applying for a position."

"A position?" His voice flattened as if he didn't understand.

"As a…an adviser, I suppose, a guide. She learned about the place from Finch. I should have mentioned that at once. Finch wrote to tell Meg that a princess from Mont Nuages is in London to make her Season and she needs an expert on such matters to teach her all the things she doesn't know."

"But—" Hunter flipped his dark blue coat back and planted his hands on his hips. He shook his head. "You have an odd sense of humor, Sibyl."

"Oh, I wasn't making a joke. Not at all. You see, since we need money if we are not to become destitute…" *My, my, my.* She forced a laugh and was certain she sounded quite jolly. "Now I *am* joking. But I wasn't before. Meg is doing exactly what I said she was. She's with Count Etranger, who is also from Mont Nuages. He's the Princess's brother."

"What did she say, Lloyd?" Adam Chillworth, the artist who lived in 7C, and who was more a friend of Meg's than of any other resident of the house, arrived behind Hunter. He was renowned for his dour countenance, but the fierce expression he wore this afternoon rivaled any he'd previously achieved.

"Everything is quite all right, thank you, Adam," Sibyl said. Please let her be able to hold her silly, fearful tongue, and rescue her own and Meg's dignity before it was lost forever. "Thank you both for calling."

"Oh, no, you don't, Sibyl," Hunter said. "I'd be obliged if you would assist me, Chillworth. Perhaps two minds can make some sense of all this. One isn't making much of a showing."

Sibyl prayed Meg would soon return, but not so soon as to confront Hunter and Adam in the parlor.

Hunter explained what she'd told him to Adam—in terribly long detail. Adam was the tallest man Sibyl recalled having met. He wore his black, curly hair rather long and had gray eyes currently turned almost the same color as that hair. Sibyl had always marveled at Meg's unlikely friendship with such an overwhelming person. True, of late the two of them were rarely to be seen laughing together as they used to do quite often, but Meg still regarded him highly.

"Blast," Adam said when Hunter was finally silent. Adam came from the north and what remained of his accent was appealing, or would be in other circumstances. "This is what comes of women being alone in circumstances suited only t'men. It's barely a week since she was all but killed by that carriage. Does she want to put her life at risk again? Where is she?"

Sibyl swallowed and felt close to tears.

"Please sit down," Hunter told her. "Chillworth is concerned for you and Meg, that's all. He doesn't mean to upset you."

"Damn you, Lloyd. Don't you take it upon yourself to decide what I do or don't mean. I mean to upset Sibyl if that's what it takes to get to the bottom of this. Speak up. Where is Meg?"

She turned away and hurried to the window. Crying was absolutely out of the question. If Meggie were here she would manage not to cry, and so would Sibyl.

"I say," Hunter said, and his evident distress brought her even closer to shaming herself. "Please let us help. We can't leave you like this, and we can't—"

"We won't leave until we know what to do to save Meg." Adam interrupted Hunter and arrived beside Sibyl at the same moment. "Cry if you must, but answer my questions. Where is Meg?"

Sibyl gulped and pointed.

"What are you pointing at?" Adam said, all sharpness. "Speak up, I say."

"N—number Seventeen," Sibyl told him. "It used to be Number Sixteen and Number Seventeen but—"

"The two houses were made into one," Adam said. "We all know that. Are you telling us Meg is in that house?"

She nodded.

"But it's empty," Hunter said.

Sibyl shook her head.

"It's not," Adam said. "Barstow twittered about there being a lot of nighttime activity over there for some weeks. Lots of beautiful furnishings delivered and craftsmen coming and going. That would have been a time back. Then Old Coot remarked on important personages being in residence. Didn't take much notice. I should have. I may have thought it would be nice to see something done with this place, but not much more—unless it was to hope I'd wake up one day and find out someone had finally pinched all those ugly animal urns on their uglier plinths. A man gets sick of falling over the things everywhere he turns in the place he calls home."

No one took any notice of Adam's occasional tirades on the subject of deterioration at Number 7.

He pulled a lace curtain aside.

Hunter hitched back the other.

They stood, one each side of Sibyl, staring across the square, past the central gardens where trees budded and early flowers teased the eye, to the white stone facade of Number 17.

"Meg isn't qualified for such a position," Hunter said.

"You're right," Adam said, "but that wouldn't stop her from applying if she had a strong enough reason."

"What reason could be strong enough to make her risk looking foolish?"

"That's what we've got to find out," Adam said, "and fast, before she gets herself into some sort of nonsense she won't recover from."

"Agreed. D'you think we should go over there? Put on a united front as friends of the young lady and demand to remove her at once?"

"Aye." Adam rested his fists on the sash. "Princesses and counts. What can she have been thinkin'? About time for a sitdown, I think. There's somethin' up here and I want t'know what it is. First we've t'get her back, Lloyd. We'd best be off."

Sibyl summoned all her courage, hurried to the door and closed it. "You will do no such thing," she said, facing them. "When Meggie returns home I will inform her of your concern for her and suggest she explain her motives for seeking out the position. And—since you have both been quick to give your opinions of my sister's inadequacies—she may not have made a Season herself, but she is very knowledgeable of the intricacies involved. If you remember, she has sewn wardrobes for several young ladies embarking on the same round. And she is observant and well-read. And genteel. A person may not have had all the advantages of some, but that does not mean that they are bound to embarrass themselves in even the most minor of roles in Society."

Color rose on Hunter's cheeks. "No, Sibyl, of course it doesn't. I apologize if I have given offense. You know that's the last thing I would set out to do."

"Well-read's one thing," Adam said. No sign of embarrassment on that face. "Bein' a part of it all's another. I take it she's hopeful of becoming this princess's companion. I doubt it'll happen, but if it did, how would our Meggie deal with dancin', for instance. She'll never have been to a dance other than in the village ye came from. Hardly the same thing."

"Meggie dances well," Sibyl said, smarting from Adam's belittling comments.

"And what if the princess decides her companion, or whatever, ought to be able to advise her on—well—the more delicate side of things?"

"I say, Chillworth," Hunter said.

"Oh, Meggie will cope with whatever comes along," Sibyl said, gaining confidence with her subject.

"Will she indeed?" Adam's nostrils flared. "From what I know of the girl, I doubt she'd be over comfortable talking about the married state."

"Chillworth." There was warning in Hunter's voice.

"Aye, I'm watchin' what I say. You and Meg are gentlewomen. Well-bred and too good for this unpleasant city. I happen to think that if the princess asked Meg what to do on her wedding night, Meg would be horrified. And I will be horrified if I think she's being exposed to any such thing. No. It won't do, and that's that. We've t'go and get her back."

Adam invariably expected the worst. Sibyl wrung her hands and spoke to Hunter direct. "Please, do not do this. I confess I'm very worried about her, but if you interfere, she will never forgive me for revealing her personal affairs."

"So, what is it you will agree to let us do?" Hunter asked.

"I didn't ask you to do anything," she reminded him. "It was Barstow's gossiping—her, yes, her gossiping about matters that are no concern of hers that brought you here. But I'm grateful to know you will come to our rescue if it's necessary."

"You mean we can help ye if some foreign count makes off with Meggie and—"

"Chillworth, please," Hunter said. "Why don't you and I discuss this elsewhere? We won't do anything without your approval, Sibyl."

"Aye, we won't," Adam said, marching to the door. He had always been one given to dramatics and expectations of unlikely disasters. "And we'll hope the wealthy, important Count doesn't have his way with her before you do approve."

4

Jean-Marc slapped his riding crop against a boot. "If I wished to be nagged, I should have a wife, Verbeux, don't you think?"

"Couldn't say," Verbeux said.

"Exactly. And what you *don't* say becomes a silent form of nagging. You make it your mission to cause me discomfort. I should discharge you, don't you think?"

"Couldn't say."

Closing his eyes, Jean-Marc fell flat on his back on top of the counterpane and sought about in his mind for a way to combat this valet without whom he would be lost, but who caused him to question too many decisions. The man had to be the only valet who employed his own valet—one Pierre who, despite being a solid sort of fellow, scuttled about and appeared perpetually nervous. Jean-Marc suspected this must be because, in private, Verbeux was a tyrannical master. Yes, Verbeux was most certainly above himself, but he was also indispensable.

"Miss Smiles is young," Verbeux said. "Good-hearted."

"So you've said. And I agree. From what I observed, Miss Smiles is a good-hearted young woman."

"The Princess is difficult."

"Not a bit of it," Jean-Marc said, but when Verbeux set up his familiar hum that meant he considered his employer to be irrational and beyond the pale, he added, "Miss Smiles is strong. I feel that in her. What possible good can I do other than give her the authority to do what must be done, then trust she will do it? If I interfere I will only undermine her confidence and stretch the process of bringing Désirée into line.''

"If you say so."

"I do say so."

"But you don't believe it."

"Damn it, but I do."

"Very well." Verbeux made for the door. "Run away. Let Miss Smiles suffer. Don't help ease the way."

"Stop where you are," Jean-Marc told him. "Come back here at once. You believe Désirée will be less stubborn if she knows I am near? All right, you win. We'll do it your way. Make the arrangements for them to accompany me to Windsor, if you please. You have wasted so much of my time that we will have to spend the night there. Of course, Miss Smiles may not want to come, but offer just the same. If this were other than her first day with us, I would not give her a choice, of course, but I must be fair. If she should decide to make the journey, allow her to send word to her sister."

"As you say." Verbeux carried on and left the massive bedchamber.

Jean-Marc stared upward at the lush, bronze satin draperies that formed an extravagant bed canopy. This bed had been a gift from his father, Prince Georges, and in place when Jean-Marc arrived in London with Désirée. He found it over ornate, but still recognized its dark, Jacobean mystery.

"Mon dieu," he said aloud, giving vent to his frustration in ringing tones. "I am not a parent, have never been a parent, and probably never will be a parent. Why must I play the role of a parent with my graceless half sister?" Because, he thought, since Uncle Louis—formerly considered next in line for the throne— since he had slipped from favor, Jean-Marc's father had decided he'd rather put his bastard son on the throne than the daughter for whom he had neither respect nor particular affection. And Prince Georges had seized the idea of a London Season for Désirée as an excuse to put Jean-Marc before eyes that should start

to respect him as the Chosen. No matter that he scarcely knew his half sister and she seemed disinclined to consider him as other than an unpleasant stranger with the authority to give her orders.

With luck Miss Smiles would refuse Verbeux's ridiculous idea and insist she could not go to Windsor today.

On the other hand, would it be so bad if she accepted? Ordinary she might be, but she had courage and ingenuity. He liked those attributes in anyone, and in a woman he found them particularly charming. If nothing else, it might divert him from his concerns if he could somehow watch her without drawing attention to his interest.

Verbeux returned. "Half an hour," he said.

"Drat," Jean-Marc responded, because it was expected of him. "I hate being made to wait."

"Miss Smiles will not stay," Verbeux said.

Jean-Marc rose from the bed. "What can you be talking about? She won't stay? You mean she won't come with us to Windsor?"

"She'll go to Windsor. Won't last here. The Princess is difficult."

"So you keep reminding me. That girl's boots are old. They need replacing. She'll need a good many things replaced."

"The Princess?"

Jean-Marc's temper grew exceedingly thin. "I refer to Miss Smiles. While she attends to Désirée's wardrobe, she must also attend to her own. You will help me devise a suitable manner in which to suggest this, Verbeux. I rather think that for all her unusual forwardness in approaching me, Miss Smiles has pride and might be embarrassed at my telling her she needs finer ensembles in order to be with Désirée in public."

"In public?"

"That's what I said. In public. At all these routs and balls and musicales and the entire round of boring events."

Verbeux fell back a step, his usually serious expression transformed to one of amazement. "A spinster nobody? Escort a princess?"

"I hope they won't be longer than half an hour," Jean-Marc said, avoiding Verbeux's eyes, "I have company awaiting me at Riverside."

When he did look at Verbeux again there was no doubt the man still awaited a response to his former questions. "Yes, damn it, a spinster nobody will escort Désirée. And I shall escort the pair of them. I will not, however, stand around as if I were her mama—who could have been sent with her, I may add."

"Couldn't."

"I beg your pardon?"

"Princess Marie. A good woman who dares not cross her husband."

Verbeux knew too much. But at least he was unlikely to gossip.

"Coach is being brought around."

"Thank you," Jean-Marc said. "Make sure Cook knows we won't be eating here this evening. But she should prepare something particularly splendid for dinner tomorrow. We'll have a guest to impress."

"Miss Smiles?"

"Certainly, Miss Smiles."

"She is to be *impressed?* A companion?"

Honesty was usually the best foil with Verbeux. "I need that woman. If she must be pampered into remaining here, so be it. You will tell Cook."

"Time Cook was supervised. You need a wife."

"I need peace, Verbeux. Enough of this interference. I think I shall sit on the box with the coachman."

Verbeux rolled his eyes.

"Regardless of your opinion, I shall sit with the coachman."

"Too much of a stir. People might talk. Might say you don't like the Princess."

"I shall do—" Unfortunately Verbeux had a point. "I agree. Don't take advantage of that. It doesn't mean I'm weakening. I'm going downstairs."

At least he could escape once they got to Riverside. He'd be amicable until then and perhaps if he attempted to become closer to Désirée, she would be less obdurate. That was what he would do.

Miss Smiles, her bonnet firmly in place, stood in the foyer. And a bright creature she was, too. The yellow outfit suited her and was of good enough quality. With the addition of a few... No, no, he'd have Verbeux tell her yellow was pleasing and she should have another dress and pelisse in the same color. A yellow ball gown! Something to show off her—to show off her best features. That would be just the thing.

The Count, Meg decided, appeared even more formidable than when they'd first met. Dressed in a dark blue coat, buff breeches and riding boots, he trailed a black cloak over one shoulder and carried a crop. He stared at her, examined her. A glittery quality made his eyes almost fearsome. "Are you well, My Lord?" Perhaps that was it. He was ill and desperate for assistance with his sister because he could not manage alone. Oh, she did hope that was not the case.

Jean-Marc frowned, then wondered how long he'd stood only steps away and stared at Miss Smiles. She was so...*feminine*. Naturally feminine and without any silly affectations. That's what drew him to her. She had none of the annoying little habits—intended to beguile but guaranteed to bore—so commonly used by the women he knew. "I'm quite well, thank you. I have a great deal on my mind. Are you making progress with Princess Désirée? Where is she, by the way? Of course, gone to find a cloak or some such thing, I suppose."

"No."

"No? You mean she hasn't gone for something warmer?"

She would do everything in her power to keep her position. She had to. Wait till she told Sibyl how their fortunes were changed. Meg winced. Wait until she told Sibyl they must live separately until the end of the Season, that the Count insisted Meg become part of his household while Sibyl was to remain at Number 7.

"My sister," the Count said, somewhat more sharply. "Did she return to her rooms for something?"

"I can't say as to that. She may have done so. But she chose to go to the coach direct, rather than wait for me." The Princess was cold and withdrawn, but at least she hadn't continued to pretend she spoke no English.

This opportunity to remove the yoke of responsibility from his shoulders should not slip away, thought Jean-Marc. "She's shy," he said. "I know she will come to consider you her closest friend."

"She told me she has no friends at all."

"As I said, you are likely to become her best friend." Sarcasm was a poor trait, but he was oppressed. "The coach awaits. We'd better join my sister."

"The coach isn't here yet. Princess Désirée went out to the mews, to the stables."

Princess Désirée would spend private and probably unpleasant time with her half brother later. "I see. I think you will enjoy the drive to Windsor. We'll pass the castle on the way and Riverside is only a short distance beyond. Next time you come down we shall take you riding."

"I have never been on a horse. I don't even have suitable clothing. I shall watch."

He stifled a retort that she would do as she was told. Rather, he said, "I want you to feel you can come to me with any questions about dealing with Désirée. I am certain that once she is sure of you, she will be a joy to instruct and assist. But, even then, I will always be available to help you."

"Thank you, My Lord."

She sighed, definitely sighed. Did that mean she intended to fulfil her commission and was grateful for his offer, or that she didn't expect to be with them long enough to seek help?

"No thanks are necessary," Jean-Marc said. Her reticule was overlarge and bulged. He could not help but wonder what it contained. "I shall do what family loyalty demands. And, to be frank,

I am very pleased with my selection of you as an able assistant. You, Miss Smiles, show signs of being more than able.''

"Thank you, My Lord." Perhaps she was really to get the chance she needed, a chance to find an agreeable, well-fixed husband who was not eligible enough to capture a bride considered a real prize. There must be such a man. Surely there was just one of them who would be pleased to marry a person who, although not a beauty, had a certain mystery about her. Oh, surely. And, after all, when he was no longer intrigued by her mystery, he would discover himself attached to a rather comfortable sort of person. Well, mostly comfortable when she wasn't preoccupied with one of the many miraculous and intriguing new subjects she would always wish to pursue.

And Sibyl could only be an added bonus. After all, until Meg and her husband married Sibyl off to someone suitably deserving, they would have the joy of her company.

"Miss Smiles?"

She jumped. "Yes?"

Now he had frightened her. "Are you a daydreamer?"

"Absolutely not. Why would you ask such a thing?"

"I simply wondered." She was very direct, he must say. And the dashed odd thing about it was that he enjoyed her lack of guile. He said, "You didn't hear me tell you the coach is here now."

She looked at the arm he extended to her and hesitatingly placed her hand there. A silent butler opened the front door and stood back, bowing, showing thin silver hair slicked back over his scalp.

"Thank you, Rench," Count Etranger said. "Please see to it that rooms are made ready for Miss Smiles in the Princess's wing."

"As you say," the butler said.

The Count swung on his cloak and tucked his riding crop beneath his arm. He covered Meg's hand in a most solicitous manner.

He was only being polite—*fiddle*. Wouldn't it be nice if he actually found her appealing? Would it? Yes, it would. He was the most formidably handsome man she had ever seen. Mature.

"Let us take our time on the steps," he said. "They are steep and I shouldn't like you to fall."

Mature. Charming. Appealing. *Desirable*. Meg's breath fought, apparently unsure whether it was supposed to go in or out. Count Etranger was positively—*edible*. Yes, she'd heard that term used by some of the young ladies for whom she'd sewn when they were preparing for their Seasons. Edible. They descended the steps.

Jean-Marc thought he felt her shiver.

"Are you warm enough?" he asked. "Just a moment." He removed a glove and touched his warm fingers to her face. Such a soft cheek, and she watched his face with concentration that was disarming. "No, you are not warm enough at all. That will not do. Let's get you into the coach and find a blanket."

Swooning would not be at all the thing, Meg thought. She wasn't a silly young girl who was likely to buckle at the knee from proximity to a man who caused some very unusual sensations in some very unusual places for her to consider having sensations at all.

Her knees felt decidedly wobbly.

"Here we go," Count Etranger said, smiling down at her, showing off those devilish dimples. They progressed to the flagway at a stately pace. *"Mon dieu,"* he said, and sounded so angry. "That girl will be taught to behave."

Meg's heart thudded. So she wasn't the only one who considered Princess Désirée a most terrible challenge. But the Count had been less than honest and she did not care for that.

Showing his temper at its worst could send the young lady fleeing across the square, Jean-Marc thought. "Princess Désirée has obviously forgotten her manners," he said. "She has settled on this side. We shall have to walk into the street to get in, but no matter. Come, I shall help you."

The coachman was already on his way to the street. He arrived at the door just in time to open it and place the steps.

Jean-Marc drew Miss Smiles to his side while he leaned in. "Désirée," he said, "what can you be thinking of? Why did you ignore our approach and make it necessary for Miss Smiles to walk in the street? Why did you not move to this side?"

"For a companion? Pah."

"Désirée," he said very quietly, "you and I shall talk—alone—at Riverside. Meanwhile, you will have a care with your tongue, hmm?"

Her response was to lower her eyes. Poor, graceless creature. He recognized how misery as much as mutiny caused her wretched behavior. She wore no bonnet or warm travel cloak. One blanket she had draped around her shoulders and crossed over her chest. A second covered her legs and feet. There didn't appear to be another.

Pressed against the Count's solid body, Meg grew more uncomfortable. She began to feel that eyes might be watching from the windows of a certain house behind her.

"Well," he said. "I am certainly not cold."

"Good," Meg said in a small voice.

He swung off his cloak and enveloped her in it. It dragged the ground—a fact he obviously noted since he swept her into his arms and deposited her in the coach.

What if Sibyl were watching? What if the entire household at Number 7 were watching? They would not know that the Princess was already in the coach.

"Comfortable?" Jean-Marc asked. He'd thoroughly enjoyed the brief but pleasant—and totally self-indulgent—process of putting her in the coach.

"Very," Meg told him. But he reached in to wrap first one side, then the other side of the cloak about her. And with each move he stroked it over her body. An absolutely unconscious and unimportant incident, of course.

She glowed. She glowed just beneath her skin—all of her skin. It felt *wonderfully wicked.*

In he climbed, and the coachman put up the steps and closed the door.

The girl radiated life, Jean-Marc thought. Life and health and— passion? Yes, there was a passion in her. He leaned toward her, beckoning. "Lend me your ear," he said when she bent forward.

Meg pulsated. She felt his breath on her face, knew his lips were barely distant from her ear. She wiggled a little on her seat.

Jean-Marc chuckled, he couldn't help himself. The young baggage. She might not be aware of herself as a woman—rather she might not *have been* aware of herself as a woman—but this day's new events had clearly awakened something in her. He could feel her responding to him.

Why would he laugh at her, Meg wondered? Her breasts pressed against the neckline of her dress—and they stung. How so? Not that the stinging was unpleasant, quite the reverse. But, *really.*

She could smell his fresh linen, feel the power in him....

Jean-Marc placed a hand on the back of her neck and whispered, "I have the greatest faith in you. I should have been a little less protective of Désirée and explained that she covers a loving nature with her sharp tongue. Will you forgive me for my omission?"

She bowed her head and was almost certain his mouth grazed her temple. Oh, my, how very extraordinary. How very...delicious. How dreadful she was. If she wasn't careful, he would know she found him so *interesting* and he would be insulted.

"Will you forgive me, Miss Smiles?"

"Yes," she whispered. "Of course, My Lord. And I shall do my utmost to please you in every way."

Would she now? What a very stimulating thought. "Thank you, my dear. And I shall attempt to assist you in your efforts."

"You will?"

She had unconsciously turned her arresting eyes up to his. "I will," he said, smiling at her. "We should be away. Otherwise we shall give Mrs. Floris less time than she requires to complain about unexpected guests. The woman is quite the tyrant over such things."

Meg had no idea who this tyrant might be, but she laughed with the Count, and enjoyed his adjustment of the cloak at her neck.

Jean-Marc rapped the roof sharply with his crop. The coach jolted, and with a clanging of tack and hoofs, and the sound of wheels grinding on cobbles, it moved on.

Meg swayed toward him and he put out a hand to steady her.

A sideways glance through the window confirmed her fears. Several faces watched from the parlor at Number 7B Mayfair Square.

They would talk. They would speculate about what they had seen, and upon her return would besiege her with questions.

At last she'd be a woman of mystery. How perfectly wonderful.

5

*S*pivey here.

Ow! That hurt. This is absolutely beyond all. I have always excelled at anything I have attempted, you know. To be foiled in tasks that should be as simple as deciding where one wants to be, and being there, is infuriating. I am bruised. Imagine that—bruised. How can that be? Well, I suppose it can't actually be. I feel bruised because I must remember how being bruised used to feel.

Bumping into a stone wall and bouncing to the flagway. How mortifying. I have to get into Number Seventeen and look around and I need to do so at once.

I have never failed at a single undertaking. Except in the matter of controlling my family. And in the, er, advanced maneuvers associated with my present state. I will not falter at either, do you hear me?

Up the steps I go again. Hmm, not perfect. Somewhat bumpy, but passable. I must work on my gliding techniques. One would think that would be easy when one can't keep one's feet on the ground anyway. Not so. Why—gadzooks! Oh, oh, I almost tipped upside down. Really, I paid handsomely for that ghastly female instructor to teach me all the necessary skills. Mary, who would be queen of England as well as Scotland. Charlatan. I've heard whisperings that she became a pauper at the end of, well, at the end. Cost her everything she had to bribe jailers for small favors. Jailers in the Tower. There for treason against Elizabeth One, of course. Naturally that was why she taught me without ever ac-

tually moving at all. She said she held still in order to keep a good head on her shoulders—as if she needed to explain.

Enough of that. I need to get into Number Seventeen. I need to hear what the servants are saying and learn just what that silly Meg Smiles is up to. If I saw what I thought I saw, and she went off with Count Etranger—alone—I shall have to start all over again. Her reputation is ruined and the Count will most certainly not bother with a publicly ruined woman unless he happens to be infatuated with her, which he can't be. I knew I should have sent the other one, that colorless Sibyl. Young men find her appealing because she arouses their need to protect. Ah, I'm glad I'm not young anymore.

I didn't think Sibyl would do it, you see. She's afraid of everything.

It is past time for me to rest, you know. I am fatigued in the extreme and long to return to my perfect place at Number Seven where I may observe all who come and go. Despite the hard nature of that haven—actually in one of the newel posts—it is mine and only mine and I enjoy it so.

There are some members of the company I must now keep who consider me inept at being what I am. Inept at being a ghost, mind you! That's poppycock. More practice is all I need. I must concentrate. Think, Spivey, think. What is the pattern here—the pattern of your inability to do what any self-respecting ghost is supposed to do?

I can come and go from Number Seven without being noticed.

I can move about the streets with ease—again, without notice. Oh, there have been one or two occasions when someone has seen me, but they always look pleased with themselves and give a secretive greeting. One wonders about those people.

I can leave any building or place at will, but... I can't go into any building but Number Seven Mayfair Square unless there is an open door, or I am borrowing a body. I don't mean what you think I mean by that. What I do mean is that if I choose to lend my mind to a person of very little brain, in an act of partial

*charity, and only if they are alone in the world and need company,
then I manage quite nicely. I look around for some vacant sort
of person who isn't likely to be missed, and, well—I move in.
Only for brief periods, of course. And I always return what I
borrow in perfect condition. In fact, I believe the subjects are
invigorated by my attention.*

*"Approach with authority," that's what Mary told me. She
appeared to be obsessed with authority. She thought herself of
the greatest importance and could not stop talking about having
been robbed of her right to the British Throne.*

*"Approach your point of entrance with authority and sweep
inside to your destination. Assume you will accomplish this and
you will. See yourself there and you will be there."*

So said haughty Mary.

*Very well. Into Number Seventeen and immediately down to the
servants' domain in the basement. All the chatter about their employer will be in full swing.*

*A warm kitchen—not that I feel warmth anymore—and red-
dened faces. A fire leaping at the great hearth and fowl turning
on a spit, dripping fat into fire and sizzling. The aroma would be
marvelous—if I could smell. Yes, that's where I will be in a moment. Agitated cook, overbearing housekeeper, hovering butler,
chattering servants. Probably all taking a cup of tea since the
master is away.*

To see is to believe and make real.

I am where I want to be....

*Hell and damnation! Ah, stop, stop. Dizziness overwhelms me.
How can I bang into a door when I am not...when I simply am
not?*

*That settles it. I know what must be done and how it shall be
accomplished, and the precise assistant who will make everything
possible. Thank goodness flying presents no problem—I will perfect the other necessities in time, you know.*

*Off I go. What a bore. No gentleman should have to exert
himself so. I'm on my way to a school for young ladies, not*

exactly to the school but to a retired employee who lives nearby—alone. One of my own relatives—from the impoverished side of the Spivey family—opened the establishment itself many years ago. She passed away fairly soon afterward. But those she employed shared her beliefs and those beliefs fit well with mine. Any sign of high spirits in a young lady should be immediately suppressed. Exactly my view.

All will be well now. All will go smoothly. Oh, really, how offensive some of these slums are. Even looking down on them repels me.

Dash it, someone's flying this way. He's shouting at me.

"Hold hard, there. Lookest whither thou goest."

Do you hear him? Damn, it's that arrogant loudmouth, Shakespeare. "I do beg your pardon, Sir. After you, of course." Really, one could hardly fail to recognize a man with such eyelashes.

How the man does posture. Look at him swooping and rolling. Now there's another one who is forever lauding himself. Why can't people stop living in the past?

6

Rather than feeling his mood lift when Riverside Place came into view, Jean-Marc suffered a deeper slide into gloom. The sensation had begun the instant they were in sight of Windsor Castle, that great, gray, castellated bastion on its green hill. This land was so familiar. With every turn of the coach's wheels, they passed over ground he'd loved since boyhood, when Riverside had belonged to his mother and her husband. On Jean-Marc's eighteenth birthday, the rambling Tudor mansion had been a gift from his mother and stepfather—together with the reminder that there was an agreement with Crown Prince Georges and his son, Jean-Marc, that the identity of his mother and her husband would never be revealed.

There had never been such a revelation, Jean-Marc thought, and there never would be. Why should he grovel for recognition from a mother who denied him and who issued a bill of sale for his wonderful gift so all could assume the property had been purchased by the young Count. Mother and son had never crossed paths since, and had no plans to do so in the future.

"How beautiful," Meg said. She couldn't help herself. Riverside Place reminded her of Puckly Hinton, of their own dear house there. Oh, The Ramblers was a tiny place in comparison to this. But it, too, dated back to the reign of Elizabeth I and was set in once lovely grounds, the skeleton of which could still be made out amid the overgrown disaster second cousin William Godly-Smythe had allowed to grow there.

The Count had been silent for some time. Silent, and sunk into morose contemplation of the landscape. His sister hadn't spoken since they left Mayfair Square. Meg decided she was grateful there would not be much time here before they must return or encounter unwelcome darkness.

The carriage bowled along a curving driveway edged with sentinel elms. Bluebells nodded in soft grass beneath the trees. Bluebells and daffodils, and here and there, patches of small, white daisies.

"I shall speak with Mrs. Floris," the Count announced. "You will show Miss Smiles to your wing, Désirée. There you will be kind, and eager to please your new companion and friend. She is to be your right hand and your left in the weeks ahead. You will need her as your champion as much as you need me—perhaps more. Do not hesitate to ask her any questions. I have asked her to work with your hair today. That seems an important step to making you look like the grown-up young woman you are. You are to be launched in Society and will find a husband very soon. The days for plaits have passed. And you will never again pretend you don't speak English. Is that understood?"

Meg's gaze shifted to Princess Désirée's face. The poor thing's mutinous expression had turned to one of despair, and she nodded like a creature whose spirit had been broken. Meg sat straighter. Her job would become making Princess Désirée confident and teaching her how to look her best.

"Do you understand, Désirée?" the Count repeated in a voice that chilled Meg. When he spoke like that he sounded more French, and much as the accent delighted her, it did not bring her comfort under such circumstances.

Princess Désirée nodded several times and even managed a small smile at Meg.

"Very well, then," her brother said. "Miss Smiles, if you need me, please ring for a servant at once and have someone dispatched to find me. My sister's affairs are my primary concern."

The carriage swept to a halt before a front door protected from the weather by a gabled vestibule enclosed with richly stained glass. Roses climbed and bloomed either side of the vestibule, and mingled with the deep green ivy that grew over much of the building's redbrick facade.

The Count didn't wait for the coachman to open the door. He leaped to the ground and put down steps before helping first Meg, then Princess Désirée to the gravel driveway.

"Mrs. Floris," he called to a rotund woman who emerged to greet them. "Good to see you. I'm sorry we couldn't be here earlier. We'll talk inside. Désirée, please look after Miss Smiles." With that, and without another glance at Meg, he strode into the house behind Mrs. Floris.

She shouldn't regret his departure, Meg knew, but nevertheless she suffered a sudden lonely longing for him to take her with him. The sooner she found some other gentleman, a gentleman not quite so removed from her own station, but interesting enough to capture her attention, the better.

Désirée stood where she was and showed no inclination to move.

The River Thames was both visible and audible. At some distance and between the budding wands of weeping willows, Meg could see the water shining glassy smooth and drifting on its way. Riverside Place had several stories and a number of wings. There were even dormer windows under the eaves and in several places in the slate-covered roof. Tall chimneys rose in clusters, and smoke curled against the blue sky.

Meg noted how Princess Désirée looked repeatedly over her shoulder at the coach, which, strangely, had not been driven to the stables as one would expect. The coachman busied himself among the horses for reasons Meg failed to understand.

"We should go inside," she said to the Princess at last. "Your brother was most insistent."

Divested of her blankets, Princess Désirée shivered in her ugly gray dress. "When you go into the 'all, you'll see a staircase that rises from the center. Go up there and turn to the, er, left. A gallery runs along each side of the second floor. Rooms on the left are for receiving, but there is a corridor before you turn to the gallery on that side and it leads to my wing. Go to the end of the corridor. Open the door there. Go into another corridor and my rooms are on either side. Per'aps my boudoir would be most comfortable. It is the third room on the right. Please rest there. I will come soon.''

Meg listened to this remarkable speech in near perfect English and was ready to insist the Princess must come with her at once— until she saw the plea in the girl's eyes. In a low voice, Meg said, "Are you all right? Are you sure I should leave you here? The Count would probably be angry."

The girl nodded. "I promise I will be there almost before you know it. Allow me this small trust, if you please."

Not at all sure she wasn't making a terrible mistake, Meg turned away and entered the house. Her fear that she would instantly encounter Jean-Marc proved unfounded. She hurried to the foot of the stairs and was startled to hear the ring of feminine laughter from somewhere nearby. Deep, male merriment joined in, and Meg didn't have to see the owner of the voice to know it was Count Etranger. No wonder he'd been in such a hurry. A lady guest had awaited him.

Breathing deeply and swallowing against a stricture in her throat, Meg went hastily up the long flight of stairs. The house was magnificent. Paintings of hunting scenes, of haughty ladies and gentlemen, of stiffly posed children and dogs hung on every wall. The hall rose three stories, past twin galleries to a ceiling painted deep blue and dotted with clouds. A huge crystal chandelier hung on a massive chain from the center.

She had no right even to have an opinion about, much less feelings for Count Etranger. He would laugh harder if he knew she was affected by him.

The Princess had given perfect directions. The way to a small jewel of a boudoir, complete with gilt daybed inlaid with jet and mother-of-pearl, was short. Meg closed herself inside and sat in a comfortable chair upholstered in rose-colored velvet.

A fire burned in the grate of a fireplace faced with dark pink rose-strewn tiles. More roses adorned oval plaster panels on the walls and glass shades that covered candles on the chandelier. The ceiling was also rose-colored with heavy gold molding where it joined the walls. A single embroidered rose embellished the center of the counterpane, and gold ropes held deep pink velvet draperies away from the pretty leaded windows.

A beautiful, feminine room and totally unsuited to the Princess for whom it had been appointed.

The door flew open. Princess Désirée rushed in, popped her head into the corridor to look in both directions, then shut the door behind her very carefully. She took shallow breaths, and her gray eyes were huge. Meg noted that some sort of excitement had brought color to the girl's cheeks, and it suited her.

Meg also noted—could hardly fail to note—a very large and squirming bundle covered with one of the blankets Princess Désirée had used in the coach.

"You may go to your own rooms now, if you please," the Princess said.

Already standing, Meg was bemused about what she should do next. "I don't have any rooms," she pointed out. "I am to remain with you."

"Of course you 'ave rooms," Princess Désirée snapped. "If I 'ave rooms, you 'ave been given rooms nearby. That's 'ow it always works when one is forced to suffer a companion."

"You are very rude," Meg said, before she could harness her words. Well, she was supposed to wield authority, wasn't she? "At the Count's request—on his orders—I am here to assist you, not to suffer your insults. It is my job to help you learn to deal with others in a pleasing manner. To charm them. At the moment your tartness would likely horrify most people. No, I shall not be leaving. We should start on your toilette. Obviously a great deal of practice will be needed."

"I am Princess Désirée of—"

"I know who you are, Your Royal Highness. You are also an

undisciplined and spoiled girl. You told me you have no friends. Little wonder. But there is no one who cannot change—including you. Where shall we work on your hair?''

The bundle the Princess held hunched and stretched, grew rounded, then pointed. What looked suspiciously like the end of a tail protruded from one side. "You have an animal there. Why are you hiding an animal?"

"It's not an animal," Princess Désirée said, and to Meg's horror, tears filled Her Royal Highness's eyes.

"Oh, dear. It *is* an animal. And you're not supposed to have it, are you? Is it dangerous?"

"It—it's 'Alibut.'' Princess Désirée's mouth quivered, and the first tears spilled over. "'E 'as no one to love 'im. 'E is alone and sad—like me. So I will care for 'im. I will. If you try to take 'im from me, I shall run away.''

The deterioration in Princess Désirée's diction was peculiarly affecting. Her tears brought matching ones to Meg's eyes. This sad creature was struggling to cope and doing very poorly.

With a wild wriggle, the interloper shot free of the blanket and the Princess's arms.

Meg gaped. The largest cat she'd ever seen landed on the rose-patterned carpet and shot instantly to the rich counterpane on the daybed. "My goodness. How. Where have you been hiding him? In some outbuilding in the gardens here? Who feeds him?"

"I feed 'im," the Princess said quietly. "And I brought 'im with me today. The coachman is always kind and keeps 'im in the stables at Mayfair Square if I cannot get 'im to my rooms. Today 'e was inside the coachman's box. 'E has traveled there often and does not mind it at all. I found 'im the day I arrived in London from Mont Nuages. 'E was in the little garden behind Number Seventeen and 'e was not well, but as soon as I got 'im dry and fed 'im, 'e became 'appy and beautiful. Just as you see. And 'e wanted to be with me so 'e 'ad to stay. But you will tell Jean-Marc, won't you?''

Meg looked at Alibut. His fur was soft and full and—naturally—gray, with faint white stripes and a circle of white on each of his sides. His eyes were the gold of amber, and he held his pink nose high.

"Why is he called Alibut?"

"Not Alibut. 'Alibut. The fish. 'E loves fish.''

Thoughtful for an instant, Meg approached the daybed and reached out tentatively. "You mean Halibut?"

"Yes, Halibut."

The dropped h's must be attended to. A pale, rough tongue went to work on Meg's fingers. "How do you intend to keep such a large cat hidden?"

"I must." Again the girl's voice was so small Meg could scarcely hear it. "I said I 'ave no friends. I lied. 'Alibut is my only friend. I love 'im and 'e loves me. I want to be with 'im. I don't—"

"Your Highness." Meg interrupted. "Pronounce your h's, if you please."

"I don't want to do all these things they say I must do. Fuss with myself. Have many new clothes to make me pretty. I am ugly. 'Ow—how can I be pretty? And wear my hair just so, because it will change me. People cannot be changed by the way they do their hair. What they are is in here—" she pressed a fist to her chest "—where it cannot be seen. I wish only to have my 'Alibut, but I know he will not allow it once he finds out."

Meg spoke with difficulty, "You mean your brother will not allow it?"

"Half brother. Our father was not married to his mother, but he is married to mine."

Meg absorbed that astonishing announcement and said, "Yes, well, Count Etranger. I hardly know him, but I have seen his concern for you. He wants you to find someone special who will look after you."

"An *'usband*." Princess Désirée cast her eyes toward the ceiling. "What would I do with an 'usband?"

"Husband," Meg told her.

"Husband. What would a husband do with me? What man could want me? I am without charm or allure. If there were wisdom in the world I would be allowed to return to my books. I am a scholar. I don't mean I am clever, only that I like to learn, to study, to discuss the affairs of my father's country, and of the world. I am not the kind of person men fall in love with. I know this and I don't care."

And this was the malleable girl, the girl excited about her debut, with whom Meg was supposed to work in the weeks to come? Well, apparently that was not to be so. Apparently by the time they returned this evening she would have told the Count how his sister felt and he would, doubtless, dismiss Meg. How could this all be otherwise?

"You are a nice person," the Princess said. "You will find someone else who needs a companion."

"I doubt it," Meg responded, gathering Halibut into her arms and suffering a thorough washing of her face and neck. The cat was almost too heavy to carry. "I got this position quite by chance. I expect you'd like me to tell the Count you refuse to make your debut."

Princess Désirée's fine eyes opened even wider. "And you will tell 'im about my cat and 'e will be taken away."

Smiling over Halibut's head and kissing the soft fur between his ears, Meg said, "No. No, I will not be mentioning a huge gray cat I could not possibly have seen. After all, who would believe such a wild claim? But I advise you to try to keep him from sight. Bringing him here today was dangerous. I will help you get him back but he should not travel in the coach again or one day he will be discovered. I had best ask to meet with the Count now."

"Stay with me," the Princess said. "I don't want you to leave."

Meg tried not to dwell on returning to London to tell Sibyl their wonderful plans had slipped away.

"Please?" Princess Désirée said. "Let me show you the

'ouse—house, and perhaps some of the gardens. My brother said I should.''

What had made the girl afraid—and she was afraid—of Count Etranger? "I'd like that," Meg said. In fact she didn't feel at all like walking about the house and possibly encountering the Count and his companion.

Princess Désirée opened the top of a window seat and Halibut jumped inside.

"He could die in there," Meg said.

"No, he could not. See?"

Drawing close, Meg did see how small pegs kept the lid from closing completely.

"And there is a comfortable blanket inside. He has hidden there before and I do believe he likes it. Come."

A rapid tour of the Princess's wing revealed a series of beautiful rooms. Eventually they encountered Mrs. Floris, who was directing several maids in preparing what were evidently two rooms intended for Meg's use on some future occasion. Mrs. Floris smiled pleasantly enough at Meg, curtseyed to the Princess, but seemed disinclined to enter into conversation.

The Princess drew Meg quickly away and once they were out of earshot of Mrs. Floris she said, "Please do not say anything to stop them preparing rooms for you."

Meg smiled, but didn't answer. She was puzzled by Princess Désirée's behavior.

Riverside Place was lovely. Very old and with a deep patina on everything from paneling to silver. Through a window at the end of the third floor gallery, Meg saw two figures on horseback. A man and a woman. She knew at once that the man was Count Etranger.

Princess Désirée stood beside her. "He loves to ride. I doubt Ila cares overly for horses, but she will do anything Jean-Marc wishes to do."

Jean-Marc. Meg considered the name and the man. They suited each other. "They have known each other a long time?" she asked, knowing she was impertinent.

"Not so very long. And not so very well, I think. They do not have things in common—but she has good qualities."

Meg sensed that the subject should not be pursued.

The tour was rapid and superficial. All Meg saw of the grounds was a small, enclosed garden. A high wall surrounded the very private bower with its rose beds among stone flags, and carved stone benches were placed to give views of those beds. The shrubs were budding and blooming, and promising a brilliant show before long.

"I should go to 'Al—Halibut," Princess Désirée said. "He will be hungry."

"You have food for him?"

"There will be food."

That oblique statement didn't invite further discussion, either. Meg hesitated and said, "We should talk, at least a little, before we go back inside."

"Yes."

She didn't enjoy the anxiety in the Princess's eyes. "Either I must tell the Count you do not wish to have me, or you will have to allow me to perform the duties he has given me. Your decision is your own to make."

Princess Désirée shifted from foot to foot, frowning and biting her lower lip.

"I will accept your wishes without comment," Meg said.

"You would like to stay?"

This was most unusual and most difficult. "Yes, but—"

"You need the position?"

"That is not something that should influence your decision."

"But you do need it?"

The interrogation was neither intended to be impolite, nor did it sound motivated by idle curiosity. "Yes, I need it. My arrangement with the Count is that I will guide you in matters of deportment, social graces, fashion, elocution, and that I will answer any questions you may have. My sister, Sibyl—oh, Your Highness, Sibyl is the sweetest of people—Sibyl is a fine musician and would assist you with your pianoforte and your voice. This would mean the best of employment for both of us at a time when we are in some difficulty. We have trusts but we are told the payments are now reduced because it was assumed we would marry by now and since we haven't, the money must be made to last longer. We have no parents, you see, and no home of our own. We live at Number Seven Mayfair Square. As lodgers. The house is owned by Lady Hester Bingham and she is very kind to us, but we are afraid we may not be able to support ourselves for too much longer and we will not accept the charity we know Her Ladyship would offer. There, now you know more than I would wish anyone to know about us." And Meg's face burned with chagrin.

"I see. Clearly you are a cultured person. Through no fault of your own you have suffered reversals. But you do not give up. Admirable."

"Thank you. I will find other positions for Sibyl and myself. I'll get a message to the Count. Please do not concern yourself for us."

"I wasn't," the Princess said. "I won't. But Jean-Marc will be very angry with me if I cause you to go away. Even though our father sent him to England for the purpose of launching me, he does not wish to spend time on a half sister he scarcely knows. He has other matters that interest him a great deal more.

"You don't have to leave. I will be kind to you—appropriately kind. In return you will give Jean-Marc the impression that I am making great progress and following instructions well. We should return now."

Meg watched the girl open the door from the walled garden to the house.

"Come along, Miss Smiles. You have to do my hair."

Meg finally remembered to close her mouth. "Yes, we should attend to that." She followed, thinking how selfish her charge appeared again, selfish and self-serving and imperious, when only a short while earlier she had been quite different. But necessity would help Meg make herself invaluable.

Once back in the boudoir, Princess Désirée retrieved Halibut, who promptly draped himself over her shoulder, clearly happy to bounce along there.

"Let us be quick," the Princess said. "We will go to my bedchamber. It will take no time to do something to my hair that will look different enough to satisfy Jean-Marc."

Meg said nothing. She traipsed in the wake of Princess Désirée and Halibut to a radiant bedchamber aglow with yellows and golds. The Princess produced a dish of fresh white fish from beneath the bed and served it to Halibut atop an exquisite gilded table. "There," she said. "Now do what you have to do, please."

Some time later, when Meg's charge sat frowning fiercely before the mirror on her dressing table, there was a knock at the door. A very young maid entered, dipped and said, "His Lordship says you're to go to dinner, Your Highness. Both of you." She left in a flurry of starched white apron.

"Dinner?" Meg said. "We can't have dinner here. We must return to Mayfair Square at once, or we shall be traveling in the dark.

"Do not be a silly," Princess Désirée said, her thin arms crossed while she glowered at her reflection. "Why would we leave Riverside tonight? It is not possible to get back to Town in safety now."

Horrified, Meg stared into the mirror, into annoyed gray eyes. "You are mistaken. Of course we are going back. Why, my sister would be beside herself if I did not return as she expects. Oh, my, I must go back."

"You will not be able to. Not unless you like very long, very dangerous walks. And why should your sister worry? Verbeux told you to send a message and you did so, didn't you?"

"Yes, but—"

"There, then. Let us not concern ourselves with that further

Kindly dismantle this ridiculousness on my head and plait my hair again.''

I must get home, Meg thought. Her message had mentioned an outing only, not an overnight stay.

"I will take the 'air down myself."

"You will *not,* Your Highness. Touch it and I shall reveal Halibut's presence." Her sly threat shocked her. "No, I won't. Of course I won't. He is a love and I understand why he is your friend. Please don't touch your hair. It probably feels uncomfortable, but it becomes you. Wait exactly where you are. Don't move."

The sooner she saw the Count and informed him of her dilemma, the better.

She went to the wardrobe and opened it, afraid she'd find nothing useful inside. Indeed, most of what hung there was as dowdy as the gray. Meg didn't give up. She scrutinized each item until she found a gown made of silk striped in two shades of brown. She pulled it out, then spied a box with no lid that contained a tangle of fripperies.

"Please allow me to help you out of your dress," Meg said. "I think this one will do very well for dinner."

"What I have on will do for dinner."

"Kindly do as you are told."

She thought a hint of a smile passed over the Princess's lips. She stood and turned her back to allow Meg to undo the tapes on her dress. Even her undergarments were too large. "Step out, if you please."

The Princess did so, and she allowed Meg to dress her in the silk gown. Stiff satin scrolls edged the bottom of the skirt, and long, tight sleeves puffed at the shoulder. Fortunately this was not so oversize as the gray, and a square neckline edged with tea lace fitted her small but nicely made body quite well.

"Hmm," Meg said, pleased. "Sit down again. I have a box of treasures here. Is it all right if I look at them?"

The Princess shrugged, but Meg noted how she studied herself and did not look quite so disinterested.

"The gown suits you," Meg said. "A little somber for such a young lady, I should think, but you are a subtle person, not at all the flamboyant kind. Here. This is just the thing."

Meg had brushed the girl's hair until it shone and drawn it up into a soft, plaited coronet that showed off a long, slender neck and small ears. A pearl-studded tortoiseshell comb Meg found looked Spanish. She settled it into the coronet of hair at the very crown of Princess Désirée's head and pulled a few wisps of hair free around the hairline.

"You are pretty," she said.

"Don't be silly. We must go down to dinner or Jean-Marc will send another servant, and then he'll be angry with me. I'll wear the ridiculous gown and leave my hair up because I want him to be pleased with your efforts."

They left the bedchamber. She no longer cared about the Count's pleasure—or not overmuch. She would throw herself on his mercy and ask to be sent back to Town. If he was pleased with what little she'd accomplished he would be more inclined to help her.

"Oh, boredom. Here is the dining room already," the Princess said when they reached the ground floor.

Footmen flanked closed double doors, but slid rapidly to open them when they saw the Princess and Meg. They walked in, apparently without being either seen or heard by the couple seated at the far end of a table long enough, and with enough chairs, to seat at least twenty people on each side.

The Princess crossed her arms and tapped a foot.

Meg wished she were elsewhere. Anywhere, elsewhere.

The Count's friend was seated on his lap with her arms around his neck. The lady's violet-blue gown displayed more pale skin and rounded flesh than Meg had ever seen in public. A great quantity of shiny chestnut hair was arranged in loops that swept back from a center part and caught up beneath white rosebuds at the crown. Ringlets cascaded past each temple.

Meg looked at the servants who stood by, ready to serve dinner. They stared straight ahead, as if they were unaware of two people embracing at the table.

"Lady Upworth," Princess Désirée muttered, "is a widow who wants Jean-Marc to marry her. If he does, Papa will be furious."

Meg heard what the Princess said, but could not draw her attention from the kiss that went on and on, or the Count's hand, which the lady held to her all but naked bosom.

"Jean-Marc," the Princess said, her voice raised. "We are come to dinner."

The Count's friend tore her lips from his and turned to see who spoke. She kept her companion's hand where it was. She began to laugh, and finally covered her mouth while she brought her mirth under control.

The Count appeared puzzled, but he smiled.

"Come here, little Princess," the lady said. "Come where Ila can see you more clearly."

"You, too," the Princess murmured to Meg. "I need you with me."

They moved down one side of the table, Meg hanging back a little.

Gorgeous Lady Upworth settled herself comfortably against the Count's chest and laced her fingers together. "Oh, dear," she said, when Princess Désirée stood before her. "Oh, dear, oh, dear. I should never have allowed you to deal with any part of your sister's preparations without my help, Jean-Marc. You look ludicrous, you poor darling. No matter, I shall supervise everything from now on."

7

"Sibyl? Is that you?"

A man's voice, calling to her in the thickening twilight, jolted Sibyl. She had waited until she was certain she could escape the house without being seen, and come to the gardens at the center of Mayfair Square. There she had chosen a bench with a view of both Number 7 and Number 17.

"Sibyl?" the man said again, closer this time. "It *is* you. Answer me at once."

He came toward the gardens from the flagway outside Number 7, a solidly built fellow of average height.

She shut her eyes tightly and willed him away. How could she suffer through two great misfortunes in so short a time? Her second cousin William Godly-Smythe's figure could not be mistaken. Nor could his big, round voice, in which he took such pride.

He entered a gate and came directly to her. "Sibyl Smiles, what can you be thinking of to be out here, alone, at such an hour? What can Meg be thinking of to allow you to be here alone—at any time? You are a gentle girl with no experience of the world. Have I not told you, on a number of occasions, that London is no place for tender souls such as yourself—or Meg, of course?"

"Good evening, William," she said. He had made a habit of issuing orders to his second cousins ever since he'd moved into the house he'd been glad to inherit on their father's death. "What are you doing in London?"

"Kindly refrain from questioning me when I am already questioning you. This is what comes of girls being allowed to live alone. Girls of refined upbringing such as yourself. Alone in *London*, mind you. I will not permit this to continue. We shall wait until morning. Then I will escort you home to Puckly Hinton."

At any other time she would inform him of how little authority he had over her and Meg. He had none. But at the moment she was anxious only to dispatch him elsewhere. He must not learn of Meggie's amazing failure to return, not learn of her absence at all, in fact, or he would become more of a pest.

"Come along, come along," he said, bending and taking hold of her arm. "We will speak with Meg at once."

"She's ill." Might she be forgiven for lying?

"Ill? She's always been as strong as a horse. What's made her ill?" William was too strong for Sibyl to resist his urging hand beneath her arm. She was forced to stand. "Oh, of course. How could I be so forgetful when this is exactly why I'm here? The terrible event near the Burlington Arcade. I was stricken to hear of it, of how close she came to being killed. That's why I left important matters to rush here and lend my support. Meg is suffering from the effects of her brush with death. Yes, I was right in coming to insist my wishes are followed."

Pompous ass. Oh, my, my, she was beyond all. Worry had turned her into a common person who thought inappropriate things. "Meg has a cold and a cough. She is sleeping and must remain asleep. The doctor said she needs lots of sleep to help her get better. There are no ill effects from what happened. It was purely an accident."

"Who suggested it wasn't?" he asked sharply. "Is there something being kept from me?"

"Not at all. It was merely that you seemed to be suggesting... How do you know about Meg's accident?"

"You are well aware how I know." William bowed over her, peered at her face. "There is more here than meets the eye, I'll be bound. Reverend Baggs said Meg didn't appear to recognize him but I told him he must be mistaken. Now I realize I should have believed him."

She could not imagine what he was talking about. "Reverend Baggs? From Puckly Hinton? When did Meg fail to recognize him?"

"At the scene of the accident, of course. Poor Reverend Baggs was in London on church matters. Imagine his amazement at seeing Meg like that. He rushed to greet her and shook her hand. He said she didn't know him. How could that be when she has known him since he came to the village?"

"Papa was kind to him when we were younger. I remember that. Then he came to the village when you offered him a living after Papa died," Sibyl told him. "We were not there so very long after that."

"Not long enough to know the man if you saw him?"

She could not pretend further. "I should probably know him."

"Of course you would. There's something wrong with Meg, isn't there? That's why she was vague, and that's why she walked into the path of a carriage."

"No," Sibyl said, truly frightened by his suggestions. "Meg has a cold. There is nothing else amiss with her." Or so Sibyl hoped—wherever Meg was.

"So you say," William said, possessively holding her arm and walking her from the park. "I have reason to believe you are short of money and in dire straits. That may be partly responsible for Meg's odd behavior. But you are both to stop worrying because I have decided what must be done."

He marched her across the street to the flagway. "We will wait until morning to tell Meg our plans. Meanwhile I shall sleep in your parlor. I cannot bear to think of you passing another night without my protection."

If only Meggie were here, Sibyl thought, she would be very firm with their cousin and know exactly how to send him packing while he thought it was his very own idea to leave.

They mounted the steps at Number 7, and the front door swung open. Adam Chillworth stood there, looking even wilder than usual.

William made a disapproving sound.

"She's not back yet, then, is she?" Adam said. "Who's this?"

"Our second cousin, Mr. William Godly-Smythe," Sibyl said, casting about for a way to stop Adam from saying anything further about Meg.

"Aye," Adam said and nodded brusquely at William. "Live nearby, does he? Never heard you mention him before. But he might as well give what help he can."

"Who is this person?" William asked, taking off his hat as he ushered Sibyl into the foyer.

"Adam Chillworth," Adam said, looking William over from head to foot. "Seven C. Sibyl and Meg are friends of mine."

"Because you are all *lodgers* in the same house?" William wrinkled his rather nice straight nose. "You could certainly have nothing else in common."

Sibyl shrugged apologetically at Adam, who smiled. On the rare occasions when Adam smiled, it was impossible not to be enthralled. He became boyishly handsome and his eyes sparkled.

As quickly as it had appeared, the smile fled. Adam said, "There's no sign of her, is there? I should have done what I thought was best and gone to make inquiries. Anyway, I was watching you in the gardens just in case."

"Just in case of what?" William said. His sleek blond hair shone. The expression in his eyes was angry.

"In case I needed to go to Sibyl's aid," Adam said. "She didn't swoon when you approached, so I thought she must know you. Otherwise I'd have been over to ask your business."

William stared at him. "Sibyl was waiting for someone, wasn't she? Who? You are waiting—both of you. Who is missing?"

Color bled along Adam's cheekbones.

"Speak up, man," William ordered.

There was nothing for it but to make sure Adam wasn't responsible for saying what Meg would hate William to hear. "Meg has applied for a position," Sibyl said. "As a companion. She went to be interviewed this morning."

"I knew I should have come days ago, as soon as Reverend Baggs told me what he'd observed." William paced. He had not made a connection between someone missing from Number 7 and Meg applying for a position. He faced Sibyl. "She's lost her mind. I must speak with her at once. Kindly awaken her while I wait in the parlor."

"I can't," Sibyl whispered. "She has secured the position. She went on an outing with her—her new mistress and—and—and she hasn't yet returned."

8

*D*amned awkward, Ila putting on an exhibition like that—particularly in front of Miss Smiles...and Désirée, of course. "Sit down, both of you," Jean-Marc said. He shifted Ila from his knees to the chair on his right with as much dignity as possible—very little dignity. "Désirée, you at my left and Miss Smiles next to you."

The blame was not all Ila's, other than for her insulting reaction to Désirée's appearance. There would be no repeat performance.

A swelling anger astounded him. Not anger at Ila. He wanted fulfillment, damn it. He wanted to walk as a man certain of his purpose. He wanted.... He wanted to care, and to know that there was someone for whom his comings, and goings, and doings, were of the utmost importance because they cared about him.

Jean-Marc thrust the foreign notion aside and smiled at Désirée. She sat beside him, her eyes downcast and her color high. Miss Smiles, in her yellow dress minus the pelisse and bonnet, took the next chair. She, too, kept her eyes lowered, but he sensed she was tired.

She conducted herself with quiet assurance. An unassuming woman. Now there was an intriguing thought. "Ila," he said, "you haven't met Miss Meg Smiles. As I told you, she is to be Désirée's companion. Miss Smiles, this is Lady Upworth."

"Miss Smiles is very good to me," Désirée announced in a rush, directing a hard look at Ila. "She 'as nothing to work with in me, yet she tries so 'ard and she is kind."

"Be calm and remember your h's," Jean-Marc told her. "Miss

Smiles has a great deal to work with, and she has already accomplished a good deal," Jean-Marc said, watching Miss Smiles's reaction with interest. With suspiciously bright eyes, she turned toward Désirée. "I knew your hair would look lovely in a mature coiffeur, young lady. And the dress becomes you. Who would have thought of putting so somber a color on one so young? Yet it suits you. I am very pleased." He avoided looking at Ila.

"Thank you," Désirée said, and smiled at him. He could not recall the last time she had smiled at him. She continued, "I am looking forward to my music lessons with the other Miss Smiles. Are we not fortunate to find such accomplished people to help us?"

"Isn't that lovely," Ila said, sounding flustered, her voice too high. "I am happy for you, Désirée, that you are comfortable with these people. But do tell me I may help. They will need some guidance on many matters and I will be glad to give that guidance."

Disaster lurked here, Jean-Marc decided. "We will discuss that later," he told Ila. "This is all new to Désirée. She has too much to think about already and not so very long to learn what she must. I shall be dealing with any help Miss Smiles needs at present."

"Of course," Ila said, sounding disappointed and perhaps cross. "Oh, the soup smells wonderful. I have such an appetite. Jean-Marc, being with you always makes me hungry."

Oh, indeed it did, Jean-Marc thought.

"Jean-Marc," Désirée said, "Miss Smiles was not prepared to spend the night here. She is concerned because her sister will worry."

He set down his soup spoon. "I thought you had informed her, Miss Smiles?"

Her breasts rose against the low neckline of her dress. He saw her throat move when she swallowed. "Yes, but I didn't know you intended to be here for more than a few hours. I assumed we would return to Town before dark."

That red hair fascinated him. "Verbeux invited you to come with us. You and my sister. Surely he told you to inform your sister of our exact plans."

"He did not say our exact plans," Désirée said, almost gleeful. She and Verbeux enjoyed a contentious relationship. "And I should have thought about it. He just said we were to come to Riverside with you. Of course, I have everything here, and I didn't think."

He contemplated Verbeux's devious behavior. The wretch had obtained his master's agreement to *invite* Désirée and Miss Smiles, then *ordered* them to come. And he'd been too pleased with himself to make the plans clear. Too bad he'd remained in Town to oversee matters at Number 17 Mayfair Square.

"Jean-Marc," Désirée said, "do comfort Miss Smiles. She is a tender person and worries a great deal about others."

Of course he was pleased at Désirée's acceptance of Miss Smiles, but he was also suspicious. Désirée had never shown an inclination to make friends before. In fact, she was remote and difficult with everyone.

"She knows so much about so many things," Désirée said. "It doesn't matter what I ask her, she answers me with such authority. And she is clever. She is going to help me with, er, my watercolors, too, aren't you, Miss Smiles?"

"Yes," Miss Smiles said. He didn't think she heard much of what Désirée said. No doubt she was unable to think of anything but the sister to whom she seemed so devoted.

"I wish it were possible to return you to London tonight," he said gently. This entire matter was too complicated for a mere man, with a mere man's interests. "You see that it already grows dark? Traveling at this time is out of the question. You are not to concern yourself. The responsibility is entirely mine. At dawn I will send a rider to reassure your sister. You will allow me to apologize to her. Meanwhile, things are progressing so well, I insist you relax. I am a happier man because of you. What fortune our paths crossed. You and I shall shepherd Désirée through her

Season. Yes, indeed, I feel confident our partnership in this will
be a success.''

"Have a care, Jean-Marc," Ila said, leaning close and lowering
her voice, "you do not know enough about her yet. In fact, you
are trusting much too much, too soon. You met her only a few
hours ago. How can you be certain she knows this Viscount Kilrood and his wife?"

The moment Ila had bent toward him and lowered her voice,
Désirée had also inclined her head in his direction to hear every
word. Unfortunately, Lady Upworth tended to be unobservant.

"Ila," Désirée said in a loud whisper, "do you think we are
in danger from Miss Smiles?"

Jean-Marc looked at Ila, who frowned and said, "Quite possibly. I'm glad you are wise enough to question such things."

"Thank you," Désirée responded hoarsely. "Perhaps we
should have her taken away."

Jean-Marc sat back in his chair and crossed his arms while his
sister and Lady Upworth strained toward each other and discussed
what should be done about Meg Smiles. He supposed he'd have
to reprimand Désirée later, but for now Ila was having far too
good a time basking in Désirée's supposed confidences.

Beyond the two women's nodding heads and gesturing hands,
Jean-Marc sought Miss Smiles's eyes. They shone, and the corners of her mouth twitched.

"A constable, do you think?" Désirée asked.

They were expressive eyes, and he'd like to see them much
closer.

Ila, whose curls bobbed, said, "I doubt it would be easy to get
a constable out here. But…"

Miss Smiles had pretty teeth and she happened to be showing
them now. She stared at him, and they grinned at each other. He
must make sure to remind himself of the dangers of employing
strangers—one day.

Her eyelashes were very dark, and they curled in a way that

added to the sparkle in her eyes—especially when she blinked. She blinked slowly and her gaze never wavered from his.

For her part, Meg delighted in looking at the Count and in his watching her. A small, shared moment of amusement. Not of his making or hers, and innocent on all parts, except for that of the Princess. A moment to remember. My, my, my, what female wouldn't remember such a face, such a powerful presence?

He was probably unaware that they were staring at each other. No doubt he was bored, his expression fixed. So vital a man was unlikely to be interested in girlishly foolish prattle, and equally unlikely to take notice of someone to whom he had granted temporary employment.

"I shall speak to Jean-Marc about it," Ila said to the Princess.

"No, *I* shall speak to him about it."

Her charge's wit must never be underestimated, Meg decided.

When Miss Smiles looked away, Jean-Marc felt regret. He would like to leave, take her by the hand and leave this room, to take her where they could be alone and talk. *Talk?* Now there was a concept. He wanted to be alone with a woman who aroused him for reasons he had yet to discover, and *talk.* Could he be ill?

The soup had been removed and the next course placed. He couldn't care less.

The Count shook his head. His expression had become serious once more, and rather mystified, Meg thought. This evening, when she couldn't expect to do other than fret about Sibyl, she would calm herself with abstract thinking. And she might also turn that period of intense concentration to an analysis of Count Etranger, for purely theoretical purposes, of course.

He wanted to be alone with her, Jean-Marc admitted to himself. That was all. That was monumentally all. They had met that morning, he had employed her because she convinced him she could do what he didn't want to do—and tonight he wanted to be alone with her.

I may have met a woman I could care for. I must be mad, but it is the kindest form of madness and perhaps I shall never re-

*cover. Such an acquaintance could only be casual, of course.
Nothing more would be suitable, but I might enjoy it nevertheless.*

"Oh, Ila, you naughty tease, I thought you meant it all but you
were only joking," his sister said loudly. "Pah! Now I feel foolish. I was trying to humor you until I could think of a way to
change your mind about Miss Smiles. How could you tease me
so?"

The true naughty tease at the table, Désirée, turned to Meg and
said, "You must forgive us. We idle people entertain ourselves
as best we can."

"How true," Lady Upworth said, her face flushed. "Oh, poor
Miss Smiles, you must have come without any of your things.
No matter, I shall lend you some of mine. I'll have my maid take
them to your rooms." She signaled for the under butler and whispered to him.

In turn the man whispered to a maid, who left the room at
once.

Meg said thank-you and tried to visualize what Lady Upworth
meant by "things." It was hard to imagine that anything of the
lady's would come close to fitting her. She made a covert inspection of Lady Upworth's magnificent figure, then looked at
herself.

Jean-Marc followed Miss Smiles's gaze and was certain he
understood her thoughts. She expected Ila's donations to be overlarge in certain places. He was inclined to doubt that.

Hovering at his shoulder, the under butler murmured something
to Jean-Marc. He nodded without considering what he'd been
asked, and again plates were removed and replaced.

"Please don't arise early in the morning, Miss Smiles," he said.
"Take a little time for yourself. Your sister shall hear from us
first thing so you might as well enjoy Riverside with us."

Meg realized she was being dismissed—and having eaten very
little supper, not that she was hungry. She got up and curtseyed
in three directions. The count rested an elbow on the table and

propped his chin in a palm. He had a very direct way of regarding someone—and he was smiling ever so slightly.

Meg turned away and made for the door. Count Etranger found her laughable.

As soon as the door closed behind Meg Smiles, Désirée rose from her chair. She studied Ila before speaking, "I choose to believe you did not intend to insult me when I arrived for supper. Miss Smiles is beautiful, a special sort of beautiful, and she must have unnerved you. You became confused and didn't think before you spoke. You are forgiven."

Ila turned to Jean-Marc and said, "You must control her. She is become more difficult, and despite her rank, few men will tolerate such arrogance."

Jean-Marc said, "Run along, Désirée. Once begun, tomorrow will be another busy day. Get your rest."

Obediently, she left, but not without hearing her brother say, "Désirée was good enough to hand you an escape from your hurtful comments to her. I suggest you should be grateful for her kindness. For the rest, you are here as my guest, not to instruct my sister—in anything."

Désirée sped upstairs to her rooms and found Miss Smiles in the bedchamber, sitting on the window seat with Halibut in her arms. She had covered her dress with a blanket from inside the seat and held Halibut's soft head to her mouth while she murmured gently. Désirée heard his purr from the doorway.

"Ah," she said. "Such gratitude. You get here a few minutes before me and my disloyal cat is happy to leap into your arms instead of mine."

Startled, Miss Smiles stood and set the cat down.

"Oh, I didn't mean it," Désirée said. "I am tired. I am not accustomed to so much conversation, especially with someone as foolish as Lady Upworth."

Meg didn't answer. She followed the Princess's progress around the room. Slippers flew in one direction, stockings in another. The comb landed on the dressing table and was followed by the pins Meg had used in the girl's hair. Désirée dismantled the plaits and rubbed her scalp hard, wincing as she did so. She turned about and said, "Undo my dress, please." And soon that joined the scattering of garments about the room.

Swathed in a childish night rail that buttoned to the neck and had a rounded collar edged in simple lace, the Princess gathered up Halibut, then stopped and frowned. "Oh, dear, how could I have forgotten?" She set him down and rummaged for a dressing robe.

"What are you doing?"

Princess Désirée waved a hand impatiently. "Don't you know anything? He must relieve himself, that's what I'm doing. So I have to wait for an appropriate moment and go out by a side door and steps leading down from this floor. Stay here."

"I will not," Meg protested. She never recalled being so tired, yet she followed her charge as she rushed along the corridor and into a small, empty room at the far end. A Gothic-looking doorway opened onto the top of a flight of steps leading to a very dark corner in the outside wall of the house. Princess Désirée hurried down with Meg close behind. She set Halibut on the ground and Meg closed her eyes, waiting for frantic shouts that the cat had run away into the darkness.

"*Vite. Vite,*" the Princess demanded.

"I doubt he understands the concept of hurrying—this or any other necessity in this life."

"He most certainly does." She jumped up and down and Meg was horrified to note that the Princess wore no shoes. "*Vite,* Halibut, *vite.* There, you see how obedient he is? He does what he is told. No, Halibut, you are not done. I want more, and I will have more. *Vite.* You will not come out again until morning, so use your opportunity well."

"You will catch cold," Meg said. "Your feet are bare."

"Pah! I am as strong as an ox—and as plain as one. Ask my father."

"Halibut is done," Meg said, avoiding saying what she thought of a father who would be so cruel to his child. "Up the stairs you go. I will carry Halibut."

His fur was cold, but his tongue on her nose was warm and as rough as ever.

Princess Désirée was quickly settled in bed with Halibut beneath the covers. Meg hadn't the heart to protest. "Should you like me to talk with you for awhile? Or read something? The Bible, perhaps."

"Thank you for being with me today," Désirée said. Her eyes were already closed. "Now I must sleep. You saw where your rooms are. Good night."

Dismissed again. Even though it wasn't seen, Meg dipped a curtsey and backed from the room. She would try not to think of how worried Sibyl must be. She wished she could believe her sister would go to Number 17 to find out what had happened, but doubted she would do any such thing for fear of displeasing Meg.

She entered her quarters by a pleasant sitting room where pink had again been employed, this time accented with posies of violets. Still chilled from Halibut's jaunt, Meg was grateful for the fire and held her hands near its warmth.

"There is nothing I can do about getting back to Sibyl tonight." Lecturing herself, even aloud, didn't deaden her anxiety one jot. She would ready herself for bed and settle to guide her thoughts. Now, of all times, she would make good use of the meditation she'd set out to embrace only as part of her assumed mystery.

Another fire burned brightly in the bedchamber. Pale green abounded, and gilded French furniture. Meg could not help but admire it all, and feel a twinge of regret that this would likely be her only night there.

Clothing caught her attention, clothing spread on the high bed, and she approached with a mixture of apprehension and curiosity. She had already decided to sleep in her chemise.

The gown and robe that lay there were of the most delicate

peach color. Embroidered silver leaves edged the neckline of both—a neckline that sank to a deep vee. Tiny silver buttons closed the robe, and silver satin ties trailed from the point of the neck. On the floor beside the bed, placed precisely, was a pair of soft slippers of the same peachy shade.

Meg touched the fabric. She had worked on such finery often enough, but never for her own use.

The voluminous garments would be so much more comfortable to think in than her chemise. And since Lady Upworth had been kind enough to offer them, Meg ought to at least try them on.

Practiced in attending to herself, she took little time to shed her own clothes and don the beautiful garments. The gown floated over her skin so softly it felt as if it were all satin rather than cotton. The robe was sumptuous. She did up the buttons and tied the satin bow that draped from the lowest point of the neckline— low enough to ensure that much of her breasts were revealed.

Meg bent to slip her feet into the silver-trimmed slippers and immediately straightened her back again. The gown and robe were not decent.

She washed quickly at the basin provided, brushed out her hair, retrieved the mantilla from her reticule and slipped into the sitting room. One could not achieve true abstraction where one slept. In fact, evading the temptation to sleep was the greatest challenge to concentration. The light was low, but not so low she couldn't see.

Too much warmth only added to the difficulty in staying awake. Meg sat on the carpet some distance from the fireplace. Spreading the borrowed finery in a flowing circle, she drew up her legs beneath the gown and crossed them. "I will not fight my mind," she said. "Mmmm." The vibration of her voice hummed in her throat. "Wander at will, and I shall draw you back when you are ready."

With the mantilla draped over her head and shoulders, she visualized a white light within her, filling her, passing along her veins. The light warmed her, softened her, expanded to fill her more and more.

The light fled. What must Sibyl be thinking by now? She would not sleep, that was for sure. The one hope that had surfaced was that Adam—who was rather stubborn and determined—might have insisted on going to Number 17. Meg gritted her teeth. He would demand to know exactly where she was and probably make a great fuss in the process.

Sibyl suffered now, but soon the morning would come and a man would go to reassure her. As the Count had sensibly pointed out, nothing could be done tonight.

This time the white light advanced quickly. She opened her hands, palms up, and began the process of relaxing her body. Starting with her feet, humming all the while, she pinched each muscle tight, held it so, then allowed it to fall limp. The sensation that followed was warm and heavy.

One day this marvelously refreshing discipline would be practiced by all.

Fiddle dee dee. Once again her concentration had failed and she must start again.

"I *am*," she murmured on an indrawn breath. She exhaled and repeated, "I am," as she breathed in again. "I am." In. Exhale. "I am." In.

A small amount of pain as a focus was always followed by deeper and deeper connection with self. Keeping her legs crossed beneath the flimsy gown and robe, she eased to lie flat on the carpet. In the places where her limbs joined her body there was much stretching. Her back hurt. But she maintained discipline and started with her feet again. Tightening, holding, releasing. Working slowly upward.

"I am."

With the serene assurance she continued to gain, she would also catch the attention of someone who sought a peaceful sort of wife. First she would draw him to her with her mystery and the deliberate enhancement of what physical attributes she possessed, then she would make him so comfortable, so sure of her loyalty and her devotion to everything he was and did, that he would celebrate the quiet order she brought him.

And in return he would make sure she and Sibyl were not forced into reduced circumstances. Oh, they would happily continue to do what they could for the financial good of them all, but they would no longer worry as they did now.

"I am," she murmured, drawing in the next breath, holding it, releasing the breath and visualizing the darkness of despair flowing out with it.

Meg spread wide her arms. "I *am*." A cooling draft passed over her body.

Behind her closed eyelids she saw the darkly intent face of Count Etranger. She certainly didn't know him. Not at all, really. But she would like to. His need for her sprang from his need to be free of caring for Princess Désirée at this time—probably at any time. He had interests of his own, yet Meg did not think Lady Upworth was more than a small part of those interests. Other, more enigmatic and perhaps more important issues were on the man's mind.

He was kind to her and on occasions today he had studied her with what appeared to be interest. But then, he had also laughed at her. She was beneath his notice. And she wished that were not so, because if she could have absolutely anything in the entire world, it would be Count Etranger.

She lay still, her body pulsing. Just thinking about him made her come alive as she had never felt alive before. But they were strangers. True, they were strangers in strange circumstances that could very well lead to an unusually speedy involvement between two people.

"I *am*." Her next breath released the band of constriction that had formed around her brow. "I *am*."

Coolness wafted over her again. She pulled aside the neck of the robe and gown to bare her shoulders and arched her torso from the carpet. Her back felt hot, and the breeze helped chill the skin pleasantly.

Standing just inside the door that had not been completely closed, Jean-Marc regarded Meg Smiles with a fascination so profound it shook him. On her back, her head swathed in black lace, she lay with her limbs drawn up beneath a voluminous and insubstantial robe. Her arms were thrown out at her sides, and her back arched from the floor.

He was transfixed. Enough of her features could be made out to show her eyes were closed. From time to time she murmured, "I am," and seemed to stiffen, then relax.

Coming here had been a whim. He was a man besieged and she was the only person detached enough to offer some hope of impartiality.

His presence was an intrusion on some very private ritual. He should not have come. And he should certainly leave at once.

She had bared her shoulders. The robe opened wide to reveal a good deal of her, dare he say, large breasts. Yes, they were large and luminous in the flickering light. It was quite possible that before long they would be entirely revealed.

His manhood responded vigorously to the notion, and his thighs jerked hard. Deep in his belly more tension gathered, spreading fullness and hardness and pumping need.

Odd she might be, but she was not a jade for his taking—not even if only with his eyes, his mind.

Meg's concentration waned. She felt the spaces around her shift, grow smaller. And there was another, a more subtle heat in the room. And a scent, as if the breezes she'd felt had swept in the essence of the flowing river and the waving grasses at its banks.

She held still, and then she heard the faintest of sounds. A sigh, or someone remembering to breath. Meg grew tense and frightened.

Jean-Marc doubted he could leave unnoticed. Already he sensed her becoming aware of him.

Meg lowered her back to the floor. Sensation climbed her spine, like fingers brushing lightly, painting fervent excitement a subtle touch at a time. Not a creation of her own, but the reaching out of another consciousness, one with the power to make her feel without the meeting of skin.

Her stillness in the firelight, the unknowing supplication in her upturned palms, her innocent voluptuousness… She moved him.

In the silence Meg felt him.

She was no longer alone. He was here.

9

"Please excuse me. I have no right to intrude on you."

Slowly, Meg opened her eyes. He stood a few feet from her, a solid, faceless silhouette, but with a glimmer of white—his shirt. He wore no coat. How could she ask him to stay without his thinking she lacked modesty? "Why did you come?"

"You should be angry." He was humbled by what she made him feel. "You don't know me at all. My presence must be a shock."

His low voice had broken—just a little, but definitely—as if with emotion. To have such feelings for a man who was a stranger must be very wrong. No doubt she was being foolish, perhaps even walking into a dangerous trap set by a man of the world for a girl of little experience.

"Miss Smiles, may I..." Did he know what he intended to ask? Why *had* he come here? Was he looking for a dalliance with an interesting girl who posed no threat to him? No threat in the form of potential demands for commitment?

Meg clutched the robe and gown together at the neck and sat up. She wasn't dressed. "Please tell me why you are here." She pulled off the mantilla and wished she had not let her hair down. This was too intimate.

"I wandered," he told her. "I didn't know where I intended to go until I arrived at your door. May I sit with you?"

He wanted to sit with her, with Meg Smiles, orphan of almost no means, seamstress ashamed of practicing her skill to make a living, a woman whom he had hired because she fabricated her experience and played on his need?

"No, of course not," Jean-Marc said, as much to himself as to Miss Smiles. "I'll go." If she decided to leave once they returned to London, it would be his fault.

"Please do sit with me," she said, and watched him pause before coming closer. "Do you find it difficult to sleep?"

"Occasionally."

Rather than take a chair, he dropped to sit, cross-legged, his knees almost meeting hers. Rank and privilege did not necessarily make a person different, less likely to feel downcast, more likely to treat those of humbler beginnings with contempt. Did it?

Count Etranger was as silent as she. Could he be as lost for words as she was?

What was he thinking?

"Miss Smiles, I am deeply sorry for what is completely inappropriate behavior." His own sudden laughter actually calmed him. "And you would be less intelligent than I know you are if you did not question my sincerity. Rather than go away and try to forget I ever blundered here, I sit before you on the floor. I have interrupted you in... I have interrupted you and you are probably frightened. Of course you are. Forgive my laughter, but I have managed to amaze myself." He propped his elbows and buried his face in his hands.

If she could, she would comfort him. Any such attempt would be insolent.

Silence settled.

Silence filled with the small sounds, the small feelings of rich awareness. Soft breathing. Settling sighs in aged wood. White linen pulled taut over hard flesh. Hands painted beautiful by shadows. Firelight on his hair. Legs so unlike her own, the muscles long and solid, legs that invited forbidden touches. She was lost in him, happily lost.

"What ritual do you practice, Miss Smiles?"

Ritual? Such a question had never occurred to her. "Ritual? I am learning the benefits of abstracted thinking. Combined with physical disciplines. One attempts to attain a quiet mind and heart—to achieve peace that allows serenity at all times.''

"Serenity at all times?" *Abstracted thinking?* Mysterious minx. He had heard of such things, but surely they were only interesting to men.

She laughed a little, and said, "I didn't say I had conquered my own darting mind, or found serenity—most certainly not at all times! But I have come to need these opportunities for solitude and thought."

"I see." And he believed he might. "I may give you another duty—to teach me how to find peace. At some later date, of course."

"I would try, and gladly."

Jean-Marc did not dare risk a glance at her. She might see just how he longed for companionship that gave as much as it took. He must have drunk too much after having unpleasant words with Ila.

Miss Smiles touched his hair so lightly he might not have noticed if he hadn't heard and felt her move. There was the briefest of hesitations before she withdrew her hand.

"No, no," he said, and caught her wrist. "Oh, no, please don't offer comfort and steal it back so soon. I should like you to hold my hand. Come, press your palm to mine just so. Perhaps I will feel your peace and serenity and take some of it for my own."

Meg trembled. He took her hand and placed his left palm against her right. If he sought to undo her, to steal away whatever logic she'd managed to cling to, be it ever so tenuous a connection, then he succeeded.

"Cold," he said, and she knew he meant her hand.

He laced his fingers through hers. The two of them remained there, arms extended, hers raised higher than her shoulder. When she would have weakened, he supported the weight for both of them without seeming to notice.

"You are warm," she said, not at all certain he would hear what she said.

With his free hand he stroked her raised forearm. Very slowly, with utter concentration. So many sensations overwhelmed Meg. He said, "Then take my warmth in exchange for your peace."

Jean-Marc covered her hand with both of his and settled them on his calf. He had already taken her beyond any acceptable boundary. What further harm could come from his sharing this innocent interlude with her?

How innocent could this be on his part?

"There is nothing acceptable about our being here, My Lord, is there?" To be less than honest would rob her of any joy she might hope to take away from the night.

"Not unless we convince each other there is. If we forget who we are, how we are different—even how we are the same—and grant ourselves permission to accept whatever we have to offer and take, then I believe our actions are not only acceptable, but necessary. And we should also have to forget that we met only hours ago." He tilted his face to the ceiling and expanded his lungs. "I am a man who is torn between two countries, and between what is expected of him and what he craves for himself. The responsibilities I am ordered to assume weigh heavily. I would like to please those who expect these things of me. But my heart is elsewhere, and I do not know what to do."

"My Lord," Miss Smiles said softly. "I feel for you in your struggle."

Yes, he believed she did. "These matters are most private. I have not shared even a hint of my true feelings with anyone else."

"Why do you share them with me?" Only a gullible person would refrain from asking, Meg thought. "A stranger?"

"Are you a stranger?" He smiled to himself. "I suppose that is so in hours and minutes, but in here—" he struck his chest "—it is as if I have been coming toward you for a long time. Oh, I didn't know it, but I do now. You are familiar to me.

Familiar yet mysterious, and I want to know you.... Meg, I should like to know you very well.''

He used her first name and the sound of it on his tongue was unbearably sweet, as sweet as it was startling. The turning, turning, turning of her stomach made her light-headed. She might well regret her impetuousness later, but for now she believed he was sincere.

"You have a great deal of hair," he told her, and she bit her lip at the almost boyish dip of his head. "That was personal. Forgive me again. But I will tell you nevertheless that I do admire your hair. It invites me to sink my fingers into its softness. Look at me, sweet Meg—you have nothing to fear."

She would not think now of Mme. Suzanne's Mixture for Fine Red Hair, or her little pots of potions for darkening the lashes and brightening the cheeks with an exquisite subtlety that vied with nature. Should she try to tell the Count that she hoped to capture the attention of a good man desirous of a gentle and supportive wife?

"Meg, would you like me to go now?"

It was her turn to tip her head back. As she did, she prayed for guidance. Already he was using her name as if they were old friends—which they were never likely to be. By right she should respectfully suggest that the moment had come for them to part.

She didn't want him to go.

"Meg?" He leaned toward her and waited until she looked into his eyes. "I will go at once if that's what you want." His unfairness should shame him. Asking her to make the decision was designed to bring her insistence that he remain.

"And that is what *you* want?"

Ah, she was not to be so easily duped. "No, it isn't. I want to stay with you for as long as is even remotely safe. I would stay until the dawn, just to sit here with you and talk. And if we fall asleep in each other's arms, I shall be the most fortunate of men."

Meg could not speak. His earnestness disarmed her. The suggestion that they might hold each other and sleep shattered every shred of her composure.

"Meg—"

"My Lord, you are most welcome to stay as long as you please. I will not sleep tonight because I am worried about my sister. I would welcome your company."

His eyes smarted, not something he'd experienced in longer than he remembered. Men didn't cry and he would not—but she moved him again and again. "You don't mind if I call you Meg?"

"Oh, no." She smiled at him. "It pleases me."

"And it would please me if you would call me Jean-Marc. I admit such a practice would raise eyebrows in public, but when we are alone, it will be as friends and confidants." His mind was becoming unbalanced, but he welcomed the loss of sanity in this instance. He went willingly to his fate as a bewitched man. And he *was* bewitched by the girl he'd employed to be his sister's companion, her guide through this dashed annoying Season. He didn't care when they had met or under what circumstances— they reached one another in ways that evaded most men and women even should they know each other for a lifetime. "Meg, speak my name."

With her thumb, Meg rubbed back and forth on his palm. What he asked was extraordinary. He was extraordinary. "Jean-Marc. A manly name. How it suits you."

"Thank you. I have fought my tasks with Désirée. She is not an unpleasant girl, but she is misunderstood—even mistreated— by some members of her family. I admire her for drawing forth a gentler side when she can. She likes you."

"I like her. I intend to be a friend to her and to make her happy when she might have been sad."

"You shall not mind attending salons and musicales, and other such nonsense?"

She giggled. "Now you will know how shallow I am. I look

forward to seeing all the grand people in their beautiful clothes. And I shall love the music. I am besotted by music."

"Do you like to dance?"

She shrugged. "I have danced in the country—at small affairs in the village, and yes, I did enjoy that very much. But I do wish to dance the waltz one day—with a partner who will all but sweep me from my feet. A foolish wish, but I believe in wishing just the same."

"So do I." He had often had nothing but his hopes and wishes to stand between him and despair. "You make me happy. I am delighted you will be Désirée's willing chaperone." He came close to telling her she must have a new wardrobe, but best to leave it to Verbeux as had been agreed.

"My sister, Sibyl, will enjoy Désirée. Sibyl is quiet but firm with her students and they come to love her. She is never impatient and has been known to find humor in the reluctant musician."

"Good," he said, but his attention wandered elsewhere. Meg had the most sensuous of mouths. The bottom lip fuller than the top, pink and soft, and expressive. When she smiled, she became an imp capable of stealing any man's heart. "Tell me something of what troubles you, just to ensure I don't become embarrassed at all I have revealed about myself."

"There would never be need for embarrassment between us." Now she sounded presumptuous, but to withdraw the statement would be to make too much of it.

"I shall put more coals on the fire. Get closer to the warmth." Moving to kneel near the hearth, he scooped coals from a brass scuttle and brought back the blaze of flame.

Meg followed his wishes and shifted to sit nearer to the grate. He rubbed his hands together and sank back to stretch out, his shoulder against her back, his long legs fully extended.

She was aware only of him, of his arm and shoulder pressing against her and of his head above hers and so close.

"My sister and I find ourselves in reduced circumstances," she told him haltingly. "Part of our living comes from Sibyl's music lessons and my design and sewing. The rest has been provided by the trusts our father set up in our names. Our home he had to leave to a male relative—our cousin, William Godly-Smythe— but there was money for us and we thought it would be adequate for a very long time, as long as we also worked."

"It's not?" These unjust inheritances were still too common.

"It was. But we misjudged. Our father had assumed we would marry. Papa was a kindly and simple man. He trusted that all would be well in all things. He did not countenance that a plain woman—or in my case, plain women—with little to bring to a marriage would be unlikely to find husbands. Anyway, the sums we receive have grown smaller and smaller and we must do something to help ourselves. This is why I came to ask if you might have a position for me."

"And I did," Jean-Marc told her. "What a good thing—for both of us."

"Yes, indeed."

"Lean on me, Meg. You will be more comfortable."

Her heart beat uncomfortably hard. She had known no such time as this—but she did want to know it, this one and many more. Oh, she was too ready to fall from the conventions she knew very well.

"Please never call yourself plain," he said, so quietly, into the hair near her ear. "Come. Don't be afraid of me. I shall never hurt you. I want only to give you comfort and beg you for a little comfort in return."

Meg could not make one of her muscles move.

Jean-Marc shifted beside her and put an arm around her shoulders.

The robe and gown she had been lent were most unsuitable now. She ached from clinging to the neck, but if she let go... Well, if she let go the neck would be low, but since the shoulders were firmly in place, she should reveal nothing more than a little womanly flesh.

He eased her closer until her head rested in the hollow of his shoulder.

Meg carefully released her grip on the robe and wriggled until she sat sideways. There she was more comfortable. She turned her face into his chest and stiffened at the ripples of raw weakness that reached into unmentionable places.

"Let me see your face," he said. "If our stolen moments are to be infrequent, I would like to have images of you to remember, images like this. Look at me, Meg."

She took so long to do as he asked, he feared she would refuse. But then she did raise her chin, and her luxurious red hair fell back to frame her face. His efforts with the coals had produced a bright blaze to heighten her cheekbones and jaw and soften the shadows between. She might not be beautiful by the standards of some, but the misfortune was theirs. The firelight glinted on her brilliant hair and stroked her full white breasts, pressed together against his chest and now so much more visible to him. A darkness slashed between those beguiling breasts.

"I don't think we'll find it easy to pretend we are not drawn to each other," he told her. And he did truly believe what he said. He also had no desire to try to douse what he felt for her. What he felt for her incorporated an attraction to her delightful openness, and it began to include a burgeoning hunger for her person. Surely she would not rebuff a simple kiss.

Meg curled against him, blotting out each warning thought that assailed her. His arm around her, he stroked her shoulder, slid the tips of his fingers lightly back and forth on naked skin too close to her breast.

He studied her face. "Would you let me kiss you?" Her instant tensing didn't surprise him. "Refuse and I shall understand, and press you no further."

Her eyes were so dark he could make out nothing of her expression. She reached up to settle a hand on either side of his neck, beneath the open collar of his shirt. And she traced tendon, bone, muscle, with a caution that suggested the form of a man was new to her. "I should like you to kiss me," she said. "But you are unlikely to enjoy the experience."

Only with difficulty did Jean-Marc contain a laugh. Before she could change her mind, he held her slender waist and covered her upturned mouth with his.

Her lips remained as they were, slightly parted but unresponsive. He breathed more heavily and grazed back and forth, back and forth, murmuring appreciation from time to time while he moved his hands upward from her waist to span a good deal of her body just beneath her breasts. He felt them, heavy and soft against his thumbs.

He was a man, not a saint.

A small, experimental movement of Meg's mouth excited him more than was safe. He could do nothing to stop her—or himself. She nuzzled him, her mouth parting a little more. Jean-Marc made a silent plea for the skill to please her without frightening her and dipped his tongue just inside her bottom lip.

Meg shuddered. Her breasts strained and stung. Only through strength of will did she stop herself from taking his hands and pressing them to her. His tongue went farther and farther into her mouth. He changed positions again, knelt and pulled her to her knees in front of him. The urgency she felt in him increased and with his ardor, her own came to a full life that rendered her panting, leaning, seeking to get her hands completely beneath his shirt, where she could learn how every inch of him felt.

She could not be normal. One of her father's lady parishioners had taken it upon herself to speak of a few very difficult matters. Ladies did not show interest in a man's person. They certainly never initiated any sign of affection.

But this lady *was* willing to initiate whatever would cause Jean-Marc to lavish her with more of the wonderful things he was doing to her.

His kisses—their kisses—rocked their mouths together. He caught her by the hips and urged her so close that she felt his body against hers—she felt part of him that was very hard. And it poked at her, rhythmically. Oh, she knew all about that. It was the part in all those books of Greek statuary, and on looking closely, she had even seen a suggestion of it in some of the books she'd secretly obtained that referenced the ancient *Rig-Veda* discipline, and the ninth-century works on yoga that were her guide to concentration.

"I feel you wandering from me," he whispered against her brow. "Come back, Meg. I need you."

"I have not wandered," she told him, and tasted his neck. She unbuttoned his shirt and stroked his chest. Very dark hair there felt soft. She rubbed her cheek over it, and deep in her belly she flamed. And she grew wet. How strange.

"This is too much," he said through his teeth. Restraint was costing him too much and failing anyway. "You obviously understand how strongly I might want to touch you, Meg. I should like to feel your breasts. They are all but naked before me and—"

"It's all right," she told him. That was what she wanted. She'd already imagined how it might be for him to do so.

Jean-Marc felt the last vestiges of his control break. The noise he heard came from his own throat, low, a growl. She remained still, her hips against his while she kept her face raised to his. The slightest passage of his fingers under the neck of the pale robe sent it slipping from her shoulders and down her arms.

"It's been too long," he muttered against her neck. He gripped her elbows, gripped her clothing where it rested there. "I have not cared for too long." Looking at her threatened to swamp his conscience, so he closed his eyes and bent to kiss her breasts. He heard her sob, but didn't stop, couldn't stop. Her nipples were pink, their centers hardened with arousal. She was a passionate woman in the making, this strange Meg to whom he might become addicted.

Releasing her for just long enough to rip off his shirt, he caught her up and carried her, then stood her on the seat of a chair. "You have never known a man?"

"No, never." She pulled her arms free and drove her fingers

into his hair. "I have lived quietly, how could I do otherwise? I don't understand... I don't."

She might not understand but she cradled his head and guided his face to rest between her breasts. His legs threatened to buckle. Another part of him threatened to explode.

Jean-Marc struggled against instincts determined to rule him.

The robe and gown slid from Meg's waist toward her feet. She kept hold of Jean-Marc and kicked the lovely clothes away. For the first time ever, she stood naked before a man, a count who employed her, a man who could have whatever woman he chose and who could not be concerned with either her reputation or her feelings.

He had offered to leave but she had asked him to stay.

"Do you understand pregnancy?" he asked.

She frowned, then grew even more heated. "Yes, of course I do."

"I doubt you understand too much. If a man and woman are together as they are meant to be. Joined. There is always the possibility that the woman will begin to increase, that they will cause the beginning of a child."

"Not if they aren't married."

He made a sound she couldn't interpret and caught her up in his arms again. "No, Meg, preferably not if they aren't married. But sometimes—as now—a man and a woman want the greatest intimacy possible. You do not know these things, but put your trust in me and all will be well. I won't say that what I intend isn't wrong, but neither is it dangerous to the well-being of you or me. Can you believe that?"

"Hold me again as you did before."

Jean-Marc kissed her, but it was a hard and brief kiss. "Can you believe I will not do either of us harm?"

"Yes." She was all nerve and wanting and open places that she felt would never close again.

He sat on the chair where she had stood and arranged her astride his hips. He undid his breeches and contrived to push them low enough to allow him freedom. Slipping his fingers into the hair between her legs, he was instantly enveloped in moisture, and surrounded by the intoxicating fullness of her most private parts. Swollen silk inviting him inside—inside where he must not go.

Meg could scarcely breathe at all. Her pulse beat so that she felt it through all of her body. She felt it between her legs in the flesh no man had touched before, but where Jean-Marc now probed. She clutched his shoulders.

"I will guide you," he said, and his voice sounded different. "Relax, my sweet." She could not, but she didn't resist when he wrapped her hand around the part of him that stood erect from his body, erect and like smooth, hot stone.

He had had little to do with inexperienced women. "Don't be afraid. When it is appropriate, what you hold is inserted inside your body, where you feel that wonderful humid sleekness. When it is not appropriate, there are other ways to satisfy what we feel. You want something, don't you?"

They shouldn't speak of such things. "I think so, but I don't know what it is. And it doesn't matter. I'm sure I will stop aching soon."

He might have yelled his triumph. Instead he buried his face in her neck and kneaded her breasts. She arched toward him, crying his name, and again he used his mouth to draw more ecstatic cries from her.

Meg panted. Jean-Marc sucked the tips of her breasts. The thought mortified her. It also excited her. Her breasts felt very full, and they throbbed. With each touch of his mouth, she experienced an echoing throb between her legs. She wished he would do something about that.

The women in his life had all been practiced lovemakers. They often led the way, ensuring they took what their greedy bodies demanded, but also attending to his needs—often until he was drained, but always satisfied.

Meg Smiles's body demanded release from the tension he'd

built. He held her with one arm and kissed her, long and deep, while he stroked her, felt her try to close her legs, then, as sensation must have built, become incapable of doing other than allow her knees to spread. Her whimperings were uttered into his mouth and he smiled as he continued to kiss her, and to increase the pace of his deliberate caress. From time to time he passed fingers inside her and her bottom jerked from his thighs.

Even when she tried to tear her mouth from his, to catch a breath, he would not allow it. She burned. Almost unbearable tension mounted. Still he kissed her, commanded and controlled her with his lips and tongue. He moved his tongue into her mouth as he moved his fingers into the passage where desperate desire pooled.

Faster and harder he rubbed over a small hot place that demanded something, something she could not do without. "Jean-Marc," she said breathing when she could, "What I feel...there. I cannot bear it if...I just don't know."

Ah, but he did. "Hold me," he told her. "Do as I'm doing to you. Rub up and down my shaft. It is the only way to find fulfillment." Not so, but perhaps there would be more occasions to continue Meg's instruction. "Yes, yes, oh, yes. Don't stop. Perfect. Oh, perfect."

Finally unable to stop himself, he replaced her hand on him with one of his own. Lunging helplessly forward, he manipulated her with the tip of his vibrating rod. Almost instantly she cried out, and he felt ripples pass through her flesh. She rocked against him, holding him once more and blindly trying to guide him inside her. Instinct could be relied upon as the great teacher. It could also be relied upon to test a man's willpower beyond endurance.

Her hair flowed wild over her shoulders. Her pale skin shone, damp and irresistible.

He was not a saint. "Sometimes there is something a woman does for a man to ease what I have just eased for you."

"Tell me," she demanded, gripping his sides with enough unconscious savagery to drive her short nails into his skin.

Gritting his teeth, he didn't protest. The pain helped gain him the slightest distance from the drive of his sex. He leaned to whisper in her ear and steeled himself for her horrified reaction.

Meg looked at his face to see if she could detect any humor there. No, he didn't joke, and what he suggested made perfect sense. Inexperienced she might be—might have been—but common sense painted a most practical picture. She looked down at him. Still pulsing from the marvelous thing he had done for her, Meg slipped to her knees between Jean-Marc's thighs. Overwhelming emotion brought tears to her eyes. Briefly she rested her face low on his belly, felt the coarser hair there and turned to kiss him in spots that caused him to jump again and again, while she smiled through her tears and vowed not to be hurried.

She would be the end of him. It was too much to feel so much. Her gentle touch, the way she kissed him in places he never recalled another woman kissing him—not at such a moment when her needs had been met—moved him deeply. Meg wanted to kiss him, she wanted to lavish sensual response upon him because... It would be best not to examine the reasons too deeply, certainly not now. After all, he would protect her from any talk, but theirs was not a story with an end that was in question.

"Thank you," she said, her lips poised a breath from the head of his rod. "You have filled me with such delight. I shall never be the same and I am glad."

Pushing his legs apart, she leaned over him, her breasts heavy on his thighs, and she drew him into her mouth. *She was glad?* Miss Meg Smiles could not possibly be as glad as he was.

10

Every member of her family might consider her distant and insensitive, Désirée thought, and she might be, but she was not so distant that she couldn't feel something very different about Miss Smiles this morning.

Yes, very different. "I would prefer my hair in braids again," she said. "This is most uncomfortable. I thought I would only have to wear it like this last night."

Dressed in the yellow once again, Miss Smiles busied herself over Désirée's hateful new coiffeur.

"I shall call you Meg," she said.

"That would be unlikely to meet with approval."

"*Your* approval?"

"My approval isn't of any importance, Your Highness." Meg Smiles looked at her in the mirror. "Of course I would not presume to approve or disapprove of your decisions." Her eyes were bright, too bright, and dark beneath.

"I can decide what to call you, Meg. You did not sleep last night, did you?"

Meg turned away, and Désirée saw how her shoulders rose. "What is it? What has happened to you?"

"Nothing," Meg said, collecting herself and preparing a lie. "I thought I should sneeze. I didn't sleep well. Thinking about my sister kept me awake."

"A rider was sent to London very early this morning so there is no point in worrying further. Your sister knows you are safe now. You will be very hungry on the journey if you do not eat."

"I'm not hungry." How petulant she sounded. "But thank you. Now you are to move around in Society as a mature woman, you will not be seen in public with your hair down." She was a hypocrite. Not so many hours earlier, Jean-Marc... The Count had left her when the dawn touched the walls in her bedchamber. Her hair had been down, caught beneath his neck when he'd awakened and dressed in silence.

"How can a female of seventeen be considered a mature woman?" the Princess said.

How, indeed? "It isn't my place to interpret conventions, Your Highness. My studies taught me that women are considered mature a great deal later than used to be the case."

The Count had taken her to bed and immediately slept in her arms. She had not slept, but that was as well because she wouldn't have liked to miss a moment of watching him, watching his dark eyelashes move, the restless turning of his head and the thrashing of his body as if he were troubled, the vulnerability that fled the moment he opened his eyes.

Not a word had he spoken to her. Of course, she had kept her eyes closed and pretended to sleep because she would not have known what to say to him. She had been a fool. A green girl deluded into shameful behavior by the immensely flattering advances of a sophisticated and...a sophisticated and wonderful man.

The fault was hers. Papa's parishioner had warned her most strongly that if she should "fall"—that was the term used—if she should fall, it would be Meg's fault because men were animals, each of them desperate to procreate, and they could not be held accountable for their urges. The Count had assured her there would not be a child. She would accept what he'd said as true although she did feel apprehensive in case it wasn't.

Mais oui, indeed there was something most strange here, Désirée decided. "Meg, are you ill?"

"I have experienced a great many things in too short a time," Meg said sharply. She lowered her eyes at once. Indeed she had experienced a great deal that was new. "Forgive me. I am usually exceedingly even tempered."

"I am not. I am a…a shrew. Ask Jean-Marc."

"If you are a shrew—" caution was not always a good thing "—well, then, you are only protecting yourself in difficult times. You do not even wish to be here going through this fantasy they have decided you will enjoy."

"Oh, Meg." Désirée turned on her plush stool and took Meg's hands. "You do understand. You are the kindest of creatures. Will you help me, please?"

Meg quaked. "Help you how?"

"If possible, to escape this thing they will have me do. Failing that, assist me in arriving at the end of my Season with no repulsive fiancé in tow."

"What if you meet a most pleasant man?"

"No such creature exists. I wish to please Jean-Marc—who is the best of my relations—by appearing to enter into the spirit of the thing. But I shall rely on you to help me discourage all advances. This will require clandestine activities, but no man is as clever as a woman, so they have not a chance against two women such as us." She suddenly clapped her hands together, startling Meg. "And I do believe we shall have fun, especially when you reveal all the secrets that have been kept from me."

Puzzled, Meg shook her head.

"Oh, you goose," the Princess said. "You know. *Their* secrets. Them. The all-hallowed male of the species. The least I expect is to learn all there is to know about how they are the same, and how they are different from women. I have managed to peek at a picture or two. Nothing very good, you know. The silly things always manage to drape their salient parts—and those who produce books with illustrations are annoying enough to place little black squares over…well, *over.*" Princess Désirée giggled in a most naughty fashion. "I want some illustrations *without* those little squares. That shall be another of your duties. Obtain some original sketches of the male minus his little black square—taken from all directions—and with clear information on the specific purpose for each of his parts. There must be specific purposes—unpleasant purposes we should not approve of—or no doubt they would be flaunting their parts all over the place. You see, I happen to believe they are exceedingly pleased with whatever it is that makes them male—and take it from me, it's under those black squares."

Meg struggled valiantly against laughter and succeeded to some degree. "We must hurry. It's time for us to go down."

"I believe I have shocked you." Désirée sounded satisfied. "But if I am to be my husband's helpmate in all things, including those I intend to discover shortly, I have no intention of being unprepared."

"We must get Halibut to the coach."

"We must have fun. Fun, fun, fun. These people of the *Haut Ton* will see me and laugh behind their hands. If a man should show interest in me, they will conclude, correctly, that he only wants what comes with me. If I am to suffer, so shall he. Or perhaps he won't suffer at all. Perhaps he will enjoy dallying with me as much as I shall enjoy his dallying with me—which will likely be not at all."

"Enough," Meg said, overwhelmed by her charge, who had become excessively garrulous. "We don't want to keep your brother waiting. He might be angered."

"Very likely," Princess Désirée said, and yawned.

"Halibut—"

"Halibut is already in the coachman's box. Isn't my sweet friend the most beautiful cat?"

Meg had no difficulty in agreeing. "Yes. Does Lady Upworth travel back with us?"

"Why," Désirée said, and sighed, "I do believe you are naive about such things. Ila is a convenience to Jean-Marc. Her fault, not his. She insists upon making herself available. She comes here when she knows he is also coming, and often waits here if she thinks he will soon return. She wants to marry him, but he doesn't want to marry her."

"You can't be sure of that."

"I most certainly can." Her Highness sounded annoyed. "I have loyal friends on the staff here. They tell me how Upworth fawns on Jean-Marc, creeps into his bedchamber, where there is laughter behind closed doors. You may be sure she could tell us a great deal about what is hidden by those black squares."

"Princess Désirée."

"I am incorrigible. But how else should I live? Anyway, word has it that Upworth and the Count had words last night and she left his chamber, so my half brother will undoubtedly be cross from having to do without whatever it is these men detest doing without. They say he walked around a great deal, then simply disappeared." The Princess shrugged. "I believe he went riding. That seems to cool him."

Meg pressed her hands into her skirts. The Count had come to her because his lady bird had ignored him. He had made Meg into a fallen woman because he did not want to be without his manly comforts for even one night. He must hold her in such contempt.

"Very well," Princess Désirée said. "Time to leave. Smile, if you please. I want you to be with me at all times. There must be no suggestion that you are not happy with your position."

"I am pleased with it."

"Even if you dislike me?" The Princess wrinkled her nose at the pale pink gown Meg had found. The dress was a little outdated, the fabric not the best, but it suited Princess Désirée.

"I not only don't *dislike* you, I like you a great deal. Now, turn around. I must check you from all sides."

Huffing, the Princess did as she was told.

Meg took several pink muslin roses and tucked them into the princess's braided crown. A small pair of diamond earrings reflected in the girl's translucent skin.

"One thing more," Meg said. "And if you mention this, I

shall deny all knowledge. Stand still and do as I tell you.'' Using a tiny brush intended for cleaning buttonhooks, Meg smeared the bristles with kohl and applied it to pale but long lashes. ''Now, don't blink.''

Princess Désirée tapped a toe, but she did not blink. Meg applied a little rouge to her charge's cheeks, and even less to her lips. With a fine linen handkerchief, she flipped any loose particles away. ''Now. Look at yourself.''

Her Highness turned and ducked to see herself in the mirror. She became rigid. ''I do not look at all myself.''

''You most certainly do.''

''No, I look...almost pretty.''

''You are pretty. And I could not make you so if you weren't. I just enhanced your beauty a little.''

Princess Désirée faced her, the space between her eyebrows puckered. ''Is this not subterfuge?''

''Somewhat.'' Meg would not lie about this. ''But no more subterfuge than is employed among most women of your class. You have beautiful eyes and such skin.''

Waving her arms, the Princess picked up a deep pink satin pelisse and Meg helped her put it on. ''You mean well, Meg Smiles, but I have no illusions. Through my marriage, Papa wishes to gain English connections in high places. Why he thinks such a person could be interested in me, I cannot tell.'' Soft white swansdown edged the sleeves and hem of the pelisse. More swansdown drifted along the narrow brim of a matching satin bonnet.

Meg was still tying her own bonnet strings when they swept from the room and went downstairs.

The staff of Riverside Place had gathered to see their employer and his sister on their way.

When she emerged into the bright light of late morning, Meg bowed her head to hide her eyes from the glare. She wanted to search for the Count but knew she must do no such thing.

When she stood beside the coach, a massive shadow fell over

Meg. She shaded her eyes to look up. Dressed in dark gray, the Count was seated upon a large brown horse. In fact, the creature seemed exceedingly large to Meg and did a great deal of snorting and whipping of its tail.

"Good morning, Désirée," he said at last, and his sister paused on the steps to the inside of the coach. "Let me see you."

The Princess found a handhold on the doorway and turned slightly.

"Lovely," he said. "Pink suits you. As soon as we get to Mayfair Square, arrangements must be made for the modistes to come in."

"I do not know why," the Princess said, and scrambled clumsily to sit in the carriage.

The Count turned his head and looked down on Meg. "You did not sleep well?"

Her skin throbbed with the power of her blush. She cocked her chin and said, "I slept quite well, thank you."

He dropped his voice, "No, you didn't. And I knew you weren't asleep this morning, but I chose not to cause you discomfort since you didn't want to talk to me."

She didn't reply.

A fine muddle, Jean-Marc thought. This day would tell the story of whether his indiscretion with this girl had been an even bigger mistake than he'd decided it was by the time he left her.

"Yellow becomes you, Miss Smiles." No one was close enough to overhear, but he would take no chances. "You should wear it often."

She ducked her head. Her hands were tight fists on the handle of her reticule.

Jean-Marc grew still and he waited, unmoving other than at the whim of his restless horse.

At last she raised her face, and the blood had all but fled her pale skin. Her chin came up even more. She met his eyes directly and he saw challenge there. Meg didn't want his concern, his pity—not that he pitied her. She was a delightful creature who presented him with complications he didn't need. But whose fault was that?

Meg would not look away first. His dark eyes didn't as much as flicker. She wondered how long they'd remained there—staring at each other—and who had noted their unusual behavior.

Count Etranger swung his leg over his horse and dismounted. Immediately a groom appeared and walked the animal away.

"Allow me to assist you inside." Moving a little behind her, with his right hand he held her forearm while he guided her up the steps with his left hand. When he hesitated, she could not carry on without wrenching away and causing a scene. "You are being foolish," he told her softly. "If you don't have a care, everyone around us will come to some conclusions—and they will be correct. Collect yourself. You make too much of too little. And remember that if you say a word to anyone, your reputation will be destroyed. That probably includes your sister, or any of your friends at Number Seven. Do you understand?"

"I understand that... Thank you, I understand. You have nothing to fear, I shall not complain."

"You consider that you have something to complain about?" Unless she heard only what she wanted to hear, he sounded angry. "You are the first woman ever to think so. Never mind. Later we will make sure you understand how these matters are handled for the best. And you will accept what I have to say."

He handed her into the coach, where she settled, expecting him to follow her. "I'll ride with the coachman," he said as he closed the door.

"When we get back, will you help me hide Halibut in my rooms?" the Princess said. "Jean-Marc looks so angry. I think he would be furious if he found out about Halibut today."

"I'll help you," Meg told her, and looked out of the window. The staff remained at the doorway, their hands respectfully folded before them. "Of course I will."

There were tears in Meg's eyes. Désirée studied her companion, and her mouth thinned. She would have to be blind not to see the way her half brother looked at Meg, to miss the manner in which he helped her into the coach. As if he was escorting a paramour—or a woman he'd like to make his paramour. A woman he might already have pursued, but who had rebuffed his attentions perhaps? Désirée did not know what happened between a man and a woman in private, but she would find out. She believed Meg knew already, but not that she had been taught by Jean-Marc. Such things took a great deal of time to learn, of that she was certain.

She leaned impulsively toward Meg, held her hands and waited for her to raise her tired, sad eyes. "We are going to have a happy time together, you and I, Meg," Désirée said. "I look forward to meeting your sister."

Meg nodded and offered a pathetic smile. "Sibyl is very talented and very beautiful."

"So are you. I think Jean-Marc also thinks so."

Meg's heart beat too hard. "I don't know what you mean."

"Certainly you do. There may be much I don't know, but I am observant. You are very aware of him. He attracts you."

"Please," Meg said and tried to pull her hands away.

Désirée held on. "If there was any doubt I am right, you have dispelled it. My brother is a very private man, but when he looks at you, his feelings need no explanation."

Meg attempted to use lightheartedness as a disguise. "Never mind, Your Highness. You are longing for a loved one in your life so you invent such a person for me. I take that as a good sign. You protest, but you are excited about the weeks to come."

Princess Désirée pushed her lips forward in a thoughtful pout. She raised her eyebrows and waggled her head like a knowing crone. "Hmm," she said and sniffed. "You think to distract me, Meg Smiles. You have not done so. I have decided I must have you with me, or insist on going home to Mont Nuages at once. Papa would be wrathful if I did that and I dislike Papa's ill temper. So, I must give you a warning and insist you take me very seriously. Now, I shall not use pretty words. No, I shall be blunt.

You have responsibilities of great import. Those must come first—regardless of Jean-Marc's designs."

"Designs?" Meg's breathing became difficult. "I don't understand, but I think it would be best if we terminated this subject."

"Oh, we will. Soon enough. And perhaps if you pay attention and do not question what I know is true, we need never concern ourselves with the matter again."

"There is nothing to say, Princess. You have too big an imagination."

"I imagine very little. I know what I saw in my brother's eyes back there. And you must foil him, or he will claim you and disaster will follow. Count Etranger's reputation suggests he is a man of lusty appetites. I have heard him described so, amid an unpleasant type of laughter and whispers about the current object of his appetite.

"Jean-Marc is a brilliant man. His talent is for diplomacy—a skill he practices so successfully for our country. He intends to get you into his bed and you could well be helpless to resist his relentless and persuasive methods. Much as I should appreciate your firsthand insights into what lies behind the black squares, I implore you not to allow him to claim your body."

11

Jean-Marc paused in the foyer of Number 17 to follow the hurried progress of his sister and Mcg. Désirée lifted her skirts and ran upstairs. Meg managed to retain more dignity while all but matching the speed of her charge.

On their arrival in Mayfair Square, he had expected her to excuse herself and go at once to Number 7, probably never to return. The relief he felt because she was still here was undoubtedly misplaced. She could leave at any moment.

Verbeux emerged from the study and said, "You're back." The audacity of the man. Not a hint of apprehension although he must expect his master's wrath at the manipulative methods used to ensure Désirée and Meg—he must be careful to address her only as Miss Smiles—would travel to Windsor.

"You and I will be meeting alone. *Now*," he told Verbeux. This was not the first time the man had overstepped the mark when he'd decided he had a brilliant idea and his master must be made to recognize the fact.

The motives had changed, or at least overlapped. Meg Smiles was needed because not only did he believe she could do a good job with Désirée, but they actually liked each other. Amazing. Désirée avoided friendships of any kind. But Jean-Marc also wanted Meg Smiles for other reasons. He wanted to know he would see her frequently. They could have no future and to form any alliance with her was unfair, and dangerous, yet he would do it if he could.

"Painful?" Verbeaux asked quietly.

Jean-Marc started. "Dash it, man, what do you mean?"

Verbeux shrugged hugely. "You want her? Your affair."

No, no, he would not allow the man the pleasure of drawing out information to which he had no right.

"You looked at her." Verbeux glanced meaningfully toward the stairs. "Not your usual."

"We will have that meeting, I think."

"You've got a visitor." Verbeux grinned. "Mr. William Godly-Smythe. Puckly Hinton."

Jean-Marc took the card his man offered. "Godly-Smythe? Puckly Hinton? Don't know the man."

"No."

"Where's he from?"

"Puckly Hinton."

"I know *that*. I meant, who *is* he?"

"Godly-Smythe." A subtle shift in Verbeux's stance suggested he knew he'd gone too far. "Miss Smiles's cousin, from what he says. Pompous."

The cousin who inherited, Jean-Marc wondered? He experienced an uncomfortable moment before he quickly discarded the notion that the man could have come to reveal knowledge of what had passed between Meg and Jean-Marc. "In there?" He indicated the study.

"Seemed best. Not social."

He scanned the tiers of galleries flanking the upper floors. Verbeux's man, Pierre, watched from the third floor. Ready as always to jump at his master's bidding. Rench stood at the foot of the stairs, eyes straight ahead, white-gloved hands crossed before him. Jean-Marc felt oppressed and in need of peace. To Verbeux, he said, "Make sure we are not interrupted, hmm?"

Verbeux went smoothly to open wide the door to the study. He walked in and swept an arm toward a very stiff-backed blond man. "Mr. Puckly Hinton to see you, m'Lord."

"Godly-Smythe *of* Puckly Hinton," the man said, and his large, light eyes swept over every inch of Jean-Marc.

Unperturbed, Verbeux said, "This is Count Etranger," and left as smoothly as a skater traversing a frozen lake.

"We have business?" Jean-Marc said, buying time in which to assess the fellow.

"We do now," Godly-Smythe said. "Where is my cousin, Miss Meg Smiles?"

He could be vague and, if Godly-Smythe mentioned Meg's post, say he was too busy with important affairs of state to concern himself with the names of servants. Yes...no. If this was Meg's relative then, much as he pitied her, he also owed it to her to show the man some respect.

"I asked where—"

"Indeed, sir, indeed." Those big, luminous eyes glowed with an almost childlike clarity that was at odds with everything else about Meg's cousin. A disturbing person. "Miss Smiles was engaged as my sister's companion during her preparation for her Season, and through the Season itself. Miss Smiles is with my sister now."

"I have come to take her home. We are not a family familiar with going into service. I cannot imagine how Meg was persuaded to accept such a post."

Another man might have paced. Godly-Smythe had a quality of stillness. A stocky man whose muscular neck bulged over his neck cloth, he stood, unmoving, his arms hanging at his sides. Jean-Marc rather thought he intended to appear ominous. The impression he gave was of egotistical eccentricity.

"My Lord," Godly-Smythe said, "I would respectfully request that you produce my cousin at once."

Outside the study, at the foot of the stairs, in fact, Meg heard her cousin's embarrassing demand. She paused and looked upward. Verbeux gave her an encouraging nod. He'd come to the Princess's rooms to say William Godly-Smythe had arrived and was giving the Count orders at that very moment.

There was nothing else for it but to confront William and lead him from Number 17 at once. She had managed to help the Princess retrieve Halibut from the coachman and tuck the cat away on a hidden cushion. Now Meg must give this up. There was no way for things to work out after last night, and after the debacle she'd just overheard.

William continued to tell—tell, mind you—the Count what he expected of him. "This may well be actionable," William said in his fulsome voice. "My cousin is not worldly. You escorted her away in a coach—alone. You were seen. And you kept her away *overnight.*"

Meg gave the lightest tap on the door and entered without being summoned. She curtseyed to the Count, looked at William and discovered her dislike for him had only increased in the three years since they had last met.

He strode toward her, hands outstretched, an expression of abject pity on his ruddy face. When she made no attempt to offer her own hands in return, he grasped her shoulders and placed a wet kiss on her forehead. He held her away and studied her.

The red hair. If he mentioned it, she would die.

William smiled at her then, and gazed into her eyes. She disliked his eyes intensely. The pale blue color of a young child's, and very big, they were essentially empty as if the man hid behind them. Surely he would remark on the color of her hair and Jean-Marc would learn what a scheming fraud she was.

"I should have visited you and Sibyl a long time ago," William said. "This is my fault. If I had assumed the responsibility for taking care of your welfare, you would not have strayed, Meg."

"I haven't strayed."

"I would have seen what a very lovely woman you have become and known you were in danger, and in need of protection."

The Count was a blurred figure just outside the range of her vision. She knew his arms were crossed and that he listened intently.

"Meg, there are always men on the hunt for attractive, unworldly young women. Why didn't you get a message to me the instant this man approached you?"

She did look at Jean-Marc then. His expression showed little of what he might be thinking, but he looked at her with the faintest of smiles.

"I want you to tell me now—in front of this defiler of innocents—tell me exactly what he did to you last night."

Jean-Marc strolled forward and leaned to sit on the edge of his desk. From this spot he could see both William and Meg. "There is no need for you to be exposed to such foul accusations," he said to her. "Please return to the Princess and I will have you informed when your cousin and I have finished our discussion."

"The hell you will," William said. "Meg is a blameless girl who had the gentlest of upbringings. She was motherless from an early age, but the ladies of her father's parish made sure she and her sister were appropriately raised."

If she lost her temper and told this posturing pigeon of a man what she thought of him, he could make more trouble for her and Sibyl. "I'm glad you approved of my father's efforts," she said evenly.

"Nothing has occurred to besmirch Miss Smiles's spotless reputation," Jean-Marc said. "And I did not travel alone with her yesterday. My sister was with us."

"Not from what I was told." William was belligerent. "You handed my Meg into the coach right before the eyes of all in the square. They did not see your sister join you."

If it were not for Meg, Jean-Marc would take pleasure in raising the man by his breeches and tossing him from the front door. "I owe you no explanation, but Princess Désirée entered the carriage in the mews. Now, kindly leave this house."

"Where did you spend the night, Meg?"

Jean-Marc sympathized with Meg for having so odious a relative, not that he didn't have his own share of impossible family members.

"At the Count's home near Windsor," Meg said. "There is more than a little work to be done to make the Princess comfortable in what is to come. We started yesterday."

"You met Meg yesterday," William said to the Count, an ugly sneer lifting his upper lip, "and you were so certain she was the perfect candidate for the position you wanted to fill that you took her at once to Windsor where she stayed the night?"

"Correct," Jean-Marc said, disgusted with the creature, but also aware that the man's conjectures were too close to truth. "My sister was in great need of female companionship. Miss Smiles was free and willing to begin at once. So the arrangement was perfect."

William spread wide his arms and guffawed. "Do I look like a fool?" He pointed at Meg and struck a pose that showed off his exceedingly muscular limbs to advantage. Waiting for his next words, she quaked. "She knows nothing of the intricacies of life in polite society. She would not know a member of the *ton* if she were closed in a room where they alone congregated."

That, thought Jean-Marc, was more than enough from Mr. Godly-Smythe. "Well, sir," Jean-Marc said, "since you have, as far as I can tell, no rights in relation to Miss Smiles, I must ask you to leave."

Godly-Smythe stood his ground, apparently quite smug to have caused annoyance. "I am her closest male relative," he said.

"She is not a minor," Jean-Marc pointed out. He looked at Meg's forlorn face and said, "Are you?"

"Hardly," she told him, and her nostrils flared.

"As I thought. Out you go, Godly-Smythe."

"Damn you to hell. I will not leave. Not without Meg."

Meg couldn't bear what was going on a moment longer. To do so at such a time was a risk, but even if Jean-Marc or Cousin William did wonder about her sanity, at least a little meditation would calm her, and she hoped, silence them. Abruptly, she closed her eyes and took a deep breath.

Jean-Marc watched, fascinated. Meg folded her hands at her waist, and her face became smooth and pale and devoid of expression.

Godly-Smythe took a step toward her, but Jean-Marc stayed

him with the digging fingers of one hand. He shook his head sharply.

"What's wrong with her?" the cousin said. "She's ill."

"No," Jean-Marc told him.

Without a sound, Meg sank to sit on the carpet. She drew her crossed limbs beneath her skirts.

Jean-Marc had to exert considerable effort to restrain Godly-Smythe. "I have seen such things before," he told the man. "Or heard them mentioned."

Godly-Smythe's vacant eyes displayed alarm. He attempted to pry Jean-Marc's fingers from his arm. "Let me go, damn your eyes. This is nothing more than a hysterical tantrum—probably brought on because her mind is weakened from the accident. I must make her collect herself."

"A trance should never be disturbed," Jean-Marc said, biting the inside of his cheek to resist any urge to laugh. "It's true I have never learned of other cases when women practiced such things, but I suppose it's possible."

"A *trance?*" Godly-Smythe whispered. "She's in a trance?"

Very slowly, Meg bent forward from the hip and flattened her entire upper body, rested her forehead on the floor, spread her rotated arms from the shoulder, turning the palms upward.

She was remarkable—in a number of ways.

"She has been bewitched," Godly-Smythe said, turning an accusing stare on Jean-Marc. "What have you done to her?"

"*I am,*" Meg said. "*I am.*" Her arms jerked, then grew utterly still.

Godly-Smythe trembled. "This is evil."

"Not so," Jean-Marc told him. "Such things are part gift, part practice. Probably unknown to anyone, Miss Smiles had studied the ancient Veda. Yoga, I believe it is called by some. She is able to pass to a higher plane."

"Good Lord." This sounded like a desperate prayer. "It cannot be natural. I shall awaken her at once."

"And risk losing her?" He might feel contempt for the fellow, but even so, this fiction he made up as he went along felt outrageous.

"Why should I lose her if I wake her up?"

"Because she is not there." Jean-Marc indicated Meg. "Not if my memory serves, and I believe it does. The practitioner of such disciplines leaves the body."

Godly-Smythe moved away violently, and twisted his arm from Jean-Marc's grasp. He stared and said, "What are you saying?"

"That to interfere with the body while the mind roams free could make it impossible for the mind, or whatever, to return." Might he be forgiven for such flagrant invention! "If you meddle, you might have her death on your soul."

"Can she hear us?" Godly-Smythe spoke softly. "Is she here?" He peered furtively in all directions.

"Yes, to both, I should think. Most likely up there."

"Up there?" Godly-Smythe stared at the ceiling. He produced a monocle and fastened it before one eye while he darted about, his head ducking and rising as if to aid a search for a being concealed by some trick of air and light. "Why would she resort to such tricks?"

"I scarcely know Miss Smiles, but from what I've been told, this sort of thing is a defense against extreme emotional discomfort. The skilled practitioner can summon a trance at will, but does so most usually to escape unpleasantness. I fear you and I are to blame here."

Godly-Smythe puffed up as if preparing for a further display of outrage. His gaze returned to Meg's still form, and he turned pale. "What explanation can I give poor, dear Sibyl?"

"None at all, I should think. Why concern the girl?"

Meg stirred and hoped she'd timed her return effectively. "I am," she murmured, drawing the second word out. There was no doubt that even though this was not a planned meditation, it had provided a measure of peace and of distance from turmoil.

She assumed a sitting position, but rested her upturned hands on her knees and kept her eyes shut.

"Is she back again?" Cousin William asked.

To giggle would be to ruin everything.

"Count Etranger? Is she in there?"

"Are you, Miss Smiles?"

She opened her eyes and looked into Jean-Marc's. He'd bent his knees and placed his hands on them to bring his face close to hers. His solemn expression was a marvel when there was such glittering laughter in his eyes.

"Miss Smiles?" he said.

"I am Meg Smiles."

Having allowed Jean-Marc to take any potential risk, William came nearer. "I shall go at once to Sibyl." He shook both hands in the air. "Never fear, I shall not mention what I have seen here. I will tell her...I..."

"Tell her I shall return shortly," Meg said, smiling at William. "Thank you for caring about me, Cousin. I must take a little time to regain my strength, then I will tell Princess Désirée where I am going."

William's smile was nervous. "Just so," he said, "just so." And he fled the room before any attempt could be made to have him shown out.

Meg did not dare look at her employer. Instead she stared at the carpet and contemplated how she might get up with some grace.

He stood where she could see his boots, boots still dusty from returning to Town on the coachman's box.

"Your sister will be anxious to see you, Meg," he said, his voice lowered. "Would you be so kind as to tell her we will look forward to meeting her in the morning?"

She said, "Yes." He was not going to dismiss her? Even following so outrageous a display?

"Désirée is difficult, has always been difficult and aloof. Yet, after a brief time, she already likes you. She actually seems light-hearted. Should you like me to help you get up?" He offered her his hand.

Meg accepted and was grateful for her agility as she rose quickly to stand.

"You are a minx, you know," Jean-Marc said.

She angled her head. "Perhaps."

He laughed and released her hand. When he didn't speak again, Meg searched for something to say but found nothing.

"My sister has never had a close friend. Oh, she hasn't pursued friends, but I cannot fault her for that. Those she should have been able to trust have kept their affection from her. She has been too much alone. It will be a blessing if she meets a man who will appreciate her for herself—if that is possible—someone who will enjoy her quick mind. She deserves a fulfilling life of her own."

"She has more to offer than a quick mind. She is also very gentle and generous, and she is ready to have fun. The Princess told me so. And she is a witty creature."

"You don't say."

"I don't believe there has been any attempt to know her. If there had been I should not have to point out what I have learned in less than two days."

"Yes," Jean-Marc said, and he wanted to ask her if she would return from Number 7 and when she would return. "I have no doubt you are right." Best not ask. Better not to invite what he didn't want to hear.

"As you say," she said, "I must go to Sibyl." What should she do, Meg wondered? How should she depart without knowing what he expected of her? She walked toward the door.

"Meg."

She stopped and said, "It would be unfortunate if your staff heard you call me that."

"Meg?"

He made a demand disguised as a question. "Yes, My Lord?" There was no choice but to turn and look at him. Again he held a hand toward her, a strong but elegant hand. Meg went slowly to him and placed her fingers on his palm.

"I am not sorry," he said, and raised her hand to his lips. He kissed her lightly, his eyes closed.

Her belly tightened. He would think her forward, but she turned their hands over and held his between both of hers. "I'm not sorry, either." She pressed her mouth to his wrist.

"You are magical, Meg Smiles. And mysterious. And a little wicked." He tilted her chin. "I could become addicted to you."

She couldn't look away, even when he bent gradually closer until she felt his breath on her lips. "I wonder," he said, "did I tell you how much I admire your eyes? They are the color of fine cognac. But you already know that."

"I know no such thing," she said, "I have been told that brown eyes, any brown eyes, are ordinary."

"Yours are not ordinary."

"Neither are yours. They are so dark, they are almost black. I like them a great deal."

"A pretty pickle," he told her. "Finally I meet a woman.... No, no, no matter about that. I want to kiss you."

For the briefest of moments, she kept her eyes lowered, but she said, "Why can't I be as remote as I should be? Why can't I refuse you and flee from you at once?"

"Can't you?"

Meg looked fully into his face, so close to her own, at the manner in which he studied her, and shook her head.

"That is very good," he whispered, and settled his warm hands lightly at her waist. He rubbed his jaw against her temple. She let out a sigh at the rough, incredibly sensitizing feel of his skin on hers.

He slipped his arms around her and pulled her onto her tiptoes. "I know we met only yesterday. Do you believe in... Do you believe two people can be instantly attracted?"

"I don't know," she lied. "But I will consider the question. For now I had best leave."

"Tell me one thing. Are your trances real, or an act?"

Concentrating while he moved on to nuzzle the hollow beneath her cheekbone took almost too much effort. "In the beginning it was all practice and learning. It has become something I need—the opportunity to take my mind to a higher place where it is cool and quiet."

"And today? What happened in front of your cousin was pure chance? A reaction to becoming overwrought, perhaps?" His widespread fingertips pressed into her back. He brought her ever closer. Her breasts flattened to his unyielding chest, and she tingled at the brush of his lips close to hers. "Meg, don't be coy now."

"I am never coy. Only thoughtful." She paused to rock her face into his, to take over the stroking of their faces together. "I was pressed. I have become accustomed to employing what I have learned at such times. But it is possible that I was moved to seek a trance in order to distract Cousin William's attention. He suffocates me."

Jean-Marc grew still. "He referred to an accident, Meg. I don't want to pry, but I should like to know what he meant."

"Nothing," she told him, in a manner she hoped would not encourage him to persist.

"Of course, there was something."

So much for her hopes.

"Please explain or I shall imagine the worst." He took the lobe of one of her ears gently between his teeth. The Count expended considerable energy on that ear, and he weakened Meg's knees. So much new sensory experience in so short a time. Could she remain here, or would her decision to do so cause Jean-Marc to assume she welcomed his attentions?

She did welcome his attentions—and for that reason, she definitely should not return.

He raised his face an inch or so, but certainly no more. "The accident, Meg, if you please."

"It was nothing," she told him, more sharply than she intended. "A brush with a carriage, that's all. I had left Burlington Arcade and thought it was safe to cross toward Piccadilly Circus.

Unfortunately I didn't expect the carriage to move so abruptly. I was bruised and shocked, but very lucky. There is nothing more to say."

Jean-Marc experienced a certain sensation he had come to regard as more of a nuisance than a benefit. He controlled the desire to prod her further on the incident. If God smiled, there would be other opportunities to pursue the subject—if he felt it necessary.

As he'd come to expect, she smelled of lemons and wildflowers. And he was going to kiss her.

Her extraordinary eyes searched his.

Restraint had already cost him too much. At first he simply pressed his lips to hers. At another time it could be enough just to feel her respond, to feel her lean into him, but he was both angry and aroused and at the very least he needed some relief from the veiled violence he held in rigid check.

Her mouth was sweet, and he felt how she wanted his kiss as much as he wanted to kiss her.

Meg wound her arms around his neck and let him support her weight. She felt the protective strength of a virile male whose very presence, his slightest glance, moved her. He showed her what he wanted. The faintest pressure opened her mouth and meeting his tongue was most natural—natural and with the power to drain all energy, all resistance from her body. He supported her weight and deepened the kiss until their breathing seemed so loud the world must hear it.

She passed her hands over shoulders that strained beneath the fine cloth of his coat—and she saw him as he'd been last night, naked beside her, his body a strange, intoxicating sight that invited a million touches she dared not give.

He drew his lips from hers so slowly she felt his reluctance to part from her. With his thumbs he tipped up her chin and bowed to kiss the soft skin of her neck, of the dip between her collarbones, and lower, to brush his lips over the tops of her breasts, revealed by the opening in her bodice.

Without warning, he straightened and stepped back, but not without finding her hand again and holding on. He shook his head, and his expression became haunted.

Meg patted his arm briefly and said, "I shall make what we have shared enough. I will never be able to forget, but the memory must satisfy me. And you, Jean-Marc."

The wildness he felt was dangerous. Wildness and rebellion. How much longer would he manage to balance his father's wishes with his own, his father's crippling expectations with his own needs?

"I cannot promise what will be enough for me," he told Meg. "Of course, I will bow to your wishes, but if you decide ours must be a polite and distant relationship, I shall suffer greatly."

A woman's heart should not sing at a declaration that ought to frighten her. And she was too close to declaring that her feelings were one with his.

His expression smoothed. "Meg," he said, and she saw that his eyes belied his calm face.

"Yes, My Lord."

"Go now." He swung forcefully away from her. "Just go. *Go.*"

12

Sibyl wished she could be alone when Meg arrived. There would be much to talk about and Meg would never even begin her story in the company of Latimer More and Lady Hester Bingham. But they were determined to be present.

"Meg is coming," Lady Hester said from her lookout at the Smiles sisters' parlor window. "Unbelievable. Walkin' this way as if it were the most normal thing in the world to disappear one afternoon, and remain gone until the followin' afternoon. And I don't care what that messenger told you, Sibyl, it just isn't good enough."

"I say," Latimer said, "Meg and Sibyl need our support, My Lady. A simple enough thing to offer to two people who are so admired by all at Number Seven."

When she recovered from what was an amazing speech from Latimer, Sibyl said, "Thank you." A tall, well-favored man with dark brown curly hair, he undoubtedly turned many a female head, but he had eyes for nothing other than the imported antiquities in which he dealt.

Lady Hester regarded him through a gold-rimmed lorgnette, her lovely blue eyes magnified by the lenses. "Do you have a tendresse for Meg, Latimer?"

Sibyl groaned aloud at Her Ladyship's bluntness.

Latimer cleared his throat and said, "The Misses Smiles are my friends. They are also my sister Finch's friends. I choose to take some responsibility for their welfare—as do you, My Lady."

Rather than appear chastised, Lady Hester smirked and said, "Pretty speech. I wouldn't have thought you had it in you."

"Odd, your cousin coming back from Number Seventeen, then racing off again," Latimer said to Sibyl. "Too bad he intends to return at all." He paused before adding, "Sorry."

"Don't be," Sibyl told him. "I don't relish the idea, either. And now we have this Miss Lavinia Ash to deal with. I'm still so muddled thinking about her arriving like that. Unannounced. We've never even heard of her before, yet she expects Meg to gain her a position in the Count's household, and that's that. That there might be any difficulty doing so doesn't occur to the woman. I hesitate to mention this, but…well…"

"She is unusual," Latimer finished for her. "Downright strange, in fact."

"Miss Lavinia Ash," Lady Hester announced in her best pompous manner, "is an example of the finest teaching that is offered to our young women of high social standing. As she told you, she taught only the best. I think the Count will scarcely believe his good fortune in having such a person sent to him. In fact, one laments that the standard of education is become so poor. That is because there are fewer people like Miss Lavinia Ash to take a firm hand with the cream of young English womanhood."

"She appears a most unlikely dancing instructor," Sibyl pointed out.

Latimer nodded. "All bone," he said. "Not an ounce of softness about her."

"And what, may I ask—" Lady Hester turned her lorgnette on him "—do you know about the instruction of young ladies in our finest academies? Nothing, that's what, so do not interfere."

Latimer hid a smile.

"Meg is here," Lady Hester said. She shook out the skirts of her dark mauve gown, a recent change from the deep mourning the widow had worn for so long. "Now be calm, everyone. Behave as if nothing is amiss. Be politely interested in her escapades—I mean her experiences at her new post."

Sibyl heard the front door open, and Old Coot welcoming Meg in nasal tones. Another voice joined in, this one lower.

In the foyer, the overwhelming sadness in Adam Chillworth's expression all but brought Meg to tears. "Good to see you," she told him, and knew at once that she sounded like a stranger meeting someone she had not encountered for a long time. "It isn't warm out there. Better wrap up." Taking care of Adam had become part of her life.

He gave the briefest of nods, his attention lingering on her hair, then ducked his head and strode from the house.

Meg met Old Coot's watery eyes. He made a face and said, "Lady Hester and Latimer More are with Sibyl up there." His right thumb hooked upward and to the left, indicating Meg and Sibyl's rooms. Hooking the same thumb to the left, this time toward Latimer More's flat on the ground floor, he said, "There's a visitor in there, but I think she's resting. Pinch-mouthed stick of a woman. She came to speak to you, but you'd better deal with them first." Again his thumb arced toward the second floor.

With a glance toward Latimer More's door, she thanked Old Coot and hurried upstairs, preparing herself for Sibyl's tears.

Crowded into the doorway of the parlor were Lady Hester, Sibyl and, most amazing of all, Latimer More.

"Meggie," Sibyl said, her voice a broken whisper. "Oh, Meggie, I've been beside myself. Come here and let me look at you."

"You ought to be ashamed, young woman," Lady Hester said. "Of course we're glad the prodigal has returned, but you are a young woman of genteel upbringing. You know better. What we are to do, I cannot imagine. Oh! Oh, my word, your *hair*. What have you done to it? Oh, I need my salts."

Sibyl managed to squeeze through the door and fling her thin arms around Meg. She cried into her shoulder. "I love you, Meggie. You are my hero. I know that whatever you did, you did for both of us, but…"

"But she is cast low at the thought of her sister destroying her reputation for the sake of a few pieces of silver."

"I say, Lady H," Latimer said, evidently relishing the use of the form of address Lady Hester disliked. "Been reading our Bible a lot, have we? Prodigal sons and pieces of silver. Bit of a mixed metaphor there, what? Personally I consider your hair lovely as it normally is, Meg. But the red is very fetching. Very dashing. So, why not, say I? Come along in, you two. Barstow is wallowing in a righteous funk and no one else shows signs of doing anything useful, so I shall make tea for all of us. What do you say?"

When Meg collected herself, she said, "Why, thank you, Latimer. Yes, thank you very much." She smiled at him, and he smiled back. He was really most attractive and charming—at least he was when he cared to be so.

"Take a seat, My Lady," Sibyl said, still sniffing and clinging to Meg's hand.

Lady Hester spread her skirts and arranged herself on a dilapidated chaise covered with aged pink brocade—faded green leaves and a faint suggestion of cream roses all but disappeared from wear. "Do make haste with the tea, Latimer. I am quite faint from all the worry this girl has caused. Now, sit before me, Meg Smiles. I have some questions to ask."

"I should like Meggie to have tea first," Sibyl said hesitantly. "I'm sure she has been through a great deal and must be exhausted. There are biscuits in the barrel on the sideboard, Latimer."

He had put a kettle on the hob and assembled cups and saucers on a tray. He popped upright when Lady Hester said, "It is the question about *what* has exhausted her that is of the greatest concern here. Now, what do you say to that, Meg? Yes, that is definitely—"

"That is none of our business, My Lady," Latimer said. "Not unless Meg chooses to tell us if something has concerned her— or brought her joy. And I remind you, with respect, that you are assuming disaster where there may be none."

"Ungrateful boy," Lady Hester said. "And so typical of men,

any men. You never hesitate to impose your will upon the weaker sex.''

"Are you all right, Meggie, dear?" Sibyl asked.

"I'm very well." She lied, but what else could she do? "Where is our cousin?"

Sibyl smiled. "William came to tell us you would soon be coming home, then left, saying he had important business elsewhere. He will return when he can."

"How unfortunate," Meg said. "He made a complete cake of himself at Count Etranger's."

"Which brings us to the question that must be answered," Lady Hester said. "We all saw the Count usher you into his carriage yesterday. Alone. Before you set off at a great rate, not to return until now. We understand you spent the night at the Count's house near Windsor."

"Yes, Riverside Place. Sibyl, dear, I'm so sorry. I just know you've been worried about me but I thought we were only to go there for an outing, and that we'd be back before dark. When I found out what was intended, it was too late to attempt a return journey."

"I know," Sibyl said. "And it's all right, really, it is—as long as you are safe and there is nothing wrong."

"There's nothing wrong," Meg told her. "What happened was an unfortunate mix-up but now it's over and, as you see, I am my old self."

"Were you alone with the Count at Windsor?" Lady Hester asked as if Meg and Sibyl hadn't intruded on her interrogation.

"Not at all alone," Meg said. "With a household full of servants. With Lady Upworth, a good friend of the Count's. And with my new charge, Princess Désirée of Mont Nuages."

Lady Hester's eyes became increasingly round and she bent a little more forward with each word Meg uttered. She shook her head and said, with some reverence, "You were in such company."

"Only as the Princess's companion."

"Surely you didn't go to dinner with them."

If her heart did not ache so, Meg decided she might enjoy this. "Yes, it was the first dinner at which the Princess wore her hair up. She is a delightful girl. Thoughtful, quiet—sometimes nervous and a little sharp-tongued—but so dear and pretty in her own way."

"Hmph," Lady Hester said. "In other words, she's a plain thing well-disguised by expensive trappings. Not that it matters how plain she is. She will have suitors clamoring for her hand."

Meg looked at Sibyl. She could bear Latimer's presence with them, but Her Ladyship made it impossible to be frank about anything.

Latimer carried a tray of tea and biscuits around the circle and each lady accepted a cup and saucer. "I have no doubt you'd like to rest, Meg," he said. "So much excitement must have left you overwrought."

"Very true," she agreed.

Lady Hester said, "Of course you need to rest. Do tell us all about the Count. He is the illegitimate son of Prince Georges of Mont Nuages, isn't he?"

An instant swell of protectiveness tightened Meg's every muscle. "It is not my affair—or yours—to be interested in such matters."

"Oh!" Lady Hester whipped her lorgnette into place.

"Count Etranger is a highborn gentleman. He is his father's ambassador to England and carries the weight of much responsibility."

"Is he good-looking?" As usual, Her Ladyship was not to be diverted. "I've heard that he is. And that he's a womanizer."

"There's a Miss Lavinia Ash to see you," Latimer said, his brow rumpled. "She's resting in Finch's old room. A bit disconcerting. Just turned up. Sibyl said you don't know—"

"Kindly desist from interrupting me," their landlady ordered. "Time enough to deal with that matter later. I have heard of this Upworth woman, Ila. I know of her. She married old Lord Upworth. He must have been near a hundred and probably out of his mind. He certainly was never seen out of a Bath chair. He didn't have much money, but it was enough to set Ila up—and he left her with a title. She'll be looking for another husband, of course. That kind will always seek out another man to…well, another man. No doubt Etranger finds her an engaging playmate. How did they behave together, Meg?"

"I hardly saw them together."

"But when you did?" The lady's brows rose significantly. "There are those little glances, the sly touches that tell it all."

Meg bowed her head and fussed with her teaspoon.

"Surely you are not already enamored of the Count yourself? Even a green girl such as you knows a man like that could never be interested in you—unless his appetites are such that he chooses to dally with servants."

Still Meg could not look up, although she knew her silence was damning.

"Hmm. You do have a charming figure, it's true. Men like that do not miss such details. And that gown is much too obvious. And that *hair*. Oh, my dear, have you gone astray already?"

"Stop it," Sibyl said, startling Meg. "How can you speak to Meg in such a manner? She is sweet and good. The very best of sisters and friends. You shall not sully her ears with terrible suggestions."

Latimer shifted uncomfortably. "Perhaps you could see Miss Ash now, Meg? She has waited a long time."

Agitated, Meg gave him her entire attention. "Who *is* Miss Ash? I don't know a Miss Ash."

"Has that man had his way with you?" Lady Hester asked. "If so, speak up at once and I shall have Hunter present your case against him. He will go if I ask him, and advise the Count to make a handsome settlement upon you or face the disgrace of having his dastardly deeds spread before all of London."

"That is enough, My Lady," Latimer said, gently enough.

"You have become too excited. Please allow me to escort you upstairs."

"I shall leave when I decide—"

Latimer took her cup and extended an elbow. "We will resume this conversation tomorrow when we've all had time to consider quietly. I know your kind heart, My Lady. You would never wish to hurt Meg, yet you are doing so because you do not have the reserves to be considerate at the moment."

At first it seemed she would not go, but then Lady Hester Bingham rose majestically, accepted Latimer's arm and let him lead her from the room.

"Oh, Meggie," Sibyl cried and ran to hug her sister. "I have never been so frightened since Papa's death. I even thought the coach might have been held up by highwaymen."

"Forgive me, please. And don't blame our new employers. It was a misunderstanding. Sibyl, if you are in agreement, you will instruct Désirée in the pianoforte and help with her voice. The Count asked me to tell you they look forward to meeting you in the morning." There was no point in holding back part of the truth. "Since I am to be the Princess's right hand, the one she leans on in these trying times—I'm sure I mentioned she is shy—because of these things I shall live at Number Seventeen, in rooms in the Princess's wing."

Sibyl clapped her hands to her cheeks. "You can't, Meggie. Stay at Number Seventeen? Why?"

"I have told you why. And it will not be for so very long." She breathed deeply and thrust away the sadness that rushed in at the thought of bidding Jean-Marc goodbye. "They will leave once the Season is over." And she would never see him again.

"But, Meggie," Sibyl said. "Live at Number Seventeen? No one will understand."

"I don't give a fig if they understand or misunderstand. At least I will bring the joy of a good gossip to their dull lives."

Sibyl turned aside. "I shall miss you."

Those were the words Meg had expected and dreaded. "I will

be close by. And we shall see each other every day. And it will not be for long."

"I know. And I know I am foolish. Sooner or later you will marry and then I must learn to be alone. I should take this as a fine opportunity to become reliant upon myself."

"No, no," Meg said, urging Sibyl to the chaise and pulling her down to sit. "Sibyl, darling, despite my brilliant schemes, it is far more likely that you will marry first. I am only concerned for our livelihood and so I have taken steps to try to make us more secure. But I do expect that the money you and I shall earn working with Princess Désirée may be the only benefit that comes out of my little experiment.

"Of course, I intend to persist in trying to find a good man to make our way easier. Think, Sibyl, if I were to find a pleasant fellow of reasonable means—and he turned out to be agreeable—then I know he would help me present you to some suitable gentlemen. You deserve the very best, dear sister, and I want to be able to give you the opportunity to find the very best."

Sibyl gave one of her sudden and impish smiles. Impetuously, she drew Meg into an embrace. "You would set the entire world to rights, if you could," she said. "No wonderful man will pine for me, dearest. You think such a thing might happen because you love me and think me better than I am. But I am going to do my best to support you in your efforts. How wonderful it would be if you did meet a pleasing gentleman whom you could love.

"And I look forward to meeting Princess Désirée. So don't worry about me anymore. All I care about is that you are safe, and you are. So, la, la, all is wonderful again."

Meg's smile began in her heart and suffused her. "If we stand together, no one will be able to foil us. We shall be unbeatable."

"Yes," Sibyl said. "Is there anything else to tell me about Number Seventeen or about the Princess."

Perhaps she would be able to tell Sibyl about Jean-Marc in time, but that could not be now. "Number Seventeen is the most beautiful house. The scale is grand and open. The Princess has charming rooms—and I'm sure mine will also be pleasant. The ones they gave me at Riverside Place—the Count's English home—those rooms—'' She caught her breath, seeing Jean-Marc in the sitting room at Riverside, then in her small, comfortable bedroom where he had eventually undressed and fallen asleep. "They are lovely rooms. Comfortable and light and obviously prepared with a woman's pleasure in mind." *Pleasure?* Meg had certainly found pleasure there, and anxiety, and longing—and self-disgust.

"It sounds lovely," Sibyl said.

"I'm sure you will also be able to visit," Meg told her. She could not dwell on the place where she had been together with Jean-Marc. And neither could she think about the kiss they'd shared immediately before she'd departed Number 17 to come here. "Cousin William was so embarrassing, Sibyl. He demanded that I be sent for, and then that I should leave with him."

"He didn't!" Sibyl whispered. "How awful. I admire you for resisting."

"The Count pointed out that William has no right to tell me to go anywhere or do anything. Which is true."

Meg felt Sibyl looking at her and when their eyes met, there was no doubt that Sibyl was puzzled by Jean-Marc's interest in Meg's affairs.

"William postured and demanded and made a frightful cake of himself."

"Yes, but William isn't a man who knows when he should gracefully withdraw. How did you manage to get him to go?"

"He didn't do so gracefully." Meg bent her head forward and smiled. "I had to—I found the necessity to go into a trance."

Sibyl stared before saying, "You *didn't*."

"I did. And very calming it was, too. I simply removed myself to a higher place."

"Right there?"

"Right there in the Count's study. I closed my eyes and

thought of Puckly Hinton. In spring, naturally. The next thing I was aware of was sinking to sit on the floor, crossing my legs—beneath my gown, of course—and resting my forehead on the carpet. Most pleasant."

At first Sibyl chuckled, but very quickly her laughter became a high, pealing sound that turned her cheeks pink and squeezed tears from her sparkling eyes. "Then—" she puffed "—then we probably do not have to concern ourselves with our positions at Number Seventeen. Surely you were dismissed."

"Not at all." Meg chuckled a little. "The Count would like me to teach him the noble art of abstracted thinking so that he may extricate himself from unpleasant situations. There. What do you think about that?"

"Only you, Meg, only you would do such a thing."

"You think me a wicked trickster, don't you?"

"I think you the most delightful sister a girl ever had." Sibyl flopped against the back of the seat and crossed her arms. "And I am to meet your Princess in the morning."

"Yes."

"Hmm. We should relieve poor Latimer of Miss Lavinia Ash. She arrived some time ago, and when she discovered you were not here but would return, announced herself exhausted by her journey and requested she be allowed to rest. Latimer was good enough to give her Finch's old room."

Meg didn't feel like meeting Miss Lavinia Ash, or any other stranger. "Who is she?"

"Apparently she is acquainted with Finch, who suggested she contact you about a position as a dance instructor to Princess Désirée. Lady Hester insists the woman is a pearl and should be snapped up by the Count at once."

"A dance instructor?" There had been entirely too much to digest in a very short time. "Sent by Finch?"

"She has a letter."

"I see." She supposed a dance teacher would be a good idea, especially since invitations to balls and such could start to arrive for the Princess any day. "But why would she come to me rather than to the Count?"

"Because Finch suggested she should."

Finch could not as yet know that Meg had become the Princess's companion. "Then I'd best see her."

A sharp rap sounded at the door, and Sibyl hurried to answer. "Oh, Miss Ash," she said, "we were about to come and invite you up."

"How very sweet of you. I heard your sister was returned and thought I should ask if she would see me now—or if I should return later."

Meg swallowed and turned to the fire. *Later, when she would probably be asleep at Number 17.* Yes, she did intend to return to… She intended to return to the Princess this evening.

"Come in," Sibyl said. "Meg and I have been chattering. Meg, this is Miss Lavinia Ash. She has a letter from Finch, recommending her for a post as a dance teacher. Finch also mentioned that Princess Désirée would be in need of such a person."

Meg faced the newcomer. "Good afternoon, Miss Ash." *Good gracious.* "Why don't you sit down?"

Miss Ash considered the possible places where she might accept the invitation, but remained standing. At least as tall as Adam Chillworth, perhaps taller, the lady was narrow. Narrow of face. Narrow of shoulder, chest and hip. A black silk bonnet with a deep scuttle brim and edged inside with white lace gave her pale face the look of a nun—except for two spots of bright and definitely artificial color high on her cheeks. Her black bombazine dress and pelisse were of an old-fashioned cut. Jet buttons fastening the pelisse were the only adornment, and her skirts were too short. Her highly polished but ancient boots were entirely revealed, as was more than an inch of sticklike limb.

"Er, you have taught dancing before, I understand," Meg said. If she was to recommend the woman then at least she must ask a few questions.

Miss Ash decided to sit after all and chose to thump herself onto a large, x-framed stool and plant her feet well apart. Her back was so stiff that Meg was certain it must hurt. "I have taught dance for many years," she said. Her voice sounded as if it rose inside her head and exited through her thinly bridged nose. "Many young ladies have passed through my hands. Very many and all of them from the best of families."

"Yet you have decided to leave the school to come to London and teach only one young lady?"

Miss Ash's mouth was of a shade of gray-white and had many vertical creases. "I should have thought that was obvious," she said, suddenly and sharply, her small blue eyes snapping. With evident effort, she took a breath, folded her hands in her lap and smiled. "One may be forgiven for deciding to make a change, even at my stage in life. I assure you, I am very good at what I do."

Meg did not think she cared for Miss Ash's smile, which reminded her of a vexed sheep curling its lip back from long teeth.

"We understand that, don't we, Meg?" Sibyl said. *Sibyl, ever the facilitator.*

"Yes, we do," Meg said. "Forgive me for asking, but are you familiar with the very latest dances?"

That earned Meg another display of sheep's teeth and a simpering, eyes-down snuffle. "I would do no less than to ask these questions myself," Miss Ash said. "Yes, my dear, there is no dance with which I am not familiar." She flapped her lashes upward, and Meg noted that face powder had been applied without consideration to where it might remain. The lady's scant eyelashes were liberally dusted.

Rather than feeling so particular, she should, Meg thought, be impressed that Miss Ash had the courage to make such a bold move. And it was wrong to be so critical of a plain but good woman.

"I would like to visit the Count in the morning," Miss Ash said. "And at that time I would expect to interview his sister."

Meg sputtered. "Interview the Princess?"

Those little eyes grew hard, then cleared. "No, no, no, my dear. I see you misunderstand me. She will want to see how we suit. Men, of course, are logical about such things. Men make up their minds based on sensible considerations, but women, particularly such young women, always want to employ some *emotional* standards." Again Miss Ash's piercing eyes assessed Meg's reaction. "And emotions must be considered. That is all I meant. In truth, I hope that if you are as impressed as Viscountess Kilrood, you will gladly recommend me."

That was a point, Meg decided. "I can certainly ask the Count to see you," she said and immediately felt she assumed far too much. "In the early afternoon, I should think. Would that be agreeable?"

Miss Ash frowned. "If that's the best that can be done."

"Well, I shall not return there myself until a little later. I—" She caught Sibyl's troubled eye. "I am here to visit my sister. She will be teaching the Princess voice and pianoforte. So perhaps the two of you will become a fine complement to my mistress's instruction. We will get a message to you in the morning. Where do you stay?"

"Mm, with a cousin in Chelsea. But she is a recluse and, apart from me, will see nobody. I will return here in the morning to await word." She stood up. "Don't worry about me. I am perfectly accustomed to discomfort. I will remain in the vestibule until you decide—until you can send for me."

"Well—"

"I'll take my leave of you. And you, Miss Sibyl. I look forward to hearing you play. I find the young pianist is generally in too much of a hurry, regardless of how good they are and of the sedate nature of the piece. I have discovered that very little music was ever intended to be other than sedate, you know. Until the morning."

Miss Ash bowed low, and departed.

"What has happened to our lovely, peaceful life?" Sibyl said as soon as they were alone. "Everything is changing and I don't like it. I don't want you to go back to Number Seventeen tonight. Why should you have to do so when you are already so near? You could be summoned in the night if necessary. But surely going early each morning would be ample."

"A companion lives with her mistress, Sibyl. Please, think of this as the most wonderful opportunity for us. We are bound to meet people and who knows, probably find further employment when the Count and his sister have left."

"Someone will want to marry you, I know they will. And I am excited for you, Meggie, honestly I am, but I have always been a silly goose when I have to think about what I should do with myself."

"I will not leave you alone," Meg said. "There. I have told you as much before, and now I tell you again. Please believe me. These are difficult times for me, also, but I know we shall be glad of them in the end." She would also never be the same. "I shall change and gather a few things to take with me."

Sibyl said nothing. She left the flat as soon as Meg had gone into her bedroom. Not so long ago Hunter Lloyd had been in the habit of passing through the house much more often than he did of late. Sibyl wished he would come this way now because she trusted him and could rely on him to listen without judgment. And, if she asked, he would advise her. But Hunter was becoming a famous barrister and so busy he did little more than rush into Number 7 to sleep. Usually he left again before the rest of the household was up.

"So thoughtful, Sibyl?" Latimer More spoke from the foyer.

Sibyl leaned on the banisters and looked down at his upturned face. "Meg will return to Number Seventeen this evening. She tells me companions must live with their mistresses."

Latimer glanced away.

"It sounds foolish, and selfish, but I am already missing her."

"Not selfish at all," Latimer said.

She studied the lean lines of his face, and the manner in which light made his dark brown hair shine a little red. Such a quiet, self-contained man, yet willing to be a friend when he was needed.

He and his sister, Finch, had shared 7A before Finch married Viscount Kilrood, who had been living at Number 8 then. "Do you miss Finch?" She was appalled at her own forwardness. "I mean—"

"Yes, I do. But I am glad for her happiness. And I have my work."

A man, Sibyl thought, would be expected to find solace in his work. "Your work, of course."

Latimer looked up at her again. "Please don't be offended, but should you ever need anything, I hope you will allow me the honor of helping you."

"I'm not offended," Sibyl said, and she appreciated his kindness, but the idea of being alone in this house, alone whenever she closed the door to the flat, made her heart heavy. She must become stronger, less dependent. "Thank you, Latimer. And if you should ever be lonely, I hope you will let me know." Again, she said what was not quite the thing.

He smiled, and the smile transformed him. Latimer More was a most attractive man and more so when he allowed himself to enjoy a congenial moment.

"Are you ready for Miss Ash?" he asked. "She's certainly rested long enough."

Sibyl frowned and said, "She came up, Latimer. And she's left to return in the morning. She didn't thank you? That really was too bad of her."

It was Latimer's turn to frown, but as quickly he cleared his brow. "I have been engrossed in my papers. No doubt she was being considerate in not disturbing me. I'll bid you good-night."

"Good night," Sibyl told him and glanced upward to the third floor and Hunter's quarters. She lacked the courage to seek him out.

Sounds of movement drew her back inside 7B. Meg had changed into a gown of poppy-colored gros-de-Naples, and her matching pelisse was ornamented with a simple ruff and Van-dyked mancherons. The material was not of high quality, but the modiste—Meg—had compensated with perfect cut. Meg glanced up and smiled while she tucked writing paper into her worn tap-estry portmanteau. "What are you doing out there?" She sounded excited. "Did I hear you talking to someone?"

"Latimer. He is a dear. Preoccupied, but kind and very much a man. Most appealing."

"Really?" Meg paused. "I have always considered him a well-favored man, but vague."

"He misses Finch."

"Ah." Meg gathered up her spectacles and her smallest sewing box. "I understand. Finch came to his rescue when money was such a problem. But it was more than that. They really care about each other."

"Just as you and I care about each other," Sibyl replied.

Meg continued to scurry back and forth from the bedroom they shared. She brought her brush and comb, the small collection of hair ornaments she'd collected over years, even several beloved ornaments that had come from the house in Puckly Hinton.

Pressing her lips together, Sibyl watched and felt close to tears. Her sister was happier than she'd seen her in too long, and she was taking everything she counted precious to a stranger's house across the square.... As if she wouldn't care if she never returned.

"I really need new shoes and boots," she said.

Sibyl blinked and said, "Then you must have them at once. Just as soon as we have a little money."

Meg stopped and looked at her. "Please, Sibyl, try to be happy. I am happy. It will all be so exciting. Imagine when you are playing and Miss Ash is instructing the Princess. Why, it will be such fun. I intend to see if I can learn a little myself. After all, I have only danced in the village."

"Of all people, you should dance," Sibyl said. "And once gentlemen see you twirling the floor on a handsome man's arm, you will be pressed to let them mark your dance card."

Meg became serious. "I shall not have a dance card, Sibyl. I am a servant. My presence will be unusual at best, and only because the Count does not wish to remain at his sister's side for such occasions."

"But you may be asked to dance?"

"I suppose, only I shall have to refuse."

"La, la, not so," Sibyl said. "That would be rude. As long as you return to your place in time to greet the Princess all will be well."

"Perhaps," Meg said. "I had best depart now. I think I have everything I need. Sibyl, I want you to take careful note of what I will tell you. Please dress your hair softly, not severely. A few white flowers tucked into your chignon would be just the thing. And the pale blue becomes you so. Will that please you, too?"

"Whatever will please you will please me. The blue will be just right, I'm sure. And I should come at eleven?"

"Just so. Now I go to see what can be accomplished with my mistress before it's time for her to retire."

Sibyl wanted to press Meg to come home then, but stopped herself.

"The Count takes such pleasure in every small success he sees in his sister. You should have seen his face when she walked into the dining room with her hair up. He has the most devilish smile, but it makes everyone around him want to smile also."

"Does it?"

"Oh, yes, and he complimented her so on the gown I managed to find. Tomorrow we arrange for modistes and a large staff to come in so that a wardrobe may be selected and rapidly prepared." She paused for breath. "He even compliments me. Can you imagine such a thing?"

"Yes, I can." And she was ashamed that she felt so threatened by this man she had never met. "He will love you in your poppy, Meg. Go. They will be waiting for you."

"You think so?"

Sibyl regarded her sister's beautiful light brown eyes and the lush effect gained by her red hair. Her lashes were darkened and rouge carefully applied to cheek and mouth. She was radiant. "I do think so. How could he not be waiting?"

Meg filled her lungs, and her bosom rose. Sibyl did not usually think of such things, but Meg had a magnificent figure.

The door wasn't entirely closed. Barstow, in the gray uniform that matched her hair and rustled over her ample frame, presented herself, deep disapproval etched into her features. "Coot is exhausted from such constant disturbance," she said. "That man of Count Etranger's is downstairs. An arrogant man. But what can one expect from these foreigners? He says he's come to escort you. *Escort* you, mind. I told him you would not be thinking of going anywhere at such an hour, but he will not leave."

"Thank you, Barstow," Meg said. "You are a dear woman and I'm glad we have you."

Once the expression of shock faded from Barstow's face, that lady said, "Hmph. It is Lady Hester who has me. But I know the value of human kindness to all I meet. I wouldn't do any less than support you, of course. Even if I do disapprove of your behavior. And that hair... Well, only my good nature and respect for Miss Sibyl stops me from telling you that I think such things as dyed hair are associated with houses of ill repute. I'll leave you to deal with that man."

Sibyl held her breath until Barstow's footsteps faded on the stairs to the upper floor. Then she sputtered and covered her mouth in an attempt to smother the sound.

"I'm glad you are amused at my expense," Meg said, but not without grinning. "I'm sure Barstow's experiences in houses of ill repute must be huge. Oh, I must be quick."

Yes, Sibyl thought, *you must be quick, and I should give a great deal to know if your enthusiasm is only for your position with the Princess.* "Is the Count a handsome man, did you say?"

"Oh, yes." Meg clasped her hands together beneath her bosom. "When I met him, all I could think of was your list of what would make a perfect man for you. Sibyl, Jean Marc could be that man. In every way including his hands, his legs, his shoulders, the dimples beneath his cheekbones when he smiles. He is *your* perfect man personified.''

Sibyl swallowed. Fear curled about her belly. ''Jean-Marc?''

Suddenly quite still, Meg turned red.

''You used the Count's first name. That is unusual, and you know it. In fact, it is ominous. Meg, surely nothing has occurred between you to encourage such an intimacy.''

The dreadful possibility of feeling forced to lie to Sibyl had never occurred to Meg. ''Princess Désirée calls him Jean-Marc all the time,'' she said. ''I used his name by accident. But thank you for reminding me. I shall be careful there is no repeat. Sibyl, I've been thinking, when you come in the morning you might as well bring Miss Ash. I will have spoken to the Count about her by then. If he doesn't wish to see her, I will send word.''

''Someone is waiting for you,'' Sibyl said. Never had she felt such a heavy weight upon her, not even when Papa died. ''You must go.''

''Yes.'' Meg cast about, her skirts flying and her face filled with anticipation. ''If I've forgotten something, it will be easy to get it. Wave me off, dear Sibyl.''

She all but skipped from the room.

''Meg.'' Sibyl caught her arm. ''Look at me a moment. Please.''

Meg did so. ''What is it?''

''You are excited about your arrangements.''

''I have said I am.''

''Because of the opportunities they offer?''

''I…'' Meg blinked rapidly. ''Yes, yes, of course.''

Sibyl had another theory. ''Be very careful, dear. Men of the world—so I'm told—cannot help but be attracted to innocent young women who are also beautiful. A flirtation with a powerful and handsome man might seem delicious now, but when he loses interest in you and you find yourself with a reputation in tatters, your prospects will be dashed. Please remember what I have said.''

"You speak as if I were already contemplating such a thing."

There was a time for direct conversation, Sibyl thought. "Yes, I do. And I believe you are. Say nothing more, but remember I often know what you are thinking, and I rather think you are dashing to return to this man. I am frightened as never before, but I shall pray and I shall also be very glad to meet him for myself. It cannot hurt for him to know you have a sensible relative who cares for you.''

Resentment toward her sibling was a new sensation. Meg struggled toward the stairs with her luggage. "Don't worry about me, if you please. I am the strong one, remember? I'll see you in the morning.''

And Sibyl knew she had come too close to the truth for Meg's comfort.

"Allow me." A man's deep voice with a heavy French accent greeted them. A moment, and M. Verbeux bounded up the stairs to relieve Meg of her burdens. "His Lordship sent me. He suggested a carriage. I told him you'd prefer to walk.''

"Thank you," Meg said, sounding subdued. When they reached the foyer, she told Verbeux, "I should like you to meet my sister, Miss Sibyl Smiles. Tomorrow she will begin the Princess's instruction in music and voice.''

Sibyl had been behind Meg. Now she emerged and dropped a brief curtsey.

Meg witnessed the amazing spectacle of Verbeux staring fixedly at Sibyl.

"Good evening," Sibyl said. "Thank you for taking care of my sister. I should not like her out alone at such a time.''

In slow motion, Verbeux reached for Sibyl's hand. When she let him raise it, he took her fingers to his lips and remained thus for so long, Meg expected Sibyl either to giggle or find a way to extricate herself. She did neither.

Meg surveyed the Frenchman with different sensibilities. Truc, he was intriguing in a foreign way, but she would not have expected Sibyl to respond to him.

"Enchanté," he said at last, before releasing her hand. He gathered up Meg's possessions again, and ushered her through the front door. He looked back at Sibyl and said, "Please be certain the door is firmly locked."

She said, "I will," but looked to Meg again.

And in that instant, Meg knew her sister sensed something of what was in her heart. "I see what you are thinking," she told Sibyl. "And I know you are afraid for me—for both of us. May God watch over us."

13

*S*pivey here.

My dear reader, you must bear with me in difficult times.

Few men would show tolerance in conditions such as these. The strain is overwhelming, yet I see no means of escape.

Meg Smiles is a trollop! Who would have thought it? While I was away, doing all that exhausting flying and so on, well, she went to Windsor with the Count and his sister. Easy enough to see why a man like that would glance her way. In the mood for a little dalliance, I should think. I got down there later than I would have chosen, but early enough to suffer a terrible shock, I can tell you.

I'm more than grateful that you were not exposed to that disgraceful exhibition. I should not have remained there myself had I not needed to assess the way the land lay between those two. You would have been amazed. They didn't exactly, well—you know. But silly Meg probably thinks they did—you know, did.

Take it from me, you don't want to know all the details.

One thing is obvious. The Count's blood heats at the sight of our Meg Smiles, but my challenge is to ensure it remains heated long enough to lure him into a permanent arrangement. Given what transpired, it's likely he intends to take her as his mistress. And I'd be satisfied with that arrangement since I'm sure Sibyl would join the household—or go wherever the man sets Meg up— but I've run into a most annoying problem: Reverend Smiles.

There I was, minding my own business—all right, possibly I was complaining somewhat (but to myself and quietly) about the difficulties associated with getting rid of the lodgers in my home, and I must have mentioned the Smiles sisters. Before I could collect myself and depart for a lecture on keeping one's feet on the ground, this Smiles fellow pops up and introduces himself. Seems he'd been listening to my private conversation with myself and now he has implored me to look out for his dear daughter's virtue.

Now there's a pickle. Smiles is one of the new goody-goody boys—duckies, we call them, because they have these fuzzy bumps where wings of honor will come if they're called Up There. Anyway, word has it he's got a good chance at higher things so I can't exactly afford to upset him, can I? When I've finally managed to do what I absolutely will do at Number Seven, and if I decide I want to take another stab at getting some celestial wings myself, I might want him to put a good word in for me. On the other hand, I may decide to let them offer them to me, then refuse. That'll let them know they should have allowed me to pass their angelic test the first time I applied. Too worldly, they called me. Not ready to let go. I never could abide judgmental people.

Smiles is too holy to play truant from his training and come down here (it's against the rules), so I promised I'd look out for Meg. And I will—all the way into the Count's bed. Well, she's already—ahem, she has shown signs of interest in that direction. I'll let you know how that progresses.

What I haven't had a chance to share with you is the business of L. Ash, the retired teacher from my relation's old school. How was I to know L. Ash wasn't a man? Caper merchants—dancing teachers to you—are always men, or so I believed. And I haven't time to find a replacement.

Do you have even the faintest idea how uncomfortable it is to wear corsets? A chemise? Frightful divided pantaloons, or whatever? And skirts? Oh, it is all so frightful. And she is so frightful— Miss Lavinia Ash. Those teeth! To have to be so close to her is a nightmare.

Fortunately I cut quite the figure on dance floors in my time.

With that woman to provide the newer steps, I shall manage perfectly well. But I will not pretend that I do not fear complications. The cousin, Godly-Smythe, could become a nuisance with his meddling. And if Miss Meg Smiles proves more unpredictable than she already has and causes matters to move too quickly, well, then... Well, then.

At least I shall return to a good bed tonight—my own bed for so very long. The woman is safely out of the way and happily sleeping. I shall bring her back in the morning. But, for tonight, the house is mine again and I do so enjoy the hard bed in my post, where I can see the front door.

Are you fond of carved beds? You haven't experienced one? Fear not, you will. Getting in can be a bit of a problem—getting the formula right, shrinking to fit and so on, but it's well worth the effort.

14

Jean-Marc closed the door to his study and leaned against it. "Damn it all, Verbeux, this house resembles a bazaar—or an asylum."

"A lot to be done. Not much time."

"True." But he didn't have to like the noise, or the flurry, or the constant questions.

"Lucky to have Miss Sibyl and Miss Meg—even Miss Ash." Verbeux shuddered. "Best not to look at her. Or listen to her."

"Meg handles her—Meg Smiles handles her well," Jean-Marc said, gauging that it was safe to leave the door and go to his desk. "Sibyl Smiles is far too gentle a creature to deal with such over-whelming arrogance. I'm not sorry I retained Ash, but I admit this has been one of the longer fortnights in my life." Not only because of the dance teacher, Jean-Marc thought. With his every coming and going, he either saw or heard Meg. He was a prag-matist. Surely it was likely that the very element of danger at-tached to pursuing her was what increased the excitement she aroused in him.

He had tried to keep his distance, other than when his opinion or decision was required.

"Artists need too much attention," Verbeux said, standing to Jean-Marc's right. "Musicians. Dancers. Designers. Writers. Pain-ters. Actors. Difficult people. Demanding."

"Also colorful," he said. "They entertain us, but I would not wish to be quite so entertained quite so close to home again. No doubt we shall soon see some finished creations for my sister? And for Meg Smiles?''

Verbeux pushed out his lips and hummed. He rolled onto the balls of his feet and jiggled.

''Verbeux?''

''Yes. We will.''

''We will see gowns for Princess Désirée, *and* Meg Smiles?''

''For the Princess.''

''You didn't arrange for Miss Smiles's wardrobe?''

''I tried.''

Damn it. ''Why must I do everything myself? Why, when I retain people who are supposedly capable of making sure I *don't* have to be involved in minutia, do I fail to get what I pay for?'' He stood up and threw down the pen he'd been holding. ''Follow me, Verbeux. You shall learn how these things are handled.''

He gained some release from anger by the mere act of making noise. He had ridden that morning and had not taken time to change afterward. Nothing quite matched the ominous sound of a pair of solid boot heels applied to wood and to stone by a man's solid weight.

Maids scurried from his path.

Verbeux pounded up the stairs just behind him. Hell's teeth, the man seemed entertained!

Jean-Marc threw open the door to Désirée's wing and shouted, ''I wish to speak to you, Désirée. And you, Meg Smiles. Kindly prepare yourselves.'' Yes, a good deal of authority loudly applied could really mollify a man's nerves. He checked his stride to avoid bumping into a gaggle of small women carrying garments in various stages of completion. ''Do you hear me, ladies?''

Désirée popped from her bedchamber into the corridor. Garbed in some sort of ugly white night robe, she confronted him with her hands on her hips. ''How could we *not* hear you, Jean-Marc? You are *shouting.* I have no doubt Papa can hear you, and we both know where he is.''

''Enough, young lady.'' This one had been rude and demanding from the day of her birth. "I am expending a great deal of effort on your behalf and I will not tolerate your insufferable impudence."

Désirée rounded her eyes. "You don't have to tolerate anything. You are the one who stamped in here. I didn't invite you. And you are the one who shouted for absolutely no reason. That was rude, was it not? Oh, I have no strength to argue with you. What has made you behave like... Hmm, what has happened, Jean-Marc?"

He'd give a good deal to know what she'd been about to liken him to, but wouldn't give her the pleasure of admitting as much.

"In fact it is Miss Meg Smiles I wish to see. I only included you because you happen to be here—and so, I assume, is she."

Fanning herself as if overcome, Désirée said, "Jean-Marc, your flattery overwhelms me. I'm so grateful to be included." She put a finger to her lips and looked behind her. She whispered, "Meg is unusual. Perhaps mysterious. Spiritlike, even. She is certainly unlike any lady I have known before, but she is also marvelous at helping me not be afraid of all I must do. But she is shy. I know she doesn't seem so, but she is. Please don't shout at her again."

He assessed his half sister's sincerity. She seemed to mean what she said, but damn it all, why should he cater to those he hired? "Thank you for your insight," he said, and passed her. "Carry on with your work, please, everyone. There is no time to waste. Miss Smiles! Miss Meg Smiles! Show yourself at once."

"My Lord," Verbeux said quietly, "could she be very shy? You would not want to frighten her away."

Meg appeared and said, "Good morning, My Lord." And she was pale and... Yes, he did believe she was shaken.

"Good morning," he said, "Do you agree that every moment counts?"

She looked at the floor. "We are using our time well."

"By ignoring my instructions?"

"Ignoring you, My Lord?" Meg met his gaze. "What can you

mean? We have done so much in two weeks. You have said you would prefer to be spared details whenever possible."

Yes, Jean-Marc thought, he had, and in good part because he had wanted to put temptation out of reach.

Regardless of the reason, he was attracted to her. Whether or not the danger of it played a part was immaterial—he must be with her again. Tears stood in her eyes. Oh, damn, damn, why did she have to start crying now when he needed to be strong and get his own way? "Kindly allow me to talk to you without such a display of emotion, if you please."

Meg swallowed, and swallowed again, and cast around for a handkerchief. It was Princess Désirée who gave her one, and Princess Désirée who faced her brother and said, "There. See what you have done? Your unpleasantness has made her cry."

"No, no," Meg said, viewing the brother and sister through a watery wash. "I'm not crying." Princess Désirée was definitely upset.

"Good," Jean-Marc said. "Answer me this. Were you told you must have a new wardrobe in order to carry out your duties to the Princess?"

"Yes," she said. "Of course, I declined."

"*You* declined? What ever made you think it was *your* place to decline an instruction?"

She held the handkerchief over her mouth. Meditation was essential. At once. If she was to survive this terrible experience, tranquillity must be attained. She bowed her head and closed her eyes and cleansed her body of breath.

"Answer me!"

This was a nightmare, Meg thought, a nightmare as awful as when she'd seen the coach and the lathering horses coming toward her as if in slow motion. "A terrible expense," she said softly. "I am an employee here and to consider placing such a burden on you is unthinkable."

Jean-Marc rubbed his face and tried to be calm. "It isn't *your place* to worry about my pockets, Miss. You will have a new wardrobe, and that is the end of the discussion."

"I will not," she told him, and wished her voice were steady.

"You are to accompany a princess to the grandest social events of a London Season. Do you imagine I would allow you to go—with the reputation of Mont Nuages at stake—dressed in cheap rags?"

Désirée exclaimed.

Then there was absolute silence. The modiste and her assistants had fled from sight.

Meg's skin burned, and her legs were weak. She considered him, his angry eyes and tight mouth. He was furious not with her, but with himself. He detested seeing her and being reminded that he had touched her intimately, spoken to her intimately. Yes, that was it. Her father had often told her she was unusually gifted in her assessments of others. The Count was not a cruel man, not cruel enough to speak so meanly of one so much below his stature, not if he were himself.

Jean-Marc loathed what he had said to her. What manner of man spoke so to a woman who had done him no harm—to *any* woman? What was becoming of him?

"I will not embarrass you," she said. "I must buy new shoes and boots. But with some ingenuity I shall make certain my clothes will draw no attention—certainly no negative attention. They are not cheap, but inexpensive. They are certainly not rags. And, after all, I am just a companion. No one will look at me."

Not only had she done him no harm, Jean-Marc thought, she had been the sweetest creature, kind and innocently responsive. "Will you please come with me?" he said.

He didn't wait for a response, but stalked from Désirée's rooms to the music room, where Miss Sibyl Smiles usually taught his sister. On the same floor he could hear another piano being played in the small ballroom. No doubt a dancing lesson was planned.

Verbeux knew when to disappear, and the fact that Jean-Marc

didn't hear his footsteps behind him meant he'd slipped away to other parts.

The music room was red and gold, the ceiling elaborately plastered with musical instruments and putti playing their angelic games. His father had spared nothing in making this house ready for his bastard son—and Désirée. But it was Jean-Marc whom Prince Georges now intended to woo into succession.

The windows in the music room overlooked gardens behind the house. Jean-Marc stared down at them and worked to collect himself. Soft feet had entered behind him. "Close the door," he said, and turned around. "Please."

Rather than hesitate to be alone with him, she did as he asked immediately. If he were her father, or even her brother, he would warn her of the danger of trusting any man—particularly one who had treated her so shabbily. But he was neither her father nor her brother and had no wish to be.

"I hear your sister playing," he said. "She is gifted. She is also a charming little bird of a thing."

"Yes," Meg said, and actually smiled.

She must love her sister dearly. He asked her, "Do you also play?"

"Badly."

"I doubt that. What of Désirée? Is she bad? Or is it at all possible that in one area she shows grace?"

"The Princess shows grace in a great many areas. All that is needed to make her shine is kindness. I shall remember her forever and be grateful to have shared just a little of her life."

This creature could disarm him with a single stroke. Why didn't she lash back at him, damn it? Why didn't she give him some reason to feel less of a cad?

"Sibyl considers Princess Désirée a wonderful young pianist. She has exclaimed to me many times since she's been coming here that she considers her new pupil brilliant and is so glad for the opportunity to help her. The Princess has a clear, sweet soprano voice. She is stiff when she sings, but that is because she is not accustomed to singing for others. Is she?"

"I... No, I suppose not. I have certainly never heard her either play or sing. But this is good news indeed. I shall throw a musicale for her and make sure our guests insist upon hearing her. Miss Sibyl shall also attend. I rather think Désirée takes great strength from both of you. I have never seen her so warm toward others, in fact."

"Perhaps she has not had opportunities to become warm to others. She is most intelligent, My Lord. In fact, her knowledge humbles me. She will make a great match and you will be very proud of her. Trust, My Lord, just trust."

"*You* are reassuring *me?*" He extended a hand to her. When she made no move to take it, he captured her fingers and took her to a richly upholstered divan. It stood a short distance from the fireplace, and was designed to be a place for listening comfort where the pianoforte keyboard could also be seen. "Sit down and rest. You have worked far too hard and will exhaust yourself. You are not a robust person."

She sat on the edge of the beautiful red and gold brocade seat, and he couldn't fail to note how she traced the gold thread pattern.

"Not good enough," he said. "Allow me to help you." Before she could protest, he moved swiftly to swing her around, settle her limbs on the seat and plump pillows behind her back and head. She relaxed not one whit.

"I really should return to Princess Désirée. We are doing very well with her wardrobe, but I feel I must be ever vigilant."

"I thank you for your vigilance," he told her. "Now I have other matters to discuss with you. Most of them will not be comfortable—possibly for either of us. I admire the manner in which you stood your ground on the subject of your clothes. Most women would be delighted at the prospect of acquiring an extensive new wardrobe at someone else's expense."

"I am uncomfortable with waste. I'm sure you intended the offer kindly, but I shall manage well enough."

"Tomorrow I'll have a coach take you out, and you'll purchase footwear. I have an account at the most suitable establishment."

"You pay me," she said, fiddling with her soft green skirts. "I can buy my own shoes."

He bit back a retort and said, "You would not choose to spend your money on such things. To me they are necessities. Please will you allow me to purchase them for you?" He *needed* to give her something, damn it. Given the chance, he would heap gifts upon her.

Meg breathed slowly in and out through her mouth and felt her eyelids lower. This calm she summoned more easily every day was a gift. The Count was waiting for an answer, and sometimes one must choose to surrender to the will of another. "If you insist, then yes."

"Good, then we are agreed. Thank you. I will make the arrangements. You are uncommon, y'know. Standing there with tears in your eyes, yet nevertheless holding your ground. I've never met the likes of you, Meg."

Her heart turned. It turned too often these days.

"You cause me to look at myself, and the exercise can be unpleasant," he said. "I had no right to speak to you as I did."

In good conscience, she could not make light of what he had done.

"What courage you have," he told her.

She didn't feel at all courageous.

"And you are beautiful, but you know that." And with every word that passed his lips he managed to dig himself into deeper trouble.

Meg laughed. "Posh, My Lord. I will not argue with you because it is not my place, but I am... I will say no more."

"We agreed that in private I should call you Meg and you should call me Jean-Marc."

Propping her elbow on the arm of the chaise, she rested her cheek in her hand.

"So? Can you forgive me and say my name?"

He didn't miss her little smile. "You are practiced at certain games, My Lord, whereas I know nothing of them. Whatever else I may not be, I am constant. Always the same. I would not give, then take back. I should be afraid of confusing someone—particularly if that person was truly special to me."

"Is it possible that I am special to you?"

Meg frowned but didn't look at him. "You should not ask me such things. My reputation is important to me. I doubt I shall ever be courted, or marry, but still I should like to be considered good. For a man such as yourself, idle triflings with females of no consequence mean nothing. They may distract you for an hour or two, and they do you no harm."

She was right, and he could neither argue nor reassure her that with her, his commitment would be different. "If I find a way to preserve your reputation, should you like to spend time with me?"

How he tempted her. But she had seen the other side of the man now and would not risk being subjected to such demoralizing abuse again. "I think it would be better if we avoided being alone together."

"We are alone together now and we shall not be interrupted." The alarm in her face maddened him. "Come, come now, be calm. They all think I am lecturing you."

"You should not have...no matter."

"I have already admitted I was wrong. I don't expect you to forget at once, but can I hope that you will forgive me in time?"

Her eyes, their color ever changing through shades of light brown, fixed on his. "I have forgiven you," she said, her voice low. "How could I do otherwise?"

"Does that mean you still like me a little?"

"You are shameless, My Lord. You pursue what you want relentlessly."

"Yes, you're right. And I want you." He could not say it plainer than that. "You are also right that I cannot offer you the kind of permanent arrangement you deserve, but perhaps we can find a certain agreeable situation where we may comfort each other."

Hope, hope actually flared in her eyes now. She knew nothing of the ways of men—the self-serving ways of men of rank and privilege who were accustomed to getting their way. Of course, if he defied his father and went his own way, what or whom he chose to be a permanent part of his life would be his affair.

Meg Smiles wouldn't fit into any life he chose, not as a wife.

"Should you like that, Meg? To be my confidante, the one to whom I can turn with the certainty that you will never betray me."

"I would never betray you," she said suddenly, sitting up and leaning toward him. "Never."

If he didn't hold her and kiss her, he might not be able to make his way through this day. "Bless you," he said. He stood before her and dropped to his knees. Their faces were scant inches apart. "You are a gift to me. You must be. What were the chances that our paths would ever cross?"

"It was inevitable that we should meet," she told him. He wouldn't understand, but she would explain anyway. "The very facts of our diverse backgrounds and unlikely meeting assures us that we were supposed to come together. But I should return to the Princess now."

He closed his eyes and leaned to rest his brow on her shoulder. "Please don't leave me yet. Comfort me, Meg. Let me feel your gentle hands on me."

She should respectfully refuse. This was neither the time nor the place for such things.

"Meg, I need you. Please don't deny me something so small."

His dark curls touched her cheek, and his lips moved against her neck. She brushed her fingers through his hair and leaned her face against his head. That very dark hair tipped over the back of his white collar. His hand, curling over her hip, was tanned, and sprinkled with smooth, black hair. Wide from the base of the thumb to the base of the small finger, each muscle and bone stood out. His wrist extended from his shirt cuff and again strong tendons were a sharp reminder of the physical power in the man.

Tentatively, Meg lifted his hand and pressed her lips into his palm. His shudder was potent enough to travel through her body, too. He reacted by planting a dozen hard little kisses against her neck, her jaw and the dip behind her collarbone.

"I should like to provide for you," he told her, opening his mouth on her cheek. He moved over her, took her lower lip between his teeth, used his tongue to excite her, to bring her back arching from the cushions. She copied each stroke of his until they each strove to take more. His breath quickened. "You should never have to worry about how you will live," he said. "Nor should Sibyl. I would be glad to provide for her, too."

His touch stole her concentration on anything but how he made her feel.

"Meg, tell me you will agree to a more permanent arrangement. After Désirée's debut, of course."

He framed each of her breasts with a hand, used his thumbs to rub back and forth through the insubstantial stuff of her gown. What he did was not enough. She needed to feel his naked chest on hers, his belly on hers, his thighs pinning hers—the part of him that both frightened and delighted her seeking her most private places.

She grew hotter and seemed helpless to stop herself from writhing to find closeness, to find a bonding with him.

"I will never let you go, Meg," he said. "Never. I will make sure you come to need me as much as I need you. You are ready to be completely awakened."

He would never let her go? "What are you telling me, Jean-Marc?"

He kissed her again, soundly, before attempting to answer. "I am very clear, my dear. I find you irresistible and therefore shall not resist. This is evidently the way you feel, too. It's true we have not known each other long, but I believe these things can be clear almost at once, at the first meeting. It was like that with us.''

Meg stiffened. She was a fool, a weak brain blinded by the attentions of a haunting man. Innocent of such matters she might be—at least on a personal level—but she understood that what he proposed was not honorable. He was asking her to abandon everything she'd ever believed about the sanctity of intimate relationships between men and women.

Jean-Marc saw when Meg fully comprehended the nature of his proposition. And he saw her reaction to the revelation. He had played his hand badly, much too rapidly and without learning all he needed to know about the girl. She was passionate, oh, very passionate, but he had misjudged her strength of character.

He lifted her chin and smiled into her eyes. "I've shocked you."

"You have caused me to disappoint myself." She straightened her clothes and tucked wisps of hair back into place.

"You are intoxicating, Meg Smiles. To look at you is a feast. When we first met I saw a demure girl who had the courage to approach a stranger. That was before I touched you. *Touched* you, Meg. And before I really looked at you. Your hair is like none other I've ever seen. And your eyes? Ah, yes, your eyes. The blackest of lashes reflect there. I am no poet, but you make a poet of me. The soft color in your cheeks and your lips… Irresistible, dearest girl.

"I see you will reject me now, but it will do you no good. Some things—as you have told me—are meant to be. *We* are meant to be."

She wanted him to be quiet. With fumbling fingers, she drove pins more firmly into "hair like none other he'd ever seen" and further smoothed her gown. In the small pouch she wore on a soft belt about her waist, there were all manner of useful items to be used in assisting the seamstresses with the Princess's new wardrobe. Meg also carried spare hairpins there, and salts to clear her head when there was no time to employ abstracted thought. She slipped her hand into the pouch and felt about for the salts.

"If you prefer, I won't press you further now. But I wish you to join me this evening for a small supper. No one will question such an occasion where we will discuss progress with Désirée and plan those events to take place here. It grows late to get out invitations, and we must hurry."

His assumptions shamed her. She had made so poor an impression that he considered her a woman without standards. How could she have thought she loved him?

Surely her heart had stopped beating. Of course she had never considered loving him. Her feelings had been those of a mooning child exposed to *l'amore* for the first time.

"We will have supper together this evening, Meg."

His expression gave not a hint of gentleness. He was dark, even saturnine of countenance, and the sharp bones in his face showed pale beneath tanned skin. Everything within him had tensed. She felt that tension. He was starkly handsome, and no woman would be able to pretend she was not undone by him.

"I will arrange the meal in my rooms. We will not be interrupted there."

"Of course, I cannot come," she said, and her hand closed around the vial of salts. "You know very well that to do so would start all manner of gossip in your household. That gossip would spread to Number Seven quickly enough. Even if I did not care for my own reputation, I will not shame Sibyl. Thank you for inviting me. I'm sure we will be able to attend to all these important matters quite well without a supper. Now I think it would be sensible if we did not leave this room together."

Jean-Marc stood up. He should be angry, but how could he be when she was so logical and reasonable, and when her straightforwardness only made him admire her more? But she would bend to his wishes. He had fought too many battles with strong and powerful men over matters of state to be thwarted by the orphan daughter of a country parson.

His expression only grew more aggressive. She felt a little faint—and who could blame her?

It was when she started to withdraw her salts that she felt something sharp sink into the pad of her thumb and the outside of her wrist. So sharp was the sensation that it shocked more than hurt. The warm stickiness of blood spread through her fingers. With as much nonchalance as possible, she inserted her other hand into the pouch, located the handkerchief the Princess had given her and clutched it tight in her injured hand.

She stood up and curtseyed. A pulse throbbed in her thumb and hand and she imagined her blood pumping. Sickness all but overwhelmed her. "Désirée has a dancing lesson with Miss Ash very soon. I would be glad to speak with you in the ballroom while they practice. Désirée would be pleased that you took the time to be there with her, and we could converse without interrupting the others. I must go. Now." If she didn't, she was almost certain to show signs of distress.

The Count took hold of her arm as she tried to slip past and jerked her injured hand into the open.

"My God," he said. "What have you done?"

Blood soaked the handkerchief. The flimsy material was sodden and would drip at any moment. "I *have* to go," she said.

Jean-Marc raised her arm with no evident concern for ribbons of blood that coursed to her elbow then dripped on the carpet. Applying pressure to her wrist, he took her with him to the bell-pull near the white marble fireplace and tugged repeatedly on the red velvet cord.

He released her for long enough to drag his shirt from his trousers and rip off a piece of the fine linen. Cradling her hand in both of his, he carefully removed the handkerchief, which had stuck to the wound.

What confronted them horrified Meg. A long, curved wound arced from the tip of her thumb, crossed both joints and reached the flesh on the outer edge of her wrist.

The Count wrapped the piece of linen around the injury,

pressed her fingers together and held them so tightly she struggled not to cry out.

"Now," he said, pulling her pouch open wide, "Let's see what dangerous weapon you arm yourself with."

"I arm myself with nothing," she whispered.

He looked at her sharply, said "damn" a deal too forcefully and backed her to sit on a stool. "Put your head down or you'll faint," he said, and made sure she did so by pressing on the back of her neck. "Stay there."

Once more he attacked her pouch. At his exclamation she raised her head, but he promptly pushed it down again.

In his hand Jean-Marc held a shaving knife, its blade open from a bone handle. He tested the steel and felt how it had been stropped to sword-edge quality. A desperate weapon indeed.

"Are you telling me this knife isn't yours?"

Meg looked up. Jean-Marc held the most vicious-looking gentleman's shaving blade. It was fully open, and there were traces of blood on the handle—her blood.

"Meg?"

"Of course it isn't mine. I can't imagine what it was doing in my pouch. I carry scissors in case I need to snip something. I have never seen that thing."

"Where the devil is Rench?"

"I don't want any fuss," she said, starting to rise. "Please, nothing that will draw attention to me."

Her reaction puzzled him. "Why? All I intend is to make sure this wound is cleaned and dressed and that the bleeding is stanched."

"I will attend to it." Even though she felt too weak to stand. Her legs wobbled, and she sat on the stool again. "I beg of you, do not arouse any suspicion among the servants."

"Now there's an odd word," he said, checking the wound again. "Suspicion? As in suspicion of a crime of some sort, an attempted crime of some sort?"

"No!"

"But of course that's what you mean. Did you open this blade and put it in your pouch?"

"I…no."

"Have you ever owned a gentleman's shaving blade?"

"No." She could hardly make herself heard.

"Ever used one at all?"

"Never."

He expanded his lungs. "Ever seen this particular blade before?"

"No."

"Very well. Someone opened this thing and put it where they knew there was a good chance you would injure yourself on it. Does that seem possible?"

"Thank you for the bandage. I will mend your shirt so the rent doesn't even show."

He released her wrist and held her face in his hands. "Meg Smiles, what happens to you happens to me. This may not have been intended as a deathblow, but it was intended to deal a serious injury. Who do you think did this thing?"

"I don't know." She grew so tired.

"But we made progress because you do see that this wasn't an accident, don't you?"

What she didn't want to see was the potential puzzle that lay ahead. "You're right. Someone put the blade where it was almost certain to inflict an injury on me. I don't know who that would be, or why, but it frightens me."

"It *has* frightened you. There is no need to be frightened anymore. I am with you. Nothing shall touch you again, my love."

She looked away.

"I will not allow you to thwart me," he said. "What I want, I get, and I want you. No matter if you aren't ready yet. I will give you all the time you need. For now I intend to discover who played this foolish trick, and deal with them."

The door opened without warning, and Verbeux trudged in, an

expression of foul annoyance on his face. "Yes?" he said, slamming the door behind him.

Later, much later would be soon enough to deal with Verbeux's inappropriate behavior. "Why didn't Rench come?"

"Because you've scared him. Scared whole household. Raging. Swearing. Rench sent for me. Don't blame him."

"Good," Jean-Marc said silkily. "Very good. You've had experience with the wounded in battle. Miss Smiles has been wounded by some manic creature who may well have sought to deal a desperately dangerous cut to her wrist. Fortunately the attempt was a failure. Damaging enough, but no threat to her life. Please bring me water."

Meg found the strength to get up, wrap her hand firmly and start for the door. "I appreciate your concern, but it isn't necessary. I will clean myself and join the others in the ballroom. My Lord, do not dwell on this, please. It must have been an accident. We will discover some perfectly reasonable excuse—you mark my words."

"We will discover a reason," he said. "You are to remain quiet today."

Scuffling and giggling sounded on the gallery outside the room. The door shot open, and Princess Désirée fell through the opening. Miss Ash, her face flushed, followed with long, determined strides.

"I must talk to you, Meg," Désirée said, and Meg could not fail to note how the girl spoke to her but stared at her brother with a narrowed, assessing gaze. "Miss Ash thinks it's time for my dancing lesson but you and I can have a little time first, can't we?"

"Your Royal Highness," Ash said, her voice thinly reverberating via her nose. "Discipline and a schedule are everything. We have several hours of hard work ahead of us and must begin."

"I will come to the ballroom," Princess Désirée said, and turned her back on Miss Ash. "I think there is something I am most clear about, Meg. We have discussed the matter before, but

I have done more study and read more, and I can read certain signs around me. I believe they are dangerous and should be unfrocked at once."

"Unfrocked?" Jean-Marc said. "What can you mean?" He did not trust his sister when she was in this mood.

"Unmasked then. I may have used the wrong word. Revealed, examined and put in their place."

"I ought to go and wash," Meg said. The wound pulsed most unpleasantly and began to sting.

"Go quickly," Désirée told her. "I am going to make Ash teach me the waltz this afternoon. It should be such fun."

"What is this obsession with speed?" Ash said. She slapped the crown of her floral cotton cap and tied the ribbons more securely beneath her chin. Her gown was the same black she'd worn every day. "Sedate. That is what is appropriate. *Waltzing.* The new King doesn't approve, I can tell you. I've heard as much. There's a man who appreciates enjoying all things to the fullest without hurrying one of them."

"Certainly," Princess Désirée said, sounding too gay for Jean-Marc's comfort. "I understand he eats all day, to get the most out of his food, and takes hours to dress, in order to annoy and frustrate his servants for as long as possible, and I'm told that in his bedchamber he is a frightfully long time about something or other—my sources refused to tell me what, which is very mean of them—but whatever it is, it takes a long time because the Prince consumes such large quantities of strong drink. Now, I can make no sense of any of that. I'm simply pointing out that the King is generally slow, so his opinions are to please himself only.

"Little wonder he doesn't want his wife at the Coronation. Queen Caroline is much too lively for him. I imagine *she* will want to waltz at the festivities."

"Thank you, Désirée," Jean-Marc said, as much amused as irritated. "You will do as Miss Ash tells you."

Meg saw Ash's sheep teeth begin to appear. Désirée said, "Oh, I know Miss Ash won't be able to teach me the waltz. I was joking. Only those familiar with the most up-to-date steps would know the waltz.''

Jean-Marc didn't give Désirée the satisfaction of arousing his temper again. "Run along," he told her. "I shall come to see how you're doing. Not you," he told Meg when she tried to join the other two women, "You are in no condition to rush about this house today.''

"And why is that?" Désirée said, peering at Meg. She ran her eyes over every inch of her companion. "You have injured your hand? What else has occurred here?" She turned her eyes from Meg to Jean-Marc.

"Not a thing," Meg said, a deal too loudly. "Absolutely not."

The Princess tipped her head on one side and studied her brother. "You are flushed, Jean-Marc."

"Not at all. Go to your lesson."

"You want me to stop questioning you about what's been going on here."

"Young lady, be quiet. You are upsetting Miss Smiles."

Meg longed to convey to Désirée that she was hurting, not helping her.

Slowly the Princess, dressed in one of her old, rather childish gowns, made a circle around Jean-Marc. Her perusal was entirely too personal. In fact, she seemed interested only in parts of His Lordship that no lady should ever look at.

Meg had looked at them. She'd like to look at them again—do a great deal more than look at them. She digressed, possibly because she was in shock.

"As I thought," Princess Désirée said. "You are covering something up, Meg. You've seen the truth of it all, but you're hiding it away again now."

"I don't understand you," Meg said, although a horrid knot formed in her stomach.

"That's because she makes no sense," Jean-Marc said. "I have instructed you to leave, Désirée. Kindly do so."

"I will, I will, I assure you. In fact, I'm on my way. Meg, I'm glad you've obviously had such a successful mission."

"Your Highness?" Meg said.

Princess Désirée grinned. "By getting behind those black squares," she said. "Now our aim must be to get rid of them altogether. If the subjects in question have no place to successfully hide their indicators, then we shall be able to see exactly what they're thinking, yes—and what moves we can expect from them next."

The Princess, Meg decided, had been reading far too much.

15

Désirée had left only moments before the Count was called away. He had already insisted that Verbeux should attend to Meg's hand. In the music room, and with a little maid named Fanny in attendance, the valet went swiftly about his task.

"Ooh, that must 'urt," Fanny said, or rather repeated. "Ain't she brave, Verby?"

The familiarity earned the girl a cold sideways glance from Verbeux's dark eyes. "Not deep," he commented, his spectacles glinting. "Blade penetrated at a shallow angle. Deeper and higher, and—" with a forefinger he made a curving line across Meg's wrist "—and she might have bled to death."

Fanny cried, "Ooh," closed her eyes and shook her head.

Meg raised her shoulders and tried not to visualize the wound he described. "Thank you," she told him when he returned to wrapping her hand. "I was fortunate."

Verbeux regarded her solemnly. "Let us hope so," he said.

Meg took advantage of an opportunity to survey the man. His interest in Sibyl became less obvious after their introduction, but Meg had observed that whenever the two crossed paths, there were subtle long glances from the man. Sibyl merely colored slightly and hastened her step.

He was self-assured, yet distant. His manner left one in no doubt that he was an educated, thoughtful person. Clothing of fine quality and cut benefited from his manly figure. Meg had not embarrassed Sibyl by prodding her about her feelings, but it was easy to see how she might be dazzled by him.

"M. Verbeux? Do you enjoy England?"

He looked startled by her personal question. "England is pleasant," he replied. "I prefer my homeland."

"Ow," she said. He wound the bandage too tightly, but glanced up when she exclaimed and loosened it again without comment. His sharp, brief stares disconcerted her.

Fanny patted Meg's shoulder, clucked and said, "You're a brave 'un and no mistake, Miss Meg."

Once more Meg received disturbingly direct scrutiny from Verbeux. His sudden and disarming smile ensured she must smile back. "You are brave, Miss Smiles," he said.

This comment so astonished Meg that she made no attempt to reply.

Fanny had no such difficulty. "That she is, Verby," she said merrily. "And nice as she can be, too."

The girl's insights earned her another withering look. Verbeux tied off the bandage. "Clean up here and return to your duties," he told her.

Smiling, Fanny went about doing as she was told.

"How does the wound feel?" Verbeux asked.

"The throbbing has almost stopped. Will it bleed a great deal more?"

He straightened his cuffs and checked the tasteful black pearl pin in his neck cloth. "Shouldn't think so. There are ways to close a laceration that promote rapid healing—and stop bleeding. I know them. Come to me if you suffer increased discomfort."

"Thank you. I should like to return to my duties. I am a calm woman but really, there is an amazing amount to accomplish. We cannot afford for the schedule to be delayed for any reason."

"Return to your duties," he said. "Good afternoon."

Meg waited and watched until Verbeux's straight back went from sight. Gaining permission to carry on lifted Meg's spirits. She so enjoyed the dance lessons and the voice lessons. Princess Désirée was truly quite talented.

Before Meg could leave the music room, Sibyl stuck her head

around the door and said, "Baggsy's here, Meggie. I heard Rench let him in not a second ago. He is come to see us, of course."

"Reverend Baggs," Meg muttered. "Why is he coming to Town so frequently?"

"I don't know. Let's go to the ballroom quickly. It would be more comfortable if we didn't have to be alone with him."

Meg was grateful Sibyl apparently knew nothing about the accident yet. "I think I should prefer our business kept from anyone else," Meg said.

Sibyl shook her head and motioned Meg to follow her. "Please, he makes me shiver—the more so if he can concentrate on me. For me, will you come?"

"Of course," Meg said, getting to her feet. She was immediately forced to trot in order to keep up with her sister's pace.

In the little ballroom, Princess Désirée went through steps while Miss Ash watched. "You see," Sibyl whispered. "Reverend Baggs will be intimidated by so much activity—and by strangers. He won't stay very long."

"Perhaps not," Meg said, unconvinced.

"Head *up*," Ash ordered, and moved in to apply a sharp rap on top of the Princess's head with a long, thin cane. "Up, up, up," she ordered, as if training a puppy.

Princess Désirée made a turn toward Meg and Sibyl, crossed her eyes and gave an evil grin. Meg struggled not to laugh.

Rench came into the ballroom and announced, "There's a Reverend Baggs here to see you, Miss Smiles—both of the Misses Smiles. He's already on his way up. Could take some time for him to arrive. The Reverend does not appear in strapping good health. If you don't want to see him, I'll stop him and turn him around."

"Oh, no!" Sibyl said. "That would be disrespectful. Please have him come to us."

"I think he's already come," Rench said.

Reverend Baggs scuffed in with the short steps Meg remembered well. Garbed in a black cassock and priestly collar and holding his wide brimmed black hat before him, he was as rotund and rosy as ever—and as out of breath.

"Meg and Sibyl," he said, bobbing as he bowed his head in their direction. "At last I find you. I called at Number Seven and was sent here. After all, your dear father was so good to me, and your dear mother, and it is my duty to make sure you are safe and have what you need."

Meg and Sibyl looked at each other. Their papa had died several years previously, and their mother some years before that. Meg had no difficulty recalling Papa's kindness to Baggsy, but this was the first time there had been a mention of his concern for his benefactor's children.

"I know what you're thinking," he said in his plummy voice. "If I have been so concerned for you, why have I taken so long to come to you? My fault entirely, and I am ashamed. My defense is that I am not so skilled at running a parish as your dear father was and it has taken me some time to feel free to leave Puckly Hinton."

"You were in London some weeks ago," Meg said. "Or so our cousin William tells us."

Reverend Baggs shook his head mournfully. "I was indeed. And I tried to contact you but had no success. William will have told you I was a witness at that terrible thing that happened near the Burlington Arcade. The coincidence of my also being there struck me immobile. I could do nothing, and then you were surrounded by people and I thought it best to depart and tell William as soon as possible."

"Yes," Meg said. She would not thank him. "Well, we are pleased to see you, I'm sure, but I hope you won't think us rude if we return to our duties. I don't think our employer would appreciate our spending time on personal visits. When you return to Puckly Hinton, please give William our regards and tell him we are quite well and happy."

"Your cousin is a most generous and pious man," said Reverend Baggs. "His kindness to a simple man of God will not go unnoticed. He is—'' he dropped his voice ''—he is deeply upset by this endeavor.'' He eyed the Princess and Miss Ash significantly. They had both withdrawn a discreet distance that nevertheless allowed them to watch and to overhear with ease.

"I certainly don't care—"

"Meg and I are touched by Cousin William's concern for us." Sibyl interrupted Meg. "He has nothing to worry about. Our position here is most agreeable, thank you."

The Reverend pushed his mouth out in a thoughtful pout and frowned. "This is awkward, young ladies, but I have also come to ask for your help. I will be spending some time here in London on church business. There is never enough—er—money for these things. Forgive me for mentioning such a matter, but I have nowhere to stay while I'm here and I had hoped you might help me locate inexpensive lodgings. Do you think there might be room for me at Number Seven?"

Horrified, Meg searched for the best way to discourage the man.

Sibyl swung her skirts and fiddled with the lace at one cuff.

Meg saw Miss Ash move. She paced to the piano and glared at Meg.

"You should go to Lady Hester," Sibyl blurted. "Latimer More is an agreeable fellow, and he has a second bedroom in his flat. He might appreciate some financial assistance. Yes, do go to Lady Hester."

"I shall," Reverend Baggs announced in excited tones. "I certainly shall. At once. How perfectly delightful to be so close to two dear girls who are so near my heart. Especially in this unkind city. Thank you, thank you." Bowing repeatedly, he backed to the door, turned and fled.

"Oh, Sibyl," Meg moaned, "you are so good. You cannot bear to think of someone being in need. But to suggest that man seek lodgings at Number Seven? Lady Hester will not turn him away, and neither will Latimer. They will both think they should take him in for us."

Sibyl crossed her arms tightly, and her expression became unexpectedly rebellious. "We were not brought up to be disrespectful to the clergy. How could we ignore him when he told us he had nowhere to stay?"

"By opening your tiresome mouth and telling him you couldn't help him. That's how." Ash's words fell like hard stones into the quiet air in the small blue and silver ballroom.

"Miss Ash," Princess Désirée said, her lips white, "how can you be so rude?"

"How? I'll tell you how," Miss Ash retorted. She paced, or rather strode in circles around the piano. "I am beside myself. Of all the hen-witted, chuckleheaded suggestions to make. What were you thinking of, Miss Smiles? Or—forgive me, I spoke in haste—of course you *weren't* thinking at all, were you? Women should know their place and remain in that place. Subservience is admirable in the female. Completely appropriate. But to be crackbrained enough to send another annoyance to Number Seven? Well! I am beside myself."

Miss Ash was quiet for a moment, although she breathed loudly. Her long steps revealed that her stockings were rolled down into unbecoming rings that resembled sausages just above her ankles. The exposed limbs were exceptionally thin, white and sinuous—and hairy. Fury emanated from her.

Sibyl moved close to Meg and slipped a hand in hers, and discovered the bandage. "Meg?" she whispered.

"It's nothing. Just a little scratch. M. Verbeux wrapped it. He was too conscientious. I'll tell you about it later."

"Slow top," Ash all but shouted, "you have probably managed to waste a great deal of time, of an important person's time." She stopped and seemed to shrug, to shake herself. She turned her bright little eyes on Meg and Sibyl, and her pale face gradually became deep red.

"You have no right to speak to Sibyl like that," Meg said. "What she says is no affair of yours."

"It's all right, Meggie."

"No, Sibyl, it isn't. It is all outrageous." She turned to the dance teacher and said, "Why would you care about who does or doesn't lodge at Number Seven?"

"I should think," the Princess said, sounding calmer, "that Miss Ash has some explaining to do."

Ash spread her long, thin arms and said, "Oh, dear, I don't know what came over me. Oh, really, I'm sorry, but I am already protective of you. That man wants to take advantage of your kindness, and you have let him do so."

"I still don't see why you would speak so to Sibyl."

"No, you wouldn't. You are too... You have led a sheltered life and may too easily be victimized. The sight of that happening made me forget myself. There, I have been honest, I can't do more."

The Princess didn't even try to conceal her fascination with the proceedings.

Sibyl, on the other hand, was visibly shaken.

Abandoning her anger, Meg said, "Yes, well, we should not speak further of this. Continue Princess Désirée's dance lesson, if you please. I am also hoping to hear her sing today."

Ash sniffed and raised her chin. She waved her pupil forward, using the cane to indicate where she wanted her to stand.

"Meg," Sibyl whispered hoarsely. "Miss Ash is really strange, don't you think? She became someone quite different. So angry, and not at all as one would expect a gentlewoman to be angry. Such expressions. I shall be some time recovering."

"She is strange," Meg agreed. "But she is also quite elderly, I believe. Perhaps she has painful joints that make her irritable. We should put this from our minds and carry on. Play for them, Sibyl. Please?"

Sibyl faltered for only an instant before going to the piano and sitting on the bench. She proceeded to play while Miss Ash demonstrated several steps from a cotillion. The woman was wooden—stiff. She placed her feet deliberately and made no attempt to allow the music to flow through her limbs and body, showed no sign of being moved by the music.

Meg was unaware of Jean-Marc's arrival until he stood at her shoulder. He bent to say, "I thought you were instructed to rest today."

"M. Verbeux told me I could return to my duties. The wound bled considerably, but it is shallow and wide, not deep."

"You realize we cannot ignore what happened?"

She had managed to set aside the incident. "I cannot imagine how I could discover anything about the origin of that shaving blade. No one would confess its ownership. And I'm sure it was accidentally placed in my pouch."

"Are you?"

"I think I shall take a seat to watch," she told him, walking toward one of the small divans covered with blue damask that were placed about the ballroom. She sat and rested her injured hand atop the other forearm. It hardly hurt at all now.

"You are doing well, Désirée," the Count said, and patted his sister's arm as he passed her and joined Meg on the divan. "Let us see how you are mastering the waltz. You mentioned you liked it. Miss Ash, the waltz, if you please."

Ash's frown conveyed her disapproval, but she took up a position with Princess Désirée.

Sibyl looked up and smiled. She changed her music and scanned the first sheet. Meg didn't recognize the sprightly piece. The swelling, swooping notes made Meg smile, too. She swayed, and did her best not to react to the Count, so close beside her.

Neither his behavior nor her reaction to him would do. Each time she saw him she recalled again in great detail their first time alone. On the first day of their acquaintance. Her stomach burned at the memory. She had behaved like a common girl with no respect for her body or her soul. And the small brushes that continued to occur, the brief interludes of intimacy, were simply wrong. Yet she could not force herself to stop thinking about them, longing for more time alone with him

"Not a spirited performance," he said into her ear while he watched his sister and Miss Ash. "I do believe Désirée does love music. And she moves well. Dash it all, though, I do admire Ash's ability to take the man's part in the dance. She does it so naturally. But then, she is not exactly a feminine creature."

Meg did not comment.

"I say, Désirée," he said loudly. "You're going to be a natural, *cherie*. But I'd like you to study how you should carry yourself. Miss Smiles and I will demonstrate for you. Watch carefully."

"No," Meg murmured. Her flesh prickled. "I cannot."

"But you can. Have you forgotten how you practiced alone in my study?"

She closed her eyes. "How could I forget?"

"Good. Very good. Now you and I shall practice together." He raised his voice when he said, "Sibyl, I think the Princess will learn more from watching a slightly slower, more graceful waltz. What do you think?"

"I agree," Meg said at once.

"So do I," Sibyl said.

"Of course she does," Miss Ash snapped, without any attempt to conceal her annoyance. "She agrees with anything any man tells her."

Jean-Marc chuckled a little. He got up, bowed to Meg and offered her his hand. She took a breath, placed her left hand on his forearm and let him lead her onto the floor.

With the subtlest of motions, he swung her to face him.

His smile slowly disappeared.

Sibyl played a beautiful waltz, a slower, much smoother piece.

Meg felt light-headed. Everything but Jean-Marc's face blurred.

He inclined his head and placed his right hand lightly at her waist. She settled her left hand on his arm.

The music swirled over and through Meg.

Jean-Marc decided he would like to hold this moment, to cling to this moment. He took her right hand in his left and resisted the urge to pull her closer.

He moved with her, firmly and smoothly—and she was light and responsive. "Smile," he said, but she didn't smile. "Why so serious?"

They revolved again. Her lissome body followed his direction, but then, he'd known it would. "Meg, I asked why you are so serious."

Those great golden eyes grew moist. "Perhaps I am serious because you are serious." She turned her face aside, and her jaw cast a faint shadow on her soft neck.

"I am not serious," he told her, although he didn't feel disposed to smile, either. "How is it that you have not been whisked away by some fine man, Meg? Surely any number have asked for your hand."

She looked at him through her dark lashes, and he felt foolish. He sounded like a moonstruck boy pressing a girl for words that would reassure him she had no other attachments.

"I have never been asked for my hand," she told him. "There has never been an opportunity for me to form such relationships. La, but I do not care."

He rather thought she did, and the idea pleased him, although he wasn't sure why. Meg was fresh, a sensuous creature who might almost have dew on her skin. He hummed, "One, two, three, one, two, three," under his breath and gave himself to the rhythm. At least this was the perfect opportunity for him to hold her without arousing suspicion.

"When you smile you are at once very young," she said, "and carefree."

"You don't say."

"I most certainly do say. One might mistake you for a sweet-tempered man." Then she did smile, and with high glee.

Jean-Marc turned her about and took advantage of a hidden moment to give her waist a little poke.

"Oh," she said, and her eyes glittered. "You are sly, My Lord. Have a care, for I have been known to be underhanded myself—in innocent ways, of course."

He raised his eyebrows. "Then I must dare you to be underhanded with me, Miss Smiles. The thought intrigues me. Did you know how charmingly your breasts rise when you breathe deeply?"

The manner in which her mouth fell open was most pleasing. She said, "My Lord, what has come over you?"

"You have come over me." And he saw storm clouds ahead, clouds that would follow the sun of whatever they could share with each other before they must go their separate ways—unless he could convince her to become part of his life on the only terms available to them. So far she had been shocked by that suggestion.

Vaguely, he was aware of Sibyl finishing one piece of music and starting another. Equally vaguely he realized they had already danced too long for the exercise to be only for the purpose of demonstration. To hell with that.

"There is a trembling about you, something so vulnerable and new."

She looked downward and said, "I am not new anymore."

He spread the fingers of his right hand wide at her side and stroked her ribs with his thumb. And he really did feel her tremble. "You are naive," he said. "You think I stole your virginity, don't you?"

"Don't!" She gripped his hand tighter. "Please don't mention such things."

"I will say one thing more and then I'll follow your wishes. Your virginity is intact. You should have trusted me. I told you there are ways to find great pleasure without my actually breaching your maidenhead."

She stumbled, and he lifted her almost off her feet, then set her down in time to change their course and fly around the floor, ballooning her skirts behind her, until she was breathless and gasping.

"I shall give you no mercy until you say you believe me."

"I believe you," she said. The color in her cheeks was delicious.

"Meg Smiles, you torment me." They danced now as if they'd been partnering each other for years. "Do you know this? That I no longer sleep well at night because I find myself reaching out to feel you. Only you are not there, and then I am entirely awake, my heart pounding, my body wet with sweat. It is like a dream that is snatched away and replaced with a nightmare."

Around and around they danced. He would so like to embrace her, to wrap her against him while they gave themselves to the music.

She raised her face. Looking down at her made him feel incredibly strong. He could, he thought, run for hours without stopping, tear trees from the ground and great rocks from deep holes.

"What is it about you that brings me in danger of losing my senses, Meg? Do you feel any of what I feel?"

She passed her pointed tongue over her lips, and her bandaged hand pressed his arm.

"Do you, Meg?"

"Since you don't know what it is you feel, how am I to know if I have such feelings myself?"

"Don't toy with me. Give me an answer. Do you feel something for me, something more than casual attraction?"

She bowed her head, then raised her chin. "What I feel for you I have never felt for another, My Lord. I shall never be the same as I was before we met."

"Tell me you're glad of this."

"I'm glad. I'm also fearful, because when we can no longer even see each other, I know my heart will be broken. And I also know that to make such a statement is foolish and puts me in a weak position."

The piece Sibyl played speeded a little and had a military tone. Jean-Marc brought Meg to a halt, smiled at her and commenced again but with more definite movements. A third piece. And so it went. There was no point in stopping now.

"I could dance with you forever," he told her. "Holding you causes the muscles in my limbs to burn and my belly to become so tight. There are other feelings I should not mention here and now. But I will say that you have my complete attention.''

She blushed. A bead of perspiration formed at the top of her décolletage and slowly trickled downward. He spun her until her back faced the others, and dipped his left forefinger between her breasts and finally beneath her gown. Her expression was more of arousal than shock. He withdrew his damp finger and slipped his hand inside his shirt, onto his own skin.

"What are you doing?'' she asked.

"Pretending your skin touches mine and that I feel you hot and slick. I would much prefer to feel your breasts against my chest. We would lie facing each other and embrace. And the embrace would brush your sensitive parts against me, and I would lay you on your back and take those aching parts into my mouth. And you would pleasure me. You do pleasure me, Meg—I am besotted with you.'' He ought to be wary of such comments, but he had no reason to fear that she could use them against him, and he did feel everything he'd told her.

Meg could scarcely bear the tingling that pinched at her nipples, and between her legs. "You dance so well, My Lord.''

"Surely you can call me Jean-Marc in such circumstances. Only you make me feel a complete man. I have asked you to allow me to ensure that I can come back to you. My offer is selfish. I cannot bear to think of being parted from you forever. I would take great care of you and Sibyl, Meg. You should have a pretty little house of your own where I could find peace and pleasure in the only true home I can hope to have. Perhaps near Riverside. Did you like the countryside at Windsor?''

"Very much,'' Meg said. He wanted her to be his mistress because she could not make a suitable wife to one of such noble birth—even if he was a by-blow.

She saw him hold his breath, felt his grip tighten on her hand.

"So you will do it? You will stay with me?''

"I will think about it,'' she said, and felt close to tears. She had never thought to speak such words. "Please do not press me."

"I won't," he said, but she heard his excitement, his anticipation of triumph. She should be ecstatic that he wanted a simple person such as herself.

"You make me a happy man," he told her. "Just knowing you would consider going against what you believe in to be with me is... Meg, I need you. Let me do things for you, things you deserve."

"You said you wouldn't press me."

"So I did. Just dance with me, Meg. Forget it all, everything out there that would ruin our dream, and dance with me, Meg."

What he asked was so simple. A test of restraint, but nevertheless not difficult. Jean-Marc did hold her closer than was probably wise, but she doubted the others would notice. He drew her against him, bowed his head until his jaw almost touched her temple and whirled her around and around. After the scare she'd suffered, she should be tired, yet her feet scarcely touched the floor, and she had no desire to stop. He did what he had done before and splayed his fingers at her side while he rubbed her ribs with his thumb and managed, whenever he knew he would not be seen, to apply a feather stroke to her breast.

At last he said, "No doubt there will already be talk by at least one of the number present. I suppose I must relinquish you. But it cannot be for long, my dearest. Not at all long or I shall have to come for you and bear you away. I think I shall make immediate inquiries about properties at Windsor—and perhaps in one or two choice areas of London itself."

"You should not be in any hurry to do so."

"Ah, but I am. If not for you, then for me. Yes, I think I should enjoy a small hideaway, a comfortable hideaway, where I could go to be alone—preferably with you."

"Jean-Marc."

"I know, I know. Surely you—" His abrupt pause jolted her. "You don't know, do you? I am pressed on all sides. The decisions I must make, and make soon, will change my life forever. Regardless, I shall lose something or someone I love. How cruel if I should also have to lose you. But enough of that for today. I must allow you an opportunity to consider carefully."

"Thank you."

"I should attend to your every wish, my sweet. You should never want for anything. Meg, more than anything I need to kiss you."

She shook her head and would not look at him. "We must bring this dancing to a close." Although she did not want to.

"I can make an excuse to have you accompany me when I leave the ballroom."

"No." But oh, how she longed to say yes.

"Come with me, Meg. I will do nothing more than kiss you and hold you."

To look at his mouth was a mistake. Her lips parted of their own volition.

"You want it, too," he said. "I see that you do. We could lie in the darkness and watch the firelight. You wouldn't have to if you didn't want to, but what I should like most of all is for us to be naked together. The sight of your body—"

"And the sight of your body inflames me," she told him. "But we both know such a thing is so very dangerous."

"Look at me," he told her.

Meg turned her face from him.

"I told you to look at me. Please?"

She did so, and he looked first into her eyes, then at her mouth, then lower to the level of her breasts. When his gaze returned to her mouth, his lips parted. Slowly, he passed his tongue over his upper lip, and what she felt resembled a blow to her stomach. Her mouth opened. He contrived to spread a hand over one of her breasts and to squeeze gently.

For seconds they looked only at each other, and they swayed back and forth without moving their feet.

"You torture me," he murmured.

"It is you who torture me, Jean-Marc." She stepped deliberately away from him and dropped into a curtsey. "Time to see what the Princess has learned from us," she said in her steadiest voice.

Jean-Marc put one hand behind his back and made a formal bow. She gave him a last, long look and hurried toward the piano, where Sibyl watched her approach with the oddest of expressions.

"Now you will dance with me, Désirée," the Count said.

Princess Désirée said, "I should like that," but there was no doubt that her attention switched rapidly between her brother and Meg. "You two dance beautifully together. It is as if you become one, move as one. And you look ecstatic with the whole affair. I should like to try a little faster piece, please, Sibyl."

Jean-Marc swung his sister into position and swept her away to the sound of Sibyl's beautiful music.

Meg glanced at her sister's tensed features and slid onto the piano bench beside her. "That was fun," she said lightly. "I have danced so little, yet I was completely at home dancing with the Count. What *is* Ash doing? She's fallen asleep, I do believe."

"I have no interest in Ash," Sibyl said. Her voice was strained and very small.

"Meg," Princess Désirée called over her shoulder, "my life is become so interesting. I declare there is the most delicious air of intrigue about everything."

"Concentrate on your dance," Meg told her. In fact, the girl danced beautifully and was obviously what Jean-Marc called a natural. Her posture was straight, and the small amount of paint Meg had started using on the Princess's face gave enough color to make her bright-eyed and pretty.

"Meg," Sibyl said in a suspiciously trembling voice. She leaned over the keys as she played. "Events are becoming disconcerting here. Too much is happening to us. I should like to give all this up and return to our quiet life."

Aghast, Meg wiped her good palm on her skirt. The wound on her other hand stung, but she didn't care. "What can you be thinking?'' she said. "Our routine is different, it's true. But the work we do here will undoubtedly assure us of similar work elsewhere. We should never want for money again. And I have not given up hope that one or the other of us will marry and that *will* be the end of all our troubles.''

"I knew it,'' Sibyl said in broken tones, "you are changed. And you frighten me.''

For some time Meg didn't know what to do. She observed how Sibyl's fingers ran over the keys—and she couldn't help but note that tears fell onto those keys and onto her sister's hands.

"Well,'' Jean-Marc called from the far side of the room. "Our debutante is bound to be a huge success. She dances like an angel. I must leave you now. Miss Smiles, are you sure we can't deal with that matter?''

She turned on the bench and even at a distance saw hope in his eyes. "I'm sure,'' she said. "We still have a good deal to do this afternoon if we are to go shopping in the morning.''

He punched one fist into the opposite palm and seemed about to say more. Instead he nodded and strode from the ballroom. Désirée continued to whirl about all on her own.

"What is it, Sibyl?'' Meg asked her quietly. "What has upset you?''

"Dear Meggie,'' Sibyl replied, "I am so afraid for you. He wants you as I have seen other men want women. You know he could never make you his wife, yet he behaved like that with you. As he did while you danced. He desired to do with you what men and women should only do if they are married.''

"Hush,'' Meg told her. "You are overwrought. I will not deny that the Count shows me more than the expected amount of attention. You have nothing to fear, because I am not a simpleton.''

Sibyl faced her on the bench. "You are not a simpleton. You are a girl of tender but powerful passions. And… Oh, Meg, you have fallen in *love* with him.''

16

An audience, Désirée thought, her half brother had taken to demanding an audience. He was most overbearing. True, she had spent very little time with him prior to their coming to London, but until then she had thought him removed from the behavior he had displayed in the past few weeks.

Meg had refused to sit down, and stood as far from Jean-Marc's desk as possible. In fact, Désirée had to turn in her chair to see her at all, where she stood in a shaded corner wearing her black lace mantilla. "Please, Meg, sit," she asked her. "Jean-Marc is late, I know, and you are irritated, but he will come soon. Do you think you might be more comfortable without your mantilla?" There, she could not be more plain than that.

"I am not irritated," Meg said. But she most certainly was agitated. "I am very comfortable in my mantilla, thank you. I have moved into a phase that requires ever more frequent withdrawal into meditation. This will help me do my very best for you. What can the Count want now? We are barely started on our day and already he is angered by something."

"Angered?" Désirée considered the term an odd choice. "Why should you think him angered? You have not even seen him yet, although you may be right. Did you know La Upworth arrived yesterday? Apparently she came quite early in the day while we were all otherwise occupied. I heard one of the servants talking about her insisting on waiting in Jean-Marc's rooms but not letting him know she was there. No doubt she wished to surprise him, but I don't think Jean-Marc likes surprises, do you?"

"I wouldn't know." And her heaviness of heart at the thought of Lady Upworth being here, and being with Jean-Marc, was more evidence of how dangerous her feelings for him had become. "Forgive me, Your Highness, but I should prefer to be silent now."

Désirée wondered how to approach what had been so evident when her brother danced with Meg. She had already had her suspicions that Jean-Marc had noticed Meg. Now she was certain they were attracted to each other.

"Oh, do come on, Jean-Marc," Désirée cried loudly.

The man came through the door as if in answer to her call. He slammed the door shut and went to his desk without looking at either of his visitors. He said, "Kindly refrain from shouting, Désirée. It is unattractive in a young woman—or in any woman."

"Oh, la," the Princess said, "but not in a young man—or any man?"

"Enough." Jean-Marc's voice thundered. "Look at this—this heap of frivolous nonsense. We did not make sufficient allowance for the high excitement that was bound to sweep London while everyone anticipates King George's Coronation. Even those who rarely come to Town for the Season have made an exception this year. I am assured that it will not do for me to pass these invitations to you, Miss Smiles."

Meg jumped at the sound of her name. He had shown no sign of even noticing her.

"No, don't protest or offer to help me. Keep silent in your corner. Ignore my trials and allow me to suffer when I have other, more critical affairs to conduct."

"No doubt," Princess Désirée said in a supposed whisper that was loud enough for all to hear. "Much more critical affairs. How is Lady Upworth today?"

Jean-Marc scowled at his sister. "How do *you* know of her presence?"

"Someone mentioned her." Her Highness was serene. "And

that she had been hiding in your rooms most of yesterday. To surprise you. Wasn't that a sweet thing to do?"

Meg smiled.

Jean-Marc took a breath and let it out. He relaxed visibly, and also smiled. "My sister is determined to annoy me, you see, Miss Smiles. It is past time for her to become another man's responsibility, one who will either be soft enough not to care if she is a meddlesome witch, or one who will be strong enough to keep her in her place. These—" he lifted a pile of envelopes and let them slip through his fingers and cascade onto the desk "—are invitations for you, witch. It appears that word of your unpleasant nature has not reached the ears of the many, many people who would consider themselves failures if they did not capture Princess Désirée of Mont Nuages for their soirees, and musicales, and routs, and balls, and salons, and so on. No doubt the very thought excites you beyond belief. For myself, I am cast into a desperate place because I shall, at the very least, have to make brief appearances at these events. Miss Smiles will accompany you to all of them and remain there for your support, of course."

Meg was grateful for her black lace. Undoubtedly she was making a name for herself in the household as an eccentric, but so much the better. Others would keep some distance from her, and she would be more serene, and have a way to hide, at least to some degree—and a disguise for what she should have expected. Her hair was fading.

"Peaceful, are we, Miss Smiles?" Jean-Marc asked. "Do warn us if you plan to crumple to the carpet and go into a trance."

She ignored his sarcasm. "You have nothing to fear, My Lord. I should be delighted to deal with the Princess's invitations. I have a great deal of time on my hands at night."

"Do you?"

His look was direct, and she blushed. Meg didn't miss his meaning. "Yes, I do. Of course I shall ensure that your own calendar is kept up to date and I presume Verbeux can inform

me of what would or would not conflict with your appointments.
There is no need for you to concern yourself."

He rocked back in his chair and clasped his hands behind his
head. "I do believe you and Verbeux would enjoy running my
life. An opportunity he has always seemed determined to obtain.
Very well, run my life, Miss Smiles. I shall endeavor to enjoy
the event. Do ensure that I know when I am to be dressed for a
ball, or to ride, or to impress a gaggle of simpering females with
my grasp of their beloved romantic poets. Why, I shall even read
this Mrs. Radcliffe, if necessary. All I ask is that you guide me
well."

Meg left her comforting corner and went to his desk. She bent
to gather what must be a hundred envelopes, all of thick and
creamy paper and elaborately lettered.

Jean-Marc righted his chair, and one of his hands came down
atop hers. "How is the wound?" he murmured. "Is it painful?"

"It is sore," she said, remaining still, her eyes downcast. "But
it is bound to be. However, Verbeux changed the dressing for
me, and the wound appears clean. Sibyl will be able to help me
with it until it is healed."

"Good," he murmured and leaned closer until she felt his
breath through the lace mantilla. "I hope you are thinking about
our discussion. How you do inflame me. You are an original, my
dear. There cannot be another like you. And I will make you
mine. Do not forget that. I have to make you mine."

"Surely Lady Upworth will have something to say about that."

He chuckled softly. "You're jealous? I like that, but Lady Upworth is not an issue here. I choose to be kind to her because—
because I have known her for some time. I believe it will cause
me little effort to allow her to remain here for the Season. And I
shall hope she will meet some suitable man to fill the emptiness
she clearly feels."

Meg said nothing. The thought of Lady Upworth being in this
house throughout the Season cast her very low.

He ducked his head and, with a finger and thumb, raised her

veil until he could see beneath. "She is nothing to me," he whispered. "Only you are of interest to me."

"What are you two whispering about?" Princess Désirée demanded. "What are you plotting? I see no reason why I should not be consulted on which affairs I wish to attend."

"I do," Jean-Marc said. "Your opinion will not be sought. If you like you can help me decide on some events to be held for you. Lady Holland has met Papa on a number of occasions and has graciously offered Holland House for your ball."

Meg stopped breathing at the thought.

"Oh, what a fuss," Princess Désirée said. "It will be so *gaudy.*"

"And you, my dear, will be *so* grateful for the honor. But we have other things to consider first. We already mentioned a musicale, and I suggest that should be the first event. How to make it different, that is my concern. Your invitations will be only for the most glittering and intriguing events, don't you agree, Miss Smiles?"

"I do, indeed." The idea excited her. "Why not a theme for the musicale? Everyone would come in costume. Perhaps an Eastern theme? I've read that some extraordinary costumes are produced for an Eastern theme. People do so love to dress up and pretend, don't they?"

Jean-Marc stared through the mantilla and said, "Apparently. That is a sterling idea, Miss Smiles. Yes, indeed, so shall it be. What do you think, Désirée?"

"If Meg likes it, then so do I," she said shortly.

He still marveled at Désirée's attachment to Meg, and there was no doubt that his sister thought a great deal of her companion. And her companion had already proved herself a brilliant find. "Good. You will inform the seamstresses that we need costumes for the two of you, Miss Smiles?"

"I will take care of that. Of course, making my own will be a simple matter. I shall be glad to advise you, if you would like."

Would he like? "Oh, yes, please Miss Smiles. Yes, I should

like that very much. I hope you have not forgotten that you will go to Bond Street today, to shop for those items you need.''

Bond Street? "I'm sure I need not go there, My Lord. There are other places where I can get what you require for so much less." Of course, if she went to Bond Street she could visit Mme. Suzanne and buy the much needed preparation for her hair.

"My coachman has been instructed to take you to Bond Street," Jean-Marc said. "Send word when you are ready to leave. Do you have any jewelry?"

She hated feeling stripped of her privacy like this. "I have a jet necklace that was our mother's and which Sibyl and I share. And some pearls, and pearl earrings. They are perfectly adequate."

"Very well," he said, rising. "Then we'd best get on."

Rench knocked on the door and entered. "There you are, Miss Meg," he said, his head bent to one side as if pained. "An Adam Chillworth has called. From Number Seven. Will you see him?"

At the sound of Adam Chillworth's name, Meg experienced a longing for familiar faces, and old friends. "I'll see him." She turned to Jean-Marc. "If you don't object, My Lord. And if there is somewhere we can talk."

"Show Mr. Chillworth in," Jean-Marc said, continuing to assemble envelopes. "I think it good form to meet the people who care so about you, Meg. Don't forget to move swiftly on the musicale. Verbeux will have Pierre help him oversee preparations for the ball at Holland House. Again, we will waste no time. I have already sent Lady Holland my most heartfelt thanks."

"Oh, dear." Princess Désirée sighed. "Such a great deal of silliness."

"If you can think of a simpler and equally effective way to meet a man with whom you can make a suitable match, please enlighten me."

"Mr. Chillworth," Rench announced.

Meg went to greet him and was grateful that he made no comment on her mantilla. "Adam," she said. "How lovely to see you. I miss all my friends."

"Aye, lass," he said. "But we're only on the other side o' the square. It's easy enough for ye to come t'us, or t'send word for us t'come t'ye."

"I know," Meg said. "And I feel reassured at the knowledge. How is everyone?" She didn't care if the Count was bored by her prattle. "Hunter and Lady Hester, and Latimer—and the servants?"

"They're well enough," he said, staring through the mantilla. "Missing you, but they know ye'll be back. I've something to tell ye, but Sibyl says I'm t'be careful not to upset ye."

Was it her imagination, or was his accent more pronounced than usual? "I can't think that anything you might say would upset me." She remembered her manners. "Allow me to present Jean-Marc, Count Etranger of Mont Nuages, and his sister, Her Royal Highness, Princess Désirée."

Adam's features became more rigid, but he approached the Count and the Princess and bowed to each of them. "I'm honored to meet ye," he said. "Ye must be nice people because you saw how our Meggie was a gem. You're lucky to have her. She'll do ye proud. The best, that's what Meggie is."

Meg cleared her throat in an effort to distract Adam from his embarrassing endorsement.

He responded at once and looked at her as if for direction.

"I expect you'd like to go somewhere private, Adam," she said.

"I can't imagine why," Jean-Marc said at once. "Surely there isn't something so awful it must be hidden from us."

"No, no," Adam protested at once. "Not at all." He looked beyond Meg to Princess Désirée, and his attention locked there.

"In that case," Jean-Marc said, "pull up a chair and I'll ring for some refreshments.

Adam murmured assent, but without taking his concentration from the Princess. And she returned his gaze. Today she wore a new morning dress, a cloud of pink sarcenet with delicate pleating around the neck and over puffed shoulders. Rows of the same pleated bands adorned the skirt almost to the knees. In the Princess's hair, Meg had wound pink flowers fashioned from the same fabric. She was a delight to behold.

"How are ye enjoying your London Season, Your Royal Highness?" Adam said, surprising Meg with his deference. "I hope ye are not too overcome by so much coming and going. Ye don't look the type to like a lot of fuss, if ye know what I mean."

"Oh, I do," Princess Désirée said, and Meg didn't fail to note how her mistress assessed every inch of handsome Adam. "I'm a quiet person. I do not much like having to rush around so."

Adam grimaced. "I don't blame you. To those of us as likes our homes and a little gentle company, a crowd can be painful."

"Oh, yes." The Princess was emphatic. "What do you do, may I ask?"

Meg saw Jean-Marc shift restlessly.

"I'm a painter, Miss—I mean, Princess. Or that's how I try to make my way. It's difficult for someone unknown who doesn't have any connections."

Protective urges spurred Meg. "Adam is a fine portrait artist. Not that he's ever let me see any of his work. Very secretive he is about that. But a friend of Lady Hester Bingham's—she owns Number Seven—her friend said Adam had painted portraits of the children of another friend and they were breathtaking. That was exactly the word she used, breathtaking."

Adam turned his head away. "Thank ye for that, Meggie, but you're biased, m'dear."

"You deny you're a fine painter?"

"I am a humble man and not given to complimenting myself. I've had my moments."

"I've got to have a portrait painted while in London," Princess Désirée said. "Papa insists. I know I'll have to sit still for hours and I hate it."

"There are ways to ease the discomfort," Adam volunteered.

"Then you shall paint me," Princess Désirée declared.

Meg looked to Jean-Marc, who raised his eyes to the ceiling.

"He can, can't he, Jean-Marc?" the Princess said. "*Please*. I can feel that I should be comfortable with him."

"We will see," her brother said, sounding almost indulgent. "Of course we would have to see examples of Mr. Chillworth's work—and find out if he is interested in such a commission."

"Will you?" Princess Désirée asked. "Show some paintings and agree?"

"Possibly," Adam said, and gave her one of his rare and charming smiles. "If the Count is serious, I'm sure he will contact me officially."

"Quite so," Jean-Marc said, a deal too quickly to make Meg comfortable.

"Meggie, I've come because I think Sibyl needs ye."

She clasped the correspondence to her. "Something's happened to Sibyl? She's due here within the hour."

"I'm sure she intends to come—if she can talk herself free of Mr. William Godly-Smythe, your esteemed cousin."

"William?" Meg said. "I thought he was in Puckly Hinton. That's what Reverend Baggs said."

"Reverend Baggs is another issue. He is to share Latimer More's digs. When he's in Town on church business. Awkward for all concerned, I should think."

Meg didn't pursue that. Later would do. "Why do you think I need to go to Number Seven."

"I don't think, I know." He glanced at the room's other two occupants. "Less said, the better. Your cousin's got some notion that he's responsible for Sibyl and ye. Sibyl excused herself on some pretense and came up to me. She tried Hunter first, but ye know how difficult he is to find at home."

"Yes, yes," Meg said, her agitation mounting. "But what did she say?"

"Pretty simple, really. He's got it all worked out, a way to make it unnecessary for ye to do work he thinks unsuitable for any member of his family. Excuse me,'' he told the Count, who gave a jerky nod. "He's decided to marry Sibyl and take the pair of ye back to Puckly Hinton.''

17

Jean-Marc had actually suggested that he accompany Adam and Meg, but she'd prevailed in convincing him that such a move would only make her already arrogant cousin feel more important. And more threatened. If she and Sibyl were to divert him from his mission with the minimum of effort, then he should be treated with kind gratitude and turned firmly away.

She crossed the square with Adam Chillworth. Would Jean-Marc wait for her response to his proposition, and if she didn't answer, be too proud to approach it again himself? Well, she would never mention it again, and she should hope he didn't, either.

That wasn't what she wished for.

"That Godly-Smythe was roaring when he came through the front door this morning," Adam said. "Frightened Sibyl fiercely. I told him he ought to take a walk and calm down. There was a moment there when I thought the man would try to punch me—but he thought better of it."

Meg looked up, way, way up at Adam's profile. "I'm glad my cousin has at least a little wisdom. No doubt he looked at you and knew he would not be the victor in any skirmish." They drew close to Number 7, and she sighed. "He has no power over us, yet he persists in dwelling on the fact that he is our closest relation, and a male, and that he feels a responsibility for us. He did not feel it when Sibyl and I had to leave Puckly Hinton because we were no longer made to feel welcome in our own home. I will never understand the rules of men, especially those who insist on such things as not passing property to female descendants. Because of that, we have been in a pretty pickle, Adam, but we could never be in so much of a pickle as to submit to becoming William Godly-Smythe's charity cases.''

"No, ye couldn't," he said vehemently.

"He's all but ignored us since we left Puckly Hinton. I don't understand why he is so changed now."

Adam glanced at her. "It's not my business, but I'd be very careful with that one if I were ye. On another subject. Forgive me for asking, but why did ye change your hair?"

She giggled at his reticence. "I can't explain it to you. It would be too embarrassing."

"Embarrassing?" He raised a single eyebrow. "Now ye have my entire attention, but I shall try to be patient. I hope ye will tell me eventually."

Meg considered, and gritted her teeth. Could she ask such a thing of a man, of Adam? "Well...will you consider a bargain?" She stopped until he did, also, and faced her. "If I promise that one day I will tell you what my plan has been, will you go to Bond Street for me? I would tell you exactly how to find the establishment I need, and give you a note to take to the proprietress."

"What sort of shop?"

"Well, I suppose I could call it an apothecary's of sorts, although not exactly. Perhaps—no, an establishment where one buys potions of a certain kind."

Adam looked blank.

"I'm sorry I asked. I shouldn't have."

"Give me the note," he said. "Whatever the place is, I'm sure I shall manage to find it and to bring back what ye need."

Meg let out a long breath. "Oh, thank you. Could you go today?"

There was laughter in his eyes, but he said, "For ye, I can."

She touched his cheek, but withdrew her hand at once. "Thank you. I shall get the note to you. Thank you, Adam."

"You've already thanked me—several times."

"If you could put it in our flat that would be perfect. There's a spare key on Old Coot's board."

"Don't worry about it."

They continued, only to pause once more and let a horse with a cart filled with coal pass.

"Look at the daffodils," he said, pointing to the park. "Now they've courage. It's been a cold winter and there's not much sun even now, but it's their time and there they are. No responsibility but to lift our spirits."

"And they do," Meg said. She looked up at Adam again. He was trying to divert her. She was tempted to share some of what was happening to her—not the intimate details, of course, but her feelings and fears. Adam had been a close ally since she'd arrived in London, and they'd had many a long talk by firelight. He was a complex and proud man. There had been a time when she'd wished he felt more for her than friendship, but she'd eventually been forced to abandon all such thoughts. Adam was wedded to his work.

They climbed the steps at Number 7, and Adam used his key to open the door. Once inside, they both glanced upward and Adam said, "I'll come and be with ye, if you like."

"If I didn't know you would faint, I should kiss you for that offer," Meg said. She smiled at him, and it felt good. "Thank you, but no. I am not afraid of my second cousin—just tired of him, although I should be kind and believe he is truly concerned for us." She took a pen and paper from her reticule and bent over a table in the vestibule to write the note for Adam.

He surprised her by stroking her cheek and smiling. "There is no one like ye, Meggie. No one more kind, more generous." He removed his hand and waved her ahead of him up the stairs. "Don't you forget that you and Sibyl are important to me. You're important to everyone in this house. If ye need help—of any kind—ye come to me. You understand?"

Meg trudged upward and said, "I understand. And I'm grateful. Should you like to paint the Princess, Adam?"

He paused, and when she looked back at him, his eyes were thoughtful. "Aye, perhaps I would. Interesting face." He snorted. "And it wouldn't be the first time I painted someone who…"

"Someone who?"

"Never mind that," he said. "If there's a chance I might get the commission, then, yes, I want it. Good day to ye, Meggie. Don't forget I'm here for ye."

For a moment or two longer, while Adam's imposing figure carried on up the next flight of stairs, Meg puzzled over what he might have meant. It was time to rescue Sibyl.

The scene in the parlor at 7A was even more disheartening than Meg had expected. Cousin William stood before the small fire in the grate, his hands beneath the tails of his coat, his muscular legs planted apart—and with a dark frown on his face. Sibyl also stood, but on the opposite side of the room and already wearing the heavy black pelisse she donned for walking because she felt the cold so deeply.

"Good afternoon," Meg said to William. She smiled widely at Sibyl and told her, "There is to be a musicale for Princess Désirée. It will be such fun. I think we are decided on an Eastern theme—since it was suggested we stage a costume event. But we can discuss all that later. I shall expect you to guide me."

"Meg," William said in his most ominous tone. "I must insist that you give me your entire attention. You and Sibyl. She has certainly refused to do so as yet, despite the sincerity with which I have come to her—and to you."

She would not, she decided, attempt any pretense with him. "I already understand you came to make a proposition to Sibyl, and to myself. I know the general nature of your suggestion, and I am flattered. I'm sure Sibyl is also flattered. And you must be disappointed that your wishes do not coincide with our wishes."

William's neck puffed up above his collar, and his face became a shiny puce. "What has happened to you, Meg Smiles?" he said. "You may always have been a rather...*definite* girl, but you were never so unpleasantly forceful. Forcefulness is not at all the thing in a female."

At his disparaging tone, Meg lowered her eyes.

"Yes, well," William said, sounding regretful, "you have been alone in a city that is no place for any gentle countrywoman. I say you, more than Sibyl, have been alone because it was inevitable that since you have the stronger will, it fell to you to take the lead and protect her. If it is possible for a girl to protect anyone in so unsuitable a city."

"We have looked after each other," Sibyl said in a small voice. She moved closer to Meg. "Haven't we?"

Meg held her sister's hand and said, "Of course we have. We're the only family we have. In Mama and Papa's memory we are bound to be upright, and to support one another."

William leaned on the mantel and looked at the fire. He had become thoughtful. "How is your hand, Meg?"

Immediately she put her injured hand behind her back.

"Reverend Baggs learned the details from a member of the Count's household. Then he had the good sense to send a rider to me with the news. And I left at once to come here. I traveled all night—at great peril, I may say."

"The wound is little more than a scratch." The occasional lie could be necessary. "You should not have taken such a risk."

He stood straight. Even if she did not like him, Meg had to admit to herself that the man had poise. "I would not have considered doing other than take the risk," he said. "There comes a time when a man must face his demons and consider his life. I have done so and I am not glad at what I've seen. For you and Sibyl to be turned out of your home for me was wrong. Oh, it was the law and carried out accordingly, but I should not have rested until I had persuaded you to remain."

Sibyl's fingers tightened on Meg's, and she knew her soft-hearted sister wanted to comfort William. Meg gave a sharp little twist on Sibyl's hand, a warning to remain silent.

Suddenly and brilliantly, William smiled. "But that is all behind us now. I have seen the error of my ways and am determined to put things to rights. Sibyl was not comfortable speaking in your absence, Meg, but she will be happy to do so now. I have asked her to be my wife, and for the two of you to return to Puckly Hinton with me. There." His smile grew even wider. "How could I have wasted so much time in bringing this news to you? I confess that I have known for some time that this was my heart's desire. Sibyl isn't strong, Meg, so you shall keep house and I know that will make you happy. You are not a girl who enjoys time on her hands. And the two of you will be such a success in the neighborhood. It will, of course, fall to you to forge bonds with all the other ladies of importance. You are both educated—quite possibly too much so, but your father had some unusual ideas—you are educated and will become sought-after hostesses. Yes, you will make me a proud man."

Neither Sibyl nor Meg spoke. Sibyl held Meg's hand even tighter.

"I have stolen your breath away—and your words." William laughed and rocked from his heels to his toes, clearly delighted with himself. "I understand completely. You are overwhelmed. Your lives will change so dramatically and you never hoped for such a magnificent chance."

"William—"

"No." He held up a hand and shook his head. "No, do not thank me. I shall only be embarrassed. But I will most definitely bask in the reflected joy you feel. Oh, my delight is so intense as to be overwhelming. I feel cleansed, and relieved. We are to forge a family." He lowered his eyelids a fraction to send Sibyl an intimate glance. "Perhaps I speak too soon on such a subject, but I cannot help myself. The thought of the children we shall have, of their growing up with loving parents such as we will be, touches my heart."

Meg turned to Sibyl, she had to, and looked for her honest reaction. Sibyl's brow was puckered, and she had drawn her upper lip away from her teeth. She shook, and her fingers were damp in Meg's. "Am I to speak for you?" Meg asked quietly, and Sibyl whispered yes, then shook her head slowly.

"Thank you for your kind offer," Meg said to William. "We appreciate your concern for us, but there is no need. We are now gainfully employed and expect to remain so."

"I have caught you both by surprise," William said. "Sit down, my dears, sit down and collect yourselves. This is not a dream. I shall not be stolen from you. It will come true. You must have wondered why one such as I had not married long before now. Well, I have certainly been sought after by many, but I could not give myself to one of them. Now I realize why. It was you, Sibyl, on whom I was to bestow the prize of my undying affection."

Sibyl released Meg's hand and walked directly to stand before William. "You are not listening," she said, amazing Meg. "I do not wish to marry you. I thank you for the generous offer, but cannot accept it."

Meg came close to applauding.

William managed to capture Sibyl's fingers and take them to his lips. He closed his eyes and settled his mouth there.

Poor Sibyl's back looked stiff. Meg said, "William—"

"No," Sibyl interrupted. "Don't worry, Meggie, this is for me to deal with. William, thank you for your flattering proposal, but I cannot accept."

"You *must* accept," he said, slowly raising his head. "I insist that you do."

"It would be better if you left at once," Sibyl told him.

"Why? What has happened to you? You are a girl who knows her place. You have never questioned the rightful order of things. It is your *duty* to accept me."

This stunning announcement rang in Meg's ears. He believed, actually believed what he said.

William's voice climbed. "You *will* come home with me. Both of you. This very day. Do you understand?"

"Sibyl," Meg said, "we really do have to return to Number Seventeen. I have to go to Bond Street and the Princess is expecting you."

"The *Princess*," William said, curling his lip. "How they must laugh at you for thinking yourselves suitable to wait upon a princess. You are country girls, both of you. I cannot imagine what these people are thinking of, retaining such unsuitable help. Or perhaps I can imagine, but I'd rather not do so."

Meg made herself meet his gaze directly. "We must go, cousin. Allow us to walk you out."

"What is being done about the shaving blade?" Now William blustered. "Has every member of the household been interrogated? Do you truly believe I could return home knowing that you are in mortal danger? There is absolutely no need for you to work like common women of no means."

"We are women of very little means," Meg reminded him. She was tempted to speak of their dwindling trust funds but pride prevented her. "There is no shame in making one's way honestly."

William's deep breath expanded his broad chest. "You bring dishonor on the family. Not one of your predecessors has ever sunk so low as to go into service."

To argue with him would be pointless. "It has never been our intention to embarrass you, William," Meg said. Why shouldn't she mention why drastic measures had been necessary? "We were informed that if our trusts were to last for at least some years, then the amounts we received must be lowered at once, and they have been. Our need has been to supplement that income. Even with Sibyl's music lessons and my sewing, we were falling deeper into distressing circumstances. We are not women who simply fade away at such times. We act. We *have* acted, and we are enjoying the knowledge that we can take our fate into our own hands."

William trembled, and Meg did not imagine it was with thwarted passion. The man was beside himself and amazed that the objects of his proposed generosity had not thrown themselves upon him and cried out their gratitude.

A tap on the door and Meg's "come in" produced Old Coot, who surveyed the room with his bulbous, hooded eyes, nodded, and said, "You are receiving, then?"

Verbeux stepped around the butler and brought his elegant and confident presence into the parlor.

"I say," William sputtered. "Get out, I say. Get out at once. This is a family discussion."

Verbeux looked to Meg. "Count Etranger sent me, Miss Smiles."

"Did you hear me?" William asked. "We are dealing with serious topics here. And Etranger be damned."

Meg and Sibyl gasped in unison.

Verbeux actually smiled. He showed no sign of retreat.

"Off with you, I say," William demanded. "Before I call a constable and have you thrown out."

"One might ask on what grounds," Verbeux said mildly. "I am to drop you at Number Seventeen, Miss Sibyl. Ash is there. Seems you must help make decisions. For the musicale. Short notice. Invitations to be hand-delivered."

"Oh, of course," Sibyl said, and only a blind person would fail to see her relief at the diversion. "I'll come at once."

"You will not leave until I tell you you may," William said.

Verbeux turned to Meg. "I am to carry on to Bond Street with you. Urgent. So the Count says. Should leave now. Appointments."

Meg understood the general gist, if not all that Verbeux said in his peculiar verbal shorthand. She smiled warmly at William and said, "Please don't doubt that Sibyl and I are deeply touched by your concern. And of course we shall never forget your kindness. Why, I even feel I would like to return to Puckly Hinton for a holiday soon. I thank you for that, William. You make me feel welcome."

"I...I..."

"Yes, indeed," Sibyl said. "A holiday in dear Puckly Hinton would be most pleasant. Perhaps late in the summer?"

William, all expression wiped from his features, marched to the door and threw it open. "Your silly heads are turned by all this folderol. Sooner or later you will regain at least some of your natural common sense. In the meantime I shall forgive you your foolishness and continue to watch over you. You have only to say the word and I shall be at your sides. And you *will* say the word. Take note of that. You have been drawn into a most unsavory situation. I feel it here—" he pounded his breast "—that you are not safe with these people, who cannot have honorable intentions toward you."

"We must leave," Verbeux said, and both Sibyl and Meg picked up their reticules.

William paused on the threshold to say, "You may tell your master—" and he pointed to Verbeux "—that if something happens to my cousin while she is in his employ, I shall hold him responsible. After all, she was in his house when someone placed a shaving blade where it was bound to injure her. Or might that be, where they hoped it might *kill* her?"

18

*S*pivey here.

Oh, it's no good. After all, I'm only human. I mean, I'm only a simple ghost…no, not simple at all. I am a highly complex ghost and I have suffered enough. You'll have to excuse me while I confront and accept my true feelings.

Aargh.

No, no, no, I cannot bear it. I cannot. I have bitten my knuckles until they bleed…well, would bleed if…if. Oh, hell's teeth and drat and dash it all.

Aargh.

How I long for the ability to stamp my feet and pound a door. Oh, for the satisfaction of giving a few servants their marching orders and watching them beg and blubber. What bliss it would be to kick a peg leg from beneath its owner, or to offer a match girl a shilling, only to snatch it away the instant her fingers touched it.

I want to feel satisfaction, triumph.

I deserve to have my way, and quickly.

I will have my way and the devil take… Slip of the tongue. I will have my way and the devil will be glad.

There—at least I am collected again. Exhausted, frustrated, robbed of the perfect solution because I—because someone wasn't aware of certain convenient possibilities—but collected.

William Godly-Smythe wants to marry Sibyl and take both of those foolish Smiles creatures away—at the same time—forever.

It would have been such a delicious event. There would have been not the slightest fear that one or the other of them would remain.

But Meg Smiles has encountered l'amore, she has tasted—passion. She fancies herself in love. And unless I can divert what seems inevitable, I have no doubt we shall soon be witnessing... Ahem. Forget what I started to say. It was nothing. Certainly I shall not be responsible for sullying your eyes or ears with such abominable exhibitions of...abominable exhibitions. Trust me. I will save your tender sensibilities.

Why didn't I know about William Godly-Smythe before I embarked on another, much more difficult course?

Well, I didn't and that's that. But now I am the more determined to bring my plan to its essential conclusion. Speed, that is the word. Speed, my friends. I shall do all in my power to plant seeds that convince our friends to turn their beloved Season into a whirl, the better to throw my willing lovebirds together as often as possible. A note here, a message there, a suggestion, perhaps.

You know, I begin to wonder if Etranger might be a less unfeeling man than I had thought. The idea makes me shudder, but it could be that he even has a dash of the—dare I say it?— Romantic. The word turns me cold. But it could help me, couldn't it? I shall definitely see if there's something I can exploit there.

Ahoy there, Mr. Marlow. Didn't see him coming at first. Fellow flies like a turtle, heavy in the middle and all flippers flipping. I'm well, thank you, Sir. Helped anyone write a good play lately? Ah, not deliberately, hmm? No, I haven't seen Mr. Shakespeare recently. No, I certainly won't tell him you're looking for him if you don't want me to.

Good afternoon to you, too, Sir. Oops, watch for tall trees, hmm? Ha, ha, yes, indeed, that was a close one, Sir. Goodbye.

There he goes. Over the rooftops and far away. Very far away from me I hope. Brawling Christopher, we call him. But I'm glad he was a better writer than he is a flyer.

Bear with me. I shall report further progress.

Aargh.

19

Meg pressed herself into dark green squabs at her back and peered through the windows of Count Etranger's carriage. If she'd considered the events ahead for Désirée, she would have expected to travel often in carriages such as this. But she hadn't really considered a great many things well enough.

Little Meg Smiles of Puckly Hinton riding to Bond Street in a most beautiful green carriage, a carriage that glistened in the afternoon sun. And beyond the windows a milling crowd of people about their business or pleasure, their faces animated, their hands keeping pace with their chatter.

Verbeux had handed her into the carriage and seated himself beside the coachman. Meg was grateful he had not joined her inside, for she was not comfortable with him.

Bond Street reached, the carriage bowled smartly past elegant shops, where both rich and poor pointed into windows filled with beautiful wares. When she felt the wheels slowing, Meg grew anxious. She had never been fond of surprises, and whatever was about to happen would undoubtedly be a surprise. Which shop was she supposed to enter? If she were choosing a place to buy slippers, it would not be on this street. Why, other than on her clandestine visit to Mme. Suzanne's, she had not bought a single item here, could not afford to buy a single item.

They stopped.

She dared not look from the carriage windows now.

The door opened, and the coachman put down the steps. The sound of excited voices burst upon Meg, and she squinted against the sun to see what caused such hubbub. Verbeux reached in to offer her his hand and said, "If you please." He assisted her to the flagway, where a whispering press leaned and craned their necks.

Meg checked behind her, glanced at the royal coat of arms on the door of the coach and back at the curious onlookers. "What are they saying?" she asked Verbeux. "Who do they hope to see?"

He laughed shortly. "You. They want to see you and discover who is so important. The proprietor and his staff await you, see? Mr. Birk is never present except to welcome very important customers."

"Then they must all be disappointed," Meg whispered and started toward the man she supposed to be Mr. Birk, two other men and a tiny woman. They all beamed. And they bowed or curtseyed. "How can they look at me and think me important? What foolishness is this?" Foolishness that caused her heart to beat hard and her skin to roast.

The bystanders edged closer, narrowing the path to the shop. "'E's a prince," Meg heard a woman say. "She must be a princess, then."

"They see what they want to see," Verbeux told her. "Do not speak."

"But they mistake me for what I'm not."

"Be flattered. And be quiet. *Bonjour,* M. Birk."

"Good day to you, My Lord. A very good day to you. I'm sure you will be pleased with our progress."

Verbeux did not correct the shopkeeper's salutation. In fact, Verbeux made no comment at all. He followed Meg into a small jewel of an establishment and guided her to sit in one of a pair of blue brocaded fauteuils Mr. Birk rushed to point out. Promptly the door was closed and locked—and faces pressed the glass.

Mr. Birk, a man of indeterminate years despite a head of thick gray hair, waved his assistants into action. The small woman brought two glasses of lemonade on a silver tray. Verbeux gave one to Meg and took the other himself.

"My instructions," Mr. Birk said, glancing at a sheet of paper he held, "are to provide slippers in every current popular shade. One of the lady's slippers was sent as a pattern, and we have several finished pairs for you to try. Once we are certain to fit your feet to perfection, my shoemakers will work day and night to complete everything you need. Boots will also be made in many colors, and we have assembled a veritable feast of lovely decorative confections for your pleasure."

"Drink," Verbeux said, causing Meg to jump.

"Yes." She did so, but not before several drops tipped on the carpet. She had been staring, amazed, at the shop proprietor. "Surely this isn't intended—"

"It is. It is lemonade. Very good." Verbeux's spectacles definitely made his dark eyes the more compelling. "Please proceed, Mr. Birk."

Much scurrying ensued. Slippers of the finest kid were placed upon Meg's feet, and buckles and bows tried—and her face watched for reactions. Finally everyone seemed very satisfied, everyone but Meg, whose temper had slowly risen. She placed her glass on the tray and said, "Exactly how many shades are popular this year, Mr. Birk?"

He pursed his lips thoughtfully. "Approximately ten are considered all the kick. Perhaps another ten to fifteen are basic essentials."

"Absolutely not," Meg said, rising.

"Absolutely," Verbeux countered, but with a smile on his face. "Thank you, sir. I am instructed to tell you that the silver slippers must be ready and delivered to Mayfair Square within three days."

"They will be," Mr. Birk said. "So will a goodly number of others."

"Three days?" Meg frowned while she pulled on her gloves,

cautious of the painful wound that at least showed signs of healing.

"In time for the musicale. The Count has decided to move quickly. Create a stir. First great event of the Season."

"But the costumes?"

"More seamstresses," Verbeux said.

"The Princess—"

"Will be ready," he finished for her. "You will make sure."

Her head spun. Costumes to be created, the Princess at least taught how to smile, whether or not she wanted to smile. Perhaps Verbeux's methods should be employed and Her Royal Highness instructed to *keep quiet,* unless she would promise to be polite and animated. So much to do, and although she had known their preparations must eventually be put to the test, she didn't feel ready.

"Come," Verbeux said, and she saw how he frowned a little, and how there seemed to be a reflection of her own anxiety in his expression. He escorted her from the shop, and to Meg's horror, she noticed even more idle watchers had assembled. Some crowded around the coach and horses.

"I will not have any part in such theatrics as this," Meg whispered. "And I will be much obliged if you go back to Mr. Birk and tell him there has been a mistake. We don't want the shoes."

"You already accepted them."

Meg stopped, and he was forced to stop also. "I don't need or want however many pairs are ordered. I cannot afford them."

"Hush," Verbeux said with a smile on his lips and a warning flatness in his eyes. "Be silent. They are paid for. And not by you."

"Is that supposed to lighten my heart?"

"The Count is a man with a great many responsibilities. You are to help him with the Princess—by accompanying her. You need appropriate clothes."

"I have clothes that will do well enough."

He sighed hugely and said, "You are unsophisticated. You will be guided. Consider your master. That is your job. To do whatever he requests. There is no more to say on the subject.''

"What is wrong with the Count that he should need so much consideration?''

"Impertinence,'' Verbeux said. "You are causing a stir.''

"I have already caused a stir, wouldn't you say, sir? I will continue this with the Count. He is a reasonable man. He understands the importance of a person's pride.''

She carried on to the coach, pretending not to hear a shout. "You let 'im 'ave it, missus. We knows 'ow men are, don't we? But 'e'll let you 'ave it later.'' Coarse female laughter followed.

Once more Verbeux closed her inside the coach and climbed up to sit on the box. Meg heard the coachman shout and knew he was warning people to clear a way for the horses and carriage.

As relieved as she was exhausted, she closed her eyes. Only her need for money would make her remain in her position. Wouldn't it? She was confounded by her own head—and heart.

She opened her eyes. The thought of speaking to Jean-Marc pleased her. She relished having a reason to seek him out. The carriage jerked forward and hoofbeats joined the din outside. Two possibilities lay ahead for Meg. She might accept Jean-Marc's invitation to become his mistress, and consign herself to a life of shame punctuated by moments of bliss, or she could refuse, retain her pride and be content never to see him again. *Content?*

The lump in her throat was no stranger. Of late she had cried too much.

Shrill screams jarred Meg. Screams, then shouts, and the sight of people in the street falling back, their eyes and mouths stretched open.

A different scream came to her, and she clutched the edge of the seat. The sound of horses snorting and whinnying, their terrified cries high, all but deadening the confused babble of the crowd.

The carriage shook, jerked forward. Outside, the faces swung at horrible angles, tipped like a bubbling pink concoction in a great glass. There would be a terrible accident, she was sure.

Meg prayed. She swallowed against sickness and prayed for stillness and silence. With every thud and jolt, her body felt bruised. Her own cries were obliterated.

She would die here, crushed inside this beautiful carriage that was about to be ruined.

More grinding sounds assailed her. Verbeux's voice rang out. "Hold them, fool." Meg knew he spoke to the coachman, exhorted him to control the cattle, who were clearly beyond panic and pulling this way and that in their struggle to be free.

The mighty jangling of tack went on and on.

The carriage swayed perilously, its top tilted toward the road, and Meg slid along the seat, unable to gain purchase. Her shoulder thudded into the polished wood that surrounded the window. She tried, without success, to quell her tears. Inch by inch the carriage tipped until she was certain only two wheels touched the ground.

Faces spun now. Stranger and stranger angles. She fastened her eyes on first one, then another onlooker. Her body twisted sideways, and the door handle thrust into her stomach. Winded, she gasped for breath and settled a fist on the window. Mothers and fathers, brothers and sisters held young babies and young children high, the better for them to view disaster.

One face, and then another, and another made vague impressions on Meg. A comely mother, a bright scarf over her head, cradling a chubby infant and laughing. Several young fops in the height of fashion, twirling their canes and lifting their lips in disdain. A serious, thin face in profile as if the man tried to appear above it all. Nevertheless he stole stares in Meg's direction.

She heard the vicious crack of the coachman's whip, and another. The carriage careened in the opposite direction, and Meg was thrust along the seat to the other side—in time to witness the extraordinary spectacle of Verbeux being thrown from the box, turning a complete backward somersault and disappearing in the throng.

Meg's opposite shoulder ached cruelly.

Again a veritable froth of all but indistinguishable faces flowed hither and thither. Meg thought she saw one that was familiar, but as quickly as she noted it, the face ceased to be there. Once more the maddened horses made a crazed lunge, and people fled, their arms outstretched.

Neighing and snorting escaped the horses in gusts, and froth from their mouths whipped backward against the windows.

Without warning, the coach shuddered almost to a halt and shot backward, grinding Meg's head into the squabs. Another pause and the vehicle surged forward once more—and Meg's head slammed forward, her chin to her chest. Pain shot up her neck and through her temples.

She screamed and fought to pull air through her mouth. Her bonnet slid sideways. She could no longer hang on. From side to side the coach wove. Meg grabbed for some handhold—with her one good hand. Useless. One more swing and she was tossed to the floor.

"Jean-Marc," she cried, and pressed a fist to her mouth. Again and again the unexpected motions of the coach sent her sliding and bumping about the floor. The soft seats were little kinder to her body than the hard floor, and she felt light-headed. Light-headed and like a woman who had been severely beaten. Each time she forgot her wound and tried to use both hands, she cried at the pain.

With no warning, the carriage took off at a great pace. Meg thudded backward, then managed to curl into a ball.

A great bellow, part animal, part man, eclipsed the babble, and the coach ground to a halt. Gasping, Meg scrambled up, thinking to leap for safety. A man with his arms curled over his head, his hat obscuring most of his face, appeared to moan and rock. Another, sharper angle, and it was a thin woman's face she fixed upon. Her arms were crossed, and she looked away, dispassionate. The carriage was tipping sideways ever more steeply. Meg looked toward the uppermost side, the side gradually rising, showing the top stories of buildings and a strip of bright blue sky.

As abruptly as they had stopped, the horses fled again, and the carriage thumped down squarely on all four wheels.

Meg's scream lodged in her throat. She could see the horses. They galloped directly toward shop windows, and clattered onto the flagway. Their flesh would be torn. People would be badly hurt by the broken glass.

Her scream ripped free, and at the same moment a man leaped between the carriage and the windows. He launched himself at the animals and managed to mount the back of one. He wrestled, and the horses veered from Meg's sight again.

Jean-Marc. Count Etranger was that man who was, as Meg prayed for him, on the back of a horse turned wild. *No, you can't die like this.* If he did, it would be for her, and she might live. She could not bear to think of being alive while he was dead.

Following the passage of the team, the carriage mounted the flagway. She felt when the horses were back on the roadway, and hope overwhelmed her. Once more the carriage followed and began to slow down. All would be saved. Jean-Marc would be spared, and so would Meg.

The right wheels bumped from flagway to road.

Almost slowly, the left wheels skipped from the ground and balance was lost. "Jean-Marc!" He couldn't hear her. No one could hear her. With the inevitability of a falling object too heavy to be stopped, the coach made a mad, sluggish arc before it crashed to its side. The windows smashed seconds before Meg's last grasp failed and she landed on her back against the door, against hard cobbles that filled the spaces where the glass had been.

Dust filled her nostrils, but what did it matter? The world became gray, a gray film that dimmed her eyes. And she coughed. Silence blessed her ears, and she rested there.

"Mon Dieu!" a familiar voice roared. "Get back. Get away. You do not help, so go. *Go!"*

He was there, close. Meg blinked. Sunlight shone directly through the windows that faced the sky. How very odd to lie on one's back in Bond Street and stare at a sun-bright sky through windows above your face.

"Damn it to hell, I will kill the next man to get in my way. Verbeux, hold the team. But do *not* touch them. You understand me?"

"As you say." Verbeux sounded quite unlike himself. "Thomas, assist me, please."

Thomas, Meg thought serenely, was the coachman. So, they were both safe, too.

Thuds on the uppermost side of the coach soon brought the Count's head and shoulders into view. He wrestled with the door, wrenched on the handle and threw the door back against the vehicle's side. Over his shoulder he barked, "Make no attempt to right this thing until I'm sure it's safe to do so."

He peered down at her. "Meg. Speak to me."

"What would you like me to say?"

"That will do nicely. How are you, how do you feel?"

"Where do I hurt? I am thrown about in here like an abandoned doll, and you ask how I am? Very well, thank you."

Jean-Marc sat carefully on the rim of the door and lowered his feet inside. He would hope that her saucy chatter meant she wasn't seriously hurt. "Please remain still. I must reach you without making your situation worse."

"Worse?" She giggled. "How could it be worse, My Lord? Look at me."

He did look at her. The dark green gown and pelisse she wore were covered with dust and ripped in numerous places. Her bonnet was nowhere to be seen, and her hair could well have been home to birds. "Dear Meg," he said. But despite her sad appearance and pallor, he thought her irresistible. "I shall get you to safety and make sure you are cared for with the greatest gentleness.'' He would take her home—to his home—and see her put to bed and attended by his own physician.

Her eyelids lowered, and he knew a bound of fear. ''Meg,'' he said urgently. ''Please don't go to sleep, not until a doctor has seen you.''

''I can't afford doctors,'' she said sharply. ''What are you thinking of? Always pushing me into inappropriate situations even when I have told you not to.''

She had probably hit her head.

''Hush,'' he told her. ''We'll soon have you out of here. Verbeux, can you hear me?''

''Yes, My Lord.''

''Procure a blanket at once.''

''Mr. Birk of Birk's Shoes here, My Lord,'' a man called out. ''We have blankets. Should I throw them to you?''

''At once, sir,'' Jean-Marc responded without looking at the shopkeeper.

''Blankets?'' Meg tittered. ''Am I to sleep here? Will the doctor climb in as you are?''

''You are hysterical,'' Jean-Marc told her. He was too anxious to control his own tongue, damn it. ''I want to cover and keep you warm on the way to another conveyance.''

Blankets landed beside him. Jean-Marc selected two large ones and let himself slide inside the sadly damaged interior of his coach. With great care he maneuvered himself to stand beside Meg and used one blanket to make a thick cushion to kneel on.

She tried to turn her face away, but he gently spread his fingers over her cheek and urged her to look up at him. ''My poor girl,'' he said. ''What can be afoot that such viciousness should touch you?''

''An accident,'' she whispered. ''The horses were frightened and they ran away.''

"No," he told her, leaning to look closely into her eyes. "Not an accident, as you will discover. Can you see me clearly?"

She actually smiled! "You find the question humorous?" he asked.

"No." Her voice was so soft it stroked him, and he quickened. "I am a little befuddled, My Lord, and since you are so near to me and I see you so well, the question seemed reason to smile. I like looking at you." Her eyes drifted shut again.

Jean-Marc couldn't take his gaze from her. What madness. A man who had left all of a young man's romantic notions behind him—if he had ever known them at all. A man whom other men knew as a cynic, whom they expected to turn his back on any hint of weakness, of vulnerability.

She said she liked to look at him because she had probably hit her head and was not quite herself.

He shook out the other blanket, put a hand behind her neck and raised her gently until her face was pressed to his shoulder.

Meg murmured and sat straight. She smiled up at him.

"Meg, what is between us will not be easy to forget—if you insist that it must be forgotten."

Her eyes narrowed a little, and she pressed her lips together. He had met a woman he could care for deeply, and who had a very good mind that would never make his way easy—if he were to have any way with her. "Do you insist, Meg?"

"Your Lordship?" Verbeux shouted. "I need to speak with you."

"Soon," Jean-Marc called back. To Meg he said, "Do you insist that we must pretend to feel nothing? Will you try to force me to forget you? I never will, you know."

"Life is cruel," she said, and there was no smile now. "It hands us impossible choices. I am supposed to take whatever I can have of you, or have nothing at all. Of course, I don't want to force you to forget me. I will never forget you, either."

"My Lord!" Verbeux cried. "There has been foul play here."

"I know," Jean-Marc told Verbeux loudly and shortly. "I told you not to touch the horses—other than to calm them. Do you understand me?"

After a slight pause, Verbeux said, "I understand perfectly. Is Miss Smiles injured?"

"She is catching her breath. She will be well." Very well. He slipped the blanket around her, swathed her and gathered her in his arms. "I cannot change what is, Meg. You deserve to understand exactly what my position is. Then you will understand why we must learn to snatch what we can."

Because she was not good enough for him, Meg thought, not good enough to be more than the mistress of Count Etranger, a prince's son. With his hair swept and tangled by the wind and his neck cloth loose and with dust on his clothes, Jean-Marc only appeared more handsome, more enigmatic, except for the intensity in his eyes when he looked at her.

"I must get you out of here now," he told her. "I will have the coach held fast and then hand you out to Verbeux. That will provide the least chance of doing you further damage."

"I am shaken, not damaged."

She watched carefully enough to unnerve him, watched his mouth when he spoke, his eyes when he fell silent. Her study of him stoked the steady rise of his passion. "Very well, Meg. Let's get you out."

Another smile tipped up the corners of her mouth.

"I humor you again?" he asked.

"Mmm. I am gathering little memories to carry with me. So many little memories."

He was but a man, and an aroused man. Jean-Marc kissed Meg Smiles, planning to take his advantage of her surprise in only a small way. But her soft lips parted, and her eyes closed. He kissed her with a power that made him tremble and felt her arms steal around him beneath his coat. Meg's sighs mingled with his low groan.

Meg gave herself up to his kiss. They had both been through a fearsome time, and it felt so right to reach for his warmth and strength. For him there must be some of the same need—to assert again his life and manliness.

He stole her breath. And he stole her heart—again. The one thing she wanted most to tell him, yet must never speak aloud, was that she had fallen in love with him. Others would laugh at such an idea. She was in his employ, a woman of a most ordinary station, while he was royalty. The scoffers would remind her that she was a joke, an example of how foolish women could so easily be bent to an important man's will.

There would never be another her equal. Jean-Marc knelt over her, held her to him, crossed his arms around her and allowed the mixture of lust and tenderness he felt flow from him. She would never know she had been the only woman to touch him, to touch Jean-Marc, the skeptic. Their desperate kiss delved at his gut. Sweet pain. Need. Longing. He would have her if he could, keep her if he could, but although there would be parts of his life he would want to share with her, he might never be able to take her completely into his confidence.

They broke from each other, their mouths parting with mutual reluctance.

"They will wonder why we take so long," she said, passing her tongue over kiss-swollen lips.

"So they will." He grinned at her. "But you do know that I must have many kisses from you, Meg Smiles. Don't you?"

And what the Count thought he must have, he would undoubtedly try to take. Meg put three fingers on his mouth. She frowned at him. "I know what would please you, I think. And I know what would please me. But I don't know what the future holds for us."

Jean-Marc stood and lifted her into his arms. "Have men hold the coach steady, Verbeux," he ordered. "Then ready yourself to take Miss Smiles from me. With great care."

They looked into each other's eyes. "With the greatest of care," Jean-Marc said quietly, for Meg's ears only. "Because she is of the greatest value to me. I have never loved anyone, Meg. I don't know how such emotion would feel. But what I become when I am with you is a different thing than I have ever been. A good thing, perhaps, although it leaves me desperate."

"Desperate? I cause you great discomfort?"

"You cause me bliss, and when we must leave each other, my bliss goes with you."

20

"Do not look so troubled," Lady Upworth said to Meg. "I am not an enemy and I am an accomplished nurse. I have certainly had a good deal of experience."

"Thank you for your kindness," Meg said, but she disliked having the woman wait upon her and could not consider the ministrations as anything other than a means to impress Jean-Marc.

"The entire household is shocked," Lady Upworth said. "You must have been terrified."

"I was." There was little point in pretending otherwise. "It was as if the horror of it would never end."

"Who can dislike you enough to do such a thing?"

Meg glanced at her but did not respond. Time enough to share her feelings and thoughts on what had happened when she spoke to Jean-Marc. "You are kind to me, My Lady, but I know my sister could manage. I can manage alone."

Lady Upworth smiled. "You are too self-sufficient, Miss Smiles. Isn't she, er, Miss Smiles?" She glanced at Sibyl, who nodded. Poor Sibyl hovered at the side of the bed and didn't take her eyes from Meg's face.

Dressed in one of her favorite night rails and a robe of soft white lawn embroidered by her own hand, Meg suffered Her Ladyship to put more salve on numerous small cuts. The coach's shattering windows had embedded small shards in the back of Meg's neck, and more fragments had slid inside her gown to cut her shoulders.

Meg stilled Lady Upworth's hands. "My Lady, do you think

you could dissuade the Count from having his doctor come to me?"

The lady's sudden laughter surprised Meg. "I see you do not know the Count well. If he has made up his mind on a certain course, then I doubt there is anyone who could divert him. Rest on your pillows now. You will have some discomfort, but all looks clean and no glass remains. Your most troublesome wound will be to your nerves, Miss Smiles. You have suffered a frightening experience."

"Thank you," Meg said, and did as she was told. Gratitude for Lady Upworth's kindness warred with a desire not to like the woman one bit.

"The Count wished to see you as soon as you were settled," Lady Upworth said. "Shall I send word that you're ready now?"

There was no help for it but to agree. "I suppose so."

Sibyl had brushed Meg's hair and plaited it. She was certain she looked like an ugly child but at least the light in her red and gold bedchamber was low enough to ensure she could not be seen too clearly.

"I'll ring," Lady Upworth said, and did so.

A tap at the door came too quickly to be in response to the bell. A maid bustled in and put more coals on the fire. The room was far too grand for a paid companion, but Meg had already been honest enough with herself to admit she enjoyed it.

"Millie, Miss," the maid said, bobbing to Meg. "I'm to tell you the doctor's coming up now."

"Fie," Meg said, then, "Forgive me, please, My Lady."

Lady Upworth laughed again and said, "You are most restrained. I might say a great deal worse. May I sit with you while the doctor is here?"

To refuse would be rude. "Thank you, yes," Meg said.

The next knock on the door was firmer and louder, and a tall, portly man with white hair came into the room, allowing Millie to escape as he did so. "How is the patient?" he asked, his voice full and jovial. His luxuriant mustache bobbed with each word.

"I am Dr. Weller. First I will give you something to calm you. I'm certain I don't have to remind you that you must accept the limitations of your gentle sex and expect to be confined to bed for some time."

Meg couldn't make herself look into his eyes for fear he would see what she thought of his assumptions.

"Quiet, I see. Only to be expected." He placed a bulging bag on the table beside Meg's bed and rooted inside until he produced a bottle filled with disgusting-looking green fluid. He glanced at Sibyl. "She is to have a spoonful of this every two hours. It will keep her asleep. Should she wake at all, give her another spoonful."

Sibyl made a small sound.

Meg made a pact with herself never to allow a drop of the green stuff to descend her throat.

"Now I shall check you for injuries."

"I've done a deal of nursing, Doctor," Lady Upworth said, and she winked at Meg. "I nursed my dear departed husband in his final weeks. I took the liberty of making sure Miss Smiles has no broken bones. She doesn't. And she has no internal pain anywhere. However, she does have some wounds on the back of her neck and her shoulders from the broken glass she fell on in the carriage."

That brought a humph from Dr. Weller—and a surge of gratitude from Meg. Really, she had been wrong about Ila, Lady Upworth. The doctor bent Meg forward and examined the numerous small cuts she had suffered.

"They appear clean," he announced through his mustache. "Are you certain you have no pain elsewhere?"

"None at all, sir," Meg said in a rush. She did not want to endure further examination.

The next knock was soft. Jean-Marc put his head around the door and said, "May I come in, please?"

"Yes," Meg said, and knew she'd spoken too quickly, too

eagerly. She also knew Jean-Marc's presence at this time was unconventional.

"She'll do well enough," Dr. Weller said. "I've left a medicine of my own making for her, My Lord. It will ensure that she sleeps. Sleep is the greatest healer for the weaker minds."

"Really?" Jean-Marc said. "I doubt Miss Smiles will need to avail herself of your prescription, then. But I thank you."

Dr. Weller showed no sign of having noted Jean-Marc's rebuke. He closed his bag. "She has a considerable number of small wounds on her back. They should be kept clean."

"They will be," Jean-Marc said. He looked only at Meg.

"I'll take my leave, then," Dr. Weller said and waited, obviously expecting Jean-Marc to accompany him downstairs. "I'll take my leave, then," he repeated.

"Good day to you," Jean-Marc said, standing over Meg, a brooding frown rumpling his brow. "I'm sure you know the way out."

His face redder and his mustache wiggling ferociously, the doctor left.

"Miss Smiles is brave," Lady Upworth said. "Much braver than I could ever be."

Sibyl broke her silence. "Meg has always been brave. She takes care of us both. How dare that doctor talk about her having a weak mind, about all women having weak minds!"

Her sister's outburst surprised and pleased her, and made Meg proud. Sibyl might be shy, but she could also be forthright when necessary.

"He is of another generation," Jean-Marc said, and although he didn't smile, humor shone in his eyes. "We forward-thinking men know better than to underestimate a woman."

Lady Upworth chuckled. "How very wise of you, Jean-Marc. And how very politic. Flattering a woman has always been the best way to impress her."

Jean-Marc studied Ila. "Am I so transparent? I suppose I am," he said. She puzzled him of late. Vocal as she was in expressing her gratitude for his championship of her, she no longer sought opportunities to flirt with him—and since her return to London and his house, she had treated him with fond deference but had made no overt approaches. What, he wondered, was her current plan? He was certain she did have a plan.

"Apparently we are to have a busy evening," he said to Meg. With her hair in two long plaits she appeared very young—not a thought that made him comfortable. "Certain events have transpired today and must be attended to. They do have a bearing on what has happened to you, but I hope you will allow me to deal with them. I see no reason for you to be involved."

"I do," she said, rising from her pillows to sit very straight in her high bed. "I most certainly do. In fact, I insist."

A fiery miss. Each time he was with her she spun him a little tighter into her web. The ardor in their responses to each other grew dangerously strong. Kissing her in the coach, and her potent response to that kiss, would cause him an uncomfortable night to come.

"You insist, do you, miss?" he said, intending to mock, but managing only to sound indulgent. "I do believe that may present difficulties unless you are comfortable with my conducting interviews in your bedchamber."

"Perfectly comfortable," she told him. "And I have a number of questions of my own to ask you."

"Ask away."

"Later would be more agreeable to me, if you please, My Lord."

What would really please him could not be voiced in present company. "We shall see." He would not allow a chit to force his hand. He went to the door to speak with an under butler, who had been stationed outside the room.

"Who is there?" Meg asked. "Why is he outside my room?"

"Because it is my responsibility to keep you safe." He looked at Sibyl, then at Ila. "Only one of you need remain. I'm sure both of you have more pressing things to do."

"There is nothing more pressing to me than Meg," Sibyl Smiles said, and her throat moved sharply as she swallowed. "But I know you will care for her if I leave for a while. Shall you mind if I do that, Meggie? The Princess awaits me in the music room. She hasn't been told about your horrid accident but I'd better inform her now and make sure she is using her time wisely. Then I need to go to Number Seven to find music I need."

"Of course, I don't mind," Meg said. "Will you please tell Désirée that the musicale and its hasty arrangements mean we must concentrate on several areas of her instruction? She should practice smiling."

Jean-Marc crossed his arms. "Smiling? Is there nothing more important than having my sister grin?"

Meg didn't as much as look at him. "Tell her she has a lovely smile and it will make up for those things she does not yet do to perfection. Look in a mirror, tell her, and smile agreeably while she considers all manner of remarks that might tempt her to use her wit inappropriately. Where is Ash?"

"She said she did not feel well," Sibyl said, and Jean-Marc sensed discomfort with the subject of the caper merchant. "Miss Ash has a delicate constitution that is not suited to visiting the sick."

Meg threw her coverlets aside and said, "Please leave me. I must dress. There is no time for this foolish lolling."

"You will loll," Jean-Marc said, and covered her again.

She tossed the bedclothes aside again and swung her limbs from the mattress. "I will not *loll.* I will tend to my duties."

Such very lovely ankles. He turned her, covered her and leaned on the edge of the bed, making it impossible for her to defy him again.

Meg made for the opposite side of the bed.

Sibyl made for the door. "I will return as soon as I can, Meggie. And I will make sure the Princess is usefully engaged. Do be sensible."

Jean-Marc met Meg as she prepared to slip to the floor again.

"Stop," he said, "or I shall assume you have done damage to your weak mind and send for the sawbones again."

"That is insupportable," Ila said sharply. "You do have a most unpleasant need to insult women, Jean-Marc."

Meg regarded Jean-Marc's face, which was entirely too close to her own for comfort, and lowered her eyes.

He said, "I'm sorry," but didn't sound subdued. "Surely you understand that I am concerned only for your health, Meg."

"Thank you," she said quickly, but knew Lady Upworth had heard the slip. She scooted to the middle of the mattress, arranged herself and decorously held the sheet to her chin. "I admit to some anxiety but I'm sure the morning will be soon enough for me to accomplish my tasks."

He stood straight.

Lady Upworth pulled a chair beside the bed and sat there.

"Um, yes," Jean-Marc said. "Verbeux is on his way. We should dispose of pressing matters quickly."

Minutes passed while the three of them avoided eye contact.

Jean-Marc added coal to the fire.

Lady Upworth reached to pat Meg's hands. "I hope you at least saw someone interesting in Bond Street," she said. "The upcoming Coronation is already bringing the most elevated personages to England. Just think how they will add to the glitter of this Season."

The Coronation was far from Meg's mind. "No," she said, "I was too busy with shoes." She looked pointedly at the Count, who did not appear to have heard her comment.

At last a knock came, and Verbeux was admitted. "You sent for me, My Lord?"

"Some time ago," Jean-Marc said pointedly, while he wiped his hands on a handkerchief. "I understood you had something of considerable importance to reveal—before we discuss the other matter."

Verbeux glanced briefly at Meg, then spent much longer looking at Lady Upworth. The lady returned his regard and lifted her chin as she did so. Meg felt a tension between the two, and it puzzled her. There was no doubt that Verbeux had a remarkable presence.

"Are you recovered, M. Verbeux?" Meg asked, somewhat tentatively. "You took a terrible fall."

"And landed on my feet." His abrupt bark of laughter startled Meg.

"You didn't say you'd fallen, Verbeux," Lady Upworth said.

"No." Verbeux's answer was a trifle too rapid. "Privacy for business, My Lord?" he said.

"Oh, no, Verbeux." Jean-Marc swept a hand before him. "We are entered into a new age when the ladies are about to knock on the very doors of our clubs and demand admittance. To attempt to spare them from the more tedious aspects of life must be avoided. We will conduct our business here."

"My Lord?" Verbeux's elegant brows shot up.

"You heard what I said. What did you want to tell me?"

"Pierre," Verbeux said, evidently uncomfortable. "Pierre must be present."

"Your man?" Jean-Marc barely remembered speaking to Pierre on more than a handful of occasions. "What has he to do with our affairs?"

Verbeux appeared to make up his mind about something. He returned to the corridor, and Jean-Marc heard him speak quietly to the under butler. The rustle of Ila's satin gown reminded him of her presence. Her attention was firmly on the door. If he were a man given to conjecture, he might think she was overly attentive to Verbeux. The very thought amazed him, since his valet—if he had any amorous connections—kept them utterly private. Verbeux and Ila? Now there was an unlikely pair.

"Must wait for Pierre," Verbeux said when he returned.

"Whatever. All facts must be set before us. Who could possibly wish Miss Smiles harm? They could not, I tell you. Far more likely that these attacks on her are intended for another." He would not expand on that in the present company.

"Or perhaps intended to get your attention, Jean-Marc," Ila said.

He regarded her thoughtfully. "Anything is possible, I suppose." No fool was Ila. He regretted that to ask her to leave would appear suspicious.

There might never be another opportunity to ask about a valet having a valet, Meg decided. After all, any unusual comment on her part could be put down to her supposed fragile condition. "Is it a French custom for a gentleman's gentleman to have a gentleman?" she asked.

Lady Upworth didn't cover her smile quickly enough.

"Not at all," Jean-Marc said. "Verbeux is assisting close family friends by training Pierre. As a kindness. Eventually Pierre will leave Verbeux and do so with the highest possible references. He will obtain an excellent position. And then, no doubt, Verbeux will decide to bestow his *kindness* on another fortunate candidate."

The well-built young man in question entered hesitantly, his good-looking face drawn, his brown eyes downcast. "You sent for me, M. Verbeux," he said, and repeatedly and nervously sucked his bottom lip between his teeth. He actually wound his hands together before him.

Meg's stomach turned. A solid person, Pierre didn't seem his usual robust self this evening. He appeared to shrink inside his immaculate clothing, and she longed to tell him to stop punishing his lip.

"For God's sake, man," Jean-Marc said. "What is it? What's happened to you?"

Pierre looked to Verbeux, who breathed through his nose before saying, "Collect yourself. Explain."

"My Lord." Pierre bowed low and stood square before the Count. "The shaving blade."

"What about it?" Jean-Marc asked.

"It belongs to M. Verbeux."

"That cannot be." Lady Upworth half rose from her chair, but dropped back.

Disbelief froze Jean-Marc.

Meg did manage to leave the bed then. Looking childlike in her simple robe, and with bare feet, she positioned herself where she could see everyone present. "Why must people of a certain station speak yet say nothing?" She pointed, actually pointed at him. "You, My Lord, have no more facts than I do, yet you are dumb from the deductions you have made. The shaving blade? Are we speaking of the shaving blade on which I cut myself?" She held her injured hand aloft.

It was Pierre who said, "Yes, Miss."

"Do not overset yourself, Miss Smiles," Jean-Marc said. "You are not well. Please return to your bed."

For an instant he thought she would argue, but she thought better of it and climbed onto the mattress once more. There she assumed her extraordinary cross-legged position with her gown and robe spread about her. Her hands she rested, palms up, upon her knees. Even as he watched, he saw her begin slow, deep breathing.

Verbeux said, "Tell your tale, Pierre. And quickly."

"I was late that morning. I was cleaning the blade when I was called to another duty. It was an accident. I left with the blade in my hand and didn't notice it until it was too late. I could not go into M. Verbeux's presence in such a manner. The pouch was open on a bench nearby. I dropped the blade inside, intending to retrieve it when M. Verbeux dismissed me. When I returned, the pouch was gone. I went in search of it, but did not know where I should look since I had never seen it before."

"There, you see!" Awash in her sea of white lawn, Meg spread her arms as if about to sing an aria. "An accident. A mishap. Oh, Pierre, don't look so glum. Humans err. So you have erred. Fiddle dee dee, let us forget the matter at once."

Fury stiffened Jean-Marc. The little madam must learn her

rightful place. "That is hardly your decision to make," he said to her. "Verbeux, you know what must be done."

The valet didn't answer, and the pained expression on his face only deepened Jean-Marc's anger.

"What must be done?" Meg asked, but her smile had fled.

"Hold your tongue," he said.

Ila had the audacity to reach for the girl's hand and share a sympathetic glance with her.

"Here?" Verbeux said. "Now?"

"Here and now. I will not be challenged, is that understood? If it were appropriate, I should do it myself. It is not appropriate."

"Pierre," Verbeux said, and his hands were tightly fisted, "I shall assist you in finding another place. We will speak more of this later."

"Oh," Meg cried. "Oh, how cruel. Mine is the hand that was cut. Mine was the blood that was shed. If Pierre must go, then I must go."

"Nonsense," Jean-Marc told her. "And that is a perfect example of why women should not be present during the decisions men must make. I have a responsibility to protect you, to protect everyone in my care."

"Then why do you not have a responsibility to protect Pierre? To protect him from callous treatment that doesn't fit his supposed crime?"

"You are unsinkable, Miss Smiles," he said. "And you overstep your place—frequently."

The fight went out of Meg. He was right, she did overstep her place, and now she felt shamed. Shamed but nevertheless determined to help Pierre, who hung his head like the most miserable man alive. "Forgive me," she said to the Count. "You are right to rebuke me. I am unaccustomed to my current position in life, but that doesn't excuse bad behavior. However, I still beg you to allow this man to keep his position. I will leave at once, but please don't punish him more than he is already punished."

Even when she probably didn't intend to do so, Meg Smiles

confounded him. "Damnation," he said. "And I do not apologize for my language. Are you inclined to give Pierre another chance, Verbeux?"

"I am, My Lord," Verbeux said, without hesitation.

"Very well, but the slightest slip and there will be no other chances. You may leave us."

Pierre nodded and murmured thanks, and rapidly left the room.

"You," Jean-Marc said to Meg, "will remain where you are. My sister needs you, and you have given your word to attend her during her time in London. Let us complete our business elsewhere, Verbeux. Miss Smiles needs to rest. Or meditate, or practice her abstracted thinking—or whatever she does to please herself."

"Thank you for changing your mind," she said. "I will be quiet while you finish dealing with whatever else must be dealt with. You intimated that it concerns me."

"Yes, you did," Lady Upworth said.

He braced his weight on one of the bedposts. "You see how it is a disaster to place any trust in a woman, Verbeux? Not only do they defy one, they also form alliances against us."

Verbeux smiled slightly. "I wish I understood the gentler sex as well as you, My Lord."

Jean-Marc wrinkled his nose. "They are no mystery. Allow me to guide you in these matters. Do we need Thomas?"

"I think not. This is what he found. The intent is obvious." Verbeux drew something from a pocket in his waistcoat and put it into Jean-Marc's hand.

"May we see?" Meg said. She grew jumpy.

Yet another tap at the door made her skin crawl. She longed for peace and an opportunity to do what pleased her.

"My Lord," the under butler said, "Mr. Rench has sent a visitor up. Says everyone else is here, so why not—"

"Quite," Jean-Marc said.

"Mr. Hunter Lloyd from Number Seven," the man said, and stood back to allow Hunter to come in.

"I say, I'm sorry for arriving unannounced." He spoke to the Count but looked at Meg. "These are from all of us at Number Seven." The bright bouquet of flowers he carried was very large and tied with a yellow satin ribbon.

Tears sprang to Meg's eyes. "Thank you, Hunter." Her emotions were too unruly. "How kind you all are. Is everyone well? I miss you." She knew she spoke with her heart rather than her head, but did not care.

Hunter's reserved manner slipped. "We miss you, Meg. We will be glad when you and Sibyl are returned to the fold. My aunt is beside herself worrying about you. Even old Barstow is moved to say almost pleasant things about you." He smiled a little, and she was reminded why she and Sibyl expected him to announce he had been captured by some eligible female. Hunter was a most appealing man.

"Kindly take the flowers, Ila," Jean-Marc said.

When she looked at him, his posture disquieted Meg. He was angry again, and although it could not be so, one might think that anger was directed at Hunter.

Lady Upworth dutifully took the flowers and set them artfully in the ewer that contained water for washing. "Just for now," she told Hunter, smiling a captivated smile. "You must be Lady Hester Bingham's son."

"Nephew," he said, and withdrew a small packet from a coat pocket. He gave it to Meg. "This is the item you sent for."

"Ah, that's right." Lady Upworth lowered her eyelids and returned, gracefully, to her chair. "I believe you are a barrister, Mr. Hunter."

"Yes, My Lady." He made what were intended to be covert glances around the room. "Should you like me to take you home, Meg? It would be more comforting among good friends at such a time."

Jean-Marc gave her no time to answer. "For the present time this is Miss Smiles's home," he said, absolutely cold. "And she is among friends here, also. I'm sure she appreciates your concern. Don't hesitate to inquire after her health again."

Rather than being quelled, Hunter stood fast and fixed Jean-Marc with a green-eyed stare that must stand him in good stead in court. "Are you asking me to leave, My Lord?"

"I'm suggesting Miss Smiles should be left alone to rest."

"Hunter," Meg said anxiously. "Please tell Lady Hester I shall visit her soon. Adam has promised to produce samples of his work, but he hasn't done so yet. Would you remind him, please? He may paint Princess Désirée's portrait."

Hunter gave her his full attention, and she saw that he understood that she was delighted to see him, but that she had reason to remain where she was. "I shall pass on your messages." He came to her side, took one of her hands and kissed it. And he gave her a significant glance. "Are you, er, comfortable? You feel, er, safe?"

"Yes, yes," she said quickly. "Don't worry about me."

"In that case, get well." He continued to take every opportunity to search about the room—who knew for what? "Promise me, Meggie."

She did not recall his ever having used her pet name before. That he did so now pleased her. "I promise," she said.

Hunter bowed to Lady Upworth, who promptly offered him her hand. If he was taken aback, he disguised his feelings well and kissed the lady's hand with enough slow enthusiasm to bring a satisfied smile to her lips.

Verbeux reached the door before Hunter and held it wide open for him. When Hunter had gone, Verbeux stared hard at Lady Upworth, who fluttered her lashes at him.

"Well." Jean-Marc cleared his throat. "You have obviously charmed the household at Number Seven." And he didn't care for their proprietorial attitude, or for smooth Mr. Lloyd's possessive attitude. That must be changed, and soon.

"May we see what M. Verbeux gave you?" Meg asked. "Before Hunter came?"

She was not to be diverted, that much was now absolutely clear. "It's nothing," he said. The strain of this day must already be too much for her. "Nothing to do with you at all. You should sleep. Perhaps Weller's elixir might be a good idea, after all."

"I choose to pretend you didn't make that suggestion," she said. "Kindly be honest. And be honest quickly. What did M. Verbeux give you?"

He shrugged. A wise man knew when to give in to a determined woman. "Where exactly was this found, Verbeux?"

"Under the noseband. Where the cheek strap crosses."

Meg had no idea what the man talked about.

"There," Jean-Marc said. "Now you know."

"I do not know anything."

Lady Upworth said, "Oh, dear."

"This," Jean-Marc said, holding out a palm in which a nail rested, "was placed against the head of one of my horses. One of the horses that pulled the coach today. Here—" he touched his own cheek a short distance above his mouth "—beneath the leather straps you have likely noticed on my animals."

She rubbed the cold skin on her arms. "It's a nail. It could be thrown up by a hoof. That's what happened. It landed where it was by chance."

"And by chance it was threaded in such a manner as to assure disaster?"

"You can't be sure it wasn't."

"Yes, I can. Explain, Verbeux."

"Nothing to explain. Nail pushed through noseband. Minute Thomas made the team move, band and cheek strap tightened. Nail drove into horse's cheek. All the way through to the inside of the animal's mouth. Horse went mad. Ran wild. No chance involved."

21

*S*pivey here.

How can such carefully made plans be going so wrong?

Something most odd is happening—all the more odd because as yet I see little evidence to guide me to those who are intent upon injuring Miss Meg Smiles. Or appear to be. But I do have a notion or two, naturally. I am a brilliant man. I must simply employ my considerable intelligence and become the observer I know so well how to be.

Imagine, I am now forced to attempt to avert exactly what I was originally so determined to promote between Count Etranger and Meg Smiles. Since the outcome will be so much more certain, I have to bring about a tryst between that odious William Godly-Smythe and Sibyl Smiles. That done, Meg Smiles will pop along with them, docile as a fat cat, and settle wherever her frightful second cousin decides to take his feeble-brained relations.

This means that what I fear may be very imminent between the Count and Meg Smiles must be stopped. If I could believe Miss Sibyl would accompany her sister, even if it were to a place where she would reside as Etranger's ladybird, all would be well. I doubt that would be so.

Ash displeases me—not at all suitable—but I have no choice and must make the best of her. I do know what I shall have her do.

By the by, I cannot begin to explain my disgust with acting as that lumpish Princess's dance master. The Count calls me—I mean, Ash—a caper merchant. Insulting fellow.

But as to Ash, I intend to turn her into a diplomat. Not, you will agree, a simple task. However, it shall be done.

Back to the mystery that surrounds certain events. There is some secret that is as yet hidden from me. That secret will reveal what it is that is bringing about these mishaps. I must know who is the target. And I am not convinced it is Meg Smiles. She is too insignificant to attract so much attention.

You know, her cousin is an upright fellow. Why she is not flattered at his wishing to marry Sibyl and care for them both, I can't imagine. I should think she has ideas above her station. Possibly she even imagines herself in love—how I hate those empty words—but in love with the Count. Ha, such audacity makes me laugh. The poor creature doesn't as much as guess at the cavalier behavior the object of her affections must be capable of employing. How could she?

No matter, the chit's feelings are of no interest to me. This very evening I expect to be called on to foil disaster. Even though it is Sibyl rather than Meg that Godly-Smythe wishes to marry, he would not wish to take a fallen woman under his protection. Or so I should think. But he must take her. Seven B Mayfair Square shall be rid of lodgers forever.

Did you see that Hunter hovering over Meg Smiles? Bringing her flowers? They must have cost a pretty penny. Oh, what have I spawned? What cruelty that I must defend a family so unworthy of my fidelity.

Enough of that. I have some instructions for you. They are not onerous. If you should see any sign of the Count and Miss Meg Smiles, er, keeping company this evening, getting together by some clandestine means, perhaps, creeping about as if they don't want to be seen... Get my attention. Just in case I am considering other matters. Use your minds. Concentrate on reaching my thoughts with your own. Of course you are incapable of attempting such an effort successfully—I'm not asking you to do so. I'm asking you to make yourselves receptive to me by calling me with a quiet voice in your head.

You know, I've had a marvelous idea. If things have progressed somewhat far by the time I arrive, I have a plan to stop the event cold—stone cold.

I appreciate your assistance.

Now, without going into details, I want you to know about the frustration I encountered last year—when I was thrust into a most unsavory position. That was when I first realized I must attempt to preserve the dignity of my home and family. I'd thought things were going quite well—until a certain young woman turned into a creature entirely lacking in decorum. She thought nothing of disporting herself on a table in… Oh, dear, I forgot myself for an instant. She disported herself with a certain man—but in the end that was as well since it was part of my plan. However, witnessing such deplorable antics upset me deeply.

There were other events I had to observe in order to gain my ends, too. I shudder at the thought. I had to watch for hours to be certain I hadn't imagined what I'd seen.

Please listen carefully. The most trying part of last year's debacle—when I managed to get Finch More out of Seven A only to have her brother, Latimer, remain—was that I couldn't control or trust those I needed to rely on for support. People rather like you, dear reader, only not as clever or trustworthy.

I request that you follow my instructions carefully. Keep a lookout for anything you think I should know. I will be very busy gathering information elsewhere. But when you become aware of potentially ruinous behavior on the part of Count Etranger and Meg Smiles, close your eyes and think of me—I will come. And, unlike your predecessors, do not shame yourselves, or risk losing my esteem, by allowing yourselves to witness acts we all abhor.

Remember, copulation between gentle people is purely for the purpose of procreation. Should a man feel the natural urge to enjoy himself more often, well, if he is a man of the world, he knows where to go.

Ladies—absent yourselves the instant you sense imminent intimacy.

Gentlemen—I understand your natural drive to seek excitement, but this business is beneath you. Make me proud, men, make me proud.

22

Jean-Marc turned the pages of his book without knowing what he read. He would remain in London until the musicale was over, less than three days from now since midnight had passed. Afterward he would remove Désirée and Meg, and essential members of his London household, to Windsor for a few days. Something treacherous had been set in motion. He needed time to explore what that might be—time and some separation from the confusion that made it much easier for villains to go about their business.

The attacks could not have been intended for Meg. Why would they be? He wanted to fight back, but feared for his sister's and Meg's safety.

Verbeux slipped into the study in Jean-Marc's apartments and leaned against the door. "Been thinking," Verbeux said. "Treason. Got to say it."

Jean-Marc sprang to his feet. "What are you talking about, man? Treason? That is what I heard you say?"

"The Duke—Louis. Prince's brother. Your uncle."

"I know who Louis is," Jean-Marc said through his teeth. "Damn him."

"You dislike him. Because you are to take his place? The place he thought was his?"

"Dislike him?" Jean-Marc sank slowly into his chair. He crossed his hands behind his head and rested them on the back of the favorite, worn leather wing chair his father had thoughtfully shipped to London.

"Dislike him," Verbeux echoed.

Firelight played among the trees in a dark pastoral scene painted on the ceiling. Jean-Marc attempted a little abstracted thinking, failed and shot to his feet once more. "I don't dislike him," he said. "I *hate* the man. I hate him for his stupidity because it has brought me to a pretty pass. It has brought me to a place I never desired. Had he not been foolish enough to act as if he already ruled Mont Nuages, instead of waiting until my father was dead, he would yet be heir to the throne. And I would not be faced with a duty Papa has decided should come to me by default."

Verbeux stared moodily into the fire.

"The Prince is determined."

"Yes." Jean-Marc did not intend to discuss, with anyone, that he continued to hope his father would finally notice that his daughter was brilliant and well-suited to rule—in time. And, despite Papa's conviction that he was not long for this world, there was no apparent reason to suspect his death to be imminent.

"The Duke has many supporters," Verbeux said.

Jean-Marc waited until the other man looked at him before saying, "Your point?"

Evidently Verbeux had donned his coat hastily—and without remembering a waistcoat. The sight of his valet in less than immaculate dress disturbed Jean-Marc. Even Verbeux's hair was rumpled.

"Your point, Verbeux?" Jean-Marc pressed.

"An attempt to go against the Prince's wishes would be treason."

"It could be."

"If the attempt was to kill you, it would be."

Jean-Marc smiled a little. "Letting our imaginations run away, are we?"

"No, damn it." Verbeux's arched brows drew down. Light caught his glasses and veiled his eyes. "I chose not to tell you because I wasn't sure. No reason to concern you. Not until I knew." He pointed toward the bedchamber. "Last week. Glass on a tray by the bed. Assumed someone being diligent. You don't make a habit of drinking before bed."

"I may start," Jean-Marc muttered.

"Thought it was Madeira. Smelled wrong."

Jean-Marc concentrated. "And?"

"Took it to an apothecary. Slow. Just got a message. Aconite."

"Aconite?" Jean-Marc grimaced. "Monkshood?"

Verbeux nodded.

"You think someone tried to poison me?"

"Know they did." Verbeux brushed back his hair. "That drink would have killed you. Since that night, I've watched everything placed before you. Then the coach."

"I wasn't in the coach."

"Your coach. Could have assumed you'd be in it."

"Conjecture." But there was no proof to the contrary. "Why would…are you suggesting my uncle may be trying to assassinate me?"

Verbeux turned red.

"You are. That's preposterous. Louis may be misguided, but he's not a murderer. He is also fond of me, as I am of him on good days. And he knows that as far as I'm concerned, no one would be more happy to see him back in line for the throne."

"Not the Duke himself." The valet made to straighten his waistcoat, discovered he didn't wear one and appeared horrified. "Excuse me, My Lord. My, er, dress."

"Couldn't care less."

"Of course. Fanatic bunch, Duke's supporters. Expected favors. Honors. What not. Angry now. Could want to get rid of you—hope for a new shot at the palace."

Jean-Marc went to a beautiful red lacquer cabinet from China. It was filled with fine crystal decanters, and he poured two glasses of brandy. "Here," he said to Verbeux. "Settle your nerves. And mine."

"Thank you." Verbeux looked into the glass and appeared disinclined to drink from it.

"Good God." Jean-Marc exploded. "You're seeing killers in every corner. If you don't want my brandy, don't have it." He tossed down his own drink and poured another.

Verbeux nodded and half drained his glass. "With respect, My Lord, what happens to you is important to me. Protecting you—one of my duties."

"The hell it is. I protect myself."

"Indeed. But I will not give up vigilance. I believe these people are desperate."

"And can you tell me exactly who these people are?"

"Not yet, but I will find them out."

"Sit down," Jean-Marc said. "You're a good man, Verbeux, but you take yourself too seriously."

Surprisingly, Verbeux accepted the invitation and sank into a leather chair. He warmed to his brandy and drank with enthusiasm.

For some minutes they both regarded the fire and the brass andirons that glittered from scrupulous cleaning. They drank in silence, although Jean-Marc expected Verbeux to expand further on his conspiracy theory.

"You grow fond of Meg Smiles," the valet said, catching his master off guard. The drink had rendered Verbeux unusually talkative, it seemed. "Interesting creature. Not a beauty, though, hmm?"

"Not a beauty," Jean-Marc agreed, wrestling with a desire to say that she was nevertheless the most intriguing woman he'd ever met.

"Unusual." Evidently Verbeux hadn't entirely missed Meg's complexities. "Otherworldly, in a way."

"Very much so. Not traditional. Did you ever know of a woman who did this abstracted thinking?"

"No, My Lord. I've been told Miss Smiles spends time each day meditating. And she has a mantra? I've read about it all. Says the same words. Like putting herself into a trance. Strange."

"Peaceful," Jean-Marc responded, and didn't care if he gave Verbeux more food for thought.

"Only peaceful?" Verbeux asked. He rose and went to the red cabinet. He refilled his glass and held the decanter toward Jean-Marc. "More, My Lord?"

"I have enough. No, she isn't only peaceful. There is more to her. Chance is a strange fellow. Our paths should never have crossed."

"She is an answer to your prayers. The Princess blooms. I see her smile. Not often, but occasionally. And she follows directions—Miss Smiles's directions."

"I know. My half sister is about to turn into a swan, and I have Meg and Sibyl Smiles to thank for that. I'm not sure what part the caper merchant plays."

"Ash provides contrast. Beside her the rest appear so desirable."

"Indeed." Jean-Marc had to grin. He leaned to pick up the poker and stir glowing coals. The room felt as comfortable as if he had occupied it for many years. The carpet was a rare piece that echoed the scene overhead. Dark green draperies made of velvet hung across casement windows. His large desk occupied the space in front of both windows. Books covered one wall, the wall into which was set the door to the bedchamber.

Verbeux cleared his throat and drank rather hurriedly. One might almost think he was boosting his courage.

Leaning back in his chair, Jean-Marc watched Verbeux and decided to allow the silence to last until the man said what was on his mind.

Verbeux shifted in his chair.

The hour grew late. Jean-Marc wasn't tired. In fact, he was very awake and filled with thoughts that made peace impossible.

"You don't want any part of ruling Mont Nuages," Verbeux said finally. He removed his spectacles and dangled them between his knees. A handsome man, Jean-Marc could not help acknowledging. "You never wanted it."

"I never expected it. I have not been prepared. Once I might have relished the possibility. Now I have other dreams."

"What dreams?"

Jean-Marc made no remark about the impertinence of the question. "I am half English. The affairs of England are of the deepest interest to me. I could be very useful to Mont Nuages as ambassador to England. I already perform the task informally. And I'd like to farm. I could do both more than adequately."

"Much more than adequately. Do it."

Jean-Marc squinted across the rim of his glass. "Do it? Simply do it?"

"You would have to give the Prince a reason to change his mind—and also to accept your value to him here in England."

"I'd like to believe he already knows my value to him here."

"That will not stop him from moving to carry out the course he intends for you."

"I suppose you intend to tell me what would stop him?"

"He wishes you to marry very well. No doubt a princess. He will want your marriage to provide an advantageous alliance."

Jean-Marc digested the idea and said, "Just as he expects Désirée to marry someone useful."

"Naturally. Sees it as the most use he will get from her."

Tempted as he was, nevertheless Jean-Marc still did not share his thoughts about his sister.

"You must defy him on the subject of your marriage."

"As you know, I have no plans to marry. At least not in the foreseeable future."

"Change your plans. Lady Upworth has shown herself more than willing to assume the position. But there was, I understand, an even earlier marriage that was annulled. The Prince would never approve of the gossip that must have caused."

Careful to disguise his curiosity about Verbeux's real feelings toward Ila, Jean-Marc said, "I'm afraid I would be deterred because the lady has a certain reputation."

"For what?"

Aha, so there might be something afoot with these two. Verbeux would be unlikely to question him otherwise. Jean-Marc shrugged. "Some call her the Grateful Widow. And they don't mean she's grateful for any kindness she receives. It is her relief at being a widow to which they refer."

"Her husband was much older. He was also sick for some time. She's finally free. That's acceptable."

"The lady is entertaining." This could be highly dangerous territory. "She is not for me. On the same topic, I have seen you regard Miss Sibyl Smiles with more than passing interest. And I shouldn't be surprised if she's developing a tendresse for you."

A deep breath expanded Verbeux's chest. "Lovely girl. Innocent. Too innocent for me. She needs gentle treatment. I am not gentle."

"Really, Verbeux?" Jean-Marc could scarcely contain his fascination at the thought of Verbeux being a forceful man with women. "Is there someone else?"

"Perhaps. You are the one under discussion. There is someone you admire. We both know this. Someone you would gladly take to your bed."

"You are too blunt."

"I am honest," Verbeux said. "And I know what is at stake here. Oh, for God's sake—what is that?"

With a flurry of feet, the largest cat Jean-Marc had ever seen catapulted itself between himself and Verbeux. Gray and white, with green eyes and a pink nose, it sat there and looked from one face to the other.

"A cat, damn it," Jean-Marc said. "Where did it come from? And who owns it? It eats a good many meals, that much is obvious. The servants know they may not keep animals. Have you seen him before?"

"I have not—and how did he get in when the door is closed?" Verbeux asked, and Jean-Marc actually thought he saw anxiety in the other man's eyes. "I don't like the look of him."

"Must have arrived earlier when the door was open. Cats like to hide. Get him out of here."

Verbeux didn't appear enthusiastic.

The cat rose slowly, arched its back and strolled to rub languorously against Jean-Marc's legs. He heard the creature begin to purr, and occasionally it looked up at him with what looked ridiculously like a smile in its green eyes.

"Finish what you were saying," Jean-Marc said and bent to stroke the cat. "I'll see to this later. I'll have to speak with Rench. No, no, not you, Verbeux, me. They need to learn that I have my fingers on the pulse of this household."

"My plan is simple," Verbeux said. "You do something that will anger your father and make it impossible for him to persist in his plan to make you his successor."

Jean-Marc laughed shortly. "What would that be? Am I to declare war on England?"

"I have already as good as told you what I have in mind. A very public wedding to someone far enough beneath you, to make the Prince withdraw his confidence in you—as his heir. He would come around soon enough and be glad to have you representing Mont Nuages here—but he would never allow you to rule if he considered your wife unworthy."

Jean-Marc looked into the cat's eyes and said, "I have little stomach for using women so badly."

"Using them badly? By providing one of them with a home she never dreamed of? Marry, have children, farm—serve your country as pleases you—but live where your heart is, in England. Marry Meg Smiles."

23

Even wearing a cloak over her gown and robe did not keep Meg warm. She crouched low to the ground beside a massive suit of armor that stood between two doors leading to Jean-Marc's apartments. Her legs felt as if they would never move again.

She should have fled the corridor some time ago. The arrival of Verbeux had sent her scurrying for cover. At first she hadn't known it was him, but when he'd entered Jean-Marc's study, she'd heard him speak.

Both men had deep voices that carried clearly. Meg had heard too much. Verbeux had made his astonishing suggestion about her, and Jean-Marc's response hadn't been clear, but from his tone she knew he had brushed the idea aside. She should not be surprised or disappointed by that.

Halibut had brought her on this chase. The cat had come into her bedchamber and peered around. Princess Désirée, who had crept to Meg an hour earlier, very upset at learning the full story of the affair in Bond Street, had crawled into Meg's bed and fallen asleep. The cat jumped onto a table near the bed, peered at his mistress, then raced from the room. Meg followed, terrified the Princess's beloved Halibut would be discovered by someone who would insist he be dispatched elsewhere. She had been appalled to see him dart behind Verbeux and into Jean-Marc's study.

"Better go about your business, Verbeux," Jean-Marc said clearly. "No, leave the cat to me. I believe I know who he belongs to. I'd appreciate it if you didn't mention seeing him."

"You will give further consideration to what I've suggested?" Verbeux asked.

"I have a great many matters to consider." That was the only response. Then, "Good night to you."

Within moments Verbeux came into the corridor. He appeared tired and disheveled and quite unlike himself. With hurried footsteps, he left the Count's apartments.

Slowly, Meg stood up, her legs tingling as blood returned. The best course would be for her to follow Verbeux and return to her quarters.

But leaving Halibut here would be unwise.

It was an excuse, but she was only a woman, with a woman's longings, and she longed to see Jean-Marc and to have him be kind to her. Even if she did know he considered her much his inferior.

Would she be prepared to toss aside her pride and accept any small crumb he offered?

Perhaps.

Meg tapped lightly at the door, and almost ran away. But Jean-Marc's command to come in stopped her. After checking her hair—still in its braids—and glancing downward at her odd attire, she held herself erect and entered. She thought fleetingly of the packet Hunter had brought. Adam had sent it—the preparation for her hair from Mme. Suzanne. She would use it just as soon as she could.

"Meg?" Sitting with Halibut on his lap, he glanced up, and his surprise was evident. "Come in and close the door. Get over here by the fire. What are you thinking of? Your feet are bare. You should not have left your bed. You've had a shock and need—"

"My Lord, could you please not speak anymore? Could you please just allow me to take the cat and leave?"

He glared at her. "No. No, I cannot allow you to tell me what to do. You insinuate yourself into my rooms, looking like…looking like…" He indicated the length of her. "Like a waif recently drenched and not quite dry. And then you expect me to be quiet while you leave without any explanation. *No, damn it.* Do as you are told. Sit in that chair—'' he pointed to one facing his ''—and be quiet. I shall be the one to talk.''

''I'm sorry Halibut found his way here. It's not like him to wander away. I do hope—''

''I do hope that you intend to follow my instructions fairly shortly. The cat is yours?''

''Oh, no… I mean, um, yes, he's mine.''

''He's not yours. And lying doesn't become you. Let me guess. He belongs to Désirée.''

''I'm sure I can't say.''

''Exactly, he belongs to Désirée. She has always been fond of animals but was never allowed to own one.''

''That's so sad.''

''If you say so,'' Jean-Marc said. ''I will discuss this creature with her in the morning. He'll sleep here tonight.'' Halibut jumped heavily to the floor and curled up before the fire. He kept his eerie eyes open, and they moved back and forth between Jean-Marc and Meg.

''That's so fair of you,'' Meg said. ''I know the Princess will be grateful for your consideration.''

''What if I tell you I require some persuasion from you if I am to allow the cat to remain in this house?''

Meg prickled all over. ''You want me to persuade you?''

''I do indeed. How are you feeling? Bruised, no doubt.''

''I feel perfectly well, thank you.'' Wrong answer. ''Fairly well, thank you. What bruises I have are minor. The cuts on my neck are annoying, but will disappear soon enough. And my hand is healing.''

He gripped the arms of his chair and locked his elbows. ''A litany of injuries for which I feel responsible.''

''You aren't responsible. Anyway, I'm sure a good night's sleep will make me completely recovered.''

''Should you like to have that night's sleep with me?''

Speech deserted her.

"I would ensure that it was very good, Meg."

His regard bewildered her, but it also excited and made her quake.

"Thank you for the offer, My Lord, but it isn't necessary. However, since we are alone and I have one or two things to discuss with you, I'd appreciate being allowed to speak."

He shifted forward in his seat and allowed his long, strong hands to relax.

Since he seemed disinclined to comment, Meg persisted. "The Princess has been invited to as many as three events in one day and evening, My Lord. M. Verbeux informed me that you wish her to attend every one of these."

"Correct."

"Impossible."

"She will accept all invitations."

"Why, My Lord?"

"Jean-Marc, remember? In order not to miss a single opportunity to find her an admirable husband, that's why. Although it may be necessary to refuse for certain days. Not many. I will inform you when I know."

Halibut got up, executed an impressive forward and backward stretching maneuver, yawned hugely and planted himself at Jean-Marc's feet. The cat stared upward into the man's face.

"Impertinent animal," Jean-Marc muttered.

Meg laughed and was too late in trying to disguise the sound.

Jean-Marc's wide grin delighted her, and she shook her head. "He is only a cat. Evidently he finds you captivating."

"Evidently. If you have finished with your questions, I should like to return to discussing my own concerns."

"The musicale. It is too soon."

"The invitations have already been delivered, and responses are arriving. Everyone is accepting. Your concern must be with costumes. Do not forget that you promised to take care of mine also. An Eastern theme? What shall you do with me, I wonder?"

Meg was overwhelmed, and confused, and exhilarated, and frightened. And she would not be anywhere but right where she was, with this man—alone. She was also foolish.

"What are you thinking?" he asked.

"Slippers." Too much was at stake for her to surrender to her desires, to the flesh. She was too warm and undid the satin frog at the collar of the green cloak. "I requested that M. Verbeux cancel the perfectly ridiculous order for more slippers and boots than any twenty women could need—in years."

"Did you, indeed?"

"Indeed, I did. And he refused because he will not go against your orders."

Halibut leaped onto Jean-Marc's lap, placed his two large front paws on the man's chest and licked his cheek. Replacing the cat firmly on his lap, Jean-Marc said, "That is the reason Verbeux is in my employ. He puts my wishes before all. He never, in fact, questions my wishes. The items I ordered will be delivered as requested. And you will wear them—as I instruct you to do."

"If you insist upon buying this foolish excess, then I must pay for it. So you will please keep my salary until the debt is discharged. And then there is the matter of silver slippers. Verbeux said they were for the musicale. I will not require them."

"Of course you will. Your costume is already under construction."

"It is not."

"It most certainly… Do not argue with me, Meg. You are not accustomed to argument and it does not become you."

Meg looked at her hands. She patted a warm cheek and lifted damp tendrils of hair away from her skin.

"Down with you for a moment, sir," Jean-Marc told Halibut and set him, with great care, before the fire once more. He came to Meg, took hold of her elbows and pulled her to her feet. "You are overheated, my dear. Allow me." And he slipped the cloak from her shoulders, then placed it over the back of his chair.

"I came for Halibut," she said. "I wish to take him and leave."

"Darling girl, we both know you don't want to leave any more than I want you to leave. It's time you gave me a response to my proposition. I must know that I shall always be able to come to you."

Meg blinked rapidly and squeezed her eyes tightly shut.

"Come now." She felt him approach her, felt him close. "Can it be so hard? Do you not want to be with me?"

"You know I do."

"Then what is there to discuss, other than dispatching immediate necessities and setting about our own arrangements?"

She bowed her head. "There is a great deal to discuss. A dangerous event has occurred, and I am so terrified for you. I may never sleep until I know you are safe."

Jean-Marc's next breath was not the easiest he had taken. "Be assured that I am accustomed to conducting my own affairs. And need I point out that it was you who were in that coach and in grave danger."

He saw her small smile and admired her courage. "I am in no danger, My Lord. I—"

"Jean-Marc. I cannot bear formality between us."

"Jean-Marc. There is no reason to think I am in any danger."

"You suffered an unfortunate incident before we met. It has been reported to me in detail by a servant who spoke with Reverend Baggs. You believe you were pushed with the intention that you would be killed."

She looked warm, yet he saw her shiver. "I did, but I was wrong," she said. "I must have tripped."

"Then there was the knife."

"But you know how that happened." Her eyes sought his. He had caused the conflicted emotions that hovered there.

"I know what Pierre said. What I don't know is why he chose to confess when there was no sign of his being discovered as the culprit. I would not be able to identify Verbeux's shaving blade."

She crossed her arms, and the voluminous gauzy stuff of her gown and robe pressed against her full bosom. He looked instantly to her bare feet, small, slender feet. He concentrated on those feet rather than on parts of her body he found all but irresistible.

"Pierre was honest," she said. "He was afraid for his position but still he told the truth and should be commended for it. All an accident."

"You cannot say this afternoon's debacle was an accident."

She pressed two fingers of each hand to her temples and said, "No."

"Meg?" Jean-Marc bent to look into her face. "You don't feel well?"

"I have a tightness here—" she tapped her brow "—and I should like to be alone to think."

"You must stay with me, at least.... Will you please stay with me?"

Tears filled her eyes, and her mouth trembled.

"Meg, Meg, have I displeased you so much?"

He didn't expect what came next. Meg held his arms and stood close enough to force her to look up at him. She chafed his arms, slipped her hands beneath his coat and smoothed his chest. He knew he must not speak, must not move.

"You owe me no explanation," she said, "but am I right in thinking you have enemies?"

Lies should only be employed out of necessity. "What I tell you is a trust, but I have no fear that you will betray me. I confess I believe it very likely that there are those who would see me dead. However, I was not in the coach today. It makes no sense that someone expected me to be."

"Sometimes people act on impulse. Seeing the coach, it could well have been assumed that you were using it—and what followed was a rash, unplanned move. Or perhaps not so rash. You could have been seen."

He inclined his head but didn't take his gaze from hers.

"How was it that you were there to avert disaster?"

His mouth dried, and words seemed unlikely to come easily. "I saw the horses madden."

"Yes." Her voice was so soft. "I know. But you were there, on Bond Street. Why?"

Closing his eyes, he settled his hands on her shoulders. "To watch over you, of course. But you already know that—you only wanted to hear me say the words."

"Perhaps. It's true that hearing them is the sweetest thing to my ears. You know that I cannot deny my feelings for you. You cause me to feel invincible, to want to be all things for you. But I should be the liar if I didn't tell you that the thought of what would be ahead if I accepted your offer of a liaison is too terrible to bear."

"I don't want to speak further of troublesome matters. You are with me now. We are safe and the night is ours—if you will let it be so."

"What do you expect me to say?"

"Yes." He held her face in his big hands. "I expect you to say yes, and then I expect you to put yourself into my care."

"Care?" She gave him a long glance from beneath her lashes. "What does that mean, Jean-Marc?"

"That I will make decisions for both of us, and that I am promising you now, with my head and with my heart—" he placed a fist on his chest "—I am promising you I will never cause you harm. I will always keep you safe."

She wanted so much to believe him, to trust him, to accept him. "I have something—one other thing I must ask you to consider. The Princess. Is there any possibility that someone might want to hurt her?"

Désirée? He wrapped an arm around Meg's neck and pulled her to him, her grazed skin held firmly but carefully by the crook of his elbow. "I can't believe that would be so. There is no reason, Meg. She is a girl. A princess, it is true, but not considered important by anyone, including our parents."

Meg held him tight. She nuzzled her face against his chest. "I cannot bear to hear you say that. Don't you know how wonderful she is?''

"I'm beginning to know very well."

"And you cannot encourage your parents to notice, too?"

"Her mother is not my mother. Verbeux makes excuses for Princess Marie, says she is a kind woman but afraid of her husband. I do intend to have a serious conversation with my father about Désirée. But first, I want her to attract a man who will capture even my father's attention."

"Oh, I'm so grateful you will help her. Do you know your own mother?"

He considered before saying, "That is a topic for another time, perhaps. I have learned to forget her, and that brings me comfort. This night will not last forever." With his free hand, he unbuttoned her robe and slipped his hand inside and over her breast. It would be easy to tuck his way under the neck of her gown, but he had time to be subtle, to discover how much more she was ready to experience with him.

"If anyone discovers we are together like this, my reputation and my authority will be ruined in this house," Meg said. "I must protect my ability to be what the Princess needs."

"That is all that matters?" He smoothed the thin fabric until he could hold one heavy breast. Beneath his stroking thumb, her nipple became hard, and she drew in breaths through her teeth. "Meg, is your only concern for my sister?"

"No," she gasped. "No, my concern is that I want this. I want to be with you and please you as much as you please me. I want you to teach me all the wonderful things I think you know, but I don't wish to be shamed."

"You shall not be," he told her, and prayed he could make it so. He went to the door and turned the key in the lock.

His clothes bound him. He shrugged out of his coat, took off his waistcoat and loosened his neck cloth. But he forced himself to remain slow and to smile at her. "I find I am also too warm." With that, he discarded the neck cloth and unbuttoned his shirt.

This removed, he stood before her in the buff riding britches that were his preferred dress.

She stared at his chest, and her lips parted. Meg Smiles was passionate, and he almost felt the aching he thought she felt in her body's most secret—most irresistible places. His warmth turned to a burning. His belly tightened until the muscles ached. He gave her no warning before capturing her and bringing his mouth down on hers. Her bottom fitted his hands nicely, and he lifted her to her toes. Their mouths sought and begged, demanded and took. In moments she fought to reach her tongue deeply into his mouth. She jutted her pelvis, but it was Jean-Marc who clamped her so close she must know every intimate inch of his swollen manhood. He rocked into her, gently but definitely, and she cried out, a faint, demanding cry.

Abruptly he released her, took her by the hand and raced her into his bedchamber. He blew out all the lights and through open curtains at the high windows, a white moon flooded the room. Again he locked the door before facing her. "Will you be whatever I guide you to be?"

She frowned at him. Meg, he thought, had no idea what he might mean. Very gently, he took her hands between his and kissed her knuckles. "What I'm telling you is that love between a man and a woman takes many forms. The most intimate expression takes many forms. Oh, Meg, will you let me make sure you wear my brand within you just as I will forever wear your brand upon me?"

Meg didn't understand anything but that he offered her passion and that now she could deny him nothing. She didn't answer him, but she held her arms toward him as a supplicant and did what felt natural. Meg Smiles went to her knees before the man she loved. She bowed her head and waited.

"My love," he said. "I cannot resist you any longer."

The next sound she heard was the removal of his belt. He hopped to remove his fine boots and throw them aside. His breeches followed, and while her mouth parted of its own accord, she watched him strip naked before her. The room was all bronzed silks, and Jean-Marc was bronzed also. Straight and tall, he stood before her, his shoulders broad, his arms and legs powerfully made, the hair on his chest silken dark and extending past his navel like an arrow guiding the way to that part of him that made no pretence of its response to her.

All but choking on each word, she said, "That happens often?" and pointed to his rod.

"It happens when the object of my arousal fills my mind, my body, my desire. Then I cannot, do not want to feel anything but what I feel now." He cupped himself. "I could not quell this if I chose to try. With you before me, it throbs out its desire for you."

This was not to be exactly like the last meeting, Meg thought, the infamous meeting when they had barely met. "I could look at you like that forever. And I have my feelings, too. Here." She covered her breasts, rubbed her nipples and hissed at the scalding sensation that followed. "And here." The hand she placed between her legs encountered moistness, and there was a place there in which extraordinary sensation mounted. She began to pant.

"Oh, no, no," Jean-Marc said, laughing. He pulled her hand away. "Time enough for that with me. Come, it is time."

He raised her hands high above her head. "To be powerless in the hands of a lover can be most arousing, Meg. Let us see if it arouses you."

She was helpless to resist when he backed her to a high casement, where her body was pressed to the wall and her shoulders bent to rest on the sloping stone window ledge.

"Hold the handles that open the windows," he told her. "Unless it hurts you."

"It doesn't hurt me, but I'm cold."

"Not for long," he said. He lifted her gown, smoothed it upward, taking liberties with each inch of skin he touched. "Growing warmer?"

"Yes," she whispered. "I can't stand it."

"Good. I want you to remember this night forever and to live trying to equal the beauty of first discovery." Her belly was slightly rounded and firm. Her waist dipped in, accentuating the flare of her hips. Upward over her ribs he persisted, taking pleasure in his ability to all but span her body there.

"Touch me," she said on a husky breath. "Oh, please touch me."

"Soon enough." She would have no idea what this restraint cost him. "It will be easier this way." And he skimmed the gown over her head and let it fall. Immediately she covered her breasts.

Clenching the muscles in his jaws, Jean-Marc dropped to his knees. He kissed her belly, rested his cheek there, stroked her buttocks and thighs again and again. He darted his tongue between her legs only once—and almost brought her tumbling on top of him.

He cast around, blessing the brilliant moon that lighted his way. Without ceremony, he swept her from her feet and stretched her out on the plush bench at the bottom of his bed. Removing a heavy silken rope from a bed drapery took only a second. He was so quick to use the rope to tie her arms and her ankles beneath the bench that she didn't cry out until he swung a leg over her and positioned himself at the entrance to her body.

Her breath rasped rapidly, and she arched her back. He put his mouth close to her ear and said, "Perfect, wild one. Just perfect. Let me see how badly you want me. Your breasts gleam in the moonlight, and your hair shines. You are mine. Whatever I want to do to you, I can do. The decision is mine to make."

He made the lightest of circles around her breasts, trailing the backs of his fingers, watching her moist lips remain parted and her face toss from side to side.

She tried to arch her breasts toward him and begged, "Please, Jean-Marc. Please put your mouth on them, please. *Please.*"

The more she begged, the more slowly he made soft circles over her large, perfectly round breasts. When she writhed from side to side, they swayed voluptuously and Jean-Marc was all but undone. At last he could restrain himself no longer and he did what she begged for—and almost disgraced himself at once. He pulled on her breasts until his mouth seemed filled and the blood pumping into his rod grew unbearably tight.

Her skin was slick with sweat, but not as slick as his. He lowered himself to rub his body over hers. Now and again he kissed her lips, but each time she bit down on his lips and rolled more furiously to touch more and more of him.

He sat on the bench between her spread thighs. He trained his pulsing tip on the engorged flesh that was no longer hidden by hair grown wet. Each time he touched himself to her, she wailed and raised her hips.

Jean-Marc loosened another silk cord. He parted the smooth flesh intended to hide her womanly place and employed the soft threads of a tassel to drive her higher and higher. And when she cried out for mercy, he gave her mercy with his tongue. Very few tiny tugs with his lips, and she raised her hips with almost inhuman strength before shudders racked her, and she keened a high cry.

He could make her with child.

Sweat turned cold on his body. A child. His child and Meg's. A child like himself with parents who would go to any length to deny him until they wanted to use him.

"Jean-Marc," Meg said quietly. "May I do what will make you happy, please?"

"Have I ever said you are overly polite?"

"No."

"I should have." Moonlight caressed every dip and rise in her body. He bent over her and kissed the shadows. Between her breasts he lavished much attention, and he held her sweet flesh while he did so.

The sudden rhythmic rise and fall of her strong hips smote any resolve he might be trying to gather. And between each upward thrust of the hip, she rubbed from side to side, sending a deep throbbing into his ballocks.

"Very well," he said, putting his face close to hers and kissing her hard. "I think this is what you want, my dear. It's certainly what I want."

He pushed inside her. Meg gasped and tried to close her legs. He pushed some more, and pushed, and pushed, until he filled her to bursting. She burned and felt as if he would break her apart.

"Jean-Marc!"

"Hush, sweet."

"I am torn. I felt it."

For an instant he held still and rested his head beside hers. "You are torn," he murmured. "And you are mine. I will never let you go."

What he did then was amazing. He rose to brace his weight on his hands, and locked his elbows, and drove back and forth inside her, rocked back at forth, his body glistening in pale moonlight. When he brought his chest down upon hers, she watched his hard buttocks move him in and out of her.

Sensation mounted. "It cannot happen again, can it?" she said.

"Yes," he told her tersely. "And again and again for some people."

And he thrust once more, hard and long, and Meg tossed from side to side, and felt something pour from him into her at the precise moment the marvelous ripples of sensation captured and flowed over her.

"Don't ever try to leave me, Meg," Jean-Marc said. "I will not allow it."

His tone disquieted her, but only for an instant. She was sore and languid at the same time.

Jean-Marc separated from her and rapidly untied her bonds. "Perhaps I was wrong to restrain you. If so, I promise never to do it again."

"I liked it," she said, and giggled. When he drew her into his arms and stood up with her, she turned her face to his neck and said, "I want to do it every day, please."

"Hell's teeth," he muttered. "An insatiable wench. Wait until you start feeling your aching muscles. You may change your mind."

Still carrying her, he got onto his bed, settled her bottom into his lap and covered them both. The most natural thing was to play with her breasts and kiss her shoulder, but she cried out—differently this time—and he remembered the cuts from the glass in the coach and whispered, "Forgive me, love. I forgot."

Meg said, "There is plenty of me that was not cut by glass. Help yourself."

He did not recall being so satiated, or feeling so right with a woman. Oh, he was wrong. He had taken a virgin who knew almost nothing of the world. But now he held her in his arms and felt the relaxed heaviness of sleep steal over her. And he wanted her exactly where she was.

No longer a virgin, yet unmarried. Her life was forever changed. Jean-Marc, Count Etranger, was also changed. For the first time he had taken a woman who had no designs upon him. But he had also created difficulties at a time when he should be avoiding any complications.

He'd forgotten the big cat. The animal's unexpected loud, thin cry sent shivers up his spine. "Hush," he told it. "Lie down and sleep."

The cat's response was to leap upon the bed, climb on top of Jean-Marc and Meg and sit there hissing quietly.

"What is it?" Meg asked sleepily. "Halibut? What do you want?"

"Whatever he wants, he won't be getting it." He leaned over her and kissed her cheek. "Sleep fast, my love. I will soon be ready to give you your turn. Next you shall tie me down and force unwanted loving upon me."

"Unwanted?" She laughed explosively.

Halibut hissed aloud and stood up. He growled and yowled.

"Good heavens," Meg said. "He never makes noises like that."

"Be still." Jean-Marc rolled over to light a lamp beside the bed.

Meg raised her head to frown about the room. Halibut sat on the bottom of the bed, the fur along his backbone standing up in spikes.

"Hey, settle down, old fellow," Jean-Marc said.

Halibut's response was to leap from the bed and stalk toward the door leading to the study. There he commenced spitting and yowling louder than ever. Then he used his front paws as if he were pummeling an unseen opponent. He pawed the air before the locked door, and his drawn claws were clearly visible.

"Ignore him," Jean-Marc said, drawing Meg into his arms again. "I think he's jealous of us."

Meg laughed, but stopped laughing almost at once. The cry she heard could not be imaginary. "Did you hear that?" she asked Jean-Marc. "That sound?"

"I couldn't have," he said.

Meg rolled toward him. He kept her close in his arms and looked down at her breasts. "Concentrate," she told him.

"I am."

"Concentrate on that noise. Oh, Jean-Marc, there it is again. Someone is hurt. Being hurt."

"We've got to deaden these imaginations of ours."

The cry came only once more.

"There," Jean-Marc said, "I told you it wasn't anything."

"You've just admitted that you heard what I heard—a man shrieking as if he was being hurt. As if he was being bitten, or scratched, perhaps."

"That's outrageous."

"Is it? You saw what Halibut was doing—behaving as if he was scratching and biting. And where is he now? Tell me that. Where has Halibut gone? Through a locked door?"

"Of course not." Jean-Marc sat up and called, "Halibut, Halibut, come here, boy."

"He isn't coming because he can't hear you," Meg said. "He's too busy chasing whoever—or whatever—was here in this room—spying on us.''

"Are you suggesting this house is haunted?" Jean-Marc laughed. "By a ghost incompetent enough to get caught by a cat?"

24

The love of a gentle woman, Verbeux thought, would be a wondrous thing. Across the square, soft-skinned Sibyl Smiles would be asleep. How he would like to go to her, to lie with her, to know how to make love to her without terrifying or hurting her— or repulsing her.

Just the idea of her looking at him with disgust sickened him. Each time they encountered each other, she turned her clear blue eyes on him, and he saw an unspoken appeal there. Without so much as understanding how her eyes invited him to respond, she beckoned him. And he thanked God he was civilized enough to do no more than return her smiles. In future he would ignore her completely—for her own good.

He could not remain in his rooms, elegant as they were. He must walk and think—perhaps outside. The night was chill, and he threw on a cloak.

When Verbeux stepped into the corridor and closed his door, the house seemed to settle about him, to whisper, to taunt. On the way to the stairs, he passed his employer's apartments. That man's desires were plain to another man of the world. It remained to be seen if the Count would succumb and seduce Meg Smiles. Verbeux prayed afresh. There lay the solution to the problem of how his master could escape his father's designs.

Encountering no one on the way, Verbeux let himself out of the house by a back door and slipped quickly through the gardens to a gate leading to the mews. The horses were stabled there, in buildings that housed married servants in second stories.

A hand settled on his back, and he started violently. By the time he turned around, he held a pistol.

"Where are you going?" Ila, Lady Upworth, was even more beautiful by moonlight.

"Get into the house," he whispered harshly. "I won't ask where you've been. It's none of my affair. You are mad to be abroad alone—at such a time."

"Only now am I abroad, and I am with you. I followed you."

He returned his pistol to the waist of his breeches and took her by the shoulders. "What are you saying? What is this game?" He shook her. "The truth, My Lady. I shall find you out in any lies. And you will suffer."

"I have already told you the truth. I followed you and could tell all wasn't well with you. I need your help, Verbeux. Whatever your price, I will pay it. Whatever."

He turned his face from her. "Do you think me a fool? Am I supposed to accept your fiction and not ask how you came to see me in the house—and so late? Go back."

"It wasn't fiction. I was coming to you and you left your rooms as I reached the gallery."

She flung herself at him, crushed her body to his and held him. "Do not send me away, I beg of you. Oh, please don't send me away. It's true that my need gave me the courage to approach you, but I have wanted you to notice me since the day we met. I tried to catch your attention by letting you see me with Jean-Marc, but you are too loyal to lust after what you think is your master's property. Of late I thought you seemed a little interested, and so I came to you tonight."

Lady Upworth was warm, her body womanly and erotic where she formed it to his. But she was right, there was at least the potential for the Count to consider her his when, and if, he wanted her. She was also right that he, Verbeux, had been watching her and found her desirable.

"I have been a fool," she told him. "I have almost nothing left of what I inherited from my late husband."

He could not make himself push her away. "How could that be, My Lady? And what do you imagine I can do about it?"

"It can be because I have fallen deep into debt. Cards. I know that shocks you, but I have had little pleasure in my life for a long time. I believe Jean-Marc would help me, but he has ceased to be interested in me. I do not hold that against him. Men and women change their minds about each other. But he does not approve of certain things—definitely not women who gamble, and in low places."

"I cannot help you," Verbeux said, but she touched him where he had thought he couldn't be touched—in a well-hidden, protective place that did not relish seeing her ruined and in poor circumstances.

"You could if you wanted to," she murmured, and he thought she cried. The moon had slipped behind a cloud, and he could no longer see her clearly. She said, "I am not a bad woman. I am—or have been—weak. And I am without money. I am not asking you for money. I am asking you for friendship and comfort. The Count will continue to give me refuge, and I hope to meet someone who will want to marry me. Then I will be saved. But there is something I need so badly and I have nothing to lose by asking for it."

He waited, but when she didn't continue, he said, "Tell me." The sound of voices came to him, the voices of more than one man entering the mews from an alley between two houses. "Hush, do as I tell you."

Throwing an arm around her, he hurried behind a lilac bush and into an utterly black corner. Afraid Lady Upworth might wear something that glittered, he wrapped her beneath his cloak and held her there.

The raucous fellows were in their cups. Their voices rose and fell depending on how recently one of them had issued a warning to be quiet. They stumbled on the cobbles, and their feet clattered between gusts of ribald laughter. Verbeux had no wish to risk a confrontation with thugs while he had a woman in his company.

Four men passed at last—he could make out the shapes of them. So drunk were they that they made slow progress, having to stop frequently to drag up whichever of them had just fallen.

"They are gone," Lady Upworth whispered when the footsteps and voices faded. "You protected me. Thank you."

He said nothing. What he'd done had been innate.

"Do you still want me to tell you what it is I have wanted?"

"Yes," he replied, and he wanted other things he must not have.

"I have wanted you, Verbeux. You are the most intriguing man I have ever met. And I think you also want me. I have seen how you look at me. There is a wildness in you that reaches out to touch my needs. I have said I am not a bad woman, but I am a passionate one. I need a man who can match my appetites. Are you that man?"

Her bluntness inflamed him. "Are you asking me for sex, My Lady? Do you want to copulate right here—in this dark corner in the open air—"

She placed her hand over his mouth. Her other hand she slipped around his crotch, and she cupped and squeezed him.

He jerked his face away from her hand and said, "For God's sake," through clenched teeth. "Are you mad?"

"Oh, no, not mad." Her breath was warm on his neck. She kissed him there, so gently he closed his eyes and held his breath. Her lips were insistent, but soft. While she kissed him she went to work loosening his breeches until he felt the air cool upon his belly. There was nothing cool about his rod.

"A new experience," he said, and set his pistol on the ground. "Taken by a woman. Used by a woman. A beautiful woman. And only because she lusts for me."

"Don't make fun. If you do I shall make you suffer later—when you want me again. I'll make you wait a very long time."

Why shouldn't he enjoy what she offered? She was beautiful, and he'd had too little time to satisfy his own considerable sexual appetite. "I do not find you humorous, My Lady. Far from it."

"Ila," she told him, wriggling beneath the cloak, evidently removing clothes. "The moon is playing with us again. Look."

Automatically he raised his face, but she laughed and said, "No. Look at me."

He did so, and she opened the cloak. Her breasts gleamed white in that flirting moon, and so did her belly and thighs. Between her legs a triangle of hair showed as a black shadow.

"My Lady!"

"Ila, if you please." Her clever fingers worked to unbutton his shirt. She kissed his chest, played the tip of her tongue over his nipples, pressed her naked breasts to his and rubbed them on his belly. Holding his buttocks, she shifted, crying small cries of ecstacy while she used the end of his rod on first one, then the other nipple. She stimulated herself close to frenzy, then took him into her mouth and bit hard enough to cause Verbeux to disengage her. He drew her up and squeezed her breasts while he kissed her.

"You are without restraint," he told her. "You are a woman in every way."

"Do you like that?"

"I like it. Don't you care if you are found like this by another?"

"No. I care only for the moment, and in this moment I have you. It is not enough, not nearly enough, but it is a start. Lift me. Lift me until I tell you to stop."

Verbeux hesitated only a moment before gripping her by the waist and doing as she asked.

"Higher," she said, panting. "Higher, damn you. *Higher*."

He did as she asked and she leaned harder against him until she could grip the top of the wall behind him. Her legs went around his neck. "Please me, Verbeux," she said, her voice husky. "Please me and I will please you. This is our beginning, but our journey will not be boring, I promise you. Yes, yes, I promise you."

Ila smothered her own scream. Verbeux was as accomplished

a lover as she had expected him to be. Not only did he use his teeth to nip at her, and his tongue to delve, and to drive her wild, but her breasts were his anchors. He held her breasts, pressed them together, used the tips of his nails on her nipples until she feared she would let go of the wall and fall.

Her thighs jerked, clamped his head. "Too much," she moaned. "No, too much. I cannot do this." And with that she bent over him and clung to his muscular shoulders.

"Too much, My Lady? How could I be too much for you?"

She would silence his jesting. "Are you ready, Verbeux? And you are to call me Ila."

"Hmm, I could be ready." He lowered her slowly, and when she reached down between his legs, she discovered how ready he was.

"You have another name, Verbeux. Don't you think I should know it?"

"Names do not matter here. Not now. One day they may."

She filled her hands with his hair and pulled, and while she pulled, she kissed his mouth hard, bit his lips and tasted his blood. He would not ever consider himself her master, the one who made rules.

"*Sacre Dieu.*" Verbeux forced her face away. "Stop, My Lady, or I shall be forced to make sure you do."

Ila laughed. She hung her head back and laughed aloud. "Make sure, Verbeux. I should like that. Hurt me. I should definitely like that."

His response was to hold her hips, lift her slightly and bring her down again. With unerring accuracy he impaled her. Ila panted and squealed. With her feet splayed wide on the wall behind him, she added the strength in her legs to the power that allowed him to hold and move her over him again and again.

"Is that what you had in mind?" he asked, clearly not short of breath.

Ila said yes, and flung out her arms, delighting in her total abandonment. She knew what he saw as he took his pleasure—

and gave Ila hers. Just imagining the vision through his eyes drove her wild.

He spilled into her, but did not stop moving until she begged him to, and grabbed his arms, and swung her feet to the ground.

"Ila," he said, enfolding her, draping his cloak around her.

Ila shuddered and held him in arms that trembled. On his lips, her name was exotic. Joined with him, she was complete. Almost complete.

"I shall want you again," he said against her temple. "Often."

"I know. I shall want that, too."

He stroked her back and her bottom and pulled her to him. His kisses were hard upon her neck and shoulders. "Come to my bed, now," he said, and she heard desperation in his voice. "Now, Ila. I will help you dress and take you there."

True to his word, he helped her. He put on her chemise and gown—which she had tossed on the lilac bush—and finished dressing her as if she were a child. When his clothes were straightened and his pistol retrieved, he took her by the hand and led her into the garden behind Number 17.

She went willingly. She went with a lump in her throat. She went with the certainty that true luck and contentment would never be hers.

Verbeux's rooms were graceful and filled with valuable paintings and furnishings. He didn't as much as speak to her again until they were in his bedchamber and he had removed her clothes once more. Once he had taken her hair down and brushed it, he placed her in his bed and undressed himself.

His face strained, his eyes so dark they appeared black, he slid in beside her and held her for so long she grew desperate. She did not want to care for him—could not care for him. Yet when he looked at her like that her resolve wavered. Never before had she known what it was like to be certain the arms that held her did so because they belonged to a man who wanted more than her body.

She was being a fool. Verbeux's approach might be different, but beneath it all he was the same as the others—just a man with a man's need for sex.

As if he heard her thoughts, he made love to her again. No, he made love to her for the first time. He took her with gentle desperation, and left her even more confused and filled with longing afterward.

He must not think she was anything but a hard, calculating woman. "You are wonderful," she told him. "You know how to use this." She manipulated him without subtlety.

"Ila," he said, embracing her. "Sleep, *cherie*. You must be tired."

"I'll sleep," she said, "after I tell you what I want. Don't worry, I intend to enjoy you often. And I'll give as good as I get—probably better."

He grew still. A candle remained alight beside the bed, and he raised her chin until he could look into her face. His steady regard caused her to flinch.

"I need your cooperation, Verbeux."

His gaze moved from her eyes to her mouth and back again. "Cooperation?"

Only with a weighty heart and a stomach that clenched did she make herself speak. "If you don't want me to turn Jean-Marc against you, you will help me."

This time he flinched. "How would you do that?"

"By telling him you forced yourself on me, then tried to ensure my silence by threatening to tell him it was my idea." Her heart beat faster and faster.

Verbeux frowned, but did not appear as angry as she had expected. "Go on," he said.

"He is enamored with Meg Smiles. I care nothing for her one way or the other. She just is. And she is here and in my way. I must have him. You will help me make sure Jean-Marc loses interest in her. Or you will help me make sure she is no longer able to interfere with my plans."

Verbeux pulled his arms from around her and sat up. He gripped his knees. "You are in love with the Count."

The violence of her emotions shocked her. She could scarcely breathe.

"Answer me," he told her quietly but in a hard voice that brooked no argument. "Do you love him? If you do, why do you think you must resort to such measures? Why make love... Why have sex with me? You could have accused me without touching me." He looked at her and there was pain in his eyes. "You didn't need me to touch you."

"Yes, I did." She finally managed to speak. The tears that coursed her cheeks felt foreign, but she couldn't stem them. Wiping at her cheeks, she said, "I never said I was in love with Jean-Marc, I said I must have him. It's you I love."

25

V irtually the entire house would be open to those attending the musicale. Sibyl stood in the grand foyer and gawked. Gawked was an ugly word, but she knew it was the right one for the occasion.

Footmen in powdered wigs and green and gold livery stood in a line for Rench's inspection. Maids in crackling, starched aprons tried not to look flustered as they hurried in every direction. Cook, rarely seen above stairs, bustled to meet yet another group of additional kitchen staff retained for the event. Seamstresses dashed up and down staircases trailing bolts of shining fabrics. Some decorators looped green garlands along the banisters while others tucked a profusion of pink roses into the foliage.

And from the second floor soared the magnificent voices of a man and woman singing alone or together.

Sibyl's head spun. The world was gone mad. How could she think otherwise when she and her sister were here in this house, surrounded by people she had never thought to meet, and beautiful things, and the best of food, extraordinary comings and goings that didn't happen in the simple lives of a clergyman's daughters?

This evening coaches would circle the whole of Mayfair Square, and the line would continue along many roads leading there. Each coach would stop and one of the boys acting as ti-gers—those who wore their master's family colors and coats of arms while they clung to the back of the carriage—would leap down and run up the front steps of Number Seventeen. They would knock for admission while their gorgeously attired masters and mistresses prepared to make an elegant entrance the moment the door opened. The door would close behind them, the next coach would take the place of its predecessor, and the ritual would begin again.

"Good morning, Miss Smiles. And a very good morning it is, don't you think?"

Sibyl looked at Count Etranger a little too long before she remembered to curtsey and say, "Indeed, My Lord."

"Have you had your final costume fitting?"

She smiled tentatively. "I hope to watch the arrivals from some inconspicuous place, My Lord. I will not require costume for that, surely."

He put his fists on his hips and strode back and forth, looking at her afresh each time he passed. "Mmm, yes, yes. Yes, I believe you will. Go at once to the Princess's apartments. I will send word that a costume is to be made for you."

"Oh, no." She simply couldn't go. "That is, thank you, no. It wouldn't be suitable for me to attend."

"Your pupil will play the pianoforte this evening."

"Yes, and she will do so very well. She is so talented."

"And you will turn the pages of her music, Miss Smiles. And you will enjoy the pageantry of it all."

"But—"

"That, Miss Smiles, is an order. Upstairs with you."

She curtseyed again and did as she was told, but her heart beat so very fast.

When she reached the first gallery, she paused and looked down. The Count mortified her by bowing and raising a hand in a wave. Sibyl waved back and gawked again. Adam Chillworth had been admitted and strode toward the Count with rolls of canvas under each arm and a large portfolio hanging from his left hand.

The Count still watched her, only he appeared puzzled. Sibyl remembered to close her mouth, only to cover it when Adam's voice rang out. "I see ye, Sibyl Smiles. There's a person wantin' t'see ye. At Number Seven. That cousin of yours."

She would gladly disappear. At once. When she shook her head at Adam, it was the Count who drew her attention. He beckoned to her, and there was no question of pretending she didn't see the gesture when Adam said, "Yes, Sibyl, come down, will ye? That William's a rare one. Wait till you hear all the plans he's got for you and Meg."

Sibyl crept back the way she'd come, doing her best not to appear as terrified as she felt. Well, bosh to William, anyway. She raised her chin and swayed a little in the manner she'd seen Lady Upworth sway. Well, not quite like that, of course.

"I brought ye the paintings, M'Lord," Adam said. "Portraits of those who couldn't afford to pay, or didn't like my work."

The Count regarded Adam very directly. "You are an honest man, Mr. Chillworth. I like that. We will look at your work in the library. Come with us, Miss Smiles. Oh, Rench." He called to the butler, who had been about to go down to the kitchens. "Kindly have a message taken to the modistes. Tell them they must make a costume for Miss Sibyl Smiles. For this evening. There are enough seamstresses in this house to outfit an army by nightfall—one, er, something or other for a small woman should be no problem."

Rench bowed, but his expression suggested he disapproved of the instruction.

Count Etranger indicated that Sibyl should enter the library, and followed with Adam. "I will look at your paintings," he said. "Please give Miss Smiles your message and let her go about her business. This is a very busy day for all of us."

Adam and Sibyl looked at each other.

"Don't mind me," the Count said. "Just carry on."

As if he were suddenly deaf, Sibyl thought, scarcely able to take her eyes from this man she was certain Meg had come to love. And he had not been clever enough to hide his feelings for

Meg from Sibyl, either. She saw how his gaze lingered on Meg's face, and how it followed her every move.

"Right," Adam said. "Well, Reverend Baggs is staying at Latimer's. But ye know that. And a nuisance the man is, too. He doesn't try to hide how he's watching you and Meg for your cousin William. Says he's doing it out of duty because William's worried about ye and it'll be a few weeks before he can move to London."

"These are good," the Count said. "Very good. Unconventional, but engaging."

"Thank you," Adam said, giving one of his rare and brilliant smiles.

"Move here?" Sibyl said. "Did you say Cousin William intends to move to London? But how can he? Where would he live? And how could he take care of the holdings in Puckly Hinton? He takes his living from them."

A hesitant tap at the open door drew the attention of everyone in the library. Meg stood there. Dressed in creamy muslin and matching slippers, and with her hair piled softly atop her head, she took Sibyl's breath away.

"Come in," the Count said, and Sibyl watched yet again as he studied her sister from head to toe. Muscles in his cheeks tightened, and he stood straight to watch while she came toward him.

"You're lovely, Meg," Adam said appreciatively. "Like an angel. One day someone ought to give ye pearls to go with that dress. On your wedding day, mayhap. Ye look as beautiful as a bride."

Color rose in Meg's cheeks. She said, "Thank you, Adam. What a flatterer you are."

"Mr. Chillworth is an honest man," the Count said, his formidable chest expanding with the deep breath he took. Abruptly, he returned to studying the paintings.

"Someone just brought a message to the modistes," Meg said

to Sibyl. "You are to have a costume for this evening, and they want you to come now."

"Your cousin William says he's moving to London," Adam told Meg. "Thought I should mention it to ye. He's at Number Seven again. Says Reverend Baggs witnessed another carriage disaster—Bond Street, that would be—and sent for him."

Meg shook her head. "Holding the sides of his hat," she murmured. "I saw him, but didn't really...see him. Then I forgot."

"Little wonder," Adam said. "You're a strong girl, but you're just a girl all the same. All this is too much for a quiet one like ye. Mr. Godly-Smythe says he's going to set up home here and have the two of you move in. Where he can keep you safe, so he says."

The Count's hands were tightly fisted on the edge of his great desk. He leaned to study another of Adam's paintings. Sibyl noted how his knuckles had turned white.

"Oh, Meg," Sibyl said.

"He can't," Meg said shortly. "He has responsibilities in—"

"He's going to sell his house, he says," Adam told them. "His only choice when he's got to think about you two. If ye won't go back home. He's waiting to see ye. Asked me to tell ye that."

Only through enormous restraint did Jean-Marc hold his tongue. What happened in Meg's and her sister's family was no affair of his and might never be—if Meg continued to treat him with glacial reserve. From the moment the damnable cat had set up its squalling in his bedchamber, Meg had been convinced their lovemaking had been observed, and he had only kept her at his side by holding her there. Once he had fallen asleep, she must have slipped away, and when next he saw her, she dealt with him as she would any stranger worthy of respect.

She was ashamed. The thought infuriated him. Meg Smiles was ashamed of having made love with him, and now she struggled to regain pride. What did a man have to do to claim the woman he couldn't live without?

"Please go upstairs, Sibyl," Meg said. "Don't worry, William has no authority over us, and he won't sell the house—that's all bluff. He would lose too much if he did so. My Lord, I apologize for the intrusion of our personal affairs. Do you think I could ask the Princess to come down and see Adam's work?''

"If you wish." He would grant her anything. All she had to do was ask, or even convey what she wanted by any means, and her desires would come true. "Sibyl, please find Princess Désirée and ask her to join us." He turned to Meg. "Tell me what you think of this."

As Sibyl left the library, Meg advanced slowly. There was a bloom on her skin, and her hair seemed an even richer red. When she lowered her eyelids and cast a shy glance at him through her lashes, he barely restrained himself from taking her in his arms.

"A young mother," he told her, indicating a plump brunet matron holding her child. "The baby is particularly engaging."

"Yes," she said, leaning down at his side.

She held the edge of the desk, and he contrived to do likewise, their hands just brushing. He expected her to move away, but she didn't.

With her head inclined to one side, she studied the mother and child. Her lips parted a little. Sunlight through the windows made her translucent. Her eyes shimmered. "Adam, you are a gifted man," she said, following the line of the baby's mouth with a finger just above the canvas.

"Indeed," Jean-Marc said. He pointed to the infant's dimpled arms, settled his hand on top of Meg's and met her eyes when she looked at him. "I think Mr. Chillworth would do a good job of painting my sister, don't you?"

Her bosom rose and fell rapidly. The neck of the strikingly simple gown was low—a pleasing thing on one so worthy of display. "I do think Adam would paint the Princess beautifully," she said at last, and glanced at his hand on hers. His skin was tanned by the sun and wind, and dark beside Meg's. Jean-Marc recalled how soft she was, how soft her entire body had felt against his, and how their differences, his hard, long-muscled limbs wound about her rounded paleness, her breasts grazing his chest—how the contrasts had inflamed him. They still inflamed him.

Meg took her hand from Jean-Marc's and turned to Adam. Her old friend was a little too slow in disguising his curiosity. "William is at Number Seven now?" she asked. "Well, he will have to wait a long time to see us because this is a very busy day. If he accosts you again when you return, tell him you spoke with me, but Sibyl and I will not return until tomorrow. Sibyl will stay with me. He must not be allowed to remain at Number Seven."

"He won't be," Adam said. "Leave it to me, Meggie."

Meg smiled at that. "Don't throw him from a window, or anything like that, Adam. A constable might take you away, and I shouldn't like that."

Princess Désirée literally erupted into the library. She trotted and twirled and trotted again. Each time she faced them all, her smile was only for Adam. "Ha, ha," she said. "I am preparing to be a charming nymph of a thing tonight. I shall smile and smile to please my dear Meg. But I hope they manage to botch the finishings on my ridiculous costume. Unsuitable thing. It would be wonderful on Ila, or on Meg, but on me it is like using a gold platter for oatmeal. I am so bland I disappear inside its glitter."

"Fiddle dee dee," said Meg. "What absolute rubbish. The costume is perfect on you. Now, you are not to say another word, because it is to be a surprise."

Adam seemed to have stopped breathing. He had followed the Princess's unusual entrance with spellbound attention.

"I have matters to attend to," Jean-Marc said. He pulled the embroidered bell sash. "And I need your assistance, Miss Smiles. I shall call for a maid to remain with the Princess and Mr. Chillworth. Discuss how you might paint her, sir. She will make the decision, anyway, so I might as well save myself the effort of giving any advice."

"Good," Princess Désirée said. "Thank you, Jean-Marc. I

think I shall be painted in my silly costume. What do you think of that?"

"As you will," he said, indicating for Meg to leave the room with him.

Rench arrived and went at once to dispatch a maid to chaperone Princess Désirée.

"Oh," the Princess cried, suddenly very serious. "I have the most perfect idea. Mr. Chillworth should attend the musicale this evening. That would give him a chance to see me in my costume and decide if it does become me. Isn't that a good idea, Jean-Marc?"

Meg expected the man to refuse. Instead he said, "If Mr. Chillworth considers it a good idea, then so do I. Here's Millie. Don't spend too much time boring Mr. Chillworth, Désirée. You do not have the whole day to waste."

He crossed the foyer with Meg behind him and went into a small receiving room that was rarely used. The windows were open to let in the spring air, and bowls of roses had been placed on every surface. Tonight this room would also be needed.

"Please close the door," Jean-Marc said. "We shall have to watch my young sister. I believe she is starting to notice well-favored men, and she may not yet be discerning enough not to moon over unsuitable companions."

Meg wanted to say that Adam Chillworth was a very suitable companion for anyone, but restrained herself. She must not prolong her time alone with Jean-Marc.

"Is there any question of your cousin having authority over you?" he asked.

"No." The question caught her off guard. "William has no right to tell us what to do. I can't think why he has become so determined to pursue us. It's true that he showed a certain favor to Sibyl even when she was several years younger. I understand his wanting to marry her. But she will not have him, and I don't blame her. His talk about moving to London is obviously a ruse. Here he would be unimportant. In Puckly Hinton he has holdings—my father's holdings—and is considered a gentleman of note. He would never give that up."

Jean-Marc listened in silence. When she had finished speaking, he continued to study Meg. She tried not to return his attention, but failed. As surely as if he touched her, she felt his hands on her body.

"Come here," he said.

She must refuse. She must sever anything personal between them.

He leaned on the edge of a table and crossed his arms. She glanced at his breeches where they strained over his thighs, and quickly looked away.

"Meg."

"Both Mr. VonWerther and Madame Clarisse Bisset are practicing in the music room. Cook is shouting at everyone, including the extra staff. The florists are everywhere. The roses overwhelm me. There are so many of them. Princess—"

"Don't chatter. Come to me, or I must make sure you do. You have nothing to fear from me, Meg, except for the hurt you cause me and its effect on my temper."

She approached him with sturdy steps, making sure she showed no particular emotion. "Of course, My Lord. I am at your disposal."

"Are you now, *cherie?* How glad I am to hear it. Are you prepared for your duties this evening?"

She was anything but prepared to stand with the Princess and act almost as if she were her mother. "Yes, thank you. I'm ready."

"You have no questions about my expectations of you?"

"None, My Lord."

"That's unfortunate. I have a great many things to ask you about your own expectations of me, Meg. Have you forgotten that we lay together only three nights ago?"

She put a finger to her lips. Her heart beat fast and uncomfortably.

"Do not tell me to be quiet. Do you expect *me* to forget how we made love? How you look naked? How it feels to be inside you?"

"Dreadful," she said, bowing her head. "This is dreadful. I don't want you to be angry. I would never willingly hurt you. We should not have done what we did. And I do not blame you more than myself. But despite... Although I am ruined, I must not panic. I must do my best to find a kind husband who will care for me, and look after Sibyl until she is also wed."

Jean-Marc stood. He stood so close they almost touched. She stared down at his booted feet and willed this to be over.

"Do you care for me at all?" he said.

She whispered, "yes," and wished she were stronger, strong enough to deny him.

"And I care for you. We don't know what the future may hold. I cannot make the promises you would like to hear, but I can offer myself to you as a companion. As a lover, Meg. I want to be the man who comes to you for comfort, and to comfort you. I will provide for Sibyl. I will give you a house. It will be yours and you will never want for anything again."

She would not want for anything but respect—and a husband.

He walked around her, and she heard him go to the door and turn a key in the lock. "We cannot be disturbed," he said. "And you will not leave me until you have admitted that you want what I offer."

"I want you," she said, and hugged herself. "I don't want what you can offer me. Not things and money."

"You want me?" He stood behind her and jerked her against him. "You shall have me. I will never want another woman as I want you."

"As a ladybird? As a courtesan with lowly beginnings? As the one you escape to when you want someone other than the woman worthy to be your wife?"

Jean-Marc spun her around. Holding her wrist hard enough to

hurt, he loomed over her. "Forgive me," she said, fighting back tears. "I don't want you to be angry."

He loosed her wrist and raised her chin. "But you want me to marry you."

Meg spread her fingers. "I know you can't do that. Why would you be so cruel as to tell me I would think of such a thing?"

"You *haven't* thought of such a thing?" His cold smile tore at her. "You are a woman. Women always think of such things."

"Very well. Yes. Yes, I have thought of it. I have thought of you, and dreamed of you, and felt you when you were nowhere near. Everywhere I go, I see you. With everything that I am, I long to discover that I will never have to live without you. But I do not expect the impossible."

He closed his eyes before he kissed her. The stark lines of his face showed how he struggled. The kiss was not harsh, as Meg expected. He didn't crush her mouth with his, or attempt to force himself upon her.

Jean-Marc pressed her fingers and palms to his chest, covered and held them there. When his lips touched hers, it was with such lightness as the brush of a butterfly's wings. His breathing was as labored as hers. With the tip of his tongue he opened her mouth, then pulled her upper lip gently between his teeth. Over and over again he kissed her so, each time more slowly than the time before.

Meg leaned on him, and Jean-Marc slowly drew back until he could look into her face. "Very well," he said, his voice soft but cold, "you shall have what you want. Perhaps it is as well. You have helped me make up my mind on a difficult matter. I wasn't certain I should take so bold a step as to offend my father in order to get my own way. You persuade me."

She watched him speak but could not believe she understood him.

"As I have told you, I prefer England," he said. "With you as my wife, I will be assured of remaining here. My father would never accept you. In time I will make my peace with him. We will wait until Désirée's Season is over before announcing my intentions. Until then we should be discreet about our times together. Easily enough accomplished."

If she attempted to speak, she would surely cry.

"Meg? Do you understand me?"

She nodded and raised her face to the ceiling. Tears ran across her temples to her hair.

His hands came to rest on her shoulders. With his forefingers he stroked her jaw. "What is it? What's wrong? You have what you want. I have said I will marry you."

If she relaxed the muscles in her limbs she would collapse.

"I will never understand women."

"No," she managed to say. "You never will."

"Tell me how you think I have wronged you now?"

Meg laughed. She put three fingertips to his mouth. "Thank you for your offer. You mean well. I should even like to accept, but I could not watch you come to hate me. And you would hate me soon enough."

Gradually his features sharpened. He raised his brows and uttered an oath. "Meg," he said. "Meg, I am a fool. I have never asked a woman to marry me before. I did it badly."

"You were honest. Marrying me isn't what you planned, but it might help you achieve the ends you want with your father. And you do enjoy me."

"Yes," he said. "And I care about you."

"I think you do. And I care about you. But we cannot possibly marry."

"Meg—"

"No. I am honored, but I must refuse."

He made to take her in his arms, but when she pushed him away he didn't persist. "You intend never to be with me again?" he asked. "Because I was clumsy in announcing my intentions, you will deny me?"

Meg walked away and unlocked the door. "I said I will not marry you. I didn't say I refuse your other offer—yet."

26

*S*pivey here.

Be grateful you are not at the mercy of creatures that sense any movement in the dark. One or two members of the new company I keep have taken pleasure in speaking of feline second sight, particularly, they say, when a ghost is clumsy enough to capture the creature's attention. Piffle! I am not clumsy, or inept—another insult that has been hurled at me. That clawed monster felt my presence.... No... No, surely that cannot be what those noddy cocks spoke of. Can it? Is it possible that cats actually see those on the other side? My, my, I shall have to keep a sharp eye open to avoid future attacks.

To think of it. Only with the utmost difficulty am I able to pass through a closed door, yet a cat manages the feat without effort. Could it be...yes, that's it, I have something back to front. I am actually drawing things to me—like the wild animal posing as a domesticated pet at Number Seventeen. Dash it all.

I am severely wounded, you know. Of course I was heroic under fire, as it were. But the animal bit me, actually bit and scratched me.

I have to go now. The business with Lady Upworth shocks me, but if it's the Count she wants, that would be most exceedingly useful. The most pressing task is to change Miss Sibyl Smiles's mind about that admirable fellow, William Godly-Smythe. To that end, the unspeakable Ash woman must carry out an essential mission for me. Oh, how I detest the thought of working with her again.

I should prefer not to consider the other Smiles girl at all. Shame, shame, say I. Such wanton behavior on the part of a clergyman's daughter.... Well, enough of that subject. After all, why should I concern myself with her?

Good day to you. Don't smile like that. You think you have outwitted me, don't you? You will have to learn a great deal more about covert behavior if you are to best me. No matter, continue to ignore my warnings. Toss your pure thoughts to the wind. Sneak into temples of depravity where the debauched cavort, and take your pleasure in sly observation. Peep away, and on your own heads be it.

27

Rows of ornate gold chairs upholstered in deep blue velvet covered the small ballroom floor. There had been much discussion as to the wisdom of using the large ballroom on the third story instead, but Meg had persuaded Jean-Marc that if some guests were rude enough to talk, those at the back of that room would have difficulty hearing the performers.

She had been right, he decided, particularly since more guests seemed engaged in preening and looking to see who observed them, and in laughing and flirting, than in listening to the music.

Where was she?

"My Lord," Verbeux said, appearing unexpectedly. "You have a success on your hands. That will stand you in good stead. All of London will talk about this evening."

"Will they?" Jean-Marc looked sideways at Verbeux, who wore white robes and a wreath of green leaves about his head. "For God's sake, man, who are you supposed to be?"

Verbeux smirked and said, "Caesar—on a visit to parts east, of course."

"Caesar? Damn, I wish I'd thought of something like that. I feel the fool in this—this thing."

"May I say you look exceedingly handsome as desert chieftain, My Lord? Or are you a slave trader on the hunt for stock?"

Jean-Marc continued to search the room for Meg. "Your fellow, Pierre whatever, seems a great deal more in evidence than used to be the case. He is never far behind you."

"It's important for him to become more sure of himself."

Verbeux didn't look in Pierre's direction. "He continues to apologize for his blunder. I take it Miss Smiles's hand is fully recovered?"

"I wouldn't know. She still wears a bandage but doesn't mention any pain. Can't say I care for your Pierre. Obsequious fellow."

"He's young," Verbeux said, sparing the briefest of glances for Pierre in his costume of some wandering camp player. "Don't give him another thought."

"Go and find someone to peel you a grape, Verbeux, there's a good man. And arrange for half of the floor to be cleared of chairs. Some seem determined to dance."

Verbeux bowed and withdrew with his shadow following along. Young Pierre might be, but now he no longer feared retribution, he carried himself with a straight back and was every inch the fit young blade.

The very accomplished pianist, together with a quartet of strings, played valiantly on, and the babble rose to an overwhelming pitch. The costumes were brilliant. Myriad silks and plumes, lustrous velvets, gems winking beneath the crystal chandeliers and swirls of diaphanous stuff of every color whirling about comely limbs. Sheiks and mandarins hobnobbed with members of desert tribes, while harem girls, many of whom had not been girls for a considerable time, enjoyed throwing themselves into their roles. Flushed cheeks and sparkling eyes attested to the triumph of the event. Flunkies dressed as Egyptian palace slaves passed among the throng carrying silver trays heaped with delicacies. Drink, strong and otherwise, flowed.

Ila came toward him. Another harem girl, but what a harem girl. She smiled, sadly he thought. A beauty in daringly sheer scarlet gauze that revealed the outline of her limbs with every step. Her bodice was also of gauze, and some abbreviated garment that barely covered her breasts showed through. Gold bangles ringed her arms and wrists, and gold coins tinkled at every hem of her costume.

When she stood before him, she tucked one pointed-toed gold slipper behind her and dropped into a deep curtsey.

"Charming," Jean-Marc said, offering her his hand. "Are you enjoying yourself?"

"No."

He looked into her eyes and believed her. "Can I help, Ila? I had thought this would be an opportunity for you to meet old friends, and some new ones. You need to make another life. You told me so."

"Did I?" She averted her face. "I suppose I must have. How simplistic of me. This is the hardest thing I've ever done—to be a widow alone at such a gathering."

"You are a member of my household."

"You tolerate me and offer me refuge. But forgive me. I must not sound ungrateful when I owe you so much."

This was not the Ila he knew. "You are changed," he told her. "Come now, show that pretty smile and look around you. Men cannot take their eyes off you. You have only to give the nod and suitors will be pounding at our doors."

"You are no longer one of those men you speak of," she said, her voice flat. "You were, and not so long ago, but you no longer find me inviting."

"Come with me," he said, "Allow me to introduce you to some people from Mont Nuages." He could not be drawn into a discussion of their dead affair, not here and now, perhaps never.

"Jean-Marc, I am not interested in anyone here but you. I thought that if I stopped pursuing you and allowed you to come to me when you were ready, all would be well again. But it is not so. Tell me what has changed your feelings for me."

He searched afresh but did not see either Désirée or Meg. "Little has changed," he said. "Our relationship was never what you apparently believed it to be. I am surprised that you insist it was. At the time you did not seem involved other than in the pleasure we shared—physical pleasure."

"We can have that again."

"Please, I do not want to hurt you—but neither will I say what I don't mean."

Verbeux chose that moment to return. He looked from Jean-Marc to Ila and said, "A stroll about the house? Both of you? Find a quiet spot? They'll think you're there. Those who are there will think you're somewhere else."

Amazed at his valet's interference, Jean-Marc said, "I am the host and cannot leave. But I think Lady Upworth is not quite herself and needs one of those quiet spots. Kindly take her there and see what you can do to make her comfortable." With that he turned from them and began passing among his guests.

From her vantage point behind a marble column, Meg watched Jean-Marc. She had found a sketch of a desert chieftain and then copied it for the Count's costume. Tall and straight, he wore dark robes that fell to his feet. Beneath a loose outer garment, he wore a tunic with a wide leather belt through which a curved dagger glimmered. Neutral bands of heavy cord bound a black headdress that swept away from his face and shoulders when he walked. He showed no sign of noticing the stir he made, or the jealous glances of men when women whispered and sighed behind their fans when the Count passed.

And this man found something desirable in her? She was a woman who did not pretend; she knew she was attractive, but not a beauty. So, the Count was a discerning man. He saw that her true worth shone from within. She was a prize! Ha. A sense of both humor and of the ridiculous was indeed a great gift, and she would need it in the weeks to come.

Seated beside Meg, Princess Désirée smiled as if the corners of her mouth were tied to her ears, and stubbornly behaved as if she didn't understand a single word of English. One gentleman after another presented himself. The Princess smiled on and on and allowed her hand to be kissed. Once the hopeful one retreated, she surreptitiously wiped her hand in the voluminous folds of her pearl-studded pink net costume.

"Princess," Meg hissed. "Your brother is coming this way."

Yet another man approached, this one young, blond and possessed of his own smile. He bent over the Princess's hand and looked up at her with bright blue eyes.

"And you are?" she asked with a wicked glance at Meg.

"Anthony FitzDurham, Your Highness. Of the Dorsetshire and Birnam FitzDurhams, but a sultan for tonight." He ruefully indicated his full white pantaloons, braid-encrusted shirt and feathered turban. "You look delightful, if I may say so, Your Highness. Pink becomes you. Very clever how the costume is made so that you appear..." He flushed bright red and was clearly aghast at his gaffe.

Princess Désirée patted the chair beside her until he collected himself enough to sit down. She leaned toward him and whispered in his ear. Meg observed how at first he frowned, then widened his eyes and, finally, laughed aloud.

This is what came of having someone with little experience of such things to watch over an eligible girl with a very naughty streak. Princess Désirée was unruly. It was Meg's responsibility to direct and protect her.

"Your Highness," she said. "A word, if you please."

Her charge's and Mr. FitzDurham's heads remained unsuitably close.

"Princess Désirée?" Meg said.

"Yes, dear Meg?"

"Whispering is not appropriate."

"Oh." The Princess stopped smiling. "I didn't think I should talk loudly about what a waste of time it is for me to wear a concubine costume that is supposed to make me alluring. All these bands, you see, where the silk under the net is rather the color of my skin—well, one is to think they *are* my skin, and—"

"You are *not* dressed as a concubine," Meg said, vaguely certain that it was undesirable to be one of those. "You are a dancing girl, and the costume is wonderful on you."

"I should say so," Mr. FitzDurham agreed.

"A concubine," Princess Désirée insisted. "Although a concubine would have considerably more flesh beneath all this so-called skin, wouldn't she? There would be curves here and here—and here, and perhaps here.'' The mischievous girl undulated her hands over various parts of her person. ''A concubine is no better than she should be. Did you know that, Mr. FitzDurham?''

Meg cast her eyes toward the ceiling and registered that a desert chieftain stood before her. She looked at his face through the space in her draping silver yashmak.

''There you are,'' he said, and dropped his voice. ''One could say we dressed each other. I understand you are responsible for this nonsense of mine. I choose to brag about your costume. You shimmer with every move, Meg, but then, you always do.''

She said, ''Thank you.'' He should not have the satisfaction of seeing her discomfort.

''Perhaps I made a mistake,'' Jean-Marc said. ''You are far too eye-catching this evening. I don't like to think of other men looking at you.''

''I doubt they are, but perhaps in future you will allow me to see to my own clothing. I wore this to please you, or rather to avoid offending you. It's beautiful. Thank you.''

He had maneuvered her until she was almost out of sight of any other soul but him. ''Don't thank me.'' He rested a forearm on the pillar beside them. ''I thought you would enjoy something very different to wear when you do whatever it is you do. Your abstraction. This—'' he touched the crystal pin that fastened the lower half of the yashmak at her temple ''—this can be moved when you wish to cover your eyes.''

''Thank you for your thoughtfulness.'' The hubbub in the ballroom seemed suddenly distant.

''I would rather you never covered your eyes. At least they give me some chance of guessing at your thoughts.''

Meg opened her fan and moved the warm air across her face. She leaned to see Princess Désirée.

Jean-Marc turned and slid his attention to poor Mr. Fitz-

Durham. "Good evening to you, sir. I trust you are enjoying the festivities."

He sounded like a stuffy—father.

FitzDurham was already on his feet and executing a smart bow to Jean-Marc. "Yes, thank you, My Lord. Quite wonderfully, thank you." He cleared his throat and rushed on. "Your sister is delightful. Such beauty and wit rarely occur in the same place."

Meg was glad of the fan that hid her smile.

Jean-Marc masterfully retained a somber expression. "I agree," he said. "Désirée is a rare creature, indeed. Have we been introduced?"

Mr. FitzDurham repeated his credentials and went on. "My father is Burris FitzDurham. Notable judge and also—in Scotland—a producer of a passable single malt."

Meg wasn't so silly that she didn't know when a man appeared impressed, and Jean-Marc definitely did appear impressed. "I've heard a good deal about your father. All of it laudatory. And you are too humble about FitzDurham. I'm never without a few bottles on hand. Very fine. Very fine, indeed."

"Thank you, My Lord. It's my intention to take over that side of the family concerns in time." He gave Jean-Marc an unwavering look. "Might I call on the Princess, My Lord?"

Meg noted that Jean-Marc looked to Princess Désirée for some sign of her wishes, but that young lady contrived to appear serene and subservient. She would, Meg thought, be a credible actress.

"Hmm, yes, yes, you may, Mr. FitzDurham. My sister does not spend enough time with young people. Now, if you'll excuse me?"

FitzDurham backed away, bowing as he went. He looked pleased with himself.

"Oh, yes," the Princess said when there was no fear of being overheard, "Désirée needs more playmates. She has no one to bowl her hoop with, or to enjoy tea parties with Halibut and Mr. Bear."

Rather than being annoyed, Jean-Marc showed how his sister

could amuse him. "You are too sharp for your own good, Désirée. And you have reminded me of a subject I've been too busy to approach. Halibut. Aha, so you speak freely of him, do you? Well, not usually to me. Where did you get that great beast, and what do you mean by hiding him in this house? I thought your mother and our father considered pets unsuitable for you."

The Princess's face grew pale. Piled on top of her head, her hair seemed too heavy for so ethereal a girl.

"My Lord," Meg said. "Please don't blame your sister. It was I who—"

"No," Princess Désirée said, and leaped up to throw her arms around Meg. "You are the best friend I have ever had but you shall not take blame for me. I found Halibut, Jean-Marc. Outside. He—he was not well. I nursed him and he got well. He was my only love. He loves me and stays with me. Please, please, say you will not make him go away. He—"

"Hush," Jean-Marc said, responding to his sister's anxious prattle. "That will not do, my dear. Do not upset yourself so. You are become different, Désirée. Gentler. Or more comfortable showing your true nature, perhaps. Keep the wretched animal, but make sure he doesn't intrude upon me again as he did. He sneaked into my apartments the other night and shocked both Verbeux and myself."

"Oh, dear. Oh, thank you. I will be very careful to keep him in my rooms," Désirée said. She shook, and swallowed repeatedly. "Thank you, Jean-Marc. Thank you."

"No, no," he said, and bent to place a kiss on her cheek. "You need not thank me further. You really love the animal. I have always considered people with a soft place in their hearts for animals as worthy of trust. He is a very handsome cat, and I understand why you admire him. Now, attend to your guests. Soon you will play for us."

"Oh, must I?" She turned the corners of her mouth down and promptly turned them up again. "There's Mr. Chillworth. He has come. He is quite shy, you know, so I wasn't sure he would."

"I was," Jean-Marc said, not quite under his breath. "Hmm. And here he is heading this way."

"Where else would he head?" the Princess asked. "He only knows me—and Meg, of course."

Jean-Marc caught Meg's eye, but if she had thoughts about his sister's excitement at seeing the painter, she didn't show them.

Chillworth had undeniable presence. He had chosen to wear what appeared to Jean-Marc to be the garb of a member of some Indian hill tribe. And quite dashing he looked in a loose white shirt open at the throat, and white trousers. Leather bands crisscrossed his chest and were belted at the waist. He carried a rifle on his back. Damned unsuitable, Jean-Marc thought. A dagger was one thing, a rifle, quite another.

Désirée clapped her hands when Chillworth reached them. "You are splendid, Mr. Chillworth. I think your true spirit shows tonight. A free creature always trying to break free of his bonds."

Chillworth's only response was an embarrassed smile.

"What do you think?" Désirée stood up and pivoted in a complete circle. Her gown was a little work of art. What looked to be a single band of fabric, flesh-colored and covered with the pink gauze, wound the length of her body from shoulder to hem. Between this, a sequin-studded pink lace made the same journey. Tight to the knee, the garment flared there. She reminded Meg of an almost transparent fish, a very beautiful fish. "Would it be interesting to paint me in this silly thing?" she asked Adam.

Jean-Marc watched Chillworth's reaction. This must be how a man felt when he first realized his daughter had changed from a child into a woman. He could not see her as other than a child, but the flicker in another man's eyes proved him wrong.

Chillworth took a long time to gather his wits enough to speak. "I see Meggie's hand in that. It's clever. Yes, I think it might do well enough."

"Only well enough?" She pouted, actually pouted like any coquettish girl.

"It might do very well," Chillworth said, and when he tilted his head and revealed in his deep gray eyes the frank pleasure he took in Désirée, Jean-Marc almost wished the fellow had a title and an advantageous position.

Désirée stood on her toes to whisper in the painter's ear. He shook his head, and Désirée whispered again, and jiggled impatiently. Chillworth looked down at her and said, "My Lord, may I dance with the Princess, please?"

Jean-Marc felt Meg shrink as if she expected him to refuse—not only to refuse but to express offense at the question. "Very well," he said. "You have my permission, but remember she is young. Be certain she does not tire you."

Désirée rushed the man away, and Jean-Marc congratulated himself on his sensible reaction to a situation that held no danger anyway.

"Don't worry about her dancing with Adam," Meg said. "He is the most honorable of men."

Jean-Marc adjusted the dagger at his waist. "I rather think it is Mr. Chillworth who is the more in danger there. If nothing else, during this evening we will have learned a good deal about just how much my sister can be trusted in social situations. She is so quixotic. She is a minx. A charming minx, but a minx nevertheless."

"They are handsome together," Meg said.

"I think so," Jean-Marc said. "With your help, Désirée has bloomed. True, she is a rebel, but perhaps we should hope that she doesn't entirely lose that strong will of hers."

"I do hope she doesn't," Meg told him, standing straighter. "The world is changing. One day women will play as important a part as men—in all areas. I should like the Princess to be a part of all that. She is very clever."

Jean-Marc chose not to comment on Meg's unconventional views, but he said, "Yes, she is clever."

"My Lord." Verbeux appeared at his side once more. "Lady Hester Bingham is here."

"Where is Lady Upworth?" Jean-Marc asked, frowning at him.

"I, er, left her spending some time alone. That was her wish. Lady Hester insists you want to meet her."

Jean-Marc looked not at Verbeux, but at Meg. The delight on her face assured him he had better be anxious to meet his neighbor. He turned and smiled at a tall, blond woman with a mature but admirable figure. Hunter Lloyd stood at her shoulder, and he nodded to the man. "My sister and I are delighted you could come, Lady Hester," Jean-Marc said, pleased with his own judgment. Just as he'd thought, the woman was pleased that he knew who she was. "I am a great believer in neighborliness. You look—extraordinary."

"Aha," she said, tapping his chest with her fan. "A flatterer, I see. You are extraordinary yourself, My Lord. If I were a much younger woman my heart would likely stop at the sight of you." Lady Hester didn't look at Meg.

"What do you call that color?" Jean-Marc asked, surveying Lady Hester's robes, a headdress bound about her head and forehead with strips of gold, and the rows and rows of crystal and jet beads that hung heavy on the lady's considerable bosom. "The shade is lilac, perhaps?"

That earned him another sharp slap with the fan. "You know entirely too much about female frippery, My Lord. Yes. Lilac. And I am a sheik's first wife." She smiled, clearly enormously pleased with herself. "What do you think of that? Do I surprise you with my knowledge of such things? First wife, ha? Such heathen behavior. I should not tolerate second, third or any other number of wives for my husband, I assure you. But I can play the part for a night, can't I?"

"Indeed you can, and play it very well," he told her. "Good evening, Lloyd. Good of you to accompany your aunt. We're honored to have you both. Meg speaks very highly of you, Lady Hester. Of your kindness and loyalty."

Lady Hester finally looked at Meg and her expression softened. "She is a wonderful girl," she said. "Skilled, versatile and good to her heart. We who are her friends worry about her. She is one of the world's gentle people, and a strong person could crush her. I'm sure you are making certain she is very safe here."

Meg looked at the floor.

The discomfort he felt surprised Jean-Marc. "I make it my own responsibility," he said, and instantly wished he'd held his tongue. "Just as I do with Sibyl when she is here. I could not have managed without them, Lady Hester. A man is not well equipped for the task of bringing a girl out."

"No, indeed," Her Ladyship agreed. "I should like you to show me the house. I am interested in how the renovations were made. My grandfather was Sir Septimus Spivey, the celebrated architect. He designed Number Seven and took great pride in the achievement. In fact, so the story goes, he had so little faith in the ability of his offspring to look after his creation that he simply wouldn't die until he was sure they had improved. He lived to be one hundred and two before he was forced to give up, but he died letting everyone know he was not at all sure they were ready for the task. A vain man by all accounts, and one who rose beyond his level of incompetence."

Jean-Marc chuckled with her. "Quite the story to tell one's grandchildren," he said.

Her Ladyship looked pained. "If one had any grandchildren."

"Yes, well," Jean-Marc said, arranging his face into a suitably sympathetic cast. "Let us view the house." He could think of nothing he'd like much less, but for Meg he would make the best of it.

"I say," Lady Hester said, clinging to his arm. "Here comes Sibyl. Who is that scarecrow of a creature prancing around her?"

Meg turned abruptly and all but lost her balance. "Ash," she said, sighing. "The Princess's dancing instructor. I had no idea she would be here this evening."

"Probably couldn't escape her curiosity," Verbeux said. "Had to see the Princess dance."

"She couldn't have known Désirée would dance tonight," Jean-Marc said. "And she isn't even looking at her."

"Nor is she wearing a costume," Lady Hester said, a lorgnette raised to her blue eyes. "I understand she is using your room during your absence, Meg, but I have yet to see her. Even Barstow hasn't seen her—which is just as well. You were always too sensitive for your own good, but you were kind to help her."

"Sibyl says she remains in her room when she isn't here," Meg said, but she was concerned by Ash's agitated capering in front of Sibyl. "Please excuse me."

She hurried to her sister's side. "I wondered where you were," she said, barely acknowledging Ash. "You are so pretty, Sibyl. You look like a nymph."

"I'm not anything, really," Sibyl said. "It was much too late to start making another costume."

"An Eastern goddess," Meg said, smiling. She kissed Sibyl's cheek. "Green chiffon. It makes you look so very small. It might have been wound on you. And your hair is almost down. Very clever. And you, Miss Ash." She turned to the other woman. "I see curiosity got the better of you, after all. I don't blame you. But where is your costume?"

"Piffle," Ash said, her thin face registering disapproval. "I am here because I had to come. My duty required me to come. I must insist that you two young women talk to me. Now. It is of the utmost importance. For your good, not mine. Someone spoke to me or I should not have known the pass things have come to."

"What do you mean?" Meg asked. "This is not the time or place to deal with anything but the matter to hand—the Princess's musicale. If you must speak to us then let it be tomorrow."

"Tonight," Ash said, and let out a yelp. "Get it away! Get rid of it!"

"Oh," Sibyl said, putting a hand over her mouth. "A cat, Meggie. A beautiful cat. What can he be doing here? We must rescue him before he's seen and thrown into the street."

"Rescue him?" Ash squealed. "Toss him from the window, I say. He's vicious. Did you see that? He bit my ankle. And now he snarls at me."

A figure in black bore down upon them, with Hunter Lloyd and Verbeux at his heel. "My cat," Jean-Marc said, sweeping Halibut into his arms. "I knew I should have given in and let him have his own costume. If he doesn't get his own way, first he sulks, then he gets mean. Kindly excuse Halibut, Miss Ash. I'm about to take Lady Hester on a tour of the house. I shall return the cat to my apartments on the way."

Meg gaped as he left, but then she smiled and once more her heart opened as if to the sun because this man she loved kept showing that he was anything but ordinary. Such a commanding man might be expected to ignore unimportant detail, yet he was too kind to do so.

"I need a few words with Miss Meg and Miss Sibyl," Ash the undaunted said. "If you wouldn't mind, M. Verbeux, I'd appreciate your making sure we are not interrupted." From time to time she hopped from one foot to the other and contrived to rub places Halibut had attacked.

Verbeux dutifully faced Hunter, who wore a round white hat, an embroidered blue vest, white shirt and trousers. Meg had no idea what he was supposed to be, but he looked as appealing as ever.

"Right," Ash said, planting her fists on her skinny hips. "I want you two to listen to me, and listen well. What I have to say is important and it is also said with your best interests in mind. Today I had a long chat with that lovely Mr. William Godly-Smythe, and I could scarcely believe what I heard. He asked you to marry him, Sibyl. A fine, upstanding man like that. And he wants to take Meg to live with you, too. And you refused? I almost fainted when he told me."

"What business is it of yours?" Meg snapped.

"Meggie." Sibyl sounded reproachful. "You mustn't mind when people care about us. We're lucky to have such kind thoughts sent our way."

"I'm glad you understand how lucky you are," Ash said. She lowered her eyes, and the corners of her mouth took a matching downward dive. "Take it from one who has lived the life of a genteel woman consigned to exist without a husband, opportunities such as this don't come often. When they do, you should thank God for His kindness and take what He's offered you. And if you ask quickly, that poor, lovesick man won't sell his home in Puckly Hinton to buy a place in London *just to please you*. He could never keep the three of you as well in London as he could in the country. Go. Don't hesitate, go to him before he sells his house and holdings. If he does that, he'll start out loving you, Sibyl—while you keep him interested in the bedroom—but after that, his unhappiness will make your marriage unhappy. Mark my words."

"I didn't think you'd ever been married," Meg said, distressed at the confusion Sibyl showed.

"I most certainly have not."

"And you wouldn't like to be?"

Ash lowered her stubby lashes. "Not all of us ever have a chance. But that doesn't mean I don't have enough goodness in my heart to want better for you. When these positions with the Count are over, I'll return to the school, but you? Who will you have to turn to? Each other, it's true, but every year you're a year older and you'll be surprised how quickly you're old tabbies, and probably sitting here in this godless city wishing you'd made other decisions."

"Miss Ash," Meg said, with a sadness in her heart. "You are a very kind woman. You want us to be happy. But you don't know our cousin. We would be slaves in his house. I doubt we should even be allowed to read. William doesn't hold with women broadening their minds. He would decide what were useful occupations for us, and he would treat us badly. Our only task in life would be to make him look better and better. He hates us. He always has, and we don't know why he is suddenly solicitous."

"He has had his fling," Ash said. "I think he is changed, and that he truly loves you, Sibyl. Now he's ready to settle down and think about having sons. You should be grateful that such a desirable bachelor chooses to bestow his favor on you. Accept him, I exhort you. Don't waste a moment. Go to him this very night. He has returned to Number Seven. He's there now, awaiting your response. In his desperation he sent me, a stranger, to you. I certainly had no wish to be here."

"He's had my response," Sibyl said. "I told him no."

Ash wound her bony hands together. She seemed oblivious of the strange stares she drew. "I feel desperately sad when I think of that man's longing. I cannot ever remember feeling so certain that this is a mission I must make, and that I must continue to try to persuade you. Change your mind. Go to him, I implore you. And don't you forget that lovely Reverend Baggs has run himself off his feet trying to watch over you, Meg Smiles. The man is exhausted. Such a lovely man."

"He's not married," Meg said, and didn't feel badly about the thought that had suddenly entered her head. "Why didn't I think of that before? Why, if you married Reverend Baggs and looked after things for William and the Reverend, he wouldn't need us."

Ash turned first a little gray, then bright pink. She smiled and flapped a hand at Meg. "Oh, you're funning me. That delightful man would never look at me. What foolishness even to suggest such a thing."

"Of course he would. In fact, I've already seen him look at you." Not a complete fib. "Run along and think about it, Ash. Or may I call you Lavinia? After all, we've shared a good deal. The Princess will play the pianoforte soon."

"Please do call me Lavinia. I don't recall the last time anyone wanted to." A faraway look entered Ash's eyes, and she wandered away to find a chair and sit down.

"Meg," Sibyl said. "That was mean."

"Baggsy doesn't have a wife. It's about time he did."

"But you know... Meg, did you know Hunter's over there—staring at us?"

Meg glanced around to find Verbeux and Hunter in conversation. "Hunter is staring at you, not at me." She caught Verbeux's eye and beckoned. He came toward her, and she saw what she'd been too involved to notice before. He limped.

Hunter passed and went directly to Sibyl. He did nod at Meg on the way. She heard him say, "Sibyl. Let me guess, some sort of deep-sea creature? One of those mysterious beings from a lost world?"

Sibyl giggled. "A lost Eastern world," she said. "How observant and clever you are." Smiling at each other, they wandered away.

Meg felt lonely. She didn't begrudge Sibyl some happiness, she just wished she could see something other than disappointment in her future.

"Your position is difficult," Verbeux said. She'd forgotten he was there.

"I don't know what you mean."

"I think you do."

Did he? He might well, since he was never far from Jean-Marc.

"If I could ease your way, I would," he said, taking her completely by surprise. He looked straight ahead. "The Count cares about you. He wants you. He has dilemmas few men even dream about."

"I'm sure he does. Thank you for your concern."

"He would like to take you away and forget all of this."

Meg looked sideways at him, and frowned. "M. Verbeux, you are injured."

"Not at all." He pulled his hair forward at both sides. "It's nothing."

But she had seen the welt on the side of his head, and the bloody crust that formed there. "What happened? I insist you tell me."

"You can insist nothing, Miss Smiles. And your protests do not divert me. You want him, too. Why not allow me to help you get what you want?"

She would not as much as answer such wild suggestions. "What happened to your head? Did someone hit you?"

"That's laughable. Of course not. Tonight you shall be with the Count."

"Leave us alone," she said, suddenly furious at his manipulation. "And seek help for your wounds."

"Your Lady Hester appears to have monopolized the Count." Verbeux said. His hair couldn't hide the bruise that darkened the side of his face. "He will be polite, but he will not allow her too much time. Miss Smiles, I think it very important for the Count to leave and take you with him."

Meg cast about for someone who might break the feeling of strangeness M. Verbeux had brought with him.

"There are things I know that even the Count does not know. Do you believe me?"

She stared at him, at the evidence that he had been involved in some violence. "Yes," she whispered.

"Good. I shall need your help. I want the two of you to leave tonight and to go into hiding. It is too dangerous for you here."

"I don't understand. I have suffered some unfortunate accidents, but they did not affect the Count."

M. Verbeux touched his face and winced. "So we thought at first. I have been assured we were wrong to miss certain signs. Those signs were intended for people other than you. You got in the way. In fact there is some annoyance that you have become a complication. Nevertheless, you and the Count will leave tonight. You are considered in the way. Convincing him of the urgency will be the largest task."

Meg backed away from him. "I think you have hit your head hard. You should see a physician."

"So you say, but before this night is out, you may think otherwise."

28

"Good evenin', miss," a distinguished gentleman wearing a kilt said to Meg. His thick white hair was at odds with his pleasant, youthful face. "I believe I've the pleasure o' speakin wi' Miss Meg Smiles."

When she frowned at him, he smiled, revealing strong white teeth. "Ye wonder how I know," he said. "I wish I could reveal some mysterious method. Unfortunately it was verra easy. I asked."

"Oh," Meg said, and smiled back. She had adjusted the veil to almost entirely cover her face and had been spending a few moments silently repeating her mantra. "Do they not say the simplest forms of detection are usually the most successful?"

"Should ye mind if I sat with ye?"

She had learned no rules for dealing with moments such as this. After all, she was a young, single woman alone. "I am Princess—"

"Désirée's companion? Yes, I know that, too. I assure you that there can be no gossip about a widower such as myself sitting to rest his feet and talk with his hostess's companion. Why, we could say—if we were asked—that I was in hopes of requesting a wee dance wi' the Princess mysel'."

Meg gathered the entirely too thin silver fabric over her limbs. "You have an answer for anything, sir."

"But ye are all alone here, are ye not? And considerin' a wee bit o' abstract thinkin'?"

"How…" She wasn't sure how to ask what he knew on the subject.

"I could tell by watchin' ye. I meditate mesel'. Have done since I was wi' the army in India. Had the pleasure of studyin' wi' a very holy man in the mountains."

Meg was impressed. "I envy you," she said.

"So," he said, "I'm sorry to interrupt ye, but I wanted to meet ye. Are ye feelin' a wee bit lonely, perhaps?"

"Possibly," she said. What she really felt was terrified. How could she tell Jean-Marc that his own valet had said he should take Meg and leave because he was in danger, and she was in the way so might also be in danger?

"Ye're troubled," the man said. "Och, forgive me. I'm Sir Robert Brodie of Edinburgh. Prince Georges, the Count's father, has been a good friend t'me."

"I see." Why was Jean-Marc taking so long?

"Who are your people, lass?"

Meg jumped and looked at Sir Robert. "My father was Reverend Smiles of Puckly Hinton. I'm afraid he passed away some years since. My mother predeceased him. So you see, I really am no one." She dropped her head and smiled up at him.

His brows were still red, and he raised them. A dashing man with exceedingly broad shoulders beneath his velvet jacket with its silver buttons. His legs were strong and well set off by tartan knee socks. Lace frothed at his throat and wrists. "So," he said, "what's the verdict? Like what ye see, do ye?"

Meg blushed so fiercely her cheeks throbbed.

Sir Robert patted her hand on her lap and laughed aloud. "I'm a wicked man t'take advantage of your youth wi' such a sly question. I've been widowed a mite too long and I've lost some o' the skills a man likes t'have around a pretty woman. And ye are pretty, Miss Smiles." He dropped his voice, and the smile disappeared. "I should like the chance to speak more wi' ye, lass. If ye'd let me. I'm no an old man—despite the white hair. I fear

I took my wife's death badly and the hair is the mark I carry now."

"I'm sure you did take it badly." She looked at him with sympathy. And he looked back with regret. "You are a most handsome man and you look young. I like your white hair—it's distinguished."

Sir Robert barked out his laughter. He took hold of her hand firmly, sputtered, "May I?" and when she nodded, kissed it lightly while smiling into her eyes. "You're wonderful. So natural. The sooner ye're no longer a part of all this, the better. A quiet life filled with love and the kindness of home is what ye need. What are ye doing here, anyway?"

"It's a long story." She leaned to see around people in hope that Jean-Marc would appear. "Mostly it's because my sister, Sibyl, and I found ourselves in reduced circumstances after my father died. We had to make our way. But we are well enough, thank you."

"I've a practice here in London," Sir Robert said. "I'm a surgeon. Now isn't that an unpleasant announcement to make?"

"You don't like being a surgeon?"

"I like it verra well, thank ye. But it doesna make for suitable conversation wi' a gentle young woman. I also teach in Edinburgh for part of each year so I've two homes to administer. They're a big responsibility for a man alone."

"Oh, they must be." Meg liked him, liked the firmness of his hand, which should undoubtedly not be holding hers, and the way he smiled and how young he looked to have white hair. And she liked his red brows and blue eyes—and his very interesting knees.

"Will ye dance wi' me, Meg?" he said. "Your charge is busy and likely t'be so from what I can see."

Meg located Princess Désirée and Adam on the floor. Completely engrossed in each other, they danced a slow waltz that could absolutely not be suitable.

"Well?" Sir Robert asked.

"I... Well, all right. But for just a short time."

Not far away Jean-Marc seethed. With Verbeux at his side insisting Jean-Marc should take Meg and leave as soon as he could see an escape, and Meg herself dancing with Sir Robert Brodie as if she were enjoying herself, he was a man besieged, a man infuriated and close to exploding. "I've never known you to be an alarmist, Verbeux. Leave? Tonight? And take Meg Smiles with me? You aren't yourself, man. What has happened to you?"

"This," Verbeux said, pulling back his hair to reveal a bloody gash beneath his hairline. "Note the bruising, too. And there are marks I can't show you here. They kicked my legs from beneath me, and my knees may never be the same."

"You have my entire attention," Jean-Marc said. "Who, in God's name, were these maniacs?"

"I couldn't see them. The room was dark. I had been sitting with Lady Upworth in very subdued light. Two people entered in cloaks. They extinguished the lamps. Lady Upworth screamed. A hand over her mouth stopped her. They warned me not to move unless I wanted her hurt. Then their message was simple. The Count is to leave, taking Miss Smiles with him. He should go into hiding and make no contact until they come for him."

"Damn them," Jean-Marc said. "Take care of that wound and say nothing to anyone. If they were sure of themselves they would have acted, not sent a warning."

"We don't even know who they are," Verbeux replied.

"And Ila." Jean-Marc turned on Verbeux. "For God's sake, man, where is Ila?"

"In her room," Verbeux said. "She's not hurt, but she is very shaken. She didn't even see anyone approach—but she heard what they said. She'll corroborate."

"I don't need her to corroborate. You have never lied to me. What's your best speculation? Who are they? What do they want?"

"Friends of your uncle's. Who else?"

"If something happens to me—my father will suspect Uncle

Louis first. But I still do not believe he is behind any of this. What has Meg to do with it?''

Verbeux shook his head.

"Why in the hell is she dancing with Brodie?''

"He's eligible,'' Verbeux said. "She could do a great deal worse. And she's unlikely to do much better, hmm?''

Jean-Marc glared at him. "What is that supposed to mean?''

"You've already made it clear you won't marry a woman to please your father, but you also don't want the kind of woman your father disapproves of. You are confused.''

"I don't know any women he'd approve of,'' Jean-Marc snapped. "If he knew Meg Smiles, he might approve of her, but he would never give her a chance.''

"I wish you'd heed the threat and get away,'' Verbeux said. "Then perhaps there will be time to convince the Prince.''

"I'm going to interrupt them,'' Jean-Marc said, looking at Meg and the Scotsman. "She's young enough to be his daughter.''

"Concentrate, My Lord. Allow me to help you get away from here.''

"Run away? Never. Let them come and get me—if they can. In case you've forgotten, I have a sister to care for.''

"You won't be any use to her if you're dead.''

"I'll try to forget you said that. Désirée needs me, and she needs Meg. Much as it might appeal, I can't disappear and take Meg with me.''

Verbeux grimaced as if with pain, and said, "So you do admit you are infatuated with Miss Smiles?''

"I admit no such thing. Leave me. Go and check on Lady Upworth. Tell her to be calm. There is nothing to worry about.''

"My Lord—''

"Do it. I have faced true fear, Verbeux, fear that crawled in hot sand in the middle of the night. I will not be daunted by this situation. However, I will find out exactly who has decided to be my enemy. Watch over Ila. I will watch over Meg.''

Verbeux stared at him for so long that Jean-Marc almost expected him to take the unprecedented step of refusing. At last the valet said, "Ignore me if you will. You can't shake my determination to give my life for yours if necessary." He dropped a bow and walked away. The man limped badly. There was no doubt that something dangerous was going on, and the only possible reason had to be tied up with the throne of Mont Nuages.

Jean-Marc crossed his arms and collected himself. Verbeux was no ordinary valet. Loyalty rarely presented itself so unwaveringly.

On the ballroom floor, Brodie had Meg smiling and reacting to him with unconscious charm. Damn the man.

"Pretty piece, that little companion of your sister's," an aged soldier said to Jean-Marc. "Nice to have around the house, is she? After all, the master should have his little benefits."

Jean-Marc came close to knocking the old fool down, then recalled moments when he'd held Meg in his arms. Little *benefits?* Well, he'd offered her marriage, and she'd refused. He'd offered her his protection, and so far she hadn't accepted.

"Sir Robert's got plenty of blunt," the old soldier said.

"Really?" Jean-Marc didn't know much about Brodie.

"Hell of a surgeon, so they say. Got a reputation for being a generous sort, too. Been a widower for a few years. Shouldn't be surprised if he's decided to look for a wife. He'd treat her well and give her everything she wanted. Of course, he never had any children, so I expect he's a mind to do something about that, too. That piece has caught his eye, I should say. Wonder who decided she ought to show a bit too much every time she moves. What a pair of—" He caught Jean-Marc's ferocious glare and snickered. "Bit possessive, are we? Well, she's got a nice pair, and everything else looks worth a romp or two. But I think you know that."

"Will you excuse me?" Jean-Marc said, and walked away. He walked directly to the area where Sibyl continued to talk with Hunter Lloyd, and Miss Ash occupied a chair but appeared to be elsewhere in her mind. He leaned on the pillar and watched the dancers. It looked less and less as if there would be further musical performances this evening.

Had the knife and the carriage accidents, or at least the second one, been intended for him? Had Meg walked into those situations and borne them on his behalf? He shifted uneasily.

Brodie held her too close, and she looked too happy for him to do so.

This was not going well. Apart from the young whiskey heir, his sister had only shown interest in an impoverished painter. The program had gone poorly, although he could have controlled that had he not been distracted.

True, the company seemed as numerous as it had at the beginning of the party. They were certainly as loud, if not louder. He supposed all were enjoying themselves. The event would be gossiped about in the morning.

Some ladies and gentlemen were becoming more amorous than he considered appropriate when there were young people present. In future the drink would not flow as readily.

The piano and strings performed with gusto and were clearly appreciated by the crowd. All chairs had now been cleared from the floor, and the largest percentage of the company danced. He caught sight of the baritone and the soprano, also dancing. The baritone entertained himself by dropping sweetmeats down the front of the soprano's considerable décolletage and retrieving them with his mouth and tongue while his partner wriggled with pleasure.

Désirée should not be here.

Flushed and chuckling, Meg turned from the surgeon and said something, evidently that she wished to stop dancing. He held her hand and led her slowly from the floor, talking to her all the way.

Something akin to blind fury overtook Jean-Marc. "There you are," he said to Meg when she and Brodie reached him. "Have you forgotten you have a job to do?"

She stood before him, her eyes huge and worried. "I watched the Princess while I danced, My Lord."

"That was not what I observed."

"My Lord," Brodie said. "If there is any fault, it's mine. I pressed Meg to dance. She didn't want to but I convinced her we would be able to see the Princess at all times."

"Her name is Miss Smiles. Such familiarity is unsuitable."

Dr. Brodie flexed his shoulders. There was no sign of a smile now. Handsome devil, Jean-Marc was forced to note. "Excuse us, if you please," he said.

"Soon enough," Brodie said in a voice of steel. "Miss Smiles, in the absence of your having a parent, I must ask you. Would you consider allowing me to call on you?"

Meg looked at the man, and Jean-Marc took some satisfaction in the battle he saw her wage. She needed a husband who could provide for her, and for Sibyl. This man might turn out to be the perfect candidate, but he wasn't the candidate she wanted.

"Yes," she said. "Yes, please. How nice that would be. I would have to arrange to be at my flat, since my employer could not be expected to welcome visitors for his employees."

"You will meet at Number Seventeen," Jean-Marc said. She'd meet the man where he, Jean-Marc, could watch over her and keep her safe.

"That's verra good o' ye," Sir Robert said. "P'raps we could walk in the park, Meg. Or ride."

"She doesn't ride," Jean-Marc said. "And she owns no horse."

"Perfect," Brodie said. "I shall teach you, Meggie Smiles. I've a little gray, a mare, that would be perfect for ye. I'll call and we'll make arrangements."

"That won't be possible," Jean-Marc said, knowing what he was going to say, knowing he would regret it, but unable to stop himself. "By all means make a brief call. But we are busy here. Meg is paid well to make up for not being allowed to take any time off."

29

Sibyl separated herself from Hunter and hastened to thread an arm through Meg's. Together they observed Jean-Marc's passage across the ballroom floor to Princess Désirée. He bent to speak into her ear, then placed a hand at her waist and ushered her before him.

Adam was left staring after the man, who parted a crowd with unconscious authority. Not a pair of eyes failed to follow his progress.

"He's hurt Adam's feelings," Sibyl said.

"Adam is stronger than you think," Meg told her, although the intense anger she felt toward Jean-Marc burned in her throat like acid. "The Count is concerned for his sister's welfare. She is very young."

"And you love him," Sibyl whispered.

Meg turned to look at her, but she couldn't deny the accusation. "Did you see Sir Robert Brodie?" she asked, desperate to change the subject. "A very nice man, and he could be interested in me."

"He is interested in you," Sibyl said. She sounded choked. "But you are not interested in him. Meggie, the Count is not for you. He...well, I don't know about these things, yet I think he wants you in some way. But he wouldn't want you as his wife, would he?"

"Not unless it were the only way to—" She bit back what she'd been about to say. "Please, Sibyl, don't make me talk about it. This is the hardest thing I have ever done, but I won't lose my head, I promise you. And you would do well to avoid long glances at M. Verbeux. He is too worldly for you—would always be too worldly for you."

Sibyl raised her chin and frowned at Meg. "Spite doesn't become you. He is an interesting man. And, as you say, seems extremely worldly. Perhaps that's what makes him worth looking at. There, think about that. I may look at him if I want to. I am a quiet woman, but I am not without imagination and I rather enjoy it. Of course we should never be suited."

Cross words rarely passed Sibyl's lips. Meg blinked at her sister and said, "Good. I mean, good for you. I was mean and I'm sorry."

"No." Sibyl shook her head. "These are difficult times for both of us and…oh, Meg, the Princess didn't play, or sing. After all her hard work."

"After all your hard work," Meg muttered. "He isn't good at dealing with these matters, poor man. I shall speak to him about it."

"It's too late now."

"I know. But there will be other opportunities."

Hunter approached uncertainly, his face very serious. "There's something wrong. I can feel it, Meg. Please, if being here isn't good for you, then come back to Number Seven."

"I can't do that," she said. "But thank you, Hunter."

"Why can't you? Is it something to do with, er, funds? Because if it is, there's no need for you to concern yourselves about such things."

Sibyl's confidence faded, and she showed signs of bursting into tears.

"Thank you, Hunter," Meg said. "We will manage nicely but we will never forget how kind you and Lady Hester have been to us."

"It's not just—" Red stained his cheekbones. "Forgive me for intruding on your private affairs. I see my aunt. I should find out if she's ready to leave."

"Hunter," Sibyl said, but he was already walking away.

"Hush," Meg said. "It will be all right. His pride may be a little wounded, but he is such a good man. A few kind words from you and he will forget any embarrassment. He is fond of you, you know."

Sibyl flapped her fan briskly. "Don't be a noddy, Meg. Hunter thinks of us as if we were his sisters, nothing more. One of these days he'll bring his bride-to-be home." She grew serious once more. "I hope she is as special as he is."

Meg didn't trust herself to say more. One would have to be blind to miss the affection in Hunter's eyes when he looked at Sibyl, and it wasn't the affection of a brother for a sister.

"Speaking of brothers and sisters," she said.

Sibyl looked into her face. "Were we?"

"I was thinking I'd better go to Princess Désirée's rescue or Jean—the Count may be too hard on her. If you're still sure you won't spend the night, please be sure you go home with Adam and Miss Ash. I'll see you tomorrow."

Meg left Sibyl, threaded a way through the still jostling crowd, and was grateful to reach the comparative cool of the gallery. She went at once toward the Princess's apartments. There was little doubt that Jean-Marc would have a good deal to say to his sister about her lack of decorum that evening.

Jean-Marc was an angry man. Even when they'd been together—she could not erase the memories of those times—but even then she had felt some disturbance in him.

Pink roses from the garlands scattered the floor. Guests wandered from the ballroom and down the stairs, laughing and leaning on each other as they went. Meg felt the rush of cold night air from the open front door and heard horses and carriages rolling to and from the house.

She paused to watch. Swansdown abounded at the necks, sleeves and hems of ladies' cloaks. Jewels winked at ears and throats and wrists. Costumes were a little rumpled after many hours in the crush, but still there was so much richness all around Meg. She carried on toward the Princess's apartments. The silver gossamer creation Jean-Marc had ordered for her felt magical. Perhaps she would put it on for occasional times when she needed to feel borne away. One day it might become her only memory of a time that should never have been.

What had she read in a translation of an ancient book she'd been allowed to see at a lecture on the mind? That the streams of the mind flow to the good and to the bad. Discrimination could lead to freedom and that was only good. She must practice harder until she went only toward goodness and freedom. Then she would learn not to crave what she couldn't have. Perhaps.

Sir Robert Brodie would come to call. Meg had no doubt he would. And she liked him, little as she knew of him. He had asked if she was lonely, but he had really been telling her that he was lonely and looking for a wife to share his life. That life would be good.

That life would banish anything but the memory of Jean-Marc.

Could she embrace what she'd tried to learn about choices, or would she always want him?

Could she have him?

She would stop dwelling on her own desperate longings and take care of her charge, who might well be suffering a lashing from her half brother's tongue. There was no doubt that Jean-Marc's anger was increased by Meg's having foiled his wishes—or at least having refused to accept either of his offers.

He did not wish to marry her unless it was the only way to keep her. What woman in love wanted to bind a man to her in such a way?

The Princess's apartments were hushed. Once inside the corridor, Meg stopped to listen. Not a sound reached her. Perhaps she had misjudged the Count and he, too, had departed for his rooms—or returned to wish more of his guests farewell. She hadn't seen him, and it would have been difficult for him to pass without her doing so.

At the far end of the corridor the door to the Princess's sitting room opened and Jean-Marc came out. Still dressed in his dark robes, he closed the door quietly behind him and looked in Meg's direction.

She started toward him, but he held up a hand as if to warn her off.

"Halibut," Meg whispered. Jean-Marc held the big gray and white cat under his arm. "No," she said quietly. "Don't take him away."

Jean-Marc turned on his heel and strode in the opposite direction, his cloak and headdress billowing about him.

Meg broke into a run. The Princess would be heartbroken to have her darling Halibut taken from her. Meg wanted to shout but knew she must not unless she thought nothing of waking the maids who slept here, or even the Princess if she was asleep and unaware of what Jean-Marc was doing.

He turned the corner at the end of the corridor. When Meg arrived there, she saw no sign of him. Close to sobbing, ignoring how her veils slipped, taking her coiffeur down with them, she hastened on. The corridor took another turn at the next corner, and she paused, catching her breath before continuing.

The flutter of something dark caught her eye. He had gone into a short passageway she'd seen before. Inside were stairs, very narrow and crooked stairs that went upward to what had once been servants' quarters, but which were now used for storage.

Meg reached the bottom of the stairs and whispered, "Jean-Marc. Stop. Please." But he was almost at the top and didn't look back.

If he was so determined to be cruel, she could not expect to change his mind, yet she had to try. She climbed as fast as she could. The steps were rough, the treads worn thin in the center. There was no banister, and she felt her way through the gloom by keeping her hands on the walls.

At the top the door was shut.

A truly horrid idea came to her. There were dormer windows up here. He could put Halibut through one of these and let the cat find a way down. After all, if he died out there, Jean-Marc could still say he'd given the animal a chance.

No, that was not the Jean-Marc she knew.

Meg opened the door and walked into darkness so complete she expected to bump into something hard. The darkness felt like a black curtain. She held still and listened. A faint sound reached her, like an infant sucking. She hugged herself tightly and whispered, "Jean-Marc? What are you doing?"

The door slammed shut and a voice said, "Waiting for you."

Standing very still, she strained and realized she was trying to feel his presence. She should know exactly where he was. There was a connection between them, but she did not sense it now. "I've come," she said, but her heart beat too fast. "I'm sorry the evening was so difficult. But do not blame Désirée for her high spirits. She has not known much joy before. I believe that is true."

"Be quiet."

She shuddered, and tried to see where he was. Her eyes did not seem to adjust.

"You will learn a lesson tonight. We are all born with a place, and we should have the sense to remain in that place."

"Where are you?" she said. "Why are you talking to me like this?"

"Silence."

"Where is Halibut?"

A sharp blow across her cheek brought tears rushing from her eyes, but not because of pain. The shock was a terrible thing.

"Now will you do as you are told and be quiet?"

This wasn't Jean-Marc.

No one knew where she was. Why, she could…she could die up here and she might not be found for a long time. "Who are you?"

She sustained a blow to the other side of her face and bowed her head. He—whoever he was—would answer none of her questions, so she might as well be silent as suffer his violence.

"Can you dance?"

"Dance?"

"You heard the question. Can you dance?"

"A little."

"Good. I like to watch a pretty creature dance."

At once she was surrounded by hard arms that bundled her from the ground. His breath on her face smelled of brandy. He did not confine his hands to carrying her, but used his opportunity to touch her unsuitably.

"Stop it," she told him.

He chuckled softly and pushed a hand up her skirts to fondle her. Meg bucked and fought him, but he only laughed and thrust inside her bodice. "No wonder you caught the Count's eye," he said. "These would be enough for any man. There are places in the world where they grow melons. If your tits were melons they'd fetch a fine price. I'd lay odds they taste better than any melon. I'll have to find out, hmm? Would you like that?"

"Let me go," Meg said, her voice a croak.

Her captor pinched one of her nipples hard enough to hurt and set her on top of a piece of furniture. "Don't worry," he said. "That's a good big table. Plenty of room to dance up there."

She shivered and couldn't think at all.

"Dance, then," he said.

"Why? Why are you doing this?"

"You'll soon understand," he said. "Dance."

She couldn't make her legs move.

A hard pinch applied to her bottom shocked her again. She shuffled her feet.

"No, no, no. Lift them up. Here, let's take off those shoes. Shoes get in the way." He held her about the waist and removed her shoes.

Meg trembled and started to cry, then grew angry.

"This should help," the man said. "Always did say a little warmth loosened a person up."

A torch flamed.

Meg feared she would collapse. He was going to do something terrible to her, and she could see no way out.

"We'll make a game of it, see," he said, and lowered the flame by knocking away some of the spill. "I move the torch and you dance over the flame."

"No," Meg said. "Please, no. My costume will catch on fire."

"You could always take it off."

"Please let me go."

The flame moved slowly toward her bare feet. Meg hoisted the divided skirts of her costume until they were almost at her knees. The flame dashed heat over her limbs.

"Dance," the man said, his voice rising. "Dance, dance, dance."

He swung the torch at her feet and she jumped, jumped over the flame.

"You'll catch something on fire," she said.

"No." He sounded utterly calm, and she did not think she had heard his voice before. "If anything catches on fire, it will be you, but you'll be very careful, won't you?"

He held the torch away, moved close and brought her face down to his. His kiss disgusted her.

As quickly as he had grabbed her, he released her and the flame came toward her ankles again. And she jumped again. The headdress he wore, so like Jean-Marc's, was pulled over his face, and even with the aid of the torch, she couldn't see him.

"What a shame," he said. "What a waste. All I do is follow orders. Why shouldn't I have some fun? Take off your clothes."

Her skin became cold and tight.

"Do as you're told."

"No." If he wanted her naked, he'd have to strip her himself and that wouldn't be easy as long as he held the torch.

His fingers hooked into the front of her bodice. She twisted free, and he snarled in the darkness.

"Not good enough for you, hmm? Only a bastard Count for you. Jump, damn you. Jump again." The torch swung back and forth and Meg watched it, timing each leap while her skin felt more scorched with each pass.

"I've got a few things I want to hear you say," the man told her. "First you say, I don't belong here. Go on, say it."

The torch hit the side of her foot, and she screamed, but she did as he told her.

"Good. Now say, I'm nothing. I'm above my station. I'm sorry for all the wrong I've done."

This time she repeated the words quickly.

"Better and better," he said. "Say, I'm going away. Tonight. And I'm going to find a way to make the Count go with me."

"I don't know if—"

The flame seared her ankle, and she screamed again.

"I'm going to find a way to make the Count go with me," the man said, and Meg repeated it.

"Don't worry, all the arrangements are made. All you have to do is persuade him without saying a word about me. It's all your idea. Understand?"

"No, I can't—ah!"

"When you don't behave yourself, I have to hurt you. Do you understand now?"

"Yes!"

"Good girl. How about another little kiss?"

Not realizing that Sibyl and Miss Ash should have an escort, Adam had left the Count's house before them and gone ahead to Number 7.

"We don't need Mr. Chillworth," Lavinia said when they were ready to go. "It isn't as if the square is deserted. And we're hardly so desirable that we'll be whisked away."

Sibyl wasn't afraid to walk home alone, either, but she didn't really care to be likened to someone many years her senior.

Rench bestowed a haughty nod upon them as they left and immediately turned his attention to someone more important.

"I thought Meg might come back," Sibyl said when they reached the flagway.

"She's got to be persuaded to return to Number Seven for good," Lavinia said. "At least until the two of you return to Puckly Hinton."

Sibyl was too tired to argue.

"We'll go through the gardens," Lavinia said. "They smell so nice at this time of night."

It was on Sibyl's tongue to ask Ash how often she wandered in the gardens past midnight. The effort would be pointless.

Arm in arm they crossed from the flagway in front of Count Etranger's house and over the cobblestone roadway to the park. In fact Lavinia was right, the flowers smelled wonderful. "Feel how soft the air is," Sibyl said. "It's a beautiful evening."

Lavinia grunted.

"Perhaps you should consider Meg's idea about Reverend Baggs," Sibyl said. "I don't like to think of you alone."

"I'm perfectly happy to be alone, thank you." Lavinia Ash walked a distance before saying, "The Reverend would never be interested in me."

"You don't know that," Sibyl said. "Oh, Lavinia, look." She pulled Miss Ash to a halt beside her. "That person's coming toward us."

Lavinia Ash snorted. "This is a public walkway. Why shouldn't he?"

A short, broad figure in a greatcoat and top hat bore down on them. When he grew near, he tipped the brim of his hat with his cane and said, "Good evenin', ladies. Better get home quickly. No place for women out 'ere in the dark. All manner of rogues abroad." He growled his words.

"Thank you," Sibyl said, but her voice broke.

"What did you say?" the man asked. He ducked his head as if straining to hear her. "That's a very little voice you 'ave, miss."

Lavinia took her arm from Sibyl's. She said, "We should hurry, Miss Smiles."

"Not at all," the man said, and rather than pass and carry on his way, he threw an arm around Sibyl and raised his voice in raucous song.

Sibyl poked his plump middle and struggled.

His response was to hold her more firmly and start a meandering route through the park—in the opposite direction from the one Sibyl wanted to take.

A wet cloth hit the side of her neck and liquid trickled inside the collar of her pelisse. The sickening scent of strong liquor tightened the muscles in her jaw.

Her companion brought his face close to her ear and said, "Might as well join in the fun, love. Come on, let's hear you sing. 'A poor little girl from the river,'" he roared. "'She were white where she weren't blue. Poor little girl from the river.' Come on love, join in."

He staggered, and she staggered with him. Struggle as she might, she could not escape his grip. She was alone with him. Miss Ash had fallen back, and when Sibyl managed a glance behind her, there was no sign of the other woman.

True terror invaded every muscle, each limb. A trembling weakness threatened to make her legs useless.

"We're goin' to a place I know," the man said. "Not so far from 'ere. People don't know 'ow close to their proper 'omes they could find good fun if they wanted to look for it. 'Poor little girl from the river,'" he sang louder. "'She were white where she weren't blue, and her fingers were food for the fishes. Poor little girl from the river. No fingers or toes, and no little nose. Down with her dreams, her fingers—and toes—and her poor little nose.'"

Sibyl opened her mouth to scream, but a hand encased in leather slapped her to silence. Thin fog rose from the ground. They left the park at the far end, where the coaches on their way to pick up guests from Number 17 had become fewer and fewer in number.

"Lean on me, love," the man said. "Ain't no one coming to

your aid. Why would they? Everyone knows a drunk when they see one and no one pities a drunken woman. Drunk, she is," he cried. "What's a man to do with a drunken wife?"

Sibyl struggled afresh and kicked his shins. She allowed herself to go limp and fell through his arms to the hard cobbles.

"No, no, no." He bent over her, and she saw he wore a mask. "Be a good girl and get up." He sounded different.

"Can't," she managed to gasp.

"Halt at once," came the shout of a familiar voice. "Halt, I say. The constables are on their way."

"Why…" Sibyl's attacker fell back, losing his hat as he did so. "Of course they aren't. You can't trick me."

William Godly-Smythe, his shirtsleeves gleaming in the cold night, piled into the man. From the ground, Sibyl looked up to see her second cousin landing a flurry of punches that amazed her. Warm drops spattered her, and she realized with distaste that it was the stranger's blood.

"All right," he cried. "All right, I've had enough."

The next sound Sibyl heard was the thud of heavy footsteps. William stood over her. The other man hurried away, donning his top hat as he went.

"I should have acted before," William said, as if to himself. "What have I done with my caution?"

Sibyl managed to sit up, and her cousin dropped to his knees beside her. "My poor, dear Sibyl," he said, and there was no doubt that he was deeply disturbed by what had happened. "Remain still, if you please, and allow me to get you home."

When he picked her up, Sibyl argued that she could walk.

"No," he said, "you cannot walk, not until I am assured you are not hurt. That no bones are broken. Where is Meg?"

"You know she must stay at Number Seventeen."

"I will get you to Number Seven and see what must be done for you. Then I shall send for Meg."

She would save her energy to argue shortly.

William reached Number 7 and carried her up the steps and into the silent house.

"How did you know?" Sibyl asked and immediately added, "Miss Ash, of course. I'm so grateful to her for coming to get you." Much as she disliked the man, she was very glad for his help.

"She spoke of having to get rest," William said. "Odd woman."

"A good woman," Sibyl said. "Please let me walk now, William."

As if she hadn't spoken, he carried her upstairs and into 7B, where he set her on the old rose-colored chaise. At once he undid her bonnet ribbons and took off the hat. He peered into her face before setting a kettle on the hob. "Tea is what you need," he said. "And a warm, wet cloth to freshen your poor face. Did that wretch throw something on you?"

"Drink, I think," Sibyl said, embarrassed to reek of the stuff. William dampened a cloth and waved her hands aside when she tried to stop him from bathing her face and neck.

As soon as the kettle steamed, he made tea and gave her a cup. "Drink that and lean back. I'll find a blanket to warm you."

He went into her bedroom and returned with a coverlet, which he arranged over her.

Sibyl drank her tea gratefully. William's care filled her with uncomfortable emotions. She owed him her gratitude but could not like him more than she ever had.

"Have you learned your lesson?" he said.

"Oh, yes," she told him. "I will not walk abroad alone—at night—again."

"Indeed you will not. Sibyl—" he approached her and sat at her feet on the couch "—Sibyl, I don't know how to say what I must say. I don't know where to begin. I am an apology for a man. My skills in such situations are without finesse."

She ought to protest, but could not find the words.

"You are the sweetest of girls. You were a sweet child and I have loved you as long as I can remember."

Her blood must surely have stopped coursing through her body. She sat very still.

"I want to protect you forever. I want to awaken to see your face, and I want your face to be the last thing I see before I sleep. You are all I have ever hoped or dreamed of in a loved one. But I have approached you in all the wrong ways. With bluster and demand. Can you forgive me? As I have said, I am without practice. I have not known how to speak to you of what is in my heart."

Sibyl looked into his sincere face and prayed for guidance. She didn't wish to hurt him, but she could not accept his pledge.

"I was a boy who couldn't speak to girls, or flirt with them. My awkwardness has been the bane of my life. If I had known how to do it, I should have begged you to remain after your father died. I have suffered like a man damned ever since you left. That is why I have made sure I knew exactly what your circumstances were at all times."

"Thank you." How inadequate that sounded. It was the best she could do.

"It is my pleasure." He removed the cup and saucer from her hands and set them aside. And he took her cold hands to his lips. "I love you, Sibyl. I will always love you. Please say you will be my wife."

30

Coaches no longer rolled to a stop before Number 17. For that, Hunter Lloyd was grateful.

He was grateful for very little else.

There were times when he actually dreamed of shocking the battalions of his friends and acquaintances who would never expect him to be other than a solid, responsible fellow of very little passion.

He was responsible. He was also passionate. Unfortunately, his responsibilities had left almost no opportunity to explore the other element of his character—passion.

Damn it all.

Of all the hellish missions to fall to him. He was to go in search of Meg and tell her Sibyl had been set upon in the park, rescued by that slimy fellow, William Godly-Smythe, and was now disposed to consider accepting the man's proposal of marriage.

When Godly-Smythe had come in search of him with his request, the man's fatuous grin had come close to causing Hunter to do something that might put him on the side of the dock to which he was entirely unaccustomed.

Fog had thickened, but continued to spread itself upon the land and rise to a height of only three or four feet. The effect was eerie, and his own footsteps thudded but produced no echo. Too bad Adam was either sleeping or sulking. Hunter rather thought it might be the latter. Adam had secured a lucrative commission to paint Princess Désirée, but now the fool might actually nurse despair because he could not actually *have* the girl.

Hunter mounted the steps at Number 17, reached the door and was delighted to find it unlocked. He had no desire to confront the Count's pompous butler, or, indeed, any other member of his household. If there should be some question about his having walked in, he would apologize. Simple enough, that.

Subdued light shone in the impressive foyer.

Why hadn't he considered what was the most difficult issue here? He had no idea where to look for Meg—and he had no right to be skulking around another man's house in the middle of the night. An apology might not seem so reasonable, after all.

But he must find Meg. She would help Sibyl repulse their second cousin's persistent demands. Meg would not allow Sibyl to be browbeaten into marrying the dolt.

Hunter reached the great central staircase, where green garlands and wilted roses hung askew, and climbed slowly upward. The staff would be at work cleaning the ballroom. He could enter there pretending to have left something behind, then ask where he'd find Meg.

The doors to the ballroom were only slightly open. Very little light showed through the crack.

Hunter pushed through the doors and went inside. He automatically closed the doors behind him.

In the deep gloom, a daunting mess confronted him. Glasses crowded every surface. They were even spread on the carpet along the walls. And plates of half-eaten food had been abandoned wherever the guests had lost interest. Chairs faced every possible way, and some rested on their backs. Tablecloths had been pulled askew, resulting in broken china, left where it had landed. Fallen flowers had been mashed in lumps of cake and then onto the ballroom floor. Streamers festooned the walls in mangled ropes. The place reeked of drink.

But there was not a servant in sight.

"Lloyd?" It was Count Etranger's voice that greeted Hunter.

"What do you want? Everyone's gone home." The man was to Hunter's right and would have been hidden by a door if it stood open.

Honesty would definitely be the best, if not the only course here. "I need a few words with Meg Smiles. I wasn't sure where to look for her so I thought I would start here."

"She's bound to have retired by now. Her duties are exacting. She needs her sleep."

"There's some queer stuff afoot, My Lord," Hunter said, not about to be put down. "I'm well aware of the various unpleasant events Meg has suffered through. I've known her for two years. I assure you she is a quiet woman who lives a quiet life. For someone to try to harm her is extraordinary."

Still swathed in his dark robes, and with his feet and a good deal of his legs dangling, Count Etranger reclined on one of a number of small, blue brocade couches in the room. He propped his head on a fist and looked not one whit comfortable. "What makes you think someone's trying to hurt her?" he said.

"You know the answer to that as well as I do."

"Perhaps those accidents were just that—accidents. There may be no recurrence."

Hunter looked down at the other man. A handsome devil in that foreign way the French, or whatever he was, had. Women fell for what they mistook for the mystique every time. "My Lord, do *you* think there's no need for further concern? Do you believe the things that happened to Meg were accidental and incredible coincidences, happening as they did to the same woman?"

"No, damn it." The Count's head slipped from his hand, and he made a graceless recovery an instant before his temple would have landed on gilded wood.

If he had to guess, Hunter might say the Count was a trifle in his cups. "You are aware of William Godly-Smythe—Meg and Sibyl's second cousin?"

"Frightful man."

"Yes, well, as we speak, that frightful man is pressing his suit with Sibyl. Another unfortunate event took place when she was returning home this evening. She was accosted by a man who tried to carry her off." He detested the thought of her being subjected to such foul advances. "Godly-Smythe came to the rescue and promptly insisted he must assume the protection of his cousins. At once. He had the audacity to come to me and all but send me in search of Meg. Evidently he intends to secure a residence in Town and take Sibyl—as his wife—to live there. He intimates that, of course, Meg would accompany them."

"The hell he does." Count Etranger pushed himself to a sitting position, swung his long legs before him and studied his feet as if they surprised him. "Hmm. Meg Smiles remains with me.... She remains here. She does not care for her second cousin."

"I don't believe this has anything to do with liking. The Godly-Smythe person is preying on Sibyl's understandably shaken nerves, and what I believe to be the peculiar condition of the sisters' finances, to get his own way. After all, who can blame the man for wanting Sibyl?"

The Count glanced up at him, and Hunter realized his own regard for Sibyl must be obvious. "Mm, quite so." Etranger swept wide an arm. "Look at the condition of this ballroom. A disgrace."

"I should say so," Hunter agreed. "No doubt the staff thought you had retired and planned to deal with the task in the morning."

"No such thing. I sent them away. Too much noise. Touchy head, you know. Too much of that infernal caterwauling, and so-called music."

Too much claret, Madeira, or whatever, Hunter thought.

The Count held up a hand. "What the devil's that? Blast it. Someone else sneaking about. With luck they won't come in here."

Scuffing and rustling noises came from the gallery. Hunter drew back and sat on the nearest chair. He had no more interest in another encounter than his reluctant host.

"Bound to stay out if we don't make a sound," the Count whispered.

"Or to come in if they're hoping the room is empty," Hunter replied.

Etranger struggled with the dagger in his belt. Evidently it had worked its way into an uncomfortable position. "You sound like one of those infernal, pedantic barristers," he said and sucked in a breath. "Damn it."

"I am a barrister," Hunter pointed out. "I hope you haven't done yourself an injury, My Lord."

"They *are* coming in. Damn it."

Hunter sat quite still while one of the doors opened slowly. This intruder didn't close the door.

"Halibut!" The whisper was desperate. "Halibut, are you here? Come, Halibut, come." A series of kissing sounds followed. "Come, sweet, come to Meg and she'll find you some fresh meat. And one of those little kidney pies you like. Come, dear little Halibut, I won't let anything else happen to you. Ouch. Ouch! Oh, do come, Halibut. I'll even find you some syllabub. You know how you love syllabub. It's bad for you but you shall have just a little."

Count Etranger had already risen to his feet. Hunter was certain they were of one mind—they did not want to shock Meg.

Almost crouching, she moved between obstacles and called softly to the cat.

Hunter stood and tapped Etranger's arm. When the man turned his face toward him, he jabbed a finger in the direction of the gallery, indicating they should attempt to leave without Meg knowing they'd been there.

Unfortunately the next assault on the ear was the clatter of a dagger as it hit the arm of the chaise.

Meg whirled about.

"Nothing to worry about," the Count said, still in a low, hoarse voice. "Only friends here, Meg, only friends. We'll help you find that—Halibut."

"Oh, my goodness," Meg said, astounded, and sat on a chair with a plop. *Jean-Marc and Hunter.* She made certain her ankles were covered, not that the blisters would be noted with so little light. They were painful and stung badly. Inside, she felt shaky. The horrid man who had tricked her into following him had stopped his attack as quickly as he began. With a final order for her to persuade Jean-Marc to go away with her—at once—he had left. By the time Meg climbed from the table, gathered up her slippers and crept down the stairs, there was no sign of him. By miracle or design, the bottoms of her feet were not harmed, but still the pressure of each step and the brush of hems on her ankles caused repeated torment.

Jean-Marc approached her swiftly. Once at her side he put a finger beneath her chin and raised her face. "You should be in your bed. Tomorrow will be an exceedingly tiring day for you."

Really, Meg thought, his behavior had been beyond all this evening. "I shall not shirk my duties," she said. Ridiculous as it seemed, she was certain he was grasping another opportunity to remind her that if Sir Robert Brodie called, his visit would be short. "Halibut… He ran from the Princess's apartments. I must get him back." Once the intruder had left, the frightened cat had shot from some hiding place and dashed past Meg.

"My Lord," Hunter said, "if I may—"

"Of course you may," Etranger said. "We'll continue our discussion tomorrow. Meanwhile I'm grateful you'll be able to take care of that other matter."

Hunter no longer wore his costume. Meg studied him and noted he showed agitation. "Is there a problem?" she asked him.

"Well—no."

"You're a good man, Lloyd," Jean-Marc said. He didn't take his eyes from Meg's face. "Time enough in the morning, hmm?"

Hunter made a noise that could be taken for agreement.

Faintness overcame Meg. Her skin turned cold. She wiped her brow and felt perspiration.

"You're ill," Jean-Marc said and dropped to one knee beside her. "Meg, look at me. Dash this gloomy room. Look at me."

Her head felt too heavy to support, but she did as he asked. "I have had an unpleasant experience," she told him. "You will insist on the truth so I might as well give it to you at once. I haven't strength left to pretend. Hunter, promise you won't say anything to Sibyl?"

He stood close to Jean-Marc and bent over her. "I promise, I promise," he said. "What has happened to you?"

"I was attacked." She allowed a moment for her announcement to make its impact. "I was on my way to help the Princess. Then I saw a man I thought was you, My Lord, coming from her sitting room. You—he held Halibut. I was afraid you were taking him away so I followed to a room in the old servants' quarters. The man—I have no idea who he was—turned on me. He hit me."

"Good God," Jean-Marc muttered. "Let me see you more closely."

She raised her face. "I was more shocked than hurt," she said.

"You are bruised. See, Lloyd, the brute has bruised her."

"He lifted me onto a table and made me dance. He used a lighted taper to make me dance."

Absolute silence followed.

Hunter found one of her hands and chafed it.

"I cannot believe this," Jean-Marc said. He touched the side of her face, and she felt the bruising then. "Did he burn you?"

"Yes." To try to make the truth less amazing wouldn't help. "My ankles and the sides of my feet."

"Hell's teeth, *burned*." Jean-Marc said. "Yet you are here looking for a cat? What else... Did he do anything else to you?"

"He—" Meg bowed her head "—he wore a headdress and it was draped across his face. I don't know who he was. But...he did not sound English."

"Meg?" Jean-Marc stroked her jaw repeatedly with the backs of his fingers. "I didn't ask you what he wore, or how he sounded—although both are of interest. I asked if he did anything else to you.''

"He kissed me," she whispered, and shuddered. "And he took certain other liberties. But he held the lighted taper and, well, it impeded him.''

Hunter's grip on her hand tightened.

"You must rest," Jean-Marc told her. Even by what little light there was, she could see that he was a man enraged. "And I must discover the criminal in my own home. Your assistance is invaluable, Lloyd. I'm sure Meg doesn't need to be concerned about her sister's welfare, but I know you will take care of that anyway.''

"Indeed I will. I'll return to Number Seven at once.''

"Thank you. Tomorrow I shall remove my household to Windsor, but first I will speak with you.''

"As you wish," Hunter said.

Jean-Marc had already turned his full attention to Meg. "We shall awaken Verbeux and have him check the burns. If you'll excuse us, Lloyd?'' He picked her up and carried her from the ballroom. Frequently looking into her face, he set off for Verbeux's quarters.

Hunter watched Count Etranger climb toward the next story with Meg in his arms. The man hardly looked like an employer dealing with an employee for whom he felt only mild responsibility and suitable disinterest.

If Hunter were asked his opinion, he might just say that the Count was taken with his sister's companion. In that direction lay heartache for Meggie—if she were to fall for the man.

There was nothing to be done about that tonight, if ever. Making a shoulder available if she needed it later might be the best he could do. He ran quickly downstairs and let himself out into the damp and foggy night. The scent of wet earth and misted roses made him smile. A flash of red in the park sobered him instantly.

A woman moved swiftly toward the other side of the square. He followed, hoping she wouldn't realize he was there.

As instinct had made him suspect, she left the park, crossed the street and mounted the steps at Number 7. That woman was Lady Upworth. Once seen, she would be difficult to forget, and they had been introduced at the musicale.

She hovered at the front door, clearly uncertain what to do next. Hunter made up his mind what action to take and hurried toward her. "My Lady?" he said, loudly enough to be heard but, he hoped, in a pleasant and nonthreatening tone. "I'm Hunter Lloyd. We met at Count Etranger's."

Lady Upworth swung toward him, one hand at her throat.

He joined her, a smile firmly in place. "Forgive me for mentioning that this is a late visit, My Lady. May I help you in some manner?"

The red he had seen was her costume, over which she wore a cape that flowed away from her shoulders. "This is so awkward," she said. A tinkling sound reminded Hunter that small gold coins decorated her hems. "I learned something that disturbed me this evening. It is by no means my responsibility to do anything about it, but I do like both of the Misses Smiles and I rather think I can save them from unpleasantness that could cause them terrible difficulty."

Hunter frowned. Lady Upworth had a most beautiful face. He had learned to protect his objectivity from assault by such faces, but there was sincerity in the lady's marvelous eyes, and an air of discomfort about her that suggested she would rather not come forward with whatever her conscience told her to do.

"I think I should speak with Sibyl Smiles," she said. "Do you know if her second cousin, Mr. William Godly-Smythe, is with her now?"

He used his key to unlock the door and ushered her inside. In lowered tones he told her, "I believe he is. Should you like me to accompany you to Sibyl? She and Meg live on the next floor."

She appeared thoughtful before she said, "If it would not be too much trouble, I'd appreciate that." And she went ahead of him to the stairs. "These are beautiful," she said. "Who do you suppose all these people are? Carved into the banisters and the newel posts?"

"My ancestors," he said wryly. "They didn't amount to much, but the architect of this house—my aunt's grandfather—considered the family extraordinary and worth immortalizing in such a fashion. Some say there are carvings of him. See?" He pointed out several faces that seemed to be of the same man. "Sir Septimus Spivey. Supposedly I look like him, which means I am not a thing of beauty." He laughed and climbed the stairs behind her.

She paused again and said, "There are babies. How sad. I suppose they represent little ones who died in infancy. And here—" she looked very closely "—here is a blank face. Perhaps it was intended for some future descendant."

"Possibly." Hunter was glad to arrive at 7B. "This is where Meg and Sibyl live. I see light beneath the door. I expect the cousin is still here. Do you know him?"

Lady Upworth raised her pretty chin. "I believe we are acquainted. He does not like me—that is why I should appreciate your presence, for me, and for Sibyl."

"You shall have it," Hunter said and knocked the door.

It opened at once, and William Godly-Smythe stood there. "About time," he said, indicating that they were to come in. "I am a busy man and must complete my business here at once. We won't detain you further, Lloyd, but Meg—" His posture stiffened and he stared at Lady Upworth. "You aren't Meg."

"I certainly am not," she said, stepping into the room. "I came to visit Sibyl. And Mr. Lloyd has kindly agreed to remain with me and then escort me back to my accommodations."

"Good evening, My Lady," Sibyl said. She stood in the center of the room, and her confusion was evident.

"I told you to bring Meg here, Lloyd," Godly-Smythe said and Hunter no longer had any doubt that he detested the man. "Where is she?"

"Asleep, I gather," Hunter said. The less said of the truth, the better. "I could hardly enter her bedchamber and abduct her, could I? Surely whatever you have to say will wait until the morning."

Godly-Smythe's full attention centered on Lady Upworth, as hers did on him. Lady Upworth's mouth curved with amusement while Godly-Smythe's discomfort was evident. "How nice to see you again," she said. "We must find an opportunity to chat about old times, hmm? After all, we were both involved in some interesting events."

"Sibyl is tired," he said. "Polite calls are never made at such an hour. I suggest you leave."

"And miss hearing your latest news?"

Godly-Smythe's naturally healthy complexion darkened. "Sibyl, you should sleep. Sleep as long as you can. We will talk in the morning—late in the morning."

"Still losing in the hells," Lady Upworth said to Godly-Smythe. "Gambling can be so difficult for some to put behind them."

Fascinated, Hunter observed both the verbal and unspoken hostility between these two.

"I am a man of strong character," Godly-Smythe said. "And you, My Lady, do you continue to pour your fortune away?"

Lady Upworth laughed. "No, no, I am reformed, sir. But I shall never forget that ugly scene at Toby Short's. When you were accused of cheating and couldn't pay your debts."

"How dare you, My Lady," Godly-Smythe said, his voice tight and low. "You have mistaken me for another, I assure you." He moved his eyes significantly in Sibyl's direction.

Lady Upworth seemed to consider. "Perhaps," she said finally. "There is always such a crush in those places—or there was. It's been a very long time since I was drawn to cover my unhappiness over the death of my dear husband by seeking raucous company."

Godly-Smythe nodded. "Quite so. Sibyl, I think I shall go down and prevail on Reverend Baggs to share his room with me.

I should not be comfortable too far away from you, my dear. Come to me at once if anything disturbs you." With a measured stare, first at Lady Upworth, then at Hunter, he approached the door. "You make your way upstairs, Lloyd. I'll see Lady Upworth out. This is no time for socializing."

Hunter thought it was indeed time for him to leave. "As you say," he told Godly-Smythe. The Count didn't intend to pursue the issue of whether or not Sibyl would accept Godly-Smythe's proposal before morning. There was nothing to be accomplished by remaining.

"You go along, Mr. Godly-Smythe," Lady Upworth said. "Mr. Lloyd will take me home. But first I must give Sibyl her instructions from the Count for tomorrow."

Godly-Smythe's discomfort at leaving Lady Upworth with Sibyl showed, but he smiled at Sibyl, inclined his head to Lady Upworth and quit the room. His footsteps were soon heard descending the stairs.

"It is extremely late," Lady Upworth told Sibyl, "but I decided I must come to you. Mr. Lloyd, I really cannot impose upon you further. Please go to your bed. Sibyl and I have a good deal to talk about."

"I'll wait," he said, "I could not countenance your walking home alone."

"I am quite safe, I assure you," she said, and produced a pistol from the folds of her cloak. She immediately tucked it away again. "I have had to learn to protect myself, and I can."

Hunter heard Sibyl draw in a sharp breath. The sight of the weapon had surprised him also, but at least he was accustomed to such things, even if not in the hands of a lady. "You want to be alone with Sibyl," he said. "Very well, but I shall be in my rooms waiting for your summons. Regardless of how fearless you are, it's out of the question for you to return to Number Seventeen alone at this hour."

The door closed behind Hunter, and Sibyl sat down. She buried her face in her hands.

"I need your full attention," Lady Upworth said. "We can't know how much time we have before your second cousin returns. I don't expect him to leave you alone for long—not if he thinks I'm still here."

Sibyl raised her face. "It's very late, My Lady. I am so tired." And she no longer trusted herself to make good choices—about anything.

"Buck up," Lady Upworth said. "I am more tired than I can tell you, but I came because you need my help. You are in danger. And I have decided on a dangerous course—to me—in order to help you. You and Meg should leave your positions at Count Etranger's at once."

Sibyl felt a chill. Exhaustion of mind and body drained her.

"Do you understand what I'm saying to you, Sibyl? You must get away from here—far away."

She needed Meg, Sibyl thought, but challenged herself to be strong, as strong as her sister would be if she were here. "I'm sure you mean well, My Lady," she said, "but please don't worry about us. We are not worried. In fact, our lives are greatly improved now, thank you. We shall manage very well."

"No." Her Ladyship's tone was harsh. "You are not listening to me. You are in danger, I tell you, grave danger. I am going to arrange for you to get away. I know you have had financial troubles but I will help you. You will have plenty of money. I can and will see to that."

Tiredness slipped away from Sibyl. She regarded Lady Upworth carefully, attempting to assess that lady's state of mind.

Lady Upworth smiled. "I can tell you are seeing the wisdom of accepting my help. I assure you, Sibyl, I should never forgive myself if I failed to help you."

Sibyl smoothed her skirts and considered how to deal with this very uncommon situation. "Why do you believe we are in danger? We are very unimportant people—ordinary people. No one would gain anything from causing us unhappiness."

"You and your sister are not ordinary," Lady Upworth said.

"You are accomplished. You possess a quiet charm that is appealing, and your sister is, I admit, quite the most unusual creature I have encountered for a long time. I can well imagine why... She is attractive to men, I think. Because of this it is important that she have an opportunity to meet suitable people."

Sibyl did not like Lady Upworth. "Meg is to have a very suitable caller. Sir Robert Brodie. He is a surgeon and is clearly interested in Meg."

"No time."

"I beg your pardon," Sibyl said, frowning. "What do you mean, no time?"

Lady Upworth pushed her cloak behind her and sat down. "I mean that there isn't adequate time to hope that a first meeting may turn into something more. Sibyl, you must take me seriously. I cannot reveal my sources, but I have discovered information that leads me to believe you and Meg are dangerous to someone, and that your very lives may be in danger."

"Who is it?" Sibyl chafed her arms. Goose bumps had sprung up on every inch of her body.

"Tomorrow the Count intends to remove his household to Windsor. He would take you all with him—and me, of course—and no doubt he'll throw some suitable event for Désirée there. I believe he thinks it will be safer for everyone at Riverside, that he will be better able to protect against enemies. I disagree. I think he is desperate and not thinking clearly—and that he doesn't want to face the truth."

Trembling, Sibyl asked, "What is the truth?"

"Oh, I don't know it all." Lady Upworth flapped a hand before her face and sounded irritated. "There is some great intrigue in progress. One unpleasant event follows another. I fear for us all, but mostly for you and Meg. It may be best to reduce the household to as few members as possible, the better to identify interlopers, or people in places where they do not belong. Now, we will discuss what is best for you."

"I'm afraid we won't," Sibyl said firmly. "And I should like to go to bed now."

Lady Upworth stood up and took off the cape. She was a magnificent creature, brilliant and impossible to ignore—and so unlike Sibyl. Sibyl smiled at the thought of any comparison being made.

"I am not wealthy," Lady Upworth said, "but I have enough money to keep the two of you comfortably until all this nonsense is resolved."

"You're very kind, but we don't need money." This was more than embarrassing, Sibyl thought. It was demeaning to think that anyone would feel free to treat her like a pauper.

"Tell me about your situation and how it came about."

The woman was without shame. "I would rather not, thank you," Sibyl said.

"You are humiliated by your reduced circumstances. I assure you that is unnecessary with me. I did not always have money. I married it. Now, enough of this silly pride. A simple explanation, please. What happened? I know you lived in Puckly Hinton and your father was a minister, apparently quite a well-fixed minister."

Sibyl considered, then said, "Yes, he was. He came from a wealthy family."

"And you and your sister were his heirs?"

How, Sibyl couldn't guess, but she suspected Lady Upworth already knew the answers to her questions. Perhaps it didn't matter. "We were left a trust that was to provide an adequate allowance for each of us. The house and the rest of Papa's holdings went to William as the closest male relative. That was a stipulation—that the house must go to a male. Unfortunately, a few months ago we learned that there was to be a reduction in our allowance. The explanation given was that we had been expected to marry by now and that, since we show no sign of doing so, if the money is to last, we must take much smaller amounts."

"I see." Trailing about the room with her diaphanous red costume floating about her fine figure, Lady Upworth frowned, and her smooth brow wrinkled.

"We are managing well, thank you," Sibyl said. "Between what allowance we do get, and our own efforts, we shall do well enough."

"A shame," Lady Upworth said. "You are genteel women and quite unsuited to such things. Now, please give me your word that you will repeat nothing of what I am about to tell you."

Orders, regardless of how they were couched, were still orders. Lady Upworth had a most authoritative air about her. She expected to be obeyed.

"Come now, Sibyl, give me your word. I promise I will help you, and you will be glad you decided to trust me."

"I do trust you," Sibyl said at once. Did she? "I believe you have a kind heart beneath a sharp tongue." Horrified, she fell silent.

Lady Upworth chuckled. "Is that so? Well, yes, I suppose it is. Now, give me your entire attention, please. You heard me speak of meeting William in the gambling hells."

"Yes." Sibyl had heard of such places but couldn't imagine what they were like.

"They are low places where foolish people gamble away what they cannot afford to lose. Oh, certainly there are very well-heeled young rakes who lose fortunes without as much as scratching the extent of their wealth. But for the rest, a night at the tables can bring about ruin."

"But William wasn't one of those, was he?" Sibyl asked. "I can imagine his being curious, but not risking the fortune he was so pleased to accept."

"The fortune to which he had no right, you mean?"

"He had a right," Sibyl said without inflection. "Because he is a man, he had the right whereas Meg and I had none."

"An outrage, one of so many visited on women. William did gamble heavily and probably still does. The last time I saw him in such surroundings, he was accused of cheating. Most unpleasant and bad for the reputation.''

"Accused?" Sibyl said. "But it was not proven."

"Your insistence upon defending the man does surprise me."

"He is a member of my family."

"Quite so. But on this occasion there was no mistake. The accusation was just. You see, he wagered a house, a house in Puckly Hinton. And he lost it.''

William wagered The Ramblers? And lost it? But he wouldn't—he couldn't have. "That's impossible. He would not do such a thing.''

"He did, I tell you, but that's when he was accused of cheating. It seemed in fact that although he had the right to call the house his own as long as he lived in it, should he decide to sell, half of the proceeds belonged in two equal parts to his second cousins.''

Sibyl and Meg had been aware of such a provision, but it had seemed of no importance since they had never expected William to sell. Sibyl longed to be silent, to think what to do next. "I beg you not to speak of these matters elsewhere," she said.

With layers of red gauze flying, Lady Upworth rushed toward Sibyl. She took her by the shoulders. "I have told you that none of this conversation must go outside this room—it must not go beyond the two of us. And I tell you that you are living under a threat.''

"From William?" Sibyl whispered.

"I'm not sure how he will go about what he must do to secure his own good reputation, but he is a desperate man and will do what he considers necessary.''

"You are correct about the terms of Papa's will. The provision was made to discourage William from letting the house go out of the family.''

"But Mr. Godly-Smythe has a plan, I believe. And since he knows his time to make good on his gambling debts is limited, he is forced to move quickly. He has asked you to marry him. That is the first step, hmm?''

Sibyl lowered her voice. "So that my share in the house would become his."

"Yes. But there would still be Meg and her share. What of that?"

"William would expect Meg to live with us and give up any rights to take the proceeds from a quarter of the sale in return for his kindness. She wouldn't do it."

"Not even for your sake? Because she thought it would be better for you?"

"Meg is clever. She will know what is best. I will not allow her to give away her inheritance for me, though."

"Then what will you do?"

"Agree to marry him, of course."

31

He did not want to put her down. As long as he held her in his arms, he would not have to wonder if she was safe.

His head wasn't clear. Too much claret. An unusual event for him, but one he recalled too well from other occasions when he'd become angry, so angry he feared he would not control his actions unless he diverted himself.

"I can walk," Meg said, and she shifted as if to encourage him to set her down.

She did not guess how dangerous it was to her safety to move against him, to do anything to arouse him.

He was already aroused. "I shall carry you, Meg. Verbeux will tell us if we need to send for the doctor."

"No doctor," she said, wriggling again. "I have a few little blisters. He can do nothing I cannot do myself."

"Meg—" he stopped and drew her higher in his arms "—rest your head on my chest. I need to feel you. You will never know how badly I need to feel you, and to know you're with me."

Her eyes grew huge, then her eyelids lowered and he saw her lips move silently. She could withdraw into herself at will. Very gently, he kissed her brow. She spoke in an unintelligible whisper while her eyes slowly closed completely. He felt her relax and grow heavier.

"You're going away from me," he breathed. "You're going because you want to. You don't trust me not to hurt you." And he couldn't blame her.

At the end of a long corridor, he entered the anteroom to Verbeux's rooms and stood still. "Pierre?" Jean-Marc frowned. "What are you doing?"

"Listening for M. Verbeux," Pierre said from a chair behind Verbeux's desk. He looked at Meg and asked, "Is there something I can do to help?"

"Yes. Watch over Miss Smiles until I can rouse Verbeux."

"Oui, monsieur," Pierre said, but he appeared puzzled and stood up.

"Miss Smiles is meditating, Pierre. She is an expert at these things and employs them to steady her nerves. Best let her sit in silence."

"As you wish," Pierre said. "I have wanted to speak with Miss Smiles about her hand."

"Understandable," Jean-Marc said. "But not tonight. I shall hope to return soon."

"I don't think you should disturb M. Verbeux," Pierre said. "He doesn't feel well."

Jean-Marc set Meg down carefully on a couch covered with purple and gold striped silk. "Foxed, is he? Happens to the best of us. Won't be the first time I've seen him the worse for a little drink."

"He told you he was set upon?" Pierre said. His coat and trousers were of the finest black kerseymere, and his neck cloth was tied *à l'orientale*. Quite the dandy.

"Verbeux did come to me," Jean-Marc said. "During the party. He'd been shaken up a little, but he has known far worse, I assure you." With that he strode to enter the bedchamber.

A lighted candle glowed brightly beside the canopied bed. More purple, velvet this time. Jean-Marc went to look down at his man. "What the... Did something else happen? You weren't—"

"As badly hurt as when I saw you in the ballroom?" Verbeux smiled wryly. "My new friends waited for me here—in my own bedchamber. They wanted to remind me what I must do."

"Make sure I leave London?"

"Yes." Verbeux's face was so white as to seem transparent. "Unfortunately, I couldn't tell them you had agreed. Even though I said I intended to discuss the matter with you again, they weren't impressed. Thus the added character to my person. I am told that next time they'll break bones."

"Here in my house." Jean-Marc shook his head, bewildered. "Villains are coming and going in this house without anyone stopping them."

"Seemed to know their way about."

"And you couldn't make yourself heard? Didn't you call out, man?"

"Difficult with rags in your mouth."

"Tomorrow we go to Windsor."

"Won't help. They'll find us."

Jean-Marc didn't say that he also thought they would be followed in short order. But it would be harder for a stranger to walk into Riverside and not be noticed. There was too much going on here, too much easy cover for someone who wanted to get lost among the host of vendors and craftsmen who came every day—to say nothing of the multitudes of guests and callers.

"Let me look at you," Jean-Marc said. "What have they done to you, apart from the obvious?"

"You can see the worst of it. They took a strap to my back, but I have a salve. I'll find a way to get it applied."

"Pierre would do it."

Verbeux shook his head. "He's not accustomed to such things."

"I've brought Miss Smiles to you. I hoped you could look at the burns on her ankles, but you're not fit."

"Burns, My Lord? How was she burned?"

"Undoubtedly by one of your friends. He made her dance over a lighted taper. Took some liberties, too, unless I'm much mistaken." He felt Verbeux's eyes upon him, assessing. "Yes, I'm angry, if that's what you're trying to decide. The thought of some foul creature putting his hands on her sickens me. And it angers me enough to know I could be dangerous—to others and to myself."

"Foul," Verbeux agreed quietly. "They are without scruples, without any honorable cause."

Jean-Marc looked at Verbeux with curiosity. "You speak as if you know these people."

"Perhaps I do," Verbeux said, defiant. "Perhaps you do, also."

Jean-Marc turned his back on Verbeux.

"They do not intend to stop," Verbeux said. "Surely you see that now. Surely you understand. They would prefer you dead. Too much risk with that. Reprisals likely. Driving you out is the next best thing."

"They will not succeed."

"*Why?* Why would you fight for something you do not want?"

"Until now the answer to that question has been unclear," Jean-Marc said, "but now I believe I know what drives me to stand my ground. It is not for myself. I will tell you that it is for my father, but there is also another, and I cannot tell you who it is. I cannot know who may be listening, or from where. To mention that name might be to put another life in even greater danger than we have so far feared."

"Your father?" Verbeux said. He winced and hunched his shoulders. "You would protect the man who has never shown you the smallest amount of affection?"

Jean-Marc's vision lost focus. "We cannot know all that is in a man's heart. He makes decisions based on what he has been taught, what he believes his duty to be. But he is just a man and can only guess the right path."

"So you think your father has been hiding a great love for you?"

"We will not speak further of this." He could not, because the bitter longing he felt was too destructive.

Pierre stepped into the room. "Lady Upworth is here. She wishes to see M. Verbeux."

"Damn it," Jean-Marc said. "What could she possibly want at such an hour?"

"Evidently she is concerned for his health," Pierre said.

Verbeux said, "I think I have become her confidant for the moment. Not a happy woman."

"She is comforting Miss Smiles," Pierre said.

Jean-Marc threw up his hands. "I said Miss Smiles should not be disturbed."

"Shall I send Lady Upworth away?"

Ila, pushing her way into the room, favored Pierre with a deeply disdainful stare. She smiled at Jean-Marc and immediately turned her attention to Verbeux. Rising to her toes, she approached the bed. "M. Verbeux? Oh, I should not have rushed away. They attacked you again, didn't they?"

"Those people used a whip on his back," Jean-Marc said. "Pierre, kindly get M. Verbeux's salve and apply it."

"Hurry," Ila told Pierre. "Bring it at once." She tugged off the cape she wore and threw it aside. "I was frightened, so I shut myself away for a time. Then I went about some errands that had to be done. Why didn't I return to you sooner? You, who are always so kind to me."

"Don't babble," Verbeux said, and Jean-Marc's lips twitched. His man was confounded by such a show of womanly concern for him.

"Remember your place, sir," Ila said. She whipped the covers back so swiftly that Verbeux's attempt to catch them was too late. "On your face. At once. I am no stranger to nursing men. My husband's final illness was long, and he would only allow me near him. Pierre?"

Obediently, Pierre produced a jar from which he unscrewed the top.

Ila considered Verbeux, who had yet to turn onto his stomach. "Do as I tell you or I shall have you held down and—"

"Yes, yes," he interrupted. "Turn your back."

She threw up her hands, but did as he asked. Verbeux shook

his head, but pulled the sheet up to his waist and rolled to his stomach.

"He's ready," Jean-Marc said, barely swallowing a chuckle.

Ila took the salve from Pierre and went to Verbeux. An instant, and his nightshirt was over his head. At the sight of his vicious wounds Ila's nostrils flared with anger. She sat beside him on the high mattress and proceeded to smooth the thick, white substance over his back.

She was exceedingly gentle, Jean-Marc noted.

Each time Verbeux sucked in a breath, she made soft clucking sounds or hushed him quietly and murmured encouragement.

Pierre withdrew.

Jean-Marc studied the two on the bed for moments longer. There was probably nothing between them—yet. "What would you suggest be used on the burns?" he said.

"Pierre will give it to you," Verbeux said. "The air will make the wounds hurt more. They should be kept covered. The preparation is well-known among some. An old remedy, but efficacious. If she suffers too much pain, brandy will at least help her not to care. Ah."

Evidently Lady Upworth's fingers, coated in salve, could do magical things for a man's wounds.

Neither Verbeux nor Ila noticed when Jean-Marc left them.

Pierre, who evidently overheard every word that had been spoken, gave Jean-Marc a bottle. "They say there is silver in it. I don't know if it is true, but many swear the lesions heal faster, and there is much less pain."

Meg's cheek rested against the back of the couch. The veils obscured her face. "She is asleep again," Jean-Marc said. "Sleep is good for her, but she would undoubtedly be less disquieted if she awakened in her own room. Between us we could lift her very carefully."

But Jean-Marc didn't want help lifting Meg.

She turned her face in his direction and said, "I am not asleep."

"Is that so?" Jean-Marc said. "Then we had best make our

way." And, although he was careful not to touch her ankles, he scooped her up without ceremony.

She didn't uncover her face, but settled it against his chest as if it were the most natural thing in the world to do.

"When Lady Upworth leaves, please keep careful watch over M. Verbeux," Jean-Marc told Pierre. "He is unlikely to complain, regardless of how much pain he suffers. Do not hesitate to send for my physician if you consider it necessary."

"You may rely on me, My Lord."

Pierre opened the door, and Jean-Marc thanked him as he passed. He went swiftly to his own rooms. There, where weapons were easily to hand, he felt more confident of reacting appropriately to any intrusion.

Meg seemed to drift and felt less substantial. When he glanced at the blistered wounds on her ankles, it was with horror. The savage fool who did this could have caught her afire, and this would be a very different moment. She would not be resting in his arms, with trusting, almost childlike serenity.

With barely a shred of conscience, he took her into his bedchamber and stretched her out on the counterpane.

The drive to keep her safe, to keep her with him, constricted his throat. All so strange in a man who had tailored his relationships to assure the least possible attachment.

He could do as Verbeux suggested and toss aside all concern for his father, for Désirée and Mont Nuages. He could make public his attachment to Meg Smiles and announce that he planned to leave public life and make his permanent residence in England. He would farm the hundreds of acres of fertile lands that were presided over by the lord of Riverside Place. No doubt his villagers in tiny Castleberry would be glad enough to know the lord of the manor was at the helm, rather than the steward who acted in his stead. There was a church to be better tended, and a village school in need of repair. Livestock should be brought in, and the workers' homes improved where necessary. He could make his life count for something simple and good, and with a supportive woman at his side, perhaps he could learn to feel complete. And if his father wanted his assistance as an ambassador, well then, he would always be willing to do his duty.

Then there was the matter of Désirée. The missish creature was probably hatching some plot to run off with an impoverished painter. A talented painter, but without substance and certainly without breeding. That Jean-Marc couldn't allow, particularly since he had definite plans for his half sister and they would not allow for any kittenish infatuation.

It was true that he doubted Adam Chillworth entertained ideas that included marriage to a seventeen-year-old and very spoiled princess.

He must not delay any longer in tending to Meg's burns. Perhaps he should clean them. If he did, it would surely cause her to cry out, and to struggle, and she might hurt herself further.

The lotion Pierre had given him had a sharp, metallic scent.

"I'm going to make you more comfortable, Meggie," he said. "If I hurt you a little in doing so, please be patient with me."

She undid the little jeweled clasp that held the veil in place and pulled it off. "Jean-Marc, what is to become of us?"

He was instantly still.

"I was told that I must leave this house—" her eyes slid away "—and take you with me. I have been warned that there is great trouble all around us and that if the wishes of certain people are not met, the result will be terrible."

"And I have been told the same thing. In my case the message was sent via Verbeux, by those who assaulted him."

"He came to me, too. But that... As I've told you, the man in the attic told me the same thing."

"I'm no longer sure how much good it may do, but we will leave here in the morning," Jean-Marc said. "I will take select members of the household. You and Sibyl will come. Ash, I suppose. No one I have not spoken to in advance."

"What do you hope to accomplish?"

"Authority. I can hope to regain authority over everyone who is there. Anyone who appears, but whom I do not expect, will be removed at once—after I have questioned them extensively. I will get to the bottom of these events. And when I do, those responsible will suffer."

"I wish you good fortune, but I cannot accompany you."

He laughed and wished he felt amused. "Of course you can."

"No. My sister is in need of me here. It seems we have important personal matters to attend." Lady Upworth had passed invaluable information while Meg waited for Jean-Marc outside M. Verbeux's bedchamber.

"How do you know?"

"By what has been said." She could not betray Her Ladyship's trust. "No matter, please don't press me on this."

With anger building in his veins, Jean-Marc poured himself a large brandy and drank half of the glass in one swallow.

Meg had already noted he appeared to have drunk more than a little strong liquor. The mood it induced disquieted her. He pressed the rim of his glass to her lips and tipped until she was forced to take an aromatic sip that burned her throat.

Jean-Marc piled pillows behind her back and, very carefully, pulled her skirts up to her knees. The silver silk stockings she wore had melted with the flame and only made her condition worse.

"They must be removed," he said and proceeded to cut them away so surely she could scarcely believe he had not done such things on many occasions. The procedure hurt, and she held her breath.

"There," he said when the silk was free of the wounds. A few more swift slices and he could remove the stockings altogether.

"This is humiliating," Meg said.

"How can that be? I have seen a great deal more of you than your naked limbs."

She covered the top of her bosom and felt the heat in her skin.

Jean-Marc was grateful the lotion went on easily, but he took his time. He caressed each foot and placed kisses on the arches before smoothing the angry wounds. She sighed with each application as if the relief was immediate, and he was heartened.

At last each blistered area was thickly coated, and he spread a white linen sheet beneath her legs. "You must stay where you are," he told her. "Whatever you need, I will make sure you have. Tomorrow you will be placed comfortably in a coach and I shall escort you to Windsor myself."

"You don't listen, do you? I will not go to Windsor."

"You *will* go to Windsor. I shall speak with Sibyl, and once she knows how much is at stake, she will insist you both go."

"Don't. Please, don't. You will sway her because she will believe it is for the best. She is too susceptible to male authority."

"I always knew I really liked your sister," he said, smiling. He was relieved when Meg smiled back. "That's better, my lovely girl. I shall look forward to showing you the full extent of the estates at Riverside. And in time you shall get to know the villagers in Castleberry. The vicar's wife will be so delighted to have you play an active part in the affairs of the parish."

He did, Meg thought, truly believe he could have his own way in this, as he did in so many things.

She would lie if she didn't admit her longing to remain with Jean-Marc, but she couldn't do so with a glad heart, not under the only terms he could offer that would not threaten them both with scorn.

He was watching her face. Meg looked at him.

"Ah, Meg," he said, and sat beside her on the bed. "You are a considerable complication to me, but I have never been more grateful to have my peace disrupted."

"You have an odd turn of compliment," she told him. "I shall be truthful. You have disrupted my quiet life. You have presented me with dilemmas I never expected to experience. But every moment I spend with you is sweet. Aren't I a fool—to present you with such power over me?"

"No." Very slowly, he bent closer, his attention on her lips until he covered them with his own. He kissed her insistently. His finesse spoke of his experience, but her breath shortened and she closed her eyes and gave herself up to the sensation that the joining of their mouths was a joining of everything they were.

His hands lightly circled her neck, and he pushed her onto the pillows. Meg ached with her longing. He brought every nerve alive until she could imagine they were all just beneath her skin and open to his touch.

Tucking a knee beneath him, he moved Meg until he cradled her head and shoulders in one of his arms. He rocked her almost imperceptibly and he studied her face in detail. Even as he held her so intimately, she felt him grow still within himself. A dark force with the power to break her. The length of her body received his appraisal. Without warning, he swept a hand up one thigh and inside her clothes to spread his fingers on her stomach.

"You know you shouldn't," she whispered.

"But I want to, and you want me to," he whispered back.

He played with the hair that sheltered her womanly places, and bent over her to kiss the swell of her breasts at the neckline of the costume.

Meg throbbed all over. "Jean-Marc, please."

"Please what?" he asked from his nestling place in the deep hollow between her breasts. He licked the tingling flesh there.

"I don't know," she told him, and she didn't, except she was losing focus on everything but what he made her feel.

Removing his hand from beneath her skirts for a moment, he quickly loosed the delicate silver buckles that closed the front of her bodice and opened it. She glanced down at her breasts and quickly away. There was, Meg thought, entirely too much of her, and he had arranged the bodice so that it accentuated her fullness, framed the straining, sensitive flesh.

"Jean-Marc?"

"Don't say that again. Not now."

His mouth on hers ensured that she said nothing for a long time. And while they kissed, he returned to the warm places that caused her to squirm at his every fleeting touch.

He parted her and stroked, and she rolled her hips away. A white line formed around his compressed lips. He took the small, tender piece of flesh that pulsated between his finger and thumb and pulled lightly.

Meg cried out.

Jean-Marc's face grew tighter yet, and he pulled again, then rubbed, first with a feathery touch that drove her wild, then with increasing vigor. He turned her in his arms and fastened his mouth on a nipple. Her self-consciousness fell away. Meg held his head against her breasts, and she kissed his hair, and raised her hips to meet the now rapid stimulation. Moist and slick, she writhed against him, and reached for him, but she could not move her legs as she wished to, and his weight held her down.

"Don't stop," she panted. "Never, please."

"Only when I have to," he murmured. "But now I should allow you to rest. You are undoubtedly shocked."

"I should be more shocked if you left me now. Could you take off your clothes, please?"

He studied her and said, "You are so polite. So, of course I must grant your wishes." Always keeping a hand or his mouth on her, he stripped. "This clever skirt I had made for you could be a nuisance."

She giggled nervously, and he took her breasts in his hands, smoothed and molded them. His strong tongue worked a magical thing that made her pant and then, when she felt she could not bear another second, a ripple of heat, burning heat, broke over her of its own volition. A great throbbing, aching wonderment pumped through the flesh he had pulled. Her stomach drew tight. Meg panted and reached for Jean-Marc. She touched whatever she could get her hands on.

"You are unusual," he told her, unsuccessfully trying to capture her roaming hands. "So passionate. I am awed by you. But if you continue what you are trying to do, my girl, I shall have to make you regret your forwardness."

As he spoke, he grew a little careless, and Meg encircled his rod. He attempted to remove her hand but she held on so tightly he let out a groan. "You are a torturer. I cannot—Meg—I should have kept my clothes on."

"You took them off because you want what I want." She knew she was abandoned, that she would come to him like this again and again if he wanted her.

The skirts of the costume were separate from the bodice. With frustrating difficulty he managed to undo the waist and slide it down. He pushed inside her, and she raised her hips to grant him easier access. Even as he moved, waves of exquisite tension flowered in Meg.

He had grown so remote, purposeful but distant.

If she could not agree to take what he could willingly give her, and she was soon left with nothing but memories of him, how would she live?

She didn't want to think such thoughts now.

The hair on his chest softly scratched her nipples. She could not get close enough to him.

"Meg, let go. Give yourself to me, now."

She might have told him she could not order the moment when that would happen, but instead her body became his to command and she was a helpless vessel gladly giving and receiving.

He thrust again, and once more, and pushed up on his locked arms to look down at her. "Fate can be cruel," he said. "I... You are my dream. *My* dream, damn it." And he lowered himself to lie half over her, his face in her neck.

Meg lay still and thought she understood his anger.

"Have I hurt your ankles even more?"

She smiled into his hair. "What ankles?"

Jean-Marc didn't laugh. He shifted until he could fold her in his arms and hold her much more tightly than was comfortable. His face remained against her neck. He embraced her almost convulsively.

They both suffered, but he would never know how powerless she felt.

"Tomorrow," he said, "there will be much to be done before we can leave. I should prefer to keep you and Désirée together. You will be guarded—by myself as much as possible."

"We will be safe in the daylight," she told him. "It would be best to behave normally so that we don't cause suspicion. But when you—"

"No one will be admitted to this house without my direct permission." Jean Marc raised his head and looked at her. "No one."

"Mr. FitzDurham and Sir Robert—"

"I shall invite Mr. FitzDurham to Windsor. Sir Robert Brodie will be told you do not wish to see him."

She didn't want Jean-Marc to behave as if she was his to command. "Under the circumstances it would only be polite to see Sir Robert as a friend."

Jean-Marc's eyes narrowed. "I don't want you to see any other men. If Brodie calls, you will have him told that you cannot receive him."

"No."

"I have made up my mind. You will never leave me now."

Meg felt the sting of tears. He waged his own battle and thought he could somehow order the future and make peace for both of them.

"I will be your protector. Always."

"I don't need a protector. Please, I have allowed—no, I have willingly abandoned all convention to be with you. I do not regret that. It will be all that I have, the memory. But my sister would never understand or agree to be part of such an arrangement, and I won't desert her."

Some mighty emotion possessed him. His dark eyes glittered in a face become stark. A faint sheen emphasized the muscular form of his rigid body.

"I am not your responsibility," she told him quietly.

His smile was not comforting. "If you think that, then you are simple," he said. "I see no reason why Sibyl can't remain where

she is. She will want for nothing. And you will visit her. If she
is not walking in your shadow, perhaps she will marry. You make
her less sure of herself than she should be. Ought to be.''

He kissed her swiftly, a demanding kiss Meg resisted, but only
for a moment before she returned the ardor, ran her fingers
through his hair and struggled for breath while they all but con-
sumed each other.

When Jean-Marc rested in the hollow of her neck once more,
she stroked the backs of her fingers back and forth over his cheek.

''You must recognize what can't be ignored,'' he said. ''We
have been together. We will be together again. There may already
be a child. My child.''

Speechless, Meg was utterly still.

''If that is so I will insist upon marriage. No child of mine will
be born a bastard. Marry me now, or marry me later. Take your
choice. In either case you are mine and I don't give up anything
that is mine.''

32

Spivey here.

I was not a vindictive man and I am not vindictive now, but I must defend my honor, the honor of the Spiveys.

That ungrateful cub, Hunter, has gone too far. He actually said his ancestors had not amounted to much! And considers it an insult for his looks to be compared to mine!

Very well, since he has no respect for the impressive accomplishments of his—well, for my accomplishments, to be frank—so be it. He can go and pay his way elsewhere. Why should he enjoy the comforts of my extraordinary house? As soon as certain other, even more unacceptable annoyances are dealt with, it will be Hunter's turn.

I grow genuinely afraid that I shall be drawn into physical action again—through the person of Lavinia Ash, of course. It happened to me once before, you know, but that is of no interest to you. What damnable luck that the caper merchant isn't a man. No matter. I shall press her into service and she will follow instructions exactly. She must be in the right places to stop whatever I want stopped—such as an arrangement between Count Etranger and Meg Smiles that would almost certainly result in Sibyl Smiles remaining at Number Seven and advance my cause not one whit.

All that need happen is for Sibyl Smiles to marry William and depart with him, and with Meg, to wherever he chooses to take them and for whatever reason. I do not care. And in case you really believe Sibyl intends to marry Godly-Smythe just because she has said she intends to accept him—think again. I could be wrong—for the first time—but my highly developed intuition tells me she plans to trick her cousin in some manner.

You, dear readers, hope Count Etranger and the strumpet, Meg, will find bliss. Together. You are romantics. Oh, how the very word makes my blood run...would have made my blood run cold. And I know perfectly well that you have approved of the abandoned behavior between these two selfish people.

The time for delicacy is past, so be prepared. You should be ashamed of yourselves. You know why.

No doubt you are also sniggering over the disgraceful antics of our would-be Queen Caroline, and anticipating the spectacle this new King George will make of his Coronation in July and the revelry to follow. You all deserve each other, say I.

33

One by one, members of the household appeared in Jean-Marc's apartments. Each one entered the study too apprehensive to do other than keep curious eyes on their master.

One by one, Jean-Marc decided who should go to Windsor and who should remain at 17 Mayfair Square. He hoped to return soon, and there was an adequate staff already in place at Windsor, but they were neither as polished nor as practiced as those at the London house. Since Désirée might receive visitors at Windsor, adding additional servants from Mayfair Square seemed sensible.

When the last of the candidates left, Jean-Marc stood and went, less confidently than he preferred, to the bedchamber door. He knocked lightly, waited for Meg's response and entered.

Dressed in the beautiful pale yellow nightgown and robe Désirée had rushed to bring earlier that morning, Meg rested against a pile of soft pillows atop Jean-Marc's bed. The night they had so recently spent there together was all too vivid. He said, "Am I interrupting? You were meditating."

She had covered her eyes with a forearm and did not immediately remove that arm.

"You are an uncommon woman," he said, "but I have already told you that often enough. Are you angry with me, Meg, and growing more so? Is that why you feel you must remove yourself from me like this?"

"No." She uncovered her eyes. "To draw all of one's strength and peace to one central part of your mind, to close out everything else, is to heal."

He approached the foot of the bed. "I still believe you are angry with me."

"Not angry. Bemused. You cannot hold what you do not trust, not really. If you think you must keep me almost a prisoner, then you must expect me to disappoint you, or to place my interests before yours. How can you think such things?"

Clumsy as he knew he had been in telling her what had become obvious to him, he could not take back the words. "You don't want me to do my duty toward you. Under the circumstances I must ensure your safety, and assume responsibility for you."

"But only because you enjoy... Because you enjoy me and intend to continue doing so. And if there should be a child, you want that child. You find it all a heavy burden. It would not be your choice, but you can't see another way to have what you desire—at least for now. That is no way to begin a life of deep commitment. I see unhappiness before me, yet I can't deny you." She pushed her hair back from her face, and her sleeves fell away from rounded arms.

"You assume more than you should. Perhaps that is because you spend too much time with your abstract thinking. I will not be forced to explain the obvious." If she insisted on pretending she didn't know he cared for her, so be it.

"I want to go about my business. I do not need to be treated like an invalid."

"You are burned. That is a good enough reason to nurse you. And we know you are in danger—by your association with me, I fear. But we can't forget the original incident that occurred before we met. I continue to question if that was an isolated event, perhaps truly an accident. Regardless, these things are a good reason to insist you remain where I can keep you safe. The household, including the Princess, has accepted your being in this room as necessary in light of what has happened."

"So they would have you believe," she said.

"They will not dare to suggest anything else, not outside the privacy of their own quarters. I think I shall have Désirée sit with you. That will comfort her and should further silence any gossip.''

A knock, or rather a pounding on the bedchamber door brought a frown to Jean-Marc's brow.

Meg sat straighter and wrapped the robe more tightly about her. She had only to look at Jean-Marc's face to see that he had slept little the night before, and that he was tensely watchful. He didn't lie when he said he considered her at risk.

Without further warning, Pierre burst into the room. When he saw Meg, he faltered and began to turn away.

''What is it now, man?'' Jean-Marc said. ''You look as if you've seen a ghost.''

''Something very troublesome,'' Pierre said, glancing uncomfortably at Meg. ''Perhaps we should speak of this elsewhere.''

The worst thing he could do for their tenuous relationship would be to close her out. ''You may speak here. I'm sure there is nothing you can say that Miss Smiles should not hear.''

Pierre did not appear at all convinced of that, but he moved closer to Jean-Marc. ''A girl has come here,'' he said, and Meg noticed that he was somewhat disheveled and that his hands shook. ''If she is to be believed, then she has a strange and terrible story, but she will not tell all of it to anyone but you, My Lord.''

''Bring her here at once,'' Jean-Marc said.

Pierre sucked in his bottom lip. He shook his head. ''I've got the gist of it. Lady Upworth gave her the message and sent her. Her Ladyship may be in serious trouble.''

''Then for God's sake, get the girl here now.''

Pierre rushed away at once, and Meg said, ''When Lady Upworth spoke with me last night she seemed well enough, and certainly not concerned over anything but M. Verbeux's condition.'' She was coming to a grudging liking for the woman. ''Oh, Sibyl should be here by now. Why hasn't she come to me?''

''She is bound to be here soon enough,'' Jean-Marc said. ''Perhaps it would be best if I saw the child in the study.''

He was, Meg knew, concerned for her peace of mind. ''I think she will be more comfortable if there is a woman present. And I would like to know what she has to say.''

Pierre settled the issue by ushering in a pretty, dark-haired girl of about twelve. Her clothes were cheap but clean, and she appeared more curious than frightened.

"This is the girl," Pierre said, as if there might be some doubt. "Her name is Betty. She works in her parents' bakery off Mount Street. Lumley's."

"How do you do?" Jean-Marc said, kindly, Meg thought. "I'm Count Etranger and this is my house."

"I know," Betty said. "That's why I come 'ere. The lady told me. And she told me to talk to you, sir."

"Speak your piece and be on your way," Pierre said sharply.

"Take your time," Jean-Marc promptly contradicted. "Thank you for coming to us."

The child had bright brown eyes and a nice smile. "She give me a shillin'. I ain't never had a shillin' for meself before."

"Good," Jean-Marc told her. "And before you leave I shall give you a sovereign to go with it."

That earned him a giggle. Betty raised her shoulders in delight at the thought of such wealth. "It was early this mornin'. We 'ave to start by three and I was taking slops out back. Imagine 'ow shocked I was when I 'eard 'er whisper to me."

"Yes, yes," Jean-Marc said. "And the lady told you her name?"

"She said I was to tell you she was Ila."

Meg clenched her hands in her lap, afraid of what was to come.

"Ila is a good friend of mine," Jean-Marc said. "What did she say?"

"It was in the alley, see. She was in one of them 'ansom cabs but the driver weren't there, only she couldn't get out on account of 'er bein' tied up. I tried to 'elp but she said there wouldn't be time and I was just to listen, then come 'ere to you."

"It's noon," Jean-Marc pointed out. "You say you got this message at three this morning. Why didn't you come at once?"

"Well, there's more, ain't there? But then I couldn't come right away because I 'ad to do me chores first if I didn't want a lashing."

"Your parents wouldn't have understood?"

She hesitated, then said, "Well, I didn't want 'em to know about me shillin', did I?"

"Just tell us your story," Meg said gently. Let Jean-Marc be annoyed at her interference. He was slowing the process with all his questions.

Betty said, "She got nabbed by this gent, see. Something about 'er goin' back somewhere for something and gettin' nabbed by this man. 'Er face was bleedin'."

Meg stifled a cry.

"A foreigner, 'e was. Sounded a bit like you, sir. I know because I 'eard 'im. That's when 'e was coming back and I was 'iding. 'E was talking to this other gent. Real angry, I could tell that. Before that the lady said to tell you not to look for 'er. She'd be going on a ship but she didn't know where. She said she deserved what she got because she 'urt people, but she just wanted you to know she'd gone so you wouldn't wonder. Can I 'ave the sovereign now?"

"Soon enough," Jean-Marc said. "This was in an alley behind Mount Street, you say?"

Betty shifted from foot to foot and said, "Yes, sir."

"The man returned to the cab. Did you see a driver come? Did you see them drive away?"

"I had to go inside."

"I thought you said you hid. If you did, surely you know what happened next."

"The cab went."

"Did you see where?"

"Just out of the alley. It was dark and I had to get inside. Can I 'ave the sovereign?"

The anxiety on the girl's face made Meg want to cry.

"Where is Verbeux?" Jean-Marc asked. He sounded distracted.

"Still in his bed," Pierre said. "I'm concerned about his reaction to this news, but he will get over it."

Jean-Marc pushed back his dark coat, planted his fists on his hips and jutted his head. "Speak plainly. Verbeux admits he has offered Lady Upworth a sympathetic ear, but he is not an emotional man. Why would he be particularly upset about her?"

Pierre sucked even harder on his lip and appeared flustered. "Not my business," he muttered. "Shouldn't have spoken."

"Well, you did. Now explain yourself."

"M. Verbeux and Lady Upworth have seemed, er, friendly."

"As opposed to seeming *unfriendly?* You can do better than that, man."

Pierre sighed loudly. "I believe M. Verbeux is fond of Lady Upworth." He averted his face and held up a hand. "I might as well tell it all. I know they are fond of each other. Perhaps more than fond."

Jean-Marc did not answer at once. He was clearly perplexed by the announcement.

"M. Verbeux trusts my discretion implicitly. If he discovers I—"

"He won't," Jean-Marc said, interrupting Pierre. "But if you are right, I have little doubt he will want to find her."

"The girl says that won't be possible," Pierre pointed out.

"Nevertheless, he will search."

"Should I say about the other gent?" Betty asked, looking to Pierre. "The one what took 'er afterward?"

Absolute stillness followed. Evidently Betty was anxious to satisfy Jean-Marc enough to make sure he produced the sovereign he'd promised.

"If you have failed to tell us everything, then you must do so," Pierre said. He shrugged at Jean-Marc. "One wonders how much of this is true."

The girl turned pink and said, "I'd better just go."

"Do you mean that two men took her?" Jean-Marc said.

"Don't worry, you're among friends and quite safe. Nothing you say will get you into trouble."

"The man come and took 'er from the man who took 'er. I mean, the foreign gent was the one who nabbed 'er first. 'E must have taken 'er to the alley—probably got lost. Then, when they was in the alley, another man took 'er."

"This isn't what you said before. You said the foreign-sounding man came back to the cab—talking to someone on the way—but that the foreigner left with Lady Upworth."

"I forgot." Betty looked at the floor. "I get muddled sometimes. That's who the foreigner was talking to, the man what took the lady away. 'E was a tubby man, but quick. 'E jumped up into the driver's seat, and off they went. Left that other one sayin' things that were 'orrible, I should think, only I didn't understand 'im. Then 'e went off, too."

Jean-Marc closed his eyes as if in deep thought. "So," he said, "Lady Upworth—Ila—told you she was going to be taken on a ship by the foreign man, the one who was left behind?"

"Yes."

"I see. In that case we can assume she hasn't been taken to a ship at all, can't we?"

"I suppose so."

"And we're looking for a quick, tubby man with a lady who has blood on her face. I should think someone might notice a pair like that."

Betty became animated once more. "Oh, yes. I think you could ask and someone might 'ave seen 'em. That tubby gent don't look like the type but 'e pushed the other one 'ard enough to knock 'im over, too. And I forgot, 'e was wearin this 'at. One of them funny ones like some preachers wear. The tubby one, that is."

At the Count's request, Sibyl entered his apartments for the first time but was too distracted to observe her surroundings closely. Oh, they were opulent, masculinely elegant, but she didn't care.

"Miss Smiles," the Count said. "I'm relieved to see you. I understood you were due here earlier. I trust you aren't ill."

He wasn't concerned about her health, Sibyl thought, or her tardiness. "Where is Meg, please?" she asked him. "She isn't in her rooms."

"That's because she's here. My sister is with her in the bed-chamber. You are not to be frightened, but she had an unpleasant experience last night and I decided that for her own well-being she should be where I could watch over her."

Sibyl was instantly cold. "Don't try to shield me." Her teeth chattered and she made a move toward the other room.

The Count arrived at her side and took hold of her elbow. He guided her to a chair. "First, I want to speak to you about Reverend Baggs. Latimer More has already been told to detain the man if he returns to his room at Number Seven—which he is unlikely to do. The man is dangerous. If you see or hear anything of him, come directly to me. You are not to confront him yourself."

What extraordinary nonsense. "Why would I confront Reverend Baggs? For what reason? He is a gentle bumbletop. And he cannot be dangerous. That is outrageous."

The Count gave her a look that left no doubt but that he was deciding what to tell her. "Kindly follow my instructions. He is not to be trusted, that's all."

She regarded the Count steadfastly. "No, My Lord, that is *not* all. Kindly explain what Baggs has supposedly done so that I know how to react if I come upon him."

The Count expected such behavior from Meg, but it surprised him in Sibyl. "You sisters should have been taken firmly in hand when you were children. You are too forward. Very well. Why not? What is there to be gained from sparing you? Reverend Baggs was described to us by a young girl who says she saw him take Lady Upworth away—against her will."

Sibyl met the Count's compelling eyes, then fiddled with the strings on her reticule.

"No response to that, Miss Smiles?"

"Reverend Baggs?" To laugh would be impolite. "Absconded with Lady Upworth?" Then she did laugh, she couldn't help it.

When she managed to reduce the laughter to a grin, she was grateful to see that the Count also grinned.

"I have warned you," he said, sobering. "I advise you not to take the warning lightly. Men are searching for Baggs and Lady Upworth now. More of that later. We have other worries. Meg was accosted by someone who caused her ankles to be burned. Unpleasant, but not life-threatening—"

"Oh, Meg. Let me see her at once."

"Soon enough. The person fled and I made her comfortable here where she would know she was protected. When you go to her it would be best if you were calm. Reassure her, please."

He spoke as if Meg were his... Sibyl studied his compelling face. This was a man who never questioned his right to take what he wanted, who had taken away the Meggie Smiles Sibyl had known all her life. He didn't care who he hurt as long as he got his own way.

"I'd give a great deal to know what you're thinking," the Count said.

Startled, Sibyl turned in her chair. Her heart beat hard. "Something tells me that I am a great trial to you." She was not accustomed to being the center of attention, certainly not the focus of rich, powerful and sought-after men.

"Sibyl," he said quietly, surprising her with the use of her first name. "Will you share your thoughts with me?"

She stood up. "I must go to Meg now."

He bowed and said, "Of course." Leading the way, he tapped on the door to the other room. The Princess called, "Come in," and they did so. Smiling, he stood back to allow Sibyl to pass him. "Your sister is here. She is anxious to hear all about what happened to you."

Sibyl refrained from telling him she could speak for herself.

"I've told her you had a shock but are recovering nicely. Be certain to explain our planned departure for Windsor. Obviously that will be considerably later than I had hoped, but we shall need her.... What the devil?"

A warbling feminine voice, issuing unintelligible words, erupted into the study. Sibyl swung around in time to see Ash make an ungainly leap. She held her hand before her and hopped from side to side.

"What is it?" the Count asked. "Please be still and quiet. Miss Smiles, Miss Meg Smiles, is not in any condition for such outbursts."

"Ooh," Ash responded, and ran this way and that. She began to shake out her black skirts, showing the rolled stockings at her ankles in the process. "I had to come. *Ooh.* Get it away."

As if insulted by Ash's mode of address, Halibut appeared from beneath her skirts. He sat back on his considerable smoky gray haunches and bared his teeth at the woman. The cat's blue-green eyes narrowed, and he looked for all the world, or so Sibyl thought, as if he were grinning gleefully at his victim.

"A crazed, vicious devil, that's what he is," Ash said. "He hates me."

"There you are, Halibut, my darling," Princess Désirée said. She sat on a chair beside the bed. "Come to me at once, naughty boy, I have worried about you. Where have you been hiding?" How she had grown up since Sibyl first saw her. Meg's influence showed in hair that was drawn sleekly up with curls cascading at the temples. The pink day dress she wore was of heavy, silk-striped chiné satin.

Ash closed the study door firmly. Keeping a close eye on Halibut, she approached until she could see all of the Count's bedchamber. "You, Your Highness," she said to the Princess, "should be in the music room. I also understand the seamstresses have been standing idle for hours while they've waited for you."

"Everyone was informed that this morning's events were to be put off," Princess Désirée said. "Including you, Ash."

Ash drew herself up. "Quite. I'm so befuddled by my heavy responsibilities that I forgot. You, Miss Smiles, are on a very dangerous path. You are risking your reputation—what little reputation you may still be able to save. I suggest you return to Number Seven at once. I'm sure your cousin, that very good man Mr. Godly-Smythe, will assist you. He is a saint and will bear your shame in the name of family loyalty. Consider yourself fortunate he is not the type to abandon a relation who has shown herself to be of dubious moral character."

The Count's restraint slipped visibly.

Halibut had gone no farther than the foot of the bed. Now he turned to look up at Ash and bare his teeth once more.

The woman took a step backward and said, "Not, of course, that it is any of my business. Take no notice of a plain woman relegated to a life of service to others. I merely wish to show that I care about you, Miss Smiles, and to offer you my considered advice."

When Meg said thank you and nothing more, Sibyl gaped. Meg never failed to put people in their places if it was necessary.

The Count gave the considerable force of his attention to Ash. "I think perhaps we should reconsider your immediate future, Miss—"

"Everything is all right," Meg said quickly, cutting off the Count. "Miss Ash is accustomed to guiding young women and has forgotten that I am no longer a child to be molded by others."

"Well, I do think—"

"Please, Ash," Meg said, "let us save this conversation for another time. You will see that I have been injured." She indicated her ankles and the heavy coating of some lotion that covered them. "Burned. The Count has been kind enough to have me tended here for reasons I will explain later. I do thank you for caring about me."

Ash made fists and pounded them against her skirts. She

frowned magnificently and showed her notable teeth in a grimace. "Well," she said. *"Well."* To the amazement of all, she stamped a foot several times and rushed away, slamming the study door behind her.

"Mad," the Count said. He bent to scratch Halibut's head. "And this clever fellow knows it."

Sibyl smiled at Meg, who radiated awkwardness. Dressed in a luxurious nightgown and robe the color of lemons, she fidgeted with long satin ribbons that flowed from the collar of the robe.

Another glance at the Princess showed that the young lady appeared deeply dissatisfied. With what, Sibyl had no idea.

"We had hoped to leave for Windsor later today," the Count said conversationally. "Unfortunately, we shall obviously be forced to delay until at least sometime tomorrow—at the earliest."

"Thank goodness!" the Princess exclaimed, flopping back in her chair and silently moving her lips as if in prayer.

"Why thank goodness, Désirée?" the Count asked.

Princess Désirée scooped up Halibut and nuzzled her face in his striped fur, more to hide herself than for any other reason, Sibyl thought.

"Désirée?"

"Oh, no particular reason, Jean-Marc. I am growing fond of the excitement here, that's all. Mr. FitzDurham called this morning, you know. He said he would like to return tomorrow if possible. Now it will be possible—as long as we do not have to leave too early."

Sibyl longed to be alone with Meg.

"Let's talk about ball gowns," the Princess said, leaning forward, animated. "Have you seen my peach and gold thread, Sibyl? I was unsure at first, but Meg convinced me it was charming with my hair."

The minx was trying to bore her brother from the room, Sibyl decided. "I'm sure it is," she said. "Those shades become you. What will you wear in your hair, or had you thought to try one of those daring evening hats?"

"Meg thinks a wreath of gold leaves, and—"

The Count cleared his throat loudly.

"Gold leaves at the hairline with small ringlets around her face and neck," Meg said, and Sibyl marveled at her sister's serious expression. "And another, smaller wreath at the crown."

The Princess clapped her hands in a gesture very unlike herself.

"Will you excuse me, please, ladies?" the Count said. "Please be sure Miss Smiles is not left alone. I shall return shortly."

The instant they had the apartments to themselves, the three women laughed self-consciously. "That wasn't nice, I suppose," Meg said.

"It was necessary," the Princess said. "We cannot talk of important matters in front of him. I am devastated and must have your advice."

Ah, the self-absorption of the young, Sibyl thought.

"Only you, Meg, and you, Sibyl, can help me because you know Adam Chillworth well."

"A moment ago I thought you were pining for Mr. Fitz-Durham," Meg remarked.

"That was… Well, you know what it was. Adam Chillworth is very handsome, don't you think?"

Sibyl and Meg's eyes met. "Yes," Meg said.

"And he is so talented. I just know his portrait of me will be a masterpiece."

Meg inclined her head and shifted her limbs as if uncomfortable. "And this is the young lady who, only weeks ago, had no interest in either her appearance or in gentlemen?"

"Do not tease me, please. If I cannot find a way to be with Mr. Chillworth, my life will be over."

The urge to laugh almost undid Sibyl.

"Surely, even if Adam were suitable for you in other ways, he is rather old for so young a girl, don't you think?" Meg said.

"I'm not an infant," the Princess announced. "I'm more mature than many females much older than me in years. And he isn't that much my senior."

Sibyl regretted that the girl had become infatuated with poor Adam, who undoubtedly had no idea of the extent of his power over the girl's feelings. He moved in his own world, and it was already filled with his painting.

"Well," Princess Désirée said, standing up with Halibut overflowing her arms, "I can see you do not take my suffering seriously. I had thought you would try to be of help, but you do not believe the depth of my regard for him. I don't blame you, of course. You are surprised by my choice, which shows you do not know me. I shall never be bound by convention. Now I will go to my rooms and meditate. Millie found me a lovely green mantilla. Yes, that's what I'll do."

The sisters were quiet until they were alone. "Meditate?" Sibyl said. "Oh, dear, not another one."

"I'll ignore that," Meg said. "I have a great deal to tell you and we must hurry before Jean-Marc interrupts us."

Sibyl took the chair where the Princess had sat. "How were you burned?"

"With a taper. It's a long, nasty story, but I'm already feeling better."

"Because the Count brought you to his bed?"

Meg's cheeks became bright pink.

Sibyl hated the tears that sprang into her eyes but couldn't stop them. "I knew this would happen. I saw how you loved him. For weeks every time I have looked at you I have seen it. And he wants you so very much. I may be an inexperienced woman, but I am not a fool, and I know when I'm looking at a man who lusts after a woman."

"Stop it," Meg all but shouted. "Sibyl, stop it at once. I can't bear to hear such words on your lips."

"True words that cause you shame? He will want you for a time—perhaps for quite a long time, but eventually he will tire of the novelty of being with someone who is naturally an innocent and pure in heart and mind. No matter what he does to you, you will always be those things. Someone else will catch his eye someone more flamboyant, more brilliant and accomplished, a triumph in society, and of high birth.''

Meg would not defend herself, she couldn't. "No doubt you are right," she said. "And of course you have guessed that I love Jean-Marc. Oh, Sibyl, I'm not ready to tell you everything. I doubt if I ever will be. Please stand beside me as you always have and try to understand."

Sibyl found a handkerchief in her reticule and blew her nose. "You are my sister and my dearest friend," she said. "I couldn't change that if I wanted to. And I don't. But I am so afraid for you."

And she was wise to be afraid, Meg thought. "I never intended to fall in love with him. But from the first time I saw him—well, I suppose I was infatuated at first. We had just spoken of what we thought made a man attractive—what you found attractive, actually. Sibyl, dear, I saw every quality you mentioned in him. And I couldn't stop thinking about him."

"He is a man no woman could ignore," Sibyl admitted grudgingly. "I saw how females mooned over him at Désirée's musicale. What do you intend to do?"

Even if she knew for sure, Meg wasn't prepared to confess either her choices, or how she wasn't sure she could refuse to be with Jean-Marc, whatever the circumstances.

"Very well," Sibyl said when Meg didn't answer. "But when you decide what you want I hope you will discuss it with me first."

Meg said, "I already know what I want. I want to be with him."

Meg's announcement carried clearly into Jean-Marc's study, where he had returned with a letter recently delivered by a messenger. He had paused on the threshold. Now he continued quietly to the russet tapestry chaise and sat down, listening.

What a desperate pass this love affair had brought him to. He was even prepared to eavesdrop in hope of hearing what he so urgently wanted to hear. She had already said enough. She wanted to be with him. It should be enough and it might be if she had said she would remain with him no matter what happened, and, perhaps, that she loved him.

He wanted too much.

Sibyl and Meg had dropped their voices, and he wondered if they had heard him come into the apartments.

He broke open the heavy seal on the letter—his father's seal— and drew out a sheet of heavy, cream-colored paper. His father's strong hand had penned confident strokes.

> Jean-Marc,
>
> I trust you are well and that your sibling has not managed to destroy your mental faculties as yet. My daughter can be a great trial.
>
> Thank you for writing to keep me informed of your progress. I read your comments on Désirée's intellect and accomplishments with interest and satisfaction. I have always known her to be intelligent but I did not realize how far she has advanced.
>
> Unfortunately, I must inform you that my brother, Louis, fell further from my favor. A foolish man with great and harmful pretensions—harmful to himself. I have proof that he planned to reclaim my throne after my death—by some dangerous and devious means that would harm my children. After consultation with my ministers, I was forced to agree to banish my relation from Mont Nuages. I trust you to repeat nothing of this at present—not until I decide enough time has passed and it seems expedient to announce his death.

Jean-Marc read the sentence several times but the only conclusion he could reach was that the Prince had used the word *banish* to mean *kill*. He read on.

On a more cheerful note, and although I grieve deeply for my brother and regret his unfortunate decisions, I have made a resolution of the utmost importance. I hope you will embrace what I have to tell you with similar joy to my own.

Try to contain your disappointment, but I have decided that my daughter, the Princess Désirée, is the natural choice to wear the crown after me. She should not be told at once. She is too young yet, and I feel a quickening of my own vitality. I hope for a few years to assist in her training.

Did I mention that Louis probably killed himself? Yes, yes, in fact we will assume that is what happened.

My decision about Désirée's future in no way alters my wish that she find a suitably important husband as soon as possible. Mont Nuages needs this connection. Naturally, as we discussed before you left, the man must be an Englishman. A prince or duke would be preferable, but I might be persuaded to accept a lesser rank as long as the bloodlines are impeccable and the association guaranteed to be invaluable to Mont Nuages.

I have decided to make the journey to England myself. I will arrive within a few weeks. This will be in time for me to give my blessing on Désirée's intended—and to make sure he understands what is expected of him as a future ruler's consort.

The letter was formally signed. "No endearment?" Jean-Marc murmured, and smiled cynically. His father had never uttered an endearment to his only son.

Almost at once, triumph overcame resentment. He had frequently tried, unsuccessfully, to make his father see Désirée's potential. From this day forth the Prince would claim the idea as his own. Jean-Marc cared nothing for this as long as his half sister took the place to which he believed she would become well suited.

From the bedchamber, the Smiles sisters' voices continued to rise and fall in quiet conversation. He folded the letter, went to his desk and unlocked a drawer. At the back there was a panel that fell away when pressure was applied just so. He hid the envelope in the compartment behind, then closed it carefully away.

Returning to the chaise, he slumped down with his head on the back. Exhaustion dulled even his uneasiness. He would not leave Meg alone in this house or anywhere else—not without someone he trusted to watch over her. Meanwhile, he would wait for reports on the search for Ila.

Abruptly, he sat up. His father's letter had done more than set him free of any responsibility to give his future to Mont Nuages. Now there were less reasons to hold back from marrying Meg. Once he found the right moment, he could tell her that her inferior social status didn't have to matter anymore.

34

"He wants me to be his mistress." Meg pressed her lips together and watched her sister's face lose all color.

"How could you be so foolish?" Sibyl said. "How could you consider throwing away everything we've believed in to gain some intrigue of the flesh that will last only as long as it takes the Count to grow bored and move on to another?"

Meg ignored what she didn't want to think about. "The Count wishes us to live in Windsor, I think. You will be with me, dear, dear Sibyl, and we shall not have to concern ourselves with how we can live."

Sibyl's pelisse was a deep green with satin frog closures. A pretty satin bonnet of the same green sported two tufts of shiny peacock feathers and set off her blond hair beautifully. She roamed the bedchamber apparently without knowing what she did.

"Think of it, Sibyl. Never another care for the necessities of life."

"And you would sell your body and soul for that!" Sibyl's voice rose as Meg had never heard it rise before. "You would forget everything Papa taught us, everything we grew to value as principles by which we would live? Go against your honest heart to chase the glamour of being with such a man? Shame, Meg, shame. It shall *not* come to pass."

Shaken by Sibyl's outburst, Meg said, "He says we should marry, but I don't think that would be right."

Sun penetrated the windows and cast shafts of warm light across the room.

"He is beneath contempt, a heartless manipulator," Sibyl said. "How can you believe a count would marry a minister's orphan, an orphan with absolutely no fortune? These people marry only for gain. What could he gain from you?"

"I don't want to talk about it anymore," Meg said. She needed to be alone, to seek the peace she knew she could induce.

"There are matters we must talk about. What is this he told me about Reverend Baggs? That poor man is frequently annoying, but he is not a monster capable of criminal doings."

"I'm afraid it may be true," Meg said. She shifted awkwardly and hung her feet over the side of the bed. "He was seen, at least I can only think it was him. He was described, and if he did take Lady Upworth, then there is something most strange going on. M. Verbeux should be in his bed—he was attacked and badly hurt last night—but I understand he has joined a search party to try to find Her Ladyship. Apparently they are friends. So many things I knew nothing about."

"M. Verbeux attacked?" Sibyl stopped pacing and stood before her. "I suppose you will tell me next that Reverend Baggs did that also. What are you trying to do?" she asked while Meg gathered her clothing about her.

"I can't be still any longer. You are more my concern than any of these matters—disturbing as they are. Don't you intend to tell me about William's latest visit?"

"How do you know about that? Who told you?"

"Lady Upworth herself. Late last evening, probably not long before she left this house again for some reason and fell into evil hands."

Spreading her skirts and sitting, straight-backed and in a stiff manner quite unlike herself, Sibyl didn't look at Meg. "That is what I want to talk to you about. I have had a change of mind. I have failed to see William for what he really is. He is a gentleman, and a very kind one. And he loves me. There."

Meg took a deep breath and slid to the floor. She went immediately to Sibyl's side. "He has not changed. You speak of my being… You are the one who is deluded. Our second cousin isn't a nice man. You should have nothing to do with him."

"You must not speak of him like that again. We are to be married, and soon."

"Oh, Sibyl." Her sister had always been transparent. "Because you think that would be a way to save me from what you consider wrong? You would submit to such a horror for me? No. No, I would not let you. Surely you know that."

A door closed elsewhere in the apartments, and a man's solid footsteps approached. "May I come in, ladies?" Jean-Marc asked.

"Yes," Sibyl said at once.

"You want him here because you think you can make things move quickly and get your own way?" Meg said softly. "Say nothing to him, please."

Jean-Marc entered, smiling and rubbing his hands in a jovial manner. "You two are so close. I wish Désirée had a sister."

Meg couldn't take her eyes from him. Her need for him stole her breath.

"I am to be married," Sibyl said. "To Mr. William Godly-Smythe. The wedding will be soon, just as soon as can be arranged."

"Ah." Jean-Marc nodded and stopped rubbing his hands. "Godly-Smythe."

"No." Meg felt self-conscious in nightclothes that were not even her own. "You will not, do you understand? You don't like him. In fact, you hate him."

Sibyl swallowed, and her eyes filled with tears. "I thought we understood that matters of the heart were private. You have told me so."

Jean-Marc picked up a chair and placed it close to Sibyl's. "Sit down, Meg. You must stay off your feet. And before you argue, I know you aren't an invalid." He perched himself on the edge of the bed. "In response to a message from me, Latimer More at

Number Seven says Reverend Baggs didn't sleep in his bed last night. In fact, Mr. More returned home quite late and saw the Reverend leaving the house. He is sure he didn't return.''

"Was he wearing his hat?" Meg asked.

"Yes, he was. When Mr. More went into the house, Mr. Godly-Smythe was in the foyer and seemed disconcerted to see—or perhaps to be seen—by someone."

"Or so Latimer concluded," Sibyl said. "He can't know for certain."

Jean-Marc watched Sibyl Smiles with interest. Again, he noted that she wasn't herself. The determined set of her features, the bright light in her eyes—not at all typical.

"Dangerous things have already happened," she told him. "And now Meg has been assaulted, and M. Verbeux, and poor Lady Upworth has been stolen away. And you believe Reverend Baggs could have done all these things?"

"Of course he doesn't," Meg said, and he allowed her to speak for him. "But Baggsy was near the Burlington Arcade, remember? And in Bond Street."

"He has said he's followed you because he and William have been concerned about us." Sibyl brought her fists down on the arms of her chair. "Did you *see* him take Lady Upworth away' With your own eyes?"

Jean-Marc said, "An observant girl saw him—or someone who sounds too like him to be anyone else we are aware of. But don't fault your need for more proof. In fact I've had simila doubts myself and I've sent Pierre to Mount Street—to the bakery owned by the child's parents—to ask if Betty can return to us.'

"What haven't you told us, Jean-Marc?"

Meg's use of his first name caused Sibyl to hold on to her chai this time.

For himself, rather than annoyance, he experienced pleasur and he smiled at her. "I have told you what you need to know,' he said. She might protest, but she was growing closer and close to him just the same.

"Not good enough," she said, as if she was unaware of her mistake. "I'll rephrase the question. Do you think there is one force at work here, or two? And who is supposed to be the victim—or perhaps the one intended to be frightened into doing or not doing something? I don't believe I am. How could I be?"

"You couldn't." But there was information that would be dangerous for her to know. He stood up. "I ask you to leave these matters in hands capable of dealing with them. I have a man keeping watch outside these apartments. Please make yourselves comfortable here."

"I am not besotted with you, My Lord."

Astounded, Jean-Marc looked at Sibyl Smiles. She rose to her feet and drew back her shoulders. Color stood high in her face. "Unlike my sister, I have nothing to lose by offending you, other than a position I intend to leave anyway."

"Sibyl," Meg said, reaching for her sister's hand. "Regardless of anything else, the Count has been kind to us. Please think before you say anything else."

"Before I say that I despise him for having his way with you, and—"

"*Sibyl.* Not another word."

"And what?" Jean-Marc asked. He knew he had little right to be angry, but he longed to put this miss in her place. "I overheard a good deal of what you said a little earlier. You think very little of me. But you don't know me, and you don't know my feelings for Meg."

There was an instant when she raised a hand and he thought she might strike him, but she put more distance between them instead. "You want her for your ladybird. You said you would marry her, but not with enough conviction to make her believe you. She loves you, and you are using that love against her."

"Situations change," he told her, finally too furious to hold back. "What do you know of love? Nothing. You will marry a man like Godly-Smythe because you think it is a safe choice. A passionless choice.

"As of today, my expectations are different. Marrying Meg will no longer have the public impact I had feared. So we *will* marry. With or without your blessing."

Meg had never seen Sibyl as she was now, but even that strange picture lost significance in the face of Jean-Marc's announcement. He could now marry her without suffering any ill effects. That was what he had said and what he meant. So, because she wasn't a threat to more important things, they would marry.

"You have nothing to say?" Sibyl asked her.

"No." Meg shook her head. She had a great deal to say, but not in front of an audience.

"This is preposterous, a tragedy. I must leave. I'm going to William at once. And I shall tell him that I want Reverend Baggs to marry us. You shall be invited to the wedding."

Jean-Marc put himself between Miss Smiles and the door. "I can't allow you to do that. For Meg's sake I ask you to remain here, at least until we have more information about Reverend Baggs—and Godly-Smythe."

They would not guess how afraid she was, Sibyl thought. They must not. It was up to her to save The Ramblers, Meg and herself, before William became desperate enough to take fateful steps against them. With difficulty she composed herself. This was a burden for her alone. William must not guess what she had learned, or that regardless of what she said, she would never marry him. What she intended was wild, deceitful, but it was the only way. And for now Meg could not know the truth or she would become afraid for Sibyl and try to interfere.

"Miss Smiles," Jean-Marc said, "will you cooperate with me in this?"

"I must return to Number Seven or William will come looking for me. I told him I would tell Meg we are to be married and persuade her to return with me."

"She will not return with you," Jean-Marc said. He would not allow the woman he loved to leave his care, not until all threat had passed. "As you see, she isn't fit to go anywhere."

"Meg, will you come?"

"I can't stop you from leaving, but I won't go with you. I'm afraid for you."

"Don't be." If only she could believe there was no reason. "I'll return as soon as I can and tell you our plans." She felt as if she stood at the edge of the sea, her feet trapped, while the tide roared inexorably inward. The fear must be overcome.

Jean-Marc studied her with deeper concentration. There was something.... No, how could he possibly have more insight into her than Meg did? Yet this was a complete reversal of attitude. From many comments Meg had made, he had gathered in what low esteem both sisters held Godly-Smythe. Why then the change of heart? Certainly not because of a sudden blooming love. The obvious reason might be that Sibyl saw the arrangement as a way to extricate Meg from his influence. No. No, he did not believe that. So there was another factor. Part of another plan, perhaps, one that he would do well to pursue?

"Forgive me, Miss Smiles," he said, avoiding Meg's eyes. "I am remiss in not giving you my blessings. I know nothing of Mr. Godly-Smythe, but if you choose him, then I'm sure he is a worthy fellow, and I wish you joy."

Meg closed her eyes. Pain crossed her features. She took visibly deep breaths.

"And so you hide, Meg," he said thoughtfully. "I do believe your secret thoughts are in your eyes and you don't want them to betray what you really think. Perhaps your skill is not so much a virtue as a weakness." He was unduly harsh, but quite possibly near the truth.

Sibyl Smiles said, "She is extraordinary. If you don't know that, then you know very little about her."

"Oh, I know. Why do you think I can't bear to think of life without her?"

Sibyl frowned. She searched his face as if for a sign to the depth of his sincerity. "If only I could hope a man such as you would not break her heart."

He would like to have met the Smiles sisters' parents. Two such impressive women didn't merely happen. They had been molded by strong people.

"I see you don't answer me," Sibyl Smiles said.

Jean-Marc inclined his head until Meg felt his attention and looked at him. This time she had not succeeded in secluding herself. Her eyes were bright and clear—and they hid nothing of the intense emotion she felt.

"I will not break your heart," he told her. "You will help me be what you need me to be. But I will never hurt you."

"You won't hurt me deliberately," she said, subdued. "Would you help me to persuade Sibyl not to do this thing?"

Sibyl's guilt at troubling Meg was overwhelming, but for both of them she must not weaken now. "Even if he could do what you ask, he knows it would be wrong. Nothing is settled. I have said I will return to you, and I will, once I have more to tell."

"My Lord!"

Jean-Marc recognized Pierre's voice calling from the study and strode to open the chamber door wide. "Yes. You have the girl?"

Pierre, substantial in a many-caped greatcoat, held his top hat in his hands. "I scarcely know how to tell you," he said.

"Go close enough to hear everything," Meg whispered to Sibyl. "I'll stand behind you."

Sibyl did as she was asked and took a place almost beside the Count.

Pierre looked at her briefly but without interest. "I went to Mount Street, as you told me, My Lord. To search for the girl, Betty."

"Yes, yes," the Count said impatiently. "Kindly don't repeat what we already know."

Pierre drew in his bottom lip and hung his head. He raised his arms and dropped them heavily. "What can it mean? She knew her ladyship's name, and her connection to you and this house.

She described the preacher. I don't understand any of it, yet I am convinced we move deeper and deeper into danger."

Only by force of will did Jean-Marc resist roaring at the man to stop tiptoeing around whatever he had discovered. "You're probably right," he said, and, given the presence of the Smiles sisters, wished he hadn't. "Just tell me what you've learned."

"I went from one end of Mount Street to the other. There are bakeries, but not one called Lumley's, and no one has ever heard of a baker's daughter called Betty."

35

"Regardless of who took her, Lady Upworth is gone," Verbeux told Jean-Marc. "Yes, this apparently nonexistent child is a puzzle, but Baggs is not at Number Seven. We have established that. And he was not there last night. I think he's involved. What I can't begin to imagine is why."

They hurried side by side across the second floor toward Désirée's apartments. Word had come of Verbeux's return and the failed search, and Jean-Marc had gone to speak to his valet. Meg had taken advantage of that opportunity to tell the man who had been left on guard that she and her sister had been given permission to go together to Meg's rooms.

"Difficult to control, My Lord?" Verbeux said of Meg. "If she is now, do you imagine there will ever be an improvement?"

"That is not your affair." He was not moved to share the contents of his father's letter with anyone so soon. "Meg!"

She appeared in the corridor almost at once. "There is no need to shout, My Lord. It doesn't become you."

"Kindly refrain from lecturing me, miss. Why did you disobey me?" At least part of the answer was obvious, in that she was dressed in a deep blue gown and matching slippers, and her hair had been simply but elegantly dressed. He wondered why it sometimes looked less red. "Well? How do you explain yourself?" he asked when he reached her.

"I don't have to, My Lord." Her curtsey mocked him. "The Princess may receive another caller, and I must be present. I cannot be if I am not suitably dressed."

"No more visitors," he shouted, turning to see what servants were present. A footman appeared at the end of the corridor and took a few steps into the apartments. "Yes, you will do." Jean-Marc pointed to the man. "Go at once to Rench and tell him no one is to be admitted to this house without my approval."

"Yes, My Lord." The man bowed almost double and backed away.

"That deals with that issue. Where is your sister?"

Meg's distress was immediately evident. "Gone home," she said. "I could not persuade her to stay."

"Why are you so nasty, brother?" Désirée poked her head from inside Meg's sitting room. Halibut was draped around her neck and made it impossible for her to hold her head up. "Why should we not receive visitors? Meg has said I may be with her if Sir Robert comes. I think that will be fun."

"The *Princess* may receive another caller?" He raised a brow, but Meg met his questioning stare unflinchingly. "It will not be fun because it won't happen, for either of you. Meg Smiles, you are to rest, is that clear? Now, into your rooms. I am a busy man. We will speak at a later hour."

He left the women and stormed to the gallery with Verbeux matching strides. The man had already insisted he was recovered enough to perform his duties, but Jean-Marc suspected it was determination to locate Ila that drove him.

"What do you intend?" Verbeux asked.

"Do you admit it would have been a poor solution for me to flee with Meg Smiles?"

"No. If you had done so, I doubt the events of last night would have occurred. They were to make you take notice, don't you think?"

Jean-Marc checked his stride. "Perhaps. Yes, yes, very likely. Now we keep our own counsel. I must be ready to move quickly and without being seen. I can't imagine why this Baggs man would take Ila, but we have nothing else to go on, so I intend to find him and see what he knows. To that end I shall observe

Number Seven. My theory is that if Miss Sibyl tells Godly-Smythe she wishes Baggs to marry them, Godly-Smythe will go to him. When he does, I shall follow. I must know a great deal more about those two.''

"I'll come with you.''

"You will remain here and ensure the safety of this household. Are you armed?''

"Of course,'' Verbeux said. "I am always armed. Unfortunately, my costume did not allow me to conceal a pistol last night, and I suffered for it. But someone else can stand guard here. I insist on coming.''

Jean-Marc caught his shoulder. "We are wasting time. The less commotion, the better. That means that one man will draw less attention than two. Do as I ask.''

He didn't await an answer before running down to the foyer and allowing Rench to hand him his cloak. "Thank you,'' he told the butler. "I trust you understand my orders that no one, *no one* is to enter the house without my permission. Since I shall be out for the immediate future, that means no visitors at all. Understood?''

Rench's face was intent. "Perfectly, My Lord. Not a soul will come here until you tell me otherwise.''

"Good man.'' Jean-Marc swung on his cloak, but rather than leave by the front door, he hurried through the house and let himself out through the back garden gate. The stables were located there, and curious grooms stopped working on his horses to stare. He waved as if there was nothing unusual about his leaving his own house by the back door.

A narrow pathway between Number 17 and Number 18, a space large enough for only a single person to pass at a time, made the perfect place for him to linger and overlook the rest of the square. He had an excellent view of Number 7 and settled in to wait.

Frequent glances at his fob watch only proved how slowly time might seem to pass on occasion.

Hunter Lloyd left Number 7 and engaged in a conversation with a man who came from Number 8. That house belonged to Jean-Marc's old friend Ross, Viscount Kilrood, and his wife. Odd to think that Latimer More was the Viscountess's brother. The Kilroods were at their Scottish estates and the man Lloyd spoke to was probably the butler in residence, although the two men communicated like familiars before each went on his way.

Rain began to fall, light rain it was true, but damned inconvenient.

The front door of Number 7 opened again. Luck, at last! This time it was William Godly-Smythe who stood there looking around. He pulled on gloves and went down the steps, where he paused to glance about him again. His gaze settled on Number 17, and he stared before setting off at a rapid rate.

Jean-Marc allowed him to reach the exit from the square to the High Street and turn right before he left cover.

Almost at once, he pulled back.

Sibyl Smiles appeared. She lifted her skirts and ran to the flagway, kept on running until she reached the point where Godly-Smythe had made his turn. She looked both ways, paused a moment, but set off in the same direction as the man she supposedly intended to marry.

Damn all interfering women. She was bound to become a liability. If he delayed any longer, Jean-Marc thought he might lose them both. He walked from the alley, his carriage confident, as if he were doing nothing more than taking the air.

The rain grew heavier. Before he turned the corner and saw his quarries, rain already dripped from the brim of his hat. He prayed Miss Smiles would not turn back, see him and slow his progress, but she seemed as determined as he was to see where Godly-Smythe was headed—without herself being seen. In fact, he took her decision to follow as potential proof that Godly-Smythe had told her he would fetch Baggs to talk about a wedding.

* * *

Meg had left the house by the steps where she and Désirée took Halibut outside whenever he demanded to go. She knew of a gate near the enclosed rose garden that opened into a yard used by sanitary workers about their unenviable duties in the early mornings.

Wrinkling her nose at the stubborn odor, she hardened herself against her sore ankles, sped to the flagway and turned left in the direction she'd seen first William, then Sibyl go. Her dear sister, unaccustomed to any clandestine behavior, had been obvious in her attempt to watch where William was going, and Meg prayed he wouldn't see Sibyl. Meg hoped that with luck she would catch up with Sibyl and they could go on together. She thought she knew what was in Sibyl's mind. If she had told William that Baggs was to marry them, then it made sense for the odious man to go in search of the Reverend. Why he was determined to marry Sibyl, she didn't know, but he was most determined and would doubtless rush to do so before there could be a change of mind. Sibyl had at least some doubt about Baggs and intended to discover if he might have Lady Upworth with him.

At the exit from the square, she turned right as she had seen Sibyl do shortly before she, Meg, had left the house. The High Street was wide, and carriages rolled back and forth, throwing up mud and water as they went. Those who hurried past on foot did so with their heads down to keep the rain from their eyes. Meg shielded hers and hurried on. In the distance she saw a flash of green she was certain must be Sibyl, and she broke into a painful trot, raising her skirts and ignoring the curious glances of passersby.

Verbeux usually avoided defying Count Etranger. Their association had been long and successful because he knew well that his master was a volatile man, and Verbeux refrained from crossing him.

On this occasion, there was no choice in Verbeux's mind but

to follow the Count and to be available if matters became out of hand. Neither of them knew what might be encountered when Godly-Smythe reached his destination. If Verbeux's hopes were met and Reverend Baggs had indeed played some part in Ila's disappearance, then going against orders would be worth the danger of dismissal.

He was farther behind the Count than he would prefer, but it had taken time to get Pierre alone and make him understand he was on watch at Number 17, and that considerable responsibility rested on his shoulders.

At least his employer was a tall man. Verbeux had seen the first direction the other man took out of the square. With any luck, since the road he took was long and straight, there might be hope of finding him—and Godly-Smythe—before they either took another street or went inside a building.

Verbeux turned right at the High Street and broke into a run that assured his dignity would be lost. He dodged to the side of the flagway and mounted a flight of steps to search ahead. He almost cheered when he saw an unmistakable tall form in black apparently hurrying toward a park in the distance. All was not yet lost, and when he caught up, the Count might be grateful to have company in the confrontation he expected.

Sibyl slipped through a gap in the high, white railings surrounding Tapwell Park. A bear and a griffin stood guard over each stone gatepost, but the gates themselves were chained shut. The park was private and belonged to the elegant if somewhat shabby house of the same name that could be seen in the distance. Almost at once the noises of the city became muted. Stands of mature oak trees rose up on grassy mounds on either side of a driveway that stretched directly toward the house. William had leaned forward to trudge up the slope to the right. He disappeared from view on the other side. Too aware of the importance of not being seen, Sibyl chose to go around the mound, which stretched for at least a mile.

Evidently William had come this way before. He used the park to take a shortcut to the streets that lay on the other side of the park surrounding Tapwell House. He let himself out by a small tradesmen's gate and entered into a rather mean cobbled way beyond. Sibyl slipped quickly and silently in his wake, never taking her eyes from the jaunty angle of his beaver hat and the sandy blond hair that showed beneath its brim.

She must take the great risk of drawing closer to him.

At the crossroads of Astly Lane and Mona Avenue, he made a left. Sibyl dashed to that corner and stuck her head around. William boldly approached a large Tudor-style inn with bulging, beamed upper stories that overhung the street. A gently swinging—and creaking—sign announced that this was The Frog's Breath. He entered the establishment confidently, and she was seconds behind him. She had only to stand outside the front doors, where the smell of old ale sickened her, to hear her second cousin jovially greeted by a man who was probably the innkeeper.

"You've got visitors," the man said. "That Reverend Baggs and a *friend*." There was great emphasis on *friend*. "Classy piece. Wouldn't have thought the Reverend 'ad it in 'im."

"Still waters run deep and silent, hmm?" William said, laughing coarsely.

"Still waters might," the other man said. "Your Reverend don't exactly keep 'is mouth shut often."

William grunted, and Sibyl heard him going upstairs. She gave him a minute before following, and the bright blush on her cheeks embarrassed her when she passed the rotund innkeeper. He clucked approvingly and said not a word.

Listening to William's footsteps, she climbed to the third floor and immediately heard voices issuing from one of two rooms on the left, the one at the front of the building. On the right there was another room, obviously larger.

She looked for a place to hide. She could assume the voices she heard belonged to Baggs and William and, in the case of feminine tones, to Lady Upworth. The latter gave Sibyl great hope.

The only possible hiding place was the room on the right. She tiptoed forward and peeked inside. This was a sitting room. A sitting room furnished, she instantly realized, with pieces from her old home, some that had belonged to the Smiles family for generations. She would *not* cry now.

Instead she slipped inside, inside and behind the door—and banged into William.

"*Sibyl,*" he whispered, his face a study in horror. He put a finger to his lips and pushed her into the corner behind him. With his mouth on her ear he whispered, "What can you be thinking of? You have a great deal to learn about obedience, my girl. I have walked into unexpected trouble here. Stay quiet and do not move. You could ruin my efforts if you disobey me."

She nodded, but longed to tell him she knew all about his criminal doings.

"There's someone else coming," William said softly. "What the devil is this?"

Head ducked, looking over his shoulder, the Count came in, his black cloak swirling about him and rain running from the brim of his hat. He walked directly across the sitting room, turned and saw William and Sibyl.

In his hand he carried a deadly looking pistol. This he leveled at William. "Get away from there, Sibyl." He kept his voice low. "Do as I say at once."

"Your time for giving orders is past," William said, and revealed that he held his own pistol on Sibyl, who opened her mouth to scream, but promptly covered it. "I suggest you get over there, Etranger—against the wall—where I can keep my eye on you."

The man irritated Jean-Marc but he didn't disturb him. "*Don't* aim that thing at Sibyl. I thought she was your intended. What can have changed?" He strolled to sit in a chair well out of sight of anyone who passed the door.

"Sorry, Sibyl, darling," William said. "I wasn't thinking there for a moment. Please forgive me."

Sibyl didn't say a word, and Jean-Marc smiled pleasantly at her. "So, our two pigeons are in the room across the hall, hmm? One wonders why they have remained there so long. But we can be relieved to hear Lady Upworth's voice and to know she is alive, if not necessarily well. Put your weapon away, Godly-Smythe. Fire and you will be fired upon, and we'll be overrun with constables."

"I wonder why Baggs has defied me," William said, as if Jean-Marc hadn't spoken. "That woman shouldn't be here."

"Where should she be?" Sibyl asked mildly.

Jean-Marc looked at her with respect for her calm demeanor. "Where, indeed?" he said.

William glowered but didn't answer. "You will both remain here while I confer with Reverend Baggs. Better yet, run along home and I will report to you later."

"Run along home?" Jean-Marc laughed. "I'm sure that would make things easier for you, but I don't think so. Hush." Light feet softly trod up the stairs.

"Hell's teeth," William Godly-Smythe said. "This must stop. I'll tell the innkeeper to turn any other strangers away."

"And draw more attention to yourself?" Jean-Marc asked.

The footsteps reached the landing and halted as the owner of the feet listened to the conversation between Baggs and Ila. Rather than turn toward the sitting room, the newcomer went the other way. A door opened, and the sound of voices grew at first louder, then stopped.

Jean-Marc rose at once and looked around the door—in time to see that beloved baggage, Meg Smiles, slip into the room with Baggs and Ila.

He looked heavenward. "Oh, my God."

"You look ridiculous," Meg announced in ringing tones. "Absolutely ridiculous. What do you think you are doing?"

Jean-Marc signaled for William and Sibyl to remain where

they were and prepared to cross the landing, only to see a flash of movement that warned of yet another approach.

"Damn it all to *hell*." He spat the words out, managing, with great effort, to hold his voice down.

Pistol in one hand and dagger in the other, Verbeux got to the top of the stairs and took several steps before he saw his master watching him narrowly. Jean-Marc kept his own weapon trained on William Godly-Smythe and hissed for Verbeux to join him.

"A pox on you," he said when his man arrived. "If we come through this without shooting one another it will be a miracle. Godly-Smythe, sit in that chair! Miss Smiles, you in that one. Verbeux, watch them. Do not allow them to move."

Godly-Smythe didn't hesitate to haul Sibyl before him and hold his pistol to her temple. "I only do this to stop you from taking dangerous steps. Don't worry, Sibyl, sweetness, I would never do a thing to hurt you."

"Then why bother to hold me like this?" she said. "You've already told everyone this is a pretense."

A number of expressions passed over Godly-Smythe's face, each one more comically confused than the one before. "Yes, well," he muttered, releasing her. "But that doesn't mean I won't shoot anyone else who gets in my way."

"Just be a good chap and sit down there," Jean-Marc said mildly.

William bumbled about a bit, but finally did as he was told. He kept his pistol out and aimed it at first one, then another of the room's occupants.

"I want to see Ila," Verbeux said. "I hear her voice. I must see her."

"You must watch this one," Jean-Marc replied.

"I want to speak to Baggs," William Godly-Smythe insisted. "He's a frightened fellow. Push him and you can't know what he will do. But I know how to manage him."

"I'm going to Meggie," Sibyl said, jumping up. "That man is wicked. He may do something to her."

"Preserve me from civilians," Jean-Marc said. "And you, Verbeux, should know better."

"I want to go to Meggie," Sibyl insisted stubbornly.

"Be quiet," he told her. "Very well. This is how we will do it. When I am certain there is no danger, you, Godly-Smythe, and Miss Smiles will go in first. M. Verbeux and myself will be behind you with the necessary weapons. A circus," he muttered to Verbeux. "We control it or the animals will tear each other apart."

"Yes, My Lord."

Godly-Smythe and Sibyl crowded close together and advanced across the landing with Jean-Marc and Verbeux close behind. In the same formation, they entered what was a bedroom.

An extraordinary tableau greeted them. Seated on the wide windowsill, his broad-brimmed hat resting on the back of his head and gray-tinged beard stubble darkening his round face, Reverend Baggs pointed an overlarge pistol at Ila. Still dressed in her red harem costume, her hair falling about her shoulders, Ila sat cross-legged on the bed, a small silver firearm trained on the minister.

Meg seemed incapable of subduing her laughter, laughter that had rendered her a helpless heap on top of an old carved chest. "They must—" She choked and hiccuped. "They must have been like that all night. They don't dare move. If one falls asleep, the other may sh-sh-shoot. Or they would if they could see."

"Baggs," William said ferociously. "Why did you bring her here?"

"I thought that's what you wanted." Baggs swayed, and from time to time his eyelids almost closed. Each time it happened, he gave himself a startled shake and peered down the barrel of his pistol with one eye while his extended arm wobbled.

"I told you to make sure she could never talk about me again."

"About what?" Jean-Marc asked at once.

"Nothing," William snarled. "Mind your own business."

"Reverend Baggs saved my life, you know." Ila turned sleepy eyes on Jean-Marc and said, "He didn't mean to, but if the other one had taken me away, well, there I should be, shouldn't I? Baggsy, we must tell the truth. Baggsy's one of the best, you know. A victim of circumstances with a golden heart. We know everything about each other. *Everything*." The hand that held her pistol started to sink. She jumped and aimed it at the Reverend again.

"Too dangerous to tell them," Baggs said, supporting one hand with the other as if the pistol grew too heavy. "I'm not talking to any of you."

"This is my fault," Verbeux said. He passed a hand over his face. "I've been too busy trying to save myself."

"Verbeux?" Jean-Marc said, bewildered. "You? You have had a hand in all this?"

Ila made soft sounds and said, "He's a good man. I am a monster. What I did, I did for gain, but it's all over. Your uncle Louis said that when he was on the throne, he would make me his princess. He said your days were numbered, Jean-Marc, and I would soon be cast out with nowhere to turn. But if I helped him, I would be richly rewarded. If I failed, as I have failed, I would die."

Jean-Marc thought of the letter in his desk drawer. So much intrigue, and for nothing now that his uncle Louis was dead. "And I was convinced you were in love with me." He made sure his voice oozed sarcasm. "I may never recover."

"Don't speak to her in such a way," Verbeux said. "She has been a woman alone and with diminishing means. She did what she thought she must to survive. If only we had found each other sooner.

"My own villainy is much longer-standing. I was also told

of your expected fall from favor and promised a place at your uncle's right hand.'' He looked the most miserable of men. ''I refused at first.''

''But you changed your mind.'' Jean-Marc knew deep disappointment.

''For the sake of another, I had to. I will not beg for understanding. I don't deserve any. I allowed them to use both an unforgivable mistake, and my position, to gain information about you. I urged you and Miss Smiles together to help make certain your father would decide never to make you his successor. I saw the opportunity the moment she came to Number Seventeen and you reacted so differently to her. I admit I wasn't sure it would come to anything—until you returned from taking her to Windsor on that excursion I engineered.''

The sound of quiet crying brought Jean-Marc's attention to Meg. She wiped her eyes with the backs of her hands.

''Marvelous,'' he said. ''I have been betrayed, made the target for assassination, and everyone present feels sorry for anyone but me!''

Ila's eyes grew moist. ''And Verbeux didn't know that the instant you should decide to arouse your father's wrath by marrying Meg, I was as good as dead. Louis didn't need me as your unsuitable wife-to-be if you found one even more unsuitable. Forgive me, Meg, I'm only telling the truth—for once.''

Meg sniffed, but would not look at any of them. ''What has any of this to do with Sibyl or me, or William or Mr. Baggs? What of the violence that has befallen me?''

Sibyl, also sniffing, said, ''Lady Upworth, I don't think I could possibly explain what you told me.''

''Well, I can,'' Ila said and, talking over Godly-Smythe's protests, regaled the gathered company with a wild story of the man's gambling and his plan to marry Sibyl, force Meg to become part of his household and trick them both out of any proceeds from the sale of The Ramblers, the house he had inherited from the sisters' father. ''He brought Reverend Baggs to London to dispose of Meg altogether because he feared she would not cooperate. And Baggsy managed to live at Number Seven, where he could watch every move she made."

"You do not know that," William snapped.

"On the contrary," Ila said sweetly. "Baggsy and I have spent the night together, hmm, Baggsy, dear? We are intimately acquainted now."

"Have a care what you say," Reverend Baggs said, his plump face shiny and pink. "My reputation is invaluable to me."

More than one chuckle followed.

Oblivious, Baggs continued. "Mr. Godly-Smythe gives me my living. I thought he did so for honorable reasons. I was wrong. He did so in case he ever needed someone to do dastardly deeds. I can't risk my living, you see, since I'm unlikely to find another. So—he gave me a choice. Leave Puckly Hinton and seek a place elsewhere, or help him recover from his gambling excesses by getting rid of Miss Meg Smiles. He would have preferred to dispose of both sisters but feared provoking too much suspicion. He doesn't have long to come up with a lot of money, so—"

"*Silence.*" Godly-Smythe seemed to shrink. "You are a fool. The worst clergyman I have ever encountered."

"Yes, yes," Meg said. "But how is it all connected?"

"Baggs arranged the accident near the Burlington Arcade." William was suddenly so expansive that his face shone with enthusiasm. "And he caused the second one in Bond Street."

"Did he plant the open shaving blade?"

"I did not," Baggs said heatedly.

"We already know Pierre did so by accident," Jean-Marc pointed out. "The attempt to poison me occurred some time prior to our meeting, Meg. Clearly these are separate issues, separate criminal activities."

"There was no attempt to poison you." Verbeux sat down suddenly and mopped his brow with a large handkerchief. "I made it up. One more little lie to make you agree to leave. I had decided that if you married someone of Meg Smiles's lowly station in life, your father would not as much as consider you his heir. I had to do it. I don't want to say why, but I couldn't bear to think of a certain event becoming public. And you were so obviously passionately involved with Miss Smiles. It seemed the perfect solution, but you would not be hurried.''

Meg watched Jean-Marc's face and saw only anger. He was angry that those he trusted had betrayed him.

He looked directly at her.

She averted her eyes.

"Meg," he said, "will you marry me?"

Groans and mutters. "What is he thinking of?"

"How can he deal with such matters now?"

Meg was shamed and bitter. She said, "Are you mad? You reveal how little you respect me, how lowly you consider me, and ask me to marry you?"

"Who beat Verbeux?" Sibyl said. "And who attacked you, Meg?"

"Quite," Jean-Marc agreed, stinging from Meg's words. "As we speak, no doubt there are others—obviously loyal to my uncle Louis—who may be closing in for the kill." He had no guarantee that Louis's followers had withdrawn their efforts against him.

"Or someone here who is waiting for the perfect moment to finish what they have started," Meg stated.

He thought the same but had not wanted to frighten either Meg or Sibyl by saying so. "Come to me, Meg," he said. When she hesitated, he added, "Quickly. Put your antagonism toward me aside. Survival is more important."

She came to him. The blue gown and a matching cloak intensified her eyes, if that were possible. "Go to the innkeeper and ask him to call the constables. Immediately. Tell him not to venture above stairs."

Meg obeyed. Limping, she left the room.

"It's all lies," Godly-Smythe said. "Her *Ladyship* knows I

saw her in the gambling hells. She decided to defend herself by defaming me. All lies. I am a man above reproach.''

"My Lord," Sibyl Smiles said. "Those sounds. Do you hear them?''

He did indeed.

Sibyl was on her feet and making for the door. "Meg. I must see if Meg needs me.''

He caught her about the waist and swung her away. "You will only cause more trouble. Silence, everybody.''

The door slammed wide open and clattered against the wall. Miss Lavinia Ash, her hair awry and sopping, rainwater running down her face and soaking her already wet shoulders, stood on the threshold. She held Pierre by the ear while he hissed with pain and tried, in vain, to dislodge her fingers.

Watch this, dear reader. Haven't I told you that I, Sir Septimus Spivey, am superior to all these fools? It is mortifying—well, yes—perhaps degrading would be better. It is degrading that I am forced to use the Ash creature, but I have no choice. Clearly, if I do not intervene, all may be lost.

"Come along, Meg," Ash said loudly. "Come in here at once. Constables only bring shame, and we've had quite enough of that. We'll deal with this in our own way.''

To a man and woman the company gaped.

Ash gave Pierre's ear a vicious twist and didn't even flinch when he howled. "I am going to reveal all," she said, "and tell each of you what is to happen. Listen carefully. You have all failed miserably in assessing the cause, and the cure, for the carelessly planned events that have taken place.''

"I appreciate your assistance, Miss Ash," Jean-Marc said, "but I don't appreciate your rudeness. Have your say—preferably without insulting anyone else.''

"Lavinia," Meg said, joining them again. "Do let go of poor

Pierre. He only did what the rest of us did, and followed because he wanted to help.''

''Th-thank you, Miss Smiles,'' Pierre said, drawing in his lower lip.

Meg stared at him, at his broad shoulders and his strongly made form.

''Buck up, Godly-Smythe,'' Lavinia snapped. ''You are going to get your way because it will suit me—I mean, because it will suit everyone best. Sibyl knows she has few choices left her. She will marry you, and Meg will live with the two of you. That's what matters most here.''

Ila waved her pistol with abandon. ''It was the good old Godly one who managed to get Meg and Sibyl's allowances reduced, you know.''

''Please,'' Reverend Baggs said, ''surely enough has been said.''

''I thought they ought to know,'' Ila said.

''Meg will go nowhere,'' Jean-Marc said. He no longer cared about Godly-Smythe's transgressions. The man was finished. But the caper merchant was an annoyance and a puzzle, and she spoke with enough authority to fool some. ''In future, Meg will go where I go.''

How easy it would be to rejoice in his declaration, Meg thought. But too much had been said about her position being vastly inferior to his, which it was. However, an accident of birth did not mean a woman didn't have a mind of her own.

''I will never marry William.'' Sibyl crossed her arms and turned her head from him. ''Never, never. Never intended to. I said I would to trick him into revealing the truth about his wrongdoings. I'm sure a criminal would not be allowed to keep what he dared to gamble away—our *home*.''

Give me the strength to carry on as long as I must. Oh, to be resting in my own beloved newel post, watching very few people come and go. I will gather my strength and do my best with this wretched woman, who has such little presence. Remind me to deal with Hunter Lloyd. It still pains me to think of his flippant disregard. He should be embarrassed to be likened to me in looks? Pah! It is I who should be horrified at the suggestion.

"Who," Meg said, growing exhausted from her efforts, "who attacked whom? At Number Seventeen." She could not help but look at M. Verbeux.

"I know," he said, "you think I must have been behind it all, but it's not so. If I were, would I arrange to have myself beaten? And no, I can't tell you who did such things."

"You allude to something you cannot reveal," Jean-Marc said. "Surely the time for secrets is past. My father's enemies know something that would be deeply embarrassing to you, is that it?"

"Deeply embarrassing—and disastrous—to another. Please don't press this, My Lord."

"That sound," Jean-Marc said slowly, closing his eyes to listen.

Meg did the same, "Yes, that. I heard it many times but didn't notice until—"

"Until this oaf set upon you in the dark when you followed him." Lavinia Ash gave Pierre another rough shake. "I can't believe how obtuse you are. He's been meeting his foreign friends, and they've been telling him what to do. I know. I've been there."

"You couldn't be," Pierre protested.

"See how the fool confesses his sins?" Ash pointed out. "He likes to work in the dark. He pushed M. Verbeux around because he hates him, and because Verbeux was careless. And he enjoyed getting his hands on the Upworth creature."

"I heard him sucking in his lip," Meg said. "In that awful room when he burned me."

Ash waved her free arm like a windmill blade. "At last you notice. I hoped he might do away with you—I mean, I *feared* he might do away with you, but he is afraid, just like the rest of you, afraid of being caught, so when victory is in his grasp, he runs away."

Jean-Marc looked narrowly at Pierre and moved slowly toward him, planning how he would inflict the greatest pain. "You enjoy attacking helpless women," he said. "Now you shall learn how it feels to be helpless."

"Oh, who cares?" Ash said. "Let's get on with things. Send him back to your father, My Lord. He'll deal with him. Mr. Godly-Smythe, kindly ignore Sibyl's protests and take her and Meg away. And you, Baggs, may get lost and be grateful for my mercy. Verbeux will have to go to the Prince, too. Obviously he comes under the jurisdiction of Mont Nuages. Too bad about Princess Marie." Her laughter held anything but pity. "Then there is Lady Upworth." Ash scratched her large nose. "Now what, I wonder, would be best there?"

"I shall go wherever you go, Verbeux," Lady Upworth said.

"Fair enough." Ash spoke with alacrity, apparently unaware that not a soul was following her instructions. "You, My Lord, had better run along and continue with the business of marrying off your unpleasant sister."

"Has something happened to my father's wife?" Jean-Marc said, referring to Princess Marie.

Verbeux surged forward. He turned a fearsome glare on Ash and said, "You are spreading tales, my good woman. I suggest you stop at once, or I may have to stop you."

Ash's smile was stunningly mocking. "How will you do that? Kill me? Oh, I am very frightened of that. I hear Princess Marie is much younger than her husband and a rather—sexual creature."

"Enough, I tell you."

"Of course," Ash said, her expression serious again. "But you shouldn't have allowed yourself to be found out by people who could use your transgressions against you. That's why you're in this pickle, young man."

Jean-Marc stared at Verbeux, who wouldn't meet his gaze. "You fool." That was all Jean-Marc said. Princess Marie was no blood relative of his.

"There," Ash said. "That's that, and all's well."

"How very tidy," Jean-Marc said, continuing to size up how he would deal with Pierre—at least for now. "If you've forgotten anything, I doubt it's important."

"Thank you, My Lord," Ash said. "You aren't as much of a dolt as I took you for."

Meg caught her breath and glanced at Jean-Marc. He frowned at Ash, but with curiosity, not anger. "Apart from being beyond rude, madam, you are gifted with an extraordinary ability to sound—"

"Like a man," Meg finished for him.

Ash's response was a loud, enraged, "Ow!" Pierre had twisted until he could sink his teeth into his tormentor's arm. He did this with ferocious intent.

"Animal," Ash roared. "Low creature who does not know his—ow!—place!"

Wild-eyed, Pierre punched her ribs and, when she doubled over, slammed his fists into the back of her neck.

Verbeux made a grab for him, but too late.

"You won't send me back to the Duke," Pierre said, speaking of Louis and laughing hysterically. "Never."

Spinning away from Jean-Marc's outstretched hands, the valet's valet dashed across the room and flung himself at the mullioned and bowed windows.

Glass shattered, spun out into the glittering rain and seemed to hang suspended around the man's form. The force of his impact tore lead cross-hatch from its frames and bent it to cradle his body.

Jean-Marc strode to look down at the street.

Pierre had died before he hit the ground.

A single spear of that lead had entered his back and exited

his chest. The final expression on his face would remain a wide-eyed, wide-mouthed mask of surprise.

Screams came from below and from within the room. Sibyl and Meg threw themselves into each other's arms. Reverend Baggs, sitting on the windowsill, stared with amazement at the opened vista upon houses and street.

Despite the sound of anguished voices outside, stillness settled on those assembled in the bedroom.

Reverend Baggs rose and leaned to look downward. "I'd follow him," he said, "if I wasn't too tired." He tossed his pistol on the bed. "And if I wasn't too much of a coward."

The tramp of multiple footsteps on the stairs announced the approach of constables, who accepted Jean-Marc's authority and removed William and Reverend Baggs. For their part, the pair departed without fight or argument. That, Jean-Marc thought, would come later. He watched Meg for some sign that she was relenting toward him, but saw no such sign. She didn't look at him at all.

If she looked at him, Meg decided, she would weaken. To do so without a great deal of thought would be to abandon all pride and risk losing herself entirely.

"Come, Sibyl," she said. "We should return home and talk."

"Talk?" Sibyl said, sounding shaky. "I like it at Number Seven, Meggie. I'm going to stay there."

Meg couldn't bring herself to say she would also continue to live in Mayfair Square. She wasn't sure she could, at least not while Jean-Marc was so close by.

"I will not give up, I tell you," Ash bellowed, not sounding at all like herself. "No, no, no, I cannot bear it. Someone is to blame for this failure, and I will find out who it is. Then heads will roll, and I know exactly who will tell me all about how that is achieved."

Bellowing in baritone, she marched to the landing and down the stairs.

"Amazing," Jean-Marc said. "For all the world like an angry...*man*."

Slipping an arm around Sibyl's shoulders, Meg cast a last look at the man she loved, and guided her sister from The Frog's Breath.

Verbeux took Ila's pistol from her, picked up the one Baggs had discarded on the bed and, together with his own weapon, handed them to Jean-Marc. "Perhaps you would like some time to think," he said. "You can trust us to return to Mayfair Square and await your wishes."

Jean-Marc nodded and turned his back on them.

They closed the door as they left, and he was alone.

36

"Meg, it's you. You've come!" Princess Désirée wrenched open the carriage door and placed the steps herself. "Come out at once and let me see you. Oh, Meg, you can't imagine what I've been suffering."

"Since only yesterday, Your Highness?" Meg asked, stepping into bright sunlight beneath a cloudless sky. The scent of fresh-mown grass rushed at her, and she breathed deeply. She looked toward Riverside, at the riot of roses in many colors covering the facade, and toward the shimmering river beyond.

"Oh, do hurry," the Princess said, her face puckered with impatience. Halibut hissed and spat at the end of a long piece of green ribbon fashioned into a harness and lead. "Hopeless. Absolutely hopeless. Of course, mostly he's silent, but he glowers so fiercely. He does say Mr. Chillworth may come to Windsor to continue painting me, but then won't send for him or tell me when he *will* send for him. He has become a bad-tempered creature I wish I didn't know."

"Has he? And who is *he?*"

"You know very well. He's miserable and making me suffer for it. You must make him buck up. You can do it. Only you can do it."

Hiring a carriage and coming at all had felt very daring to Meg. Not coming had been out of the question. The idea of never seeing his face again had kept her awake all night, and she could not bear the thought of such sleepless nights stretching ahead forever.

"Thank goodness you didn't wait longer to come," Princess Désirée said, hopping from foot to foot. Her pink and lavender dress became her. The wild condition of her hair did not. "Everything that happened yesterday has been reported to me. Ash was furious and told it all to Millie, who, of course, told *everybody*. I truly feared I might never see you again. I can scarcely believe that poor wretch, Pierre, was in the employ of my wicked uncle Louis. Actually, and I'm ashamed to admit it, I rather liked my uncle. He was kind to me—when he noticed me at all. And now he's dead."

From the Princess's manner, Meg didn't think Ash had spoken of Princess Marie and Verbeux. Meg wished she need never again think of all she had learned. "Your uncle was a very bad man who intended to have your brother killed or disgraced—whichever would dispose of him most efficiently." She did not say what she could not forget, that she had become the chosen method of disgracing Jean-Marc.

"I feel sorry for Verbeux," Princess Désirée said. "He is already on his way back to Mont Nuages—with Upworth, of course. I am surprised at her bravery."

"She is in love," Meg said.

They were quiet.

Her Royal Highness cleared her throat. "I actually thought Verbeux liked Sibyl."

"I'm sure he did. He must have known they could never be suited because he stopped looking at her in that way he has. And she lost interest in him. Just as well."

"And Sibyl will remain at Number Seven. Will she be sad? And lonely?"

"I will not allow her to be," Meg said, and felt guilty because it was not Sibyl who filled her heart and mind today. "But yes, she will remain there. She insists that's her home now."

Princess Désirée set her lips so tightly a white line formed around them. She said, "I tell you, since we arrived last evening, that brother of mine has been impossible. Come, we'll walk into Castleberry and find him.''

For a moment Meg hung back, unsure she could carry out what she'd promised herself she'd do.

Princess Désirée caught Halibut up into one large armful, grabbed Meg's hand and led her to a path across the fields. ''He is very, very difficult,'' she said seriously. ''I know he is a great burden, but you have a way with him. You don't allow him to get too far above himself. I have never seen anyone else deal so perfectly with him.'' She paused and raised a hand. ''Now I have to encourage you to give him a little time to return to being a human. He isn't one at the moment, or he wasn't when I last saw him. He went to the village in a great flurry. Everything must be put right—yesterday at the latest, you understand. The school, the church, the cottages, the shops, and on and on. A sawbones for the villagers. Livestock. Weekly audiences when people may come to him personally with their complaints. He's already had notices posted to that effect. And he has offered himself to Reverend and Mrs. Smothers to work in and about the church in capacities useful to them. He pretends his anger is at himself for neglecting those who depend upon him. He may have done so—a little. But the truth is that he is madly, wildly in love with you and fears he may have lost you, which he should have after the silly things that were said, and which he does not deny were said.''

Meg grew breathless just listening to the girl, who had been transformed from an irritable, uncertain creature into a confident young woman in a matter of weeks.

''It was all foolish, you know,'' Désirée continued. ''How could someone as sweet, intelligent, honorable, talented and lovely as you not be a suitable—well, suitable for Jean-Marc? Oh, do hurry, Meg. You aren't an elderly lady to move so slowly!''

They raced through a meadow, beating a new path. Brilliant flowers, daisies and poppies, wild blue irises and golden buttercups bobbled their heads in the bright light. Butterflies flaunted their pretty wings, and the sweet perfumes of wildflowers mingled with that of the grass.

A lane was reached by a five-barred gate, which Désirée climbed without decorum. Meg clambered over with only slightly more grace. Then they were off again, holding hands, keeping their skirts from tangling about their feet. The blistered skin hurt less today, but her hems still stung raw spots.

The first cottages they saw were widely spaced. Billowing blossoms crowded tiny gardens. Birds sang in thatched roofs. Pink-faced children played while their mothers talked across walls and paused to watch Meg and the Princess pass.

Closer and closer together the stone homes became until they stood in tight rows that encompassed shops. And in the center of the village, a broad green, a white fence, gravestones and a tiny church with a spire that dwarfed the rest of the building.

"He's in there," Princess Désirée said, panting. "There's Wellington."

A massive gray cropped grass outside the churchyard fence. "The Count has a horse called Wellington? How odd."

The Princess shrugged. "He admires Wellington, so why not?" She opened the gate and trotted inside. Meg followed halfway along the path to the open church door before she stopped.

"*Come* along," Désirée urged. "Please, Meg. You have no idea how serious this is. The longer you wait, the worse he'll become."

The girl assumed Jean-Marc's ill humor was because he wanted Meg. Meg could not be so sure.

"He is determined to redo everything, *everything*—including me." She spread her arms. "I forgot to tell you. I'm to be my father's heir. Jean-Marc's glad, although he doesn't want to be, I think. Papa isn't a kind man. He is never gentle, or giving. And he never thanks anyone—including my mama. Poor Jean-Marc. He wants you, Meg."

Meg raised her face and walked straight ahead and into the church. A pretty little place, where the sun cast colored rays through stained-glass windows. A peaceful place, where the care of many hands showed in tapestry kneelers, in highly polished brass and in starched altar linens.

Meg saw Jean-Marc at once. With puffed-up cheeks, he stood at the end of the nave closest to the altar. Flowers were heaped on a table before him, together with a tall green vase that held several blossoms.

Approaching by a side aisle, hoping he wouldn't see her until she had gained more courage, Meg observed him pick up a large white rose on a thorny stem and stick it into the vase. He poked it this way and that, stood back to study his handiwork and poked some more.

She turned to whisper to the Princess. She wasn't there.

"Penance," she heard Jean-Marc mutter. "Penance, penance." He hauled all the flowers from the vase and started again. This time he gathered blooms into one large hand, evidently without a care for thorns. He added more and more until almost every daisy, rose, iris, dahlia, chrysanthemum and heaps of greenery were crushed together. This chaotic bouquet he thrust into the vase all at once, squashing the stems and giving the whole a few extra shoves. He slapped his palms together and stood back once more. "There," he said. "Flowers by Etranger in the latest style—complete confusion."

Meg smiled and shuffled her feet.

Jean-Marc swung around and saw her. He hitched at his neck cloth, then scowled at the green stains on his fingers.

"I didn't know you liked to arrange flowers," she said, when she could find her voice.

"I don't. I made the mistake of telling Mrs. Smothers—the Reverend's wife—that I wanted to help. Look at this." He indicated the crowded vase.

Meg went slowly to his side and contemplated his efforts. "Perhaps you should start yet again. I'll help you."

He studied her for far too long, so long that her skin turned burning hot. "Very well. Why not?" Once more he removed the blossoms and set them down.

"First, the flowers," she told him, holding out the white rose he had chosen before. "In the base of the vase there are spikes. Make sure you secure the bottoms of the stems on those."

A jab, and the rose stood like a sentinel in the middle of the vase. He actually looked pleased with himself. Several more stems joined the first, and from her direction, Meg noted a list to starboard.

Next she handed him an iris, but this time she curled her hand around his and guided the way he placed the purple beauty. Flower after flower was dealt with in this manner, with Meg standing at his shoulder, the top of her head level with that shoulder, her breast pressed to his arm.

She didn't expect him to swiftly change positions with her, placing her in front of him, with his hand over hers as they finished the task. His breath moved the curls at her temple and brushed the side of her face. Her back melded with his solid chest, her bottom with his groin. She attempted not to notice that she felt him respond to her.

"What a lovely job you've done," she told him. "You are obviously a natural."

He snorted. "Yes, indeed, a natural. The question is, a natural what?"

"A natural whatever you wish to be or do."

His free arm stole around her, and he spread his fingers on her tummy.

"We are in church," she pointed out.

"Yes," he said, but didn't stop holding her.

"I hired a coach to come to Windsor," she said. "In fact, one of yours was in front of Number Seventeen. When I asked the coachman to recommend where I might find a suitable vehicle, he said he was allowed to take fares and brought me to

Windsor. He said I was to pay him after the return journey. That was a forward thing for me to do. I'm sorry."

Forward? He thought not, particularly since he had told the coachman to be much in evidence in case Miss Smiles showed the slightest sign of wanting to come to Windsor.

"I'm glad you came, Meg." Glad she'd come before he was forced to give up controlling himself and go after her.

"Thank you."

So formal.

"I realize that you are no longer interested in me," she said.

That would probably be, Jean-Marc decided, because he was pressing her against his erection and massaging her belly and thighs while his breathing grew heavier—as did hers.

"How could you be interested after all that has happened? But just in case you have any bad feelings about what has passed between us, and the way it all turned out, I hoped you would give me a few minutes of your time so that I could tell you all the reasons why you shouldn't have considered getting involved with me in the first place."

"Do you like the church?" he asked.

Meg didn't look around but said, "Well, yes, very much, thank you."

"Good. So do I. What about Castleberry?"

"Pretty and inviting."

"It will improve shortly. Did you like Riverside when you were there before?"

"I thought it beautiful. A comfortably elegant place with the feeling of…a home."

Ah, good, good. "Very observant of you. When did you last bleed?"

A silence fell, so thick it roared, and Jean-Marc released Meg, aghast at the bald manner of his very personal question.

She bowed her head, but not before he saw how her cheeks turned red.

"That was unpardonable," he told her. "Please forgive me."

"We should leave the church and find a suitable place to talk."

"Yes, yes." He offered her his arm, and she decorously placed her hand there.

Désirée waited outside, apparently trying to train Halibut to walk at her heel on his ribbon. Jean-Marc met his sister's eyes and made a decision. "Go ahead with it," he told her, giving her two sharp nods, the sign they had agreed upon. "I'll bring Meg back myself."

Désirée smiled broadly, but more or less contained her excitement. She gathered up the cat and rushed away without another word. At Riverside she would set great activity in motion.

Jean-Marc was grateful Meg had been too preoccupied to notice his sister's high spirits.

"Would the river suit you?" he asked. "There are so many quiet spots there, and it's a perfect day." *A perfect day for a man to sabotage his last chance at happiness.*

Without agreeing or disagreeing, Meg took her hand from his arm and led the way. He fell in at her side, and they went the length of the village street to the lane beyond. No word passed between them, other than Meg's thank-you when Jean-Marc helped her over the stile, and his, "A pleasure," in response.

Apprehensive as he was, he couldn't help noticing how Meg's pale yellow skirts swished through long grass threaded with bright flowers, how the flowers flattened beneath her hem, only to spring up again as she passed.

She held her head high. From this angle, her straw bonnet hid her face. A single stray curl at her nape flirted with the skin of her tender neck.

Too soon they reached the river, and she paused, looking to him for direction.

He longed to take her hand, but pointed instead to a place beneath a willow, a bower where branches arched and dropped their tips into the satiny waters.

Jean-Marc reclined on the grass and rested his back against

the tree. He held out a hand to Meg. "It's so peaceful here," he said. "Join me."

She stood over him and said, "I'll stand, thank you."

"Then I must also stand."

"I'd prefer it if you didn't. Have you ever thought that a woman might like the advantage of looking down on a man occasionally?"

"You say the most extraordinary things." He thought about it. "But you may be right."

"I am a fraud," she said. "I tricked you into hiring me. Finch…Viscountess Kilrood, that is, didn't suggest I apply to you for a job. She simply mentioned that you and the Viscount are friends, and that you had moved into the square. And, of course, she wrote about your sister and how difficult it would be for you to do all you must. So, I saw an opportunity and took it. I apologize."

"I needed you. Regardless of how you came to me, you were a blessing. And I soon found out you had fabricated your introduction. I chose to do nothing about it."

"Oh."

"Yes, oh. I lied about Désirée. I pretended she was charming and malleable and excited about her debut. She hated all of it."

"Yes, I know. I knew almost at once because of the way she behaved, but it was my choice to stay because I wanted the money."

"Please sit down, Meg."

She turned from studying the river and did as he asked. She tucked her legs beneath her gown in her abstract thinking position and proceeded to tear up blades of grass. "My plan," she said, "was to use the connections I would make through you and the Princess to meet an eligible man and marry him. That seemed the only way to overcome our financial disaster, and I decided to take it. I had every intention of taking advantage of you."

"Did you?" he asked softly.

Their eyes met, then he looked at her lips, her pointed chin, her full breasts.

"I did," she told him.

"I see. And I soon had every intention of taking advantage of you—which I did. I enjoyed it. Didn't you?"

Little beads of perspiration broke out on her upper lip. Her smooth skin bloomed, and the slight tremble he felt more than saw heightened his desire for her.

"Well, anyway, I did," he said.

"And so did I. Or I did once I knew what it was. Then I just wanted you to keep on doing it."

He managed not to laugh at the odd turn of phrase. "Why did you really come to me today, my love?"

Her great golden brown eyes shimmered a little too much. "I thought... That is, I had some foolish notion of asking if you still wanted me even the tiniest bit."

Have a care, Etranger. If he overwhelmed her, she could be frightened into retreat, and the whole process of wooing her would take longer than he could bear.

He intended to get his way.

"Of course I've embarrassed you," she told him. "You need someone who is far more a woman than I am. I had planned to tell you that if I could be of some comfort to you, I'd..."

"What would you do?"

"I'd be with you on whatever terms you chose and I wouldn't expect anything permanent from you, ever. There, it's said. I should go at once."

"Ah, Meggie, you aren't going anywhere. Not without me. Never again." He saw how rigidly she held herself, but he took her by the arms and tipped her toward him. "You've just told me you'll be with me on any terms. I accept. Now I must make arrangements at once. Rooms here, a house to your liking somewhere in Town. Perhaps a Scottish hideaway."

Meg's heart thundered, and her body responded to him, and great emotion welled up within her, making her head light. He

removed her bonnet, and reason prevailed once more. "Everything about me is a lie," she told him. "I am a very ordinary
woman. My eyelashes are not nearly so dark without kohl. The
Egyptians used it, you know, and now a lot of ladies in other
countries do. I used it to make my eyes look more alluring. And
I put paint on my cheeks to make my complexion more enticing.
And I did the same on my lips."

"Your lips," he murmured, moving closer with evident intent
to kiss her. "Yes, your lips. But you forget that I have seen you
without kohl or paint, and found you just as irresistible."

She watched his mouth draw closer, and her lips parted. Her
breathing quickened, and her pulse, and she throbbed in places
where only Jean-Marc had ever made her throb.

"No!" Meg snapped her lips together and pulled away to look
over her shoulder at the river once more.

"What is it?" he asked. "Are you going to tell me your
meditation and veils and sudden silent withdrawals are also a
trick?"

"They are not," she said angrily. "They are real and a part
of me."

He settled a hand on the back of her neck. To make love to
her here, in the sweet, warm grass, would be both beautiful and
erotic.

"What you do not know, Count Etranger, is that my hair is
a dull, mousy brown, or perhaps chestnut, I suppose. Like some
street strumpet, I *dye* it red."

All of the ground-floor rooms at Riverside had been thrown
open and extravagantly decorated with the field blooms that had
been Meg's choice. In the forty-eight hours since she'd arrived
from Town, the entire house was transformed into a fairyland
of flickering candles, of silver garlands and puffs of white tulle
with poppies and daisies at their centers.

Sibyl still felt stunned by it all. She and Hunter kept company
with Adam, Latimer and Lady Hester—who continually ex-

claimed at the wonders of Riverside, and the marriage that had taken place in St. Simian in the Fields. Her questions about banns had been put to rest by the information that those banns had, indeed, been called three times prior to the wedding, and that the wedding license was in perfect order. The romantic Count Etranger, she'd been told, had surprised his bride with a dream day designed by himself alone. Meg had not as much as seen her finished gown until today.

What Lady Hester didn't know, but Sibyl did, was that to be ready in time, Meg's dress had been modified from another, using a drawing Princess Désirée found among her music. She didn't recall where it came from, but was correct in thinking it would become Meg.

A short distance from Sibyl, Jean-Marc lifted his bride's chin and smiled down at her. "I think we should leave our guests to enjoy themselves. Our presence forces them to be too decorous."

"Not at all," Meg said. "We must watch the Princess with poor Adam."

"Why *poor* Adam?"

She looked at her husband with pity. "Because he sees an interesting subject in her—to paint—whereas she looks at him and thinks he's in love with her."

"I spoke to Chillworth about that."

Meg winced. "You did?"

"Nothing to worry about there. Don't give it another thought. Let's retire to our rooms."

Meg's stomach flipped. "Latimer is a lonely man, you know."

"Really. Good enough looking fellow. Quite a presence. I do believe I'm growing tired."

"Once I thought Hunter and Sibyl would make a match."

"The world is full of disappointments."

"I'm glad Sir Robert came, and Anthony FitzDurham. Now there's a man who can't keep his eyes off the Princess."

"The devil you say." Jean-Marc craned his neck to locate the hapless FitzDurham. "Yes, well, there'll be time enough for that. Aren't you tired, my love?"

Rench, who had taken complete control of the household at Riverside, hurried toward them through the small crowd. "My Lord," he said, "there's a person to see you. I managed to keep her at the door. She seemed likely to make quite a fuss."

"Not to worry," Jean-Marc said and clapped Rench on the back, causing the man to stumble. "I'll have a word as the Countess and I make our way upstairs."

Meg didn't miss the instant flicker in the man's eyes, or the faint knowing smile. "Thank you, My Lord," he said.

Jean-Marc raised his voice. "We're going to leave you now. Time you could really get down to the business of revelry."

Chuckles abounded.

"They know where we're going," Meg whispered fiercely. "How embarrassing."

"Because they're all jealous? Hardly."

Amid cheers and laughter, they left the gold reception room. At the open front door, Rench barred Lavinia Ash from entering.

"There you are," she called.

"Her voice has really changed," Meg said. "I've never heard that happen before."

"You deliberately kept it from me," Ash said. "The wedding."

"Sorry," Jean-Marc told her. Later he'd have something to say to Rench, who knew very well who the "person to see you" was. "You'd have been more than welcome, Miss Ash."

"No, I wouldn't. I'd have stopped it. I'd have told how the two of you are already married to other people."

Meg gasped.

"We're not," Jean-Marc said shortly. "Good day to you."

"I'd have said it just the same. It would have stopped you. Where did you get that dress?"

Meg's knees shook. "It was made for me."

"Lies. It's mine. I designed it, and not for you."

"She's mad, Meg. Come away."

Ash shouted, "Don't you dare leave me like this. Very well, I'll give you my blessing. There, see how generous I am. Sibyl's coming to live with you, isn't she?" Her voice boomed through the foyer. "And why not set Adam Chillworth up with a studio here? And perhaps Latimer More could be useful to you."

"Sibyl will remain at Number Seven," Meg told her. "So will Latimer and Adam. They have lives of their own. Not that these things concern you."

"No," Ash insisted. "Sibyl must come to you. A young woman shouldn't be alone in a city like London."

Without another word to Ash, Jean-Marc swung Meg into his arms and said, "I shall have to be overbearing with you or I shall never get you into my bed."

"Shush." She placed a finger to his lips.

He began to climb the stairs.

"This is an outrage," Ash bellowed. "After all I've done for everyone, this is the thanks I get. It's going to stop, I tell you. And don't think I don't know where you two are going. More debauchery. And I'm left trying to control the unruly Peeping Toms who will not behave themselves."

"Absolutely mad," Jean-Marc said, and paused to give Meg a long, deep kiss that stole her breath.

"Laugh if you want to," Ash shouted after them. "I'm going now. But you haven't heard the last of me. Ash will return to oak and a familiar, hard resting place. Nothing like it for renewing vigor. You don't know the restorative properties of a good newel post—yet."

Meg looked up at Jean-Marc and said, "Newel post?"

Dozens of yellow-gold candles illuminated the bedchamber. He had given instructions for plenty of light, and a fire. The evenings always grew chill inside the thick walls of the house. Besides, he liked Meg by firelight.

He closed them in and could not help but see how nervous she was. She looked for all the world as if they had never lain together before.

The bridal gown was of lush ivory satin cut low to a point between her breasts, the entire bodice finely pleated. A belt of matching satin closed in front with a diamond and pearl-encrusted buckle. He approached her, smiling into her eyes all the while, and unclasped that buckle, removed the belt.

"It's so bright in here," she said.

"I wanted it so. I want to see you well—for the first time."

Meg looked at the floor.

Her sleeves were extravagantly puffed and stiffened beneath with net. Tight bands of satin clipped the fullness to her wrists. Insets of lace showed skin at her shoulders, and the same lace edged the yards and yards of satin that made up her fabulous skirts.

"The gown is perfect for you," he said. "But I believe it will be more perfect when I take it off."

This time she shuddered and held unnaturally still. He walked behind her to undo the many satin-covered buttons that closed the bodice and extended past her waist. Then he eased the wedding dress down her arms.

It caught at her wrists.

"This feels so strange," she told him. "Let me undress myself. I will be quicker."

"Exactly. I don't want you to be quicker."

He released the sleeves from her wrists and freed her arms. The gown fell in a frothy cloud, and he held her hands while she stepped through it.

She stood in a heavily embroidered chemise and layers of petticoats. Tape after tape fought with his fingers until all the stiffened skirts were removed. What remained were her chemise, drawers, white silken hose and slippers, and on her head the gold, camellia-shaped pins that held the chignon at her crown. Diamonds filled the heart of each precious flower, and more diamonds and pearls hung like rows of tiny buds from her ears. About her neck was the rope of diamonds he had given her as a wedding gift.

He reached for the chemise, but Meg pushed him away. "Take off your own clothes," she told him, her voice shaky with emotion. "At once, you understand?"

"Oh, I understand, My Lady," he told her, and followed instructions.

She removed the earrings and the pins from her hair, unlaced the chemise until it hung loose and her breasts were outlined by firelight through fine lawn. Off came the chemise. She stepped out of the drawers. The slippers she kicked away.

Jean-Marc was already naked, and there could be no question of hiding his feelings.

Meg's hair tumbled about her shoulders. He pushed his fingers into its heaviness and brought a handful to his lips. "You are a minx, do you know that? A companion and seamstress with dyed hair."

She didn't appear contrite now.

He studied every inch of her, from her wide eyes and wanting lips to her enticing breasts and lower, to her small belly and rounded thighs and the darkness between. She had forgotten her stockings, and the sight of them—and the diamonds that reached into the deep valley between her breasts—excited him more than ever.

"I love you," she said.

Jean-Marc couldn't smile. He couldn't speak. His throat felt frozen. Dropping his hands from her, he bent forward and nuzzled a nipple with his closed mouth, then with the tip of his tongue. Meg gasped and made fists. He moved to the other breast and drew the nipple gently between his teeth. Whenever he touched her, she jumped, as if her flesh was too sensitive to bear.

He stroked that dark place where her thighs met, and knew they would soon seal their marriage.

He didn't expect that she would throw her arms around hi neck and kiss him with her mouth open wide, or nibble his lip again and again until she stole his breath and left him panting

His body strained to join hers, and she stroked him until hi legs threatened to fold beneath him.

"Closer to the fire," she whispered. "Let me look at you face. You are the most handsome man in the world."

"You, wife, are the most beautifully infuriating woman in th world. I would like to be a considerate, careful husband wh takes his time to fully initiate you to his ways, but my restrair is failing."

Meg passed her tongue over her lips, raised her chin an kissed him again.

Almost before he could brace himself, she jumped to clutc his neck and hung there. She folded her limbs around his wai and kept on kissing him, and moving against him, until he gav up being strong and sank with her to stretch out on the gown.

"Considerate," she said, "and careful." She took a sho breath. "A careful husband who—takes—his—time. And so w are initiated. Again."

"I love you, Meg."

She didn't try to stop the tears. "Thank you. And I haven't."

Jean-Marc rose on his elbows. "What haven't you?"

"What you so indelicately asked about in the church. haven't for a number of weeks."

Epilogue

7 Mayfair Square
London
August, 1821

*G*reetings, readers.

I have been betrayed—by all of you. My mistake has been to treat you with kindness, you and my relatives and others.

Some might say I should rejoice at the departure of even one lodger from Number Seven. Why? That's what I want to know. Why would I celebrate when I have yet to empty even one flat? Sibyl was supposed to go with Meg, you all know that, but I failed. No, no, I didn't fail. Fate conspired against me.

No doubt you are smug at your supposed victory. You wanted this foolish marriage between a nobleman and a completely unsuitable nobody. And you wanted to see me thwarted. Enjoy your triumph. It will be short-lived. This time I shall not wait so long to mount another attack on the interlopers at Number Seven—and my next plan will be successfully accomplished. Had you treated me with deference, well then, I might have told you who will be the next to benefit from my extraordinary attention. But...

Did you note the outrageous extravagance at the Etranger wedding? I intend to find out exactly what was served, and how much blunt Count Etranger dropped in the pockets of the merchants who provided such excess. One might think the affair involved a blushing bride and her ardent groom, the latter an-

ticipating the discovery that waited ahead. Blushing? Pah! Di
covery? Ha!

I do believe I know who is responsible for sabotaging m
efforts, and they have been sabotaged on more than one occa
sion. That damnable scribbler. She tells you things behind m
back, doesn't she? And she goads you to rebel against the wi
dom of my principles. If not for her, you would have followe
my wishes and alerted me when certain events were about t
take place, events I could have averted.

Very well. I shall no longer treat her with polite if distar
respect. We shall soon see how she enjoys the next merry chas
I have planned.

And another thing. I have already told you this once, but sinc
your attention seems to wander so easily, I'll share the conf
dence again. If I don't, I have little doubt my "friend" will fin
a way to make this personal fact appear ridiculous. My carve
newel posts are peerless in their beauty, and the family member
depicted are a handsome lot—including myself. There is nothin
puzzling about my choosing to rest there, where I have a perfec
location to keep my fingers on the pulse of the household, so t
speak.

Until we meet again—soon. Don't become complacent.
Spivey.

Frog Crossing
Watersville
Out West

Dearest friends.

Don't allow the man to disconcert you. He is a pompous
blunderer. Fear not, we'll outwit him, but not, I fear, without further intrigues. Let him creep away into his beloved
newel post. While he's there, you and I will sharpen our
wits and prepare for whatever he intends next.

I am, as ever, your fond and faithful scribbler,

Stella Cameron

A daughter who's run away from home.
A mother who's run away from herself.

RACHEL LEE

Snow in
September

The tragedy of her husband's death has taken its toll on
both Meg Williams and her teenage daughter, Allie.
Now Allie has run away.

Sheriff Earl Sanders feels a responsibility to look after
Meg and Allie. Though he's determined not to let his love
and desire for his best friend's widow make her life even
harder, he's doing all he can to find her daughter. And as
days and nights pass, some startling secrets come to light.
Truths too painful to accept have stretched a family to
the breaking point, until a woman who nearly lost
everything discovers what matters most.

"A magnificent presence in romantic fiction.
Rachel Lee is an author to treasure forever."
—Romantic Times Magazine

On sale mid-April 2000 wherever paperbacks are sold!

HELEN R. MYERS

Six years ago the town of Split Creek, Texas, was rocked to its core when a young woman was brutally murdered. Her killer was never found. Now another girl has disappeared....

When Faith Ramey's abandoned car is discovered, the town feels an unwelcome sense of déjà vu. Police Chief Jared Morgan doesn't want to believe there's a connection, but Faith's sister Michaele is beginning to suspect otherwise.

LOST

As secrets and scandals are exposed, old fears—and new—spawn doubt and suspicion. Is a sinister stranger lurking behind the murder and Faith's disappearance—or does someone in Split Creek have blood on their hands? Only Michaele's fierce determination—and her trust in Jared—will help her see the truth hidden in plain sight.

"Ms. Myers gives readers an incredible depth of storytelling."
—*Romantic Times*

On sale mid-March 2000 wherever paperbacks are sold!

MIRA®

New York Times
Bestselling Author
LINDA
MACKENZIE'S
MOUNTAIN
HOWARD

Wolf Mackenzie is an outsider, a loner who chooses to live with his son on top of a Wyoming mountain rather than face the scorn of a town that dismisses him as a half-breed criminal. Until Mary Elizabeth Potter comes storming up his mountain. The proper, naive schoolteacher couldn't care less about the townspeople's distrust—she's just determined to give Wolf's son the education he deserves. But when Mary meets Wolf, an education of another kind begins. Now Mary and Wolf are teaching each other—and learning—about passion, forgiveness and even love.

"Howard's writing is compelling." —*Publishers Weekly*

Available mid-March 2000 wherever paperbacks are sold!

| 66463 | MOONTIDE | ___ $5.50 U.S. ___ $6.50 CAN. |
| 66495 | UNDERCURRENTS | ___ $5.99 U.S. ___ $6.99 CAN. |

(limited quantities available)

TOTAL AMOUNT	$_____
POSTAGE & HANDLING	$_____
($1.00 for one book; 50¢ for each additional)	
APPLICABLE TAXES*	$_____
<u>TOTAL PAYABLE</u>	$_____
(check or money order—please do not send cash)	

To order, complete this form and send it, along with a check or money order for the total above, payable to MIRA Books®, to: **In the U.S.:** 3010 Walden Avenue, P.O. Box 9077, Buffalo, NY 14269-9077; **In Canada:** P.O. Box 636, Fort Erie, Ontario L2A 5X3.

Name:_____
Address:_____ City:_____
State/Prov.:_____ Zip/Postal Code:_____
Account Number (if applicable):_____
075 CSAS

  *New York residents remit applicable sales taxes.
   Canadian residents remit applicable GST and provincial taxes.

MIRA